THE CLARINET ON THE GLACIER

The sounds of music just went out of tune

First Published in Great Britain 2025 by Mirador Publishing

Copyright © 2025 by J. E. MacKenzie

First edition: 2025

ISBN: 978-1-917411-43-1

THE CLARINET ON THE GLACIER

J. E. MacKenzie

CONTENTS

CHARACTERS

The narrative is told from two perspectives, those of Jessica and of Harris. Most characters, though not all, are referred to by their first names. To make the character list user-friendly, it is presented in alphabetical order by first name except where no first name is given and so the surname is used. Characters are described from the perspective of Jessica, Harris or both, depending on how they engage with them during the story.

Alice Morrison	Jessica's niece, piano student taught by Harris
Annelise (no surname given)	Waitress in Le Parisien restaurant in Zürich Airport
Bethany Morrison	Sister of Jessica, mother of Alice
Bodega (Mrs)	Headmistress of the school where Harris teaches in Bristol
Brendan (no surname given)	Employee in Lyon Airport
Captain Borisovich	Commercial helicopter pilot, based in Interlaken
Charles (no surname given)	Friend of Harris
Colin Morrison	Father of Alice, husband of Bethany
Daniel (no surname given)	Paragliding instructor, based in Interlaken
Gerlinde Mumpitz	Water-skier on the Thunersee
Harris Beadlesby	Secondary school music teacher, based in Bristol
Ingeborg Früggelberger	Retiree in Interlaken

Isabel (no surname given)	Fiancée of Harris
Jessica Morriston	Linguistic specialist, based in Liverpool
Jöchi Hägervongelschmidt	Waiter in an Interlaken hotel
Katie Porter	Piano student taught by Harris
Montague (Mr and Mrs)	Neighbours of Jessica in Huyton, Liverpool
Oliver (no surname given)	Boyfriend of Brendan
Pierre-Luc (no surname given)	Customer service agent in Lyon Airport
Plummer (Mr)	Representative of the Board of Governors of the school where Harris teaches
Rhonda (no surname given)	Employee at the Pig & Blanket pub in Huyton, Liverpool
Robert Fletcher	Piano student taught by Harris
Sammy Tuffnall	Friend of Harris

GUIDE TO CULTURAL AND GEOGRAPHIC REFERENCES

Almost all readers will be familiar with at least some, if not most, of the references made throughout the book to various places, people and aspects of culture, both classical and modern. However, few will be fully aware of all of them and so this guide is provided to fill the gaps. It is not intended to be exclusive. Particularly where geographical terms are concerned, those listed are only those whose reference is not immediately obvious in the text but necessary to follow it. Those references made to places which are fictional and only found in this story are also noted.

Please do not think that you're supposed to read all of the below. You're obviously very welcome to do so but the chances are that you probably know quite a bit of it already. There can't be that many people out there who have never heard of at least one out of Mozart, James Bond, London City Airport or K-Pop. The only thing is, there probably aren't all that many who have heard of all of them either. Nor had the author before writing this, although let's keep quiet as to which bits did or didn't figure in his less than encyclopaedic knowledge. However, to save you interrupting your enjoyment of the story by having to look up a good internet search engine too often, the list below has been prepared. It didn't cause the price of the book to increase in any way so please consider it a free bonus.

"A Tale of Two Cities"	Novel by Charles Dickens (1859)
Académie Française	Literary academy which officially defines the French language

"Aida"	Opera by Guiseppe Verdi (1871)
Alcatraz	Famous prison island in San Francisco Bay
Alcoholics Anonymous	A global fellowship established to help those struggling with alcohol abuse
Aldi	A German supermarket chain with branches in multiple countries
"Alien"	Film concerning a killer alien (1979)
Amati Instruments Ltd	Dealers in high-end and collectors' musical instruments
API	Advance Passenger Information
"Apocalypse Now"	Viet Nam War movie (1979)
Arbon	Municipality in Saint-Gallen Canton next to Lake Constance, Switzerland
Ascot	Racecourse for horses in England, well patronized by upper classes
Aston Martin	Luxury car brand, favoured by James Bond
"A-Team, The"	Television series about a group of Viet Nam War veterans for hire (1983 – 1987)
Bach, Johann Sebastian	German composer (1685 – 1750)
Bananarama	English pop group formed in 1980
Baroque Period	Period of Western classic music from the 17th to first half of the 18th centuries
Battenberg cake	Sponge and jam cake, wrapped in marzipan
Beatenberg	Swiss village in the Canton of Bern, overlooking the Thunersee
Beatles	English band, originally from Liverpool, UK (1962 – 1970)
Beckham, David Robert Joseph	English footballer (1975 –)
Beethoven, Ludwig van	German composer (1770 – 1827)
Bellini, Vincenzo	Italian composer (1801 – 1835)

Benidorm	Spanish beach resort town, popular with UK tourists
Berkshire	County in southern England
Berner Oberland	Bernese highlands, mountainous area of the Canton of Bern, Switzerland
Bezos, Jeffrey Preston	American entrepreneur and owner of Amazon (1964 –)
Bird's Eye Potato Waffles	Grilled potato slices sold in UK supermarkets
Black Friday	Friday following US Thanksgiving, marked by retail discounts
Blackpink	South Korean girl pop band formed in 2016
Blackpool	Beach resort town in northwest England
Blofeld, Ernst Stavro	Fictional villain and opponent of James Bond
Blyton, Enid	Iconic, British children's fiction writer (1897 – 1968)
Bob the Builder	Fictional children's character
Bollocks	Slang term for testicles, also used to indicate spoken words of no value (UK)
Bond, James	Fictional, British spy, featured in books and films since 1953
Bougie	Slang term for upper class style which is often affected
Bowie, David Robert	British glam rock singer and songwriter (1947– 2016)
Brahms, Johannes	German composer (1833 – 1897)
"Braveheart"	Film concerning the war for Scottish independence (1995)
Brexit	Slang term for the withdrawal of the United Kingdom from the European Union (2020)
"Bridgerton"	Eight novels by Julia Quinn, subsequently televised, 19th century drama

Brienzersee	German for Lake Brienz, next to Interlaken in Bern Canton, Switzerland
Bristol	Port town in western England
Brit	Slang term for a British national
Brosnan, Pierce Brendan	Irish actor, played James Bond between 1995 and 2002 (1953 –)
Brothers Grimm	19th century German writers of children's fairy tales
Brunel, Isambard Kingdom	British engineer (1806 – 1859)
BTS	South Korean boy pop band formed in 2013
Bucket list	Slang term for list of things somebody wants to accomplish before dying
Burj Khalifa	The world's tallest building in Dubai, United Arab Emirates
C-3PO	Robot character in the "Star Wars" series of movies, with an awkward gait
Calvin Klein	Designer brand of fashion
Canton	Administrative/political entity in the Swiss federal structure; similar to a US State
Care Bears	Fictional teddy bear characters created for young children
Carmen	Title character of the opera of the same name by Georges Bizet (1875)
Carnegie Hall	Concert hall, New York City, USA
"Carry On"	A series of somewhat vulgar, British comedy films made between 1958 and 1973
Cartier	Luxury jewellery brand
"Casino Royale"	James Bond novel by Ian Fleming (1953), filmed in 1954, 1967 and 2006
Cervantes, Miguel de	Spanish writer (1547 – 1616)
ChatGPT	Freely available Artificial Intelligence engine

Chav	Derogatory slang term, indicating a typically young person of low class (UK)
Cheddar Gorge	Deep gorge with a river flowing through it in southwest England
Chilchegg	Alp next to Interlaken, Switzerland
Chopin, Frédéric François	Polish-French composer (1810 – 1849)
Christie, Dame Agatha Mary Clarissa	English detective novelist and playwright (1890 – 1976)
Chum	Slang term for vomit
Chur	Capital city of Graubünden Canton in eastern Switzerland
Clarinet parts	Mouthpiece, barrel, upper joint, lower joint, bell
Clarke, Zelah Caroline	English actress (1953 –)
Classicals Weekly	Fictitious magazine concerned with classical music
Click	Slang term for a kilometre
Colonel Sanders	American founder of the Kentucky Fried Chicken brand (1890 – 1980)
"Combine Harvester Song, The"	Number one hit for The Wurzels (1976)
Connery, Sir Sean	Scottish actor, played James Bond between 1962 and 1971 (1930 – 2020)
Cougar	Slang term for a woman who seeks intimate relations with younger men
COVID	Coronavirus disease which caused a global lockdown in 2020
CPR	Cardiopulmonary resuscitation
Craig, Daniel Wroughton	English actor, played James Bond between 2006 and 2022 (1968 –)
Cruise, Tom	American actor, notable for his role in, "Top Gun" in 1986 (1962 –)
Cup-a-Soup	Snack food marketed by Bachelors

Daily Mail	Right-wing, British, tabloid newspaper
Daisy's	Fictional café in East Dawlings
Dalton, Timothy Peter	Welsh actor, played James Bond between 1987 and 1989 (1946 –)
de Gaulle, Charles André Joseph Marie	Président of France, 1959 – 1969 (1890 – 1970)
"Debbie does Dallas"	Comedy pornography movie (1978)
del Toro, Benicio	Puerto Rican actor (1967 –)
Deluc, Xavier	French actor (1958 –)
Descartes, René	French philosopher (1596 – 1650)
Dickens, Charles John Huffam	English novelist (1812 – 1870)
DMZ	De-Militarized Zone, dividing North Korea from South Korea
Double-O 7	Code number given to James Bond as a British agent, licensed to kill (written "007")
"Dr No"	James Bond film (1962)
DUI	Driving Under the Influence (of alcohol)
Dumas, père, Alexandre	French author (1802 – 1870)
Dvořák, Antonín Leopold	Bohemian (now Czech) composer (1841 – 1904)
"E.T."	Film concerning an extraterrestrial landing on Earth (1982)
East Dawlings	Fictional village within commuting range of Bristol
Eastwood, Clinton	American actor and director (1930 –)
Eiger	Alp in the Berner Oberland, translates as, "Ogre" in English
"Eiger Sanction, The"	American action film set in the Berner Oberland, Switzerland (1975)
Einstein, Albert	German-American physicist (1879 – 1955)
El Dorado	Legendary land of gold in the Americas, used to refer to a dream world

Elgar, Sir Edward William	English composer (1857 – 1934)
"Eye of the Tiger"	Song by Survivor, popularized for sports training by the movie, "Rocky" (1982)
F1	Shorthand for Formula 1 motor racing
F-14	Jet fighter made famous by the movie, "Top Gun" (US)
Falklands War	War fought between Argentina and the UK over the Falkland Islands (1982)
Famous Five, The	Series of stories about child detectives by Enid Blyton (1942 – 1963)
Farage, Nigel	Leader of the Reform UK political party (1964 –)
Faust	Title character of an opera by Charles Gounod, who sells his soul to the Devil (1859)
Flash Gordon	Title character of comics and films, including a 1980 film featuring Timothy Dalton
Fleming, Ian Lancaster	British author of James Bond novels (1908 – 1964)
Flims-Waldhaus	Alpine village in Graubünden Canton, Switzerland
"For Your Eyes Only"	James Bond film (1981)
Frosties	Breakfast cereal made by Kellogg's
Frosty the Snowman	Character in a song of the same name (1950)
Fulda Gap	Mountain pass in Graubünden Canton, Switzerland
"Game and Country"	Fictional magazine concerning rural lifestyles and pastimes
G&T	Slang term for a gin and tonic drink
GCSE	General Certificate of Secondary Education (UK)
Geneva	Switzerland's second largest city, located in the Canton of the same name
Georgina Café, The	Fictional café in East Dawlings

GI	Slang term for an enlisted soldier, several definitions proposed (US)
Gibson, Mel Columcille Gerard	Australian actor and director (1956 –)
Givret, Karl	Fictional French clarinet player
Glastonbury	Town in southwest England which hosts an annual rock festival
Glitter, Gary	British glam rock artist, convicted of sex offences in 2015 (1944 –)
"Goldfinger"	James Bond film (1964)
"Gone with the Wind"	Romance novel (1936) filmed in 1939
Google	Internet search engine
Goose	Character in "Top Gun" killed in flying accident, played by Anthony Edwards (1986)
Gounod, Charles-françois	French composer (1818 – 1893)
"Great Escape, The"	Film based on an escape by captured, Allied airmen in WWII (1963)
Greggs	British bakery chain
Gucci Homme	Luxury perfume brand
Guevara, Ernesto "Che"	Argentine-Cuban revolutionary; wearer of famous beret style (1928 – 1967)
Gyno	Slang term for a gynaecologist
H&M	Fashion chain
HALO	High Altitude Low Opening, type of parachute drop
"Hamlet"	Tragedy written by William Shakespeare between 1599 and 1602
Händel, Georg Friedrich	German-English composer (1685 – 1759)
Harrier	Vertical/Short Take-Off and Landing jet fighter (UK, later UK/US)
Hazmat	Shorthand for hazardous material protection
Heathrow	Airport outside London, largest in UK

Heidi	Title character in a children's novel by Johanna Spyri, set largely in the Swiss Alps (1880)
Hillary, Sir Edmund Percival	New Zealand explorer, one of the first to climb Mt Everest (1919 – 2008)
HMV	"His Master's Voice", UK music and entertainment retail chain
Hochdeutsch	Literally, "High German"; accepted, standard German
Höhematte Park	Public park in central Interlaken, Switzerland
Hoi polloi	Slightly snobbish term used to refer to the general public
Hopkins, Sir Philip Anthony	Welsh actor (1937 –)
Huyton	Suburb of Liverpool, UK
Ibiza	Spanish resort island, popular with UK tourists
Ikea	Swedish, home furniture retail chain, operating in multiple countries
Imperial War Museum	Museum of war and conflict in London, UK
Incredible Hulk, The	Title character of comics and films; noted for physical strength
Instagram	Internet social media service
Interlaken	Resort town in Bern Canton, Switzerland
Isolde	Title character of the opera, "Tristan and Isolde" by Richard Wagner (1859)
ITV	Independent Television; group of television companies (UK)
IVF	In vitro fertilization
Jack the Ripper	Unidentified London serial killer (1888)
"Jailhouse Rock"	Movie musical starring Elvis Presley (1957)
Jane Eyre	Title character of a novel by Charlotte Brontë, filmed several times (1847)
"Jaws"	Novel by Peter Benchley (1974) and filmed in 1975, concerning a great white shark

Jet Ranger	Helicopter type (US/Canada)
JFK	Shorthand term for John F. Kennedy Airport, New York, USA
John, Sir Elton Hercules	English musician (1947 –)
Johnson, Alexander Boris de Pfeffel	UK Prime Minister, 2019 – 2022 (1964 –)
Jungfrau	Alp in the Berner Oberland, translates as, "Maiden" or, "Virgin" in English
Jura	Mountain range between Switzerland and France
Karen	Slang term for a middle-aged women who is very demanding
Kazoo	Cheap, musical instrument often played for comic effect
KB'd	Slang term meaning, "Knocked Back", essentially refused entry
Kent	County in southeast England
Kermit the Frog	Lead character in, "The Muppet Show", designed for children
Knights Club	Fictional dining club in Bristol
Krueger, Freddy	Character with a disfigured face in the "Nightmare on Elm Street" series of films
Lake Constance	Lake between eastern Switzerland and Germany
Lake Geneva	Lake between western Switzerland and France
Lake Lucerne	Lake in central Switzerland
Lauterbrünnen	Alpine village in the Canton of Bern, south of Interlaken
Lazenby, George Robert	Australian actor, played James Bond in 1969 (1939 –)
Le Chauffaud	French town on the border crossing with Neuchatel Canton, Switzerland

Le Locle	Swiss town next to the French border in Neuchatel Canton
Le Parisien	Fictional restaurant in Zürich Airport
Lennon, John Winston Ono	English musician and singer in the Beatles (1940 – 1980)
Lenzburg	Town in Aargau Canton, Switzerland
"License to Kill"	James Bond film (1989)
Liverpool	Port town in northwest England
"Living Daylights, The"	James Bond film (1987)
Loggins, Kenneth Clarke	American musician (1948 –)
London City Airport	Small airport located on the River Thames, east London
"Love Island"	Reality TV show concerning couples dating
Luton	Town in Bedfordshire, England, with one of five airports serving greater London
Madame Tussaud's	Famous waxworks museum in London
"Magic Mike"	Film about exotic male dancers (2012)
Mahler, Gustav	Austrian composer (1860 – 1911)
Malaga	Spanish beach resort town, popular with British tourists
Margate	Beach resort town in southeast England
Marks and Spencer	Upmarket groceries and home goods retail chain
Mars Bar	Chocolate bar confectionery brand
Matterhorn	Iconic Swiss Alp in Valais Canton, Switzerland
Maverick	Callsign of the pilot played by Tom Cruise in "Top Gun" (1986)
McCartney, Paul	English musician and singer in The Beatles (1942 –)
McDonald's	Chain of fast-food restaurants
Meder, Johann Valentin	German composer (1649 – 1719)

Mendelssohn-Bartholdy, Jakob Ludwig Felix	German composer (1809 – 1847)
Merlot	French wine
Michael, George	British singer and composer (1963 – 2016)
Michelin Man	Character used as a brand ambassador by the Michelin company for its tyres
Migros	Swiss supermarket chain
Mönch	Alp in the Berner Oberland, translates as, "Monk" in English
Moonies	Slang term for the controversial Unification Church, founded in 1954
Moore, Sir Roger George	English actor, played James Bond between 1973 and 1985 (1927 – 2017)
Mozart, Johann Chrysostom Wolfgang Amadeus	Austrian composer (1756 – 1791)
MRI	Magnetic Resonance Imagery, a form of radioactivity scan
Mulder, Fox	Fictitious FBI paranormal investigator in, "The X-Files", played by David Duchovny
Musk, Elon	American entrepreneur and richest man in the world
'Nam	Slang term for what is now Vietnam during the US military intervention in the 1960s - 1970s
NASA	National Aeronautics and Space Administration (US)
NATO	North Atlantic Treaty Organization
Netflix	Online media streaming service
Noddy	Children's fictional character created by Enid Blyton
Nookie	Slang term for sexual intercourse (UK)
Norris, Carlos Ray "Chuck"	American actor and martial artist (1940 –)

Novichok	Type of poison allegedly employed by Russian intelligence agents
OAP	Old Age Pensioner (UK)
"On Her Majesty's Secret Service"	James Bond film, partly shot in the Berner Oberland (1969)
Ötzi	Name given to a man whose body was frozen in the Ötzal Alps in Austria for around 5,300 years
Palézieux	Small town in Vaud Canton, Switzerland
PD	Police Department
Pétanque	Sport similar to English bowls, popular in France
Peter	Friend of Heidi in the novel of the same name
Pig & Blanket	Fictional pub in the area of Huyton, Liverpool
Pimm's	A British cocktail mixer made from gin and fruit extracts
"Pink Panther"	Series of films portraying an over-the-top French detective (1963 – 1982)
Pixar	American animation studio
Pizza Hut	Chain of fast-food restaurants
Plato	Greek philosopher (428/427 BC – 348/347 BC)
"Platoon"	Viet Nam war movie (1986)
Poirot, Hercule	Fictional character created by Dame Agatha Christie
Postbus	Public transportation network operated by Postauto Switzerland
Potter, Harry	Fictional character in print and film, created by J K Rowling
Powers, Austin	Fictional spy played by Mike Myers in three films (1997 – 2002)
Premier League	Top tier professional football league in England

Presley, Elvis Aaron	American singer and actor (1935 – 1977)
PTSD	Post-Traumatic Stress Disorder
Puccini, Giacomo Antonio Domenico Michele Secondo Maria	Italian composer (1858 – 1924)
Purcell, Henry	English composer (1659 – 1695)
Queens Park Rangers	Football team in northwest London
Quid	Slang term for a pound in British currency
Ralph Lauren	Designer fashion brand
Regency	Political period between 1811 and 1820 (UK)
Renaissance	Period in European history from around the late-1400s to early 1600s
Rhônexpress	Shuttle train linking Lyon Part-Dieu station to Lyon-Saint Exupéry airport
Rochester, Edward	Suitor of Jane Eyre in the novel of that name (1847)
Rocky Road	Dessert made from marshmallows, chocolate and nuts
Rolex	Luxury watch brand
Rotenegg	Alp next to Interlaken, Switzerland
Rowling, Joanne Kathleen	British author (1965 –)
Royal Navy	Maritime service of the British military
RSPCA	Royal Society for the Prevention of Cruelty to Animals (UK)
Sainsbury's	UK supermarket chain
Salvation Army	Religious and charitable organization, running several charity/thrift stores
Santoni	Designer footwear brand
Sartre, Jean-Paul	French philosopher and author (1905 – 1980)
Satan	Name given to the Devil in religious writing
SBB	German acronym for Swiss Federal Railways

Schengen Agreement	Convention to reduce passport control between most European countries
Schubert, Franz Peter	Austrian composer (1797 – 1828)
Scully, Dana	Fictitious FBI paranormal investigator in, "The X-Files", played by Gillian Anderson
Shakespeare, William	English author and playwright (1564 – 1616)
"Sharknado 2"	Second in a series of movies about tornadoes full of sharks hitting land (2014)
She-Ra	Animated lead heroine character in the series, "She-Ra: Princess of Power" (1985 – 1987)
Sigriswil	Small town in Bern Canton, Switzerland
Simmental	Alpine valley in Bern Canton, Switzerland
Sistine Chapel	Religious building in Rome, Italy, with a famous ceiling painted by Michelangelo
S'mores	Biscuit treat made with marshmallows and chocolate
Snow angels	Outlines of angels made by spreading limbs while lying in snow
Somerset	County in western England
SOP	Standard Operating Procedure
Spätzli	Egg-based pasta (Switzerland)
Spiez	Resort town with a marina on the Thunersee in Bern Canton, Switzerland
Spiezerberg	Small, forested hill on the side of Spiez next to the Thunersee
"Star Trek"	American science fiction series which originally ran from 1966 to 1969
"Star Wars"	Science fiction saga told mainly through movies starting in 1977
Starr, Ringo	English musician and drummer in The Beatles (1940 –)
Statham, Jason Michael	English actor (1967 –)

Steinach	Municipality in Saint-Gallen Canton next to Lake Constance, Switzerland
STI	Sexually-Transmitted Infection
"Strictly Come Dancing"	British competitive dancing show
Styles, Harry Edward	English singer (1994 –)
Swift, Taylor Alison	American singer (1989 –)
Swiftie	Slang term for a follower of Taylor Swift
Swingball	Leisure device consisting of a tennis ball attached to a pole by a length of cord
"Take on Me"	Song by a-ha (1985)
Take That	Boy band formed in Manchester, UK in 1990
Teletubbies	Characters in a television show of the same name for young children (1997 – 2001)
Tensing, Norgay	Nepali-Indian who accompanied Sir Edmund Hillary on Mt Everest (1914 – 1986)
Tesco	British supermarket chain, founded in 1919
Thunersee	German for Lake Thun, next to Interlaken in Bern Canton, Switzerland
TikTok	Social media app released in 2016
Tim	Shorthand name used by Jessica to refer to Timothy Dalton
Tinder	Online dating app released in 2012
Tinny	Slang term for a beer and its container (UK, Australia)
Titanic	Luxury liner which sank in the Atlantic Ocean (1912)
Toke	Slang term for smoking drugs
Ted Baker	Designer clothing and accessories brand
"Top Gun"	US Navy Fighter Weapons School, popularized in the movie of the same name (1986)
"Tosca"	Opera by Giacomo Puccini (1900)

Tristan	Title character of the opera, "Tristan and Isolde" by Richard Wagner (1859)
Uber	Transportation, ride-sharing company
Vagisil	Hydrocortisone cream used to relieve discomfort in intimate, female parts
van Gogh, Vincent Willem	Dutch painter (1853 – 1890)
Vaud	French-speaking Canton in Switzerland
Verdi, Giuseppe Fortunino Francesco	Italian composer (1813 – 1901)
Viagra	Medication to counter male, erectile dysfunction
Victoria's Secret	Chain of exotic underwear stores
Viet Cong	Guerilla movement fighting for North Viet Nam in the Viet Nam War (1955 – 1975)
Viet Nam	Country in south-east Asia, now Vietnam
Village People	American disco group formed in 1977, popular with the gay community
Vimto	Fruit-flavoured soft drink, first produced in 1908 (UK)
Vivaldi, Antonio Lucio	Italian composer (1678 – 1741)
Voltaire, François-Marie	French philosopher (1694 – 1778)
von Trapp	Family and lead characters in, "The Sound of Music" (1965) by Rodgers and Hammerstein
Waitrose Ltd	Upmarket supermarket chain (UK)
"War and Peace"	Epic novel of Russian society in the 19th century by Leo Tolstoy (circa 1865)
Wars of the Roses	Dynastic civil wars in England (1455 – 1485)
WASP	White Anglo-Saxon Protestant
Weber, Baron Carl Maria Friedrich Ernst, Freiherr von	German composer (1786 – 1826)

WECPA	West Country Performing Arts, fictional monthly catalogue of events
Weissenburg	Small village in the Simmental valley in Bern Canton, Switzerland
Wham	British pop duo (1981 – 1986)
"Who Wants to be a Millionaire?"	Quiz show originally launched in the UK in 1998
Wilby, James Jonathon	English actor (1958 –)
William Tell	Legendary, national hero of Switzerland
WKD Blue	Alcoholic fruit drink, readily available in the UK (Spain)
"World Is Not Enough, The"	James Bond film (1999)
Wurzels, The	Comic music band with an agricultural theme formed in 1966 (UK)
Yank	Slang term for an American
Yeovilton	Site of a Royal Naval Air Station in Somerset, UK
Yeti	Unconfirmed, large and dangerous creature, allegedly living in cold climates
YMCA	Young Men's Christian Association; song by the Village People (1978)
Yves Saint Laurent	Designer perfume brand
Zermatt	Town below the Matterhorn Alp in Valais Canton, Switzerland
Zoomerzet	Reference to the English County Somerset in the local pronunciation (alleged)
Zürich	Largest city in Switzerland; located in the Canton of the same name
Zweisimmen	Swiss town in the Simmental valley in the Canton of Bern

GUIDE TO GERMAN PRONUNCIATION

THE STORY IN THIS BOOK takes place mainly in the UK and in Switzerland, with a small amount in France. Although written in English, it refers to several names of people and places in German, and the pronunciation may not be immediately clear to anglophone readers who do not speak the language. Some of it may not even be immediately clear to those who do speak German since the variant encountered in the story is that spoken in Switzerland. With due respect to those Swiss who insist that Swiss German is another language and not a form of German, this perspective is duly acknowledged but for the benefit of less aware anglophones, the language spoken east of Fribourg is considered German here, just one spoken with a very unique accent. The guide below seeks to give a rough overview of how this sounds.

Where there are multiple possibilities (e.g. pronunciation of the letter "o"), these are simply left out. The guide below is not exhaustive but should provide sufficient elements to give a reasonable overview.

Although French and Spanish are also used in the course of the story, their use is much less frequent and relatively easy to determine from its presentation. If this isn't good enough, you do of course have the remaining options to find your own native speaker or go online. Both work very well.

Sound	Sounds like	Comparable English	German example	Translation
a-	Short a	And	Hallo	Hello
e-	Short e	End	Denn	Then
-e	Uh	Huh	Eine (Eye–nuh)	An
i-	Short i	In	Bin	Am
u-	Oo	Boot	Hund	Dog
ä/ae-	Eh	Pale	Hände	Hands
ö/oe-	Long uh	Curt (approximate)	König	King
ü/ue-	Clipped oo	Put (approximate)	Brücke	Bridge
au-	Ow	Loud	Baum	Tree
ee-	Eh	Say	Tee	Tea
ei-	I	Tight	Nein	No
eu-	Oi	Boy	Deutsch	German
ie-	Ee	Meet	Sie	She/they
d-	T	Ant	Und	And
j-	Y	Yard	Jahr	Year
qu-	Kv-	No real equivalent	Bequem	Comfortable
v-	F	Fun	Von	Of
w-	V	Van	Wenn	When
z-	Ts	Hats	Zwei	Two
-ch	Scottish -ch	Loch	Ich	I
-sch	Sh	Shine	Fisch	Fish
sp-	Shp-	Ship (close)	Spiez (Shpeets)	Name of town
th-	T	Tin	Thun	Name of Lake Thun

Chapter 1
I LOVE TO GO A-WANDERING

Jessica

I look ahead of me. The stony shingle of the path stretches into what looks like a low gateway made up from two aster bushes of a tender, dark green hue. The trees above stretch down their branches like overgrown arms which have long since lost their grasp on some dear, departed offspring but which reach out in a mixture of hope and despair which can never be realised but which will never depart either.

The smell is a surprisingly fresh one. Even though there is not the slightest breath of any form of air current, there is a wisp of lavender which plies its way gently but deliberately into the nostrils, coaxed and led on by an alternating scent of pine and larch. It feels as though it is swirling slowly around my chest as I breathe in its powerful yet wavering aroma. Somehow it feels as if the forest before me is breathing itself as my sensations collide to create a sense of overwhelming life around me. I look at a berry which is hanging from the branch of a scrawny yet surprisingly sturdy, grey-green bushel. Its bright red lustre defies the cooler colours surrounding it and reminds me of the real scope of life which surrounds me, whose essence I am breathing in, seeing before me and feeling envelop me.

Oh what the hell? Why am I thinking all this? I can't myself be bothered with authors who insist on picking out every minute detail and elaborating on it to a level of breathtaking boredom worthy only of an axed, Lithuanian soap opera. If you want one of those stories where you spend the first four chapters getting told what a running goat smelled like in Wales in 1754, then go and buy some romantic fiction or a museum guidebook. I'm always impressed by how people can recreate the experience of being in another existence through picking out the details of minutiae which I would never notice even if I were there myself. When was the last time you actually stopped to appreciate the broach of hazel delving into the running stem of darker brown in the elbow of a branch? Does anyone actually notice the growing torsion of knotted muscle which flexes almost imperceptibly across the shoulder blades of a metal worker whose gaze is absorbed in the writhing flow of almost molten iron over a glowing charcoal furnace? I suppose if he's fit enough and covered in sweat, well then I might notice a growing torsion or two which could absorb my gaze, although it likely wouldn't be between his shoulder blades. But it's not that kind of story, all right?

This is meant to help the reader to feel drawn in and to experience in his or her mind the actual reality of Wales in 1754 or whatever else it is. But I ask, how? First of all, it concerns a fictitious detail which, even if real, I would never notice or pay the slightest bit of attention to anyway. Why spend twenty pages describing the rear end of a goat just so I can feel as though I'm on a farm in Wales in 1754? Personally, I have no intention of sticking my head up a goat's rectum whether I find myself in 1754, the present day or any other time period, thank you all the same. Nor do I care whether said goat is Welsh, French or Italian. What are you going to do? Have another Brexit vote on it? And finally, how does said author even know what any of these experiences were actually like when he or she can never have existed in 1754, either in Wales, El Dorado or some other cheese dream?

By way of contrast, what I genuinely like about the Alps is that like anywhere else, what you see is what you get. And the Alps are pretty, even beautiful. They're serene and peaceful. They remind you of how small a part of creation you are yet permit you to go and have a look. Nonetheless, you don't have to be a poet or have a degree in Regency literature from Oxford to appreciate it. You go there, you hike yourself up the path and you enjoy the scenery. I do. What I don't do is try to break down every last molecule into a show-and-tell session to demonstrate what I'm drawing into my conscious being. Ultimately, I'm a tourist, not an existentialist tour.

However, I'm getting a little ahead of myself here. I come here to relax, not to complain. It's just that you need to air your frustrations, to vent and so forth. Then you can appreciate the good bits, and there are a lot of those. One of the things I love most about the Swiss Alps is that you can actually find silence. It's something you don't really notice until there's absolutely nothing else there. If you get far enough into woodland in particular and there's no wind, if there are no streams nearby either, you can stop and stand still and realise that suddenly there's just nothing at all. Not a whisper. You don't get that elsewhere. It may not be obvious, but all habited areas have some sort of background noise. There's nearly always traffic somewhere. Your fridge may be humming. Somebody walking down the street may generate just a bit of sound. There's always something rattling away there. Plus, if you live anywhere near the sea, you've got basically no chance as you never get a complete lack of wind and air currents.

This is not always easy to find, even in the Alps. The mountains are covered in fast-moving streams. The Swiss seem quite keen on light aircraft and helicopters, whose engine noises carry for miles. It's not as if the wind never blows either. In fact, even without any of these, you still won't even notice it yourself unless you stop completely because your own footsteps and heavy breathing as you head upwards will deafen you to the silence. And if you will insist on burping when you reach a quiet spot, just forget it. You might as well keep your headphones on and continue listening to Taylor Swift.

Still, the pure silence is something pretty much unique when you find it. The sights, of course, are awesome as well.

If you put it simply, there are more or less three stages to an Alpine walking route in summertime. From the bottom up, there's the forest line. This is quite extensive usually and will appear impenetrable until you're in it and you realise that there's actually a whole network of paths there. These lead not just upwards but also along different directions, taking you to all sorts of wonderful views and pastures.

Pastures are indeed what you hit next. Once the trees stop growing so thickly, you reach the Alpine meadows. These are surprising. There's so much more up there than you could ever imagine from standing at the bottom, looking skywards. Slogging upwards through the woods, you could never imagine that there would be any sort of space up there to accommodate more than a couple of mountain foxes but no, there's a whole range of fields and meadows. It's not flat, of course. It's still heading towards the peaks, just not quite as steeply as the side of the mountain in the forest. It's a beautiful area to walk through and head up across.

Above that is the glacier range. No longer beautiful exactly but definitely majestic. There are no trees here and barely any grass once you get high enough, just bleak but huge slopes, carved out on an annual basis by ice floes over millions of years and which stretch above you like a ridge of teeth into the sky. At their bottom, they form huge gullies, where the icy glaciers lie.

Still, I'm almost getting poetical again here so let's cut to the less salubrious end of the spectrum.

For all their beauty, there are a few other things you need to remember about the Alps. First is the fairly obvious but rarely appreciated fact that almost all the photos of them are only ever taken in good weather. However, as anyone who's stayed awake for more than half an hour in a geography class will know, if you mix up various altitudes, lakes, and fauna, you get quite a variety of weather patterns. You often see these archaic, little farmhouses a few kilometres higher than the rest of civilisation and wonder how, at least until the latter part of the twentieth century, anyone ever survived there without Wi-Fi, a fridge or decent plumbing. The Wi-Fi can be explained away by pointing out that if that's what you're thinking, you're clearly no older than about nineteen and think that TikTok preceded the Bible (assuming you've heard of the latter these days since I understand that it's rarely read on "Love Island" either). There was, however, a period of life between the Stone Age and the invention of Instagram which is known as human history and where a few things happened, believe it or not, kids.

The plumbing, however, is a different matter. Wouldn't it be pretty gross to live in a wooden shack so high up that you could look down on passing aircraft but without a decent shower? Well, no actually. Why not, you may ask? The answer is because if you stay out long enough, you can get a perfectly convincing shower free of charge, courtesy of Mother Nature. It's just usually quite badly timed, at least in my case. I don't know how many times I've turned up at a mountain village hotel where I've booked a room, looking as though I just forgot to take my clothes off before I put them into the washing machine.

All that, though, is a minor irritation compared with the one thing which is a definite blot on the Alps' otherwise excellent copy book. Again, it's not something you see in the pictures unless you look carefully and think for a moment. Consider all the postcards and screenshots you've seen of the Swiss Alps. OK, go and look it up on Google for a minute if you've somehow never seen any up to now.

Now that we're all on the same page, how many cows have you seen? Probably quite a few and you have to give the Swiss credit. They certainly know how to farm them. Almost any patch of grass which is on a slope less than 60 degrees in gradient is probably being used or has just been used to graze cattle in summertime. Makes sense for sure – where do you think all that cheese comes from and the milk which forms the basis of all that Swiss chocolate?

Of course, you don't see the ring of the cowbells round their necks which also forms part of the Alpine experience. But that's not all.

These things produce a phenomenal amount of dung. They stand around all day, hoovering up every last blade of grass over a fifty square kilometres patch of mountainside and they convert it all into a load of instant manure which comes pouring out of their backsides like a production line of shit. It's reminiscent of a talk show with politicians. In fairness to the farmers, they keep these things in clearly defined areas which you can usually skirt around but if you do find yourself in one of them, forget the scenery. You have to watch every footstep to make sure you're not about to find yourself up to the ankles in something which was in Daisy's lower intestine ten minutes ago.

There's also something psychopathic about these bovine crapping machines. I can accept that they're not people and so relieving themselves in vast quantity in a public space is not considered as anti-social as it would be if you or I were to try it out in the local high street. Fair enough but even so, why do they then sit next to it for an hour or so and chill out with their pals? Would you do that? What the hell are they thinking of? Admiring their handiwork, well bumdiwork or whatever you call it? Talk about mad cow disease.

So there's the scene. You know what to expect while I flit around the Alps. They may have their imperfections, but I love them. I'm not Swiss myself. I don't know if you were wondering but I'm not. I live in Liverpool, from where the Beatles originated in fact. Not many Swiss people live in Liverpool although whether that's relevant here, I don't know. Intellectualism is not really for me.

I hasten to point out that it doesn't make me stupid, however, at least not totally. There are some who might argue with that assessment. Mainly former teachers and ex-boyfriends. All the same, I have my strongpoints. I can speak both French and German, not just as in I once got a C grade in a GCSE exam about twenty years ago but as in I work as a linguistic specialist. It's basically a trendy term for what used to be known as a professional translator except that these days it also involves writing new material for people in other languages as well. Got to stay ahead of ChatGPT somehow these days.

Regrettably, I do have a somewhat stupid name. Jessica Morriston. That's right, Morriston, not Morrison. Why, oh why? Well, I wish I knew but I've been struggling with it on just about every piece of bureaucratic form-filling, every bank account registration and every pizza takeaway loyalty card I've ever had to fill in since I learned to write. Anyone reading it automatically thinks it's a mistake. It's even caused me problems in coffee shops. You know how when you order your medium latte, after a ten-minute wait behind some trainee accountant who pays in coppers, you need to give your name to the server on the till so they can write it on the plastic cup they serve up about half an hour later? Well, in doing so, I've realised just what a popular name Jessica is. There's nearly always another Jessica, Jess, Jessie or even Jesse ahead of me. This being the case, they tell me, "Oh, just put your surname." Only in my case, that confuses them even more, and I do not want confusion. That's what leads to accidentally getting a poison ivy tea with slug-skin crumbs, which some crazed idiot has been persuaded to order as part of a spring-time special offer. The best solution is to go with something which is quite distinctive even if clearly not your name. I tend to go with one of the Care Bears. Most of the servers in these shops are too young to remember who the Care Bears were in the first place. It just really irked me one time when I gave my name as Grumpy Bear but the kid who noted it may not have been too good at English. Or perhaps I was just mumbling. Either way, I ended up with a large cappuccino marked for, "Grumpy Bore". The worst bit was that I was in quite a bad mood that day, so it wasn't all that inappropriate either. Still, what I can say? I have my faults but at least I'm self-aware.

My other strongpoint is that I'm physically fit. Let's not get too excited, though. I don't mean that I'm promenading a 38 Double D chest size with a curved backside swinging seductively as I wander along the mountain paths in little more than a tight pair of shorts and a sports bra. No, I mean that when I programme a route on my hiking app, I don't blanche at the prospect of a 20+ clicks (aka kilometres), 1,500m climb trail in blazing summer heat or a raging thunderstorm. And I can even do it while I'm having my period. So go me. I also do it in proper, protective gear, including full-length trousers, a proper shirt and insect repellent wristbands. Where horse flies and ticks are a possibility, better safe than sexy. Besides, if you've been walking up a steep gradient in full summer heat for a couple of hours, then you're going to need to be the definitive model of female, sensual perfection to attract any male who hasn't lost his sense of smell completely. And that's just the male goats.

All this explains why I'm currently heading along a trail just above the treeline, a short distance away from the famous Fulda Gap. Switzerland just is my kind of place for a holiday, and I love it here. I can walk for miles, I can see for miles, I can think and reflect, or I can moan like hell to myself, but I can pretty much do what I like because for the most part, you're on your own. There's a sense of freedom when you can choose between forest paths or valley roads, take a break for five minutes or five hours, or even just drink out of mountain streams as you feel like it. At least, provided you're not next to a cow field. Best leave the streams alone in that case unless your idea of fun is admiring the snowline on the other side of the valley while you blow out half the contents of your intestines into a different form of avalanche on this side.

It's taken me ages to get up here today. I can't remember how many hundreds of metres the climb was, but it was steep as hell, and it just kept going. I was skirting a cliff face so there can't have been much room to extend the path horizontally as it climbed. That's the usual way to make a steep climb manageable. It's as though you zig-zag your way to the top. It's not the fastest way to travel but it won't kill you. Today's trek was more like climbing a spiral staircase and I'm feeling it, especially in my legs. There's a certain irony when taking some really serious exercise is highly recommended by the world's greatest medical sources, yet it leaves you feeling like you've just contracted arthritis.

The numbing ache in my legs aside, things are now looking pretty good. I'm trekking with the side of the mountain on my left and, on my right, the range on the other side of the valley curving gently in across the line of the route I'm following. It's a great day and I can see a whole range of Alpine meadows across the valley, the snowline a decent but not massive way above them, and the forests stretching down to the floor between us. What's nice is that it's roughly in front of me. I really hate it when there's great scenery by your path, but the angles mean that you're more or less walking away from it.

Of course, nothing lasts forever, and my great view is interrupted when the path descends gently into the forest itself. Then again, it's getting a bit hot out here, so the shade is welcome. The forests are always peaceful too. I like it there. I don't bother taking pictures like I sometimes do further up on the meadow ranges but that's only because one forest looks just like another in a camera shot. It doesn't mean I don't like being there. I suppose that's kind of like the experience of a pub crawl in Ibiza. One chav passed out on the beach looks fairly similar to the next but they're all still having fun. The main difference is that I'm sober.

Not that vulgarity is entirely absent, not even in Switzerland, and I'm soon reminded of that. What was a mountain stream further up above the treeline has metamorphosed into a full torrent with a cascading waterfall, which has, over a couple of million years I suppose, cut a very deep gorge through the forest, down the side of the mountain. After the waterfall, it passes into a mini-valley, at the bottom of which is the rivulet itself and a set of rocks next to it.

There's more than one bottom to be seen down there. I'm walking way above the side of this drop, and I must be out of sight of anyone below. Either that or they really don't care because there's some woman stripping down beside the water. I mean stripping right down. I can see a very deep gorge of a sort I was not expecting for a moment.

What the hell, woman? Perhaps you think you're all alone out here but I'm feeling faintly offended in fact. You just don't expect this sort of thing in a socially conservative, staid part of the German-speaking world. Talking of Ibiza, isn't that one of the principal roles of southern Spain? To get this sort of dodgy behaviour farmed out to a set of quasi-colonies where drunken Brits, Germans and Dutch can re-enact World War Two over the swimming pool deckchairs and who's first in line for a beer and a shag?

I'm about to carry on in a state of offended disgust when she's joined by a man. I haven't been paying much attention to what she looks like beyond the areas which I shouldn't have been able to see, I was that taken aback. However, his features suddenly captivate me and it's as though a massive overdose of oestrogen is surging through my veins. No way! He can't be, it isn't surely? Timothy Dalton! The best James Bond there's ever been and the one for whom I would have happily dropped my underpants and climbed into the back seat of the Aston Martin in an instant, even in my arch-feminist days back at university.

I'm getting a hot flush strong enough that you could fry an egg in my undies. Actually, that's quite a gross thought but I can't come up with any really elegant descriptions while my brain is overheating like this. And he's taking his shirt off now as well! If I could get down there, knock the girl unconscious and cover her up with the clothes I'd be shedding, could I just maybe get lucky?

Hold on, hang on a moment, Jessica. Let's take one step back here. Try and free a small portion of your brain for just an instant. Your idea of carnal ecstasy is with Timothy Dalton as James Bond, right? Timothy Dalton only played Bond in "The Living Daylights" and "License to Kill". They were released at the end of the 1980s. So unless Mr Dalton somehow discovered the secret of eternal youth shortly after he'd finished his vodka martini, the chances are that he must look a bit older some three to four decades later. The guy down there can only be looking like him.

Oh yeah. It just shows what a huge fan of Tim's I am that I somehow missed that. All the same, I'm busy fanning myself with the smock I wear round my neck. What a rush. It occurs to me that if I could somehow extract a litre or two of my blood to store somewhere right now, I could maybe make quite a bit of cash by selling it to a hormone replacement therapy clinic. I'm still considering how that might be done when the effect is cut short. I look back over the side of the cliff and it seems that while he's got his shirt off, that little tart next to him has decided to become very friendly with him and – bloody hell! I don't know if he's licensed to kill but he'd better have a license to commit some form of anti-social behaviour in a public place or else pray that the Swiss cops don't catch up with him in the near future.

Oh well, let's leave them to enjoy a form of self-fulfilment which is extremely unlikely ever to feature in yet another movie take on "Heidi". I doubt the goats could take the strain. I move on, wistfully considering my unfulfilled, and never to be fulfilled, passion for Tim.

I wouldn't say I'm a diehard James Bond fan. I've always liked the films but that may be for little more reason than that I once overheard my elder sister dismiss them as, "scummy and rude." This was at an early age where more adult modes of expression hadn't been adopted yet, plus Bethany has never quite had my talent for irritating repartee. Whatever, the main point was that if she had a low opinion of them, the chances were that they were pretty good. So I started watching them whenever one showed up on TV.

Not bad overall, was my childhood assessment. I had to lay off for a bit during my aforementioned flirtation with serious feminism at university. Bond has never really been the poster boy for a truly enlightened, male outlook on life. However, who then is? Some bougie actor out of Hollywood with a passion for vegan canapés and a textbook liberal speech on everything from public restrooms to throwing up a deep-fried Mars Bar? The gay one out of Take That (I'm going no further on that)? The problem is that these people just don't know how to have a good time like Bond does. They don't know how to hand it out like he does either.

So why Timothy Dalton? The poor guy is sadly way down the list of favourite Bonds in most surveys. Usually above George Lazenby but George was lucky to come in above Blofeld. Be all that as it may, I think that Tim does take the prize for being the most hard-edged Bond, yet still with a sense of likeability about him. True, Daniel Craig has always been the most dramatic Bond but that's as much thanks to the scripts as Dan the Man himself. Anyway, I can't help feeling that it's a bit overdone. If I go to see 007, I don't expect a soap opera. I want someone a little bit out there, who's on the right side of things but still gets away with killing, drinking and shagging to an extent not usually seen beyond a cup final night when Newcastle United are playing. In my opinion, Tim got it just right. Not least when he took his shirt off although sadly, that didn't happen as often as I would have liked. I reflect on all this as I wander along the forest path. I do like the fact that you can sometimes just let your mind wander as you do so.

Another great thing about being up here is that you get away from all the tourists. The towns aren't necessarily all that quiet but most of them, certainly all the smaller ones, are already connected to the nearest Alps by clearly marked routes. Said routes will get you onto an upwards climb within about ten minutes at most. Once you're climbing, suddenly everyone else seems to vanish. I don't mean that you never run into anyone at all. Assuming you're not unlucky and/or stupid enough to be making your way along some path a couple of kilometres into the sky just as a thunderstorm strikes, there are enough other hikers out there but they don't get in your way, they don't have annoying dogs with them and they show you some basic courtesy and respect. You're clearly a million miles away from the local discount supermarket. You just need to remember to greet everyone with a polite, "Grüzi," in German Switzerland or, "Bonjour," in French Switzerland and you're well aligned with the hiking culture. It's a nice culture too. You'll rarely encounter the smallest piece of litter in the mountains because littering is just not the done thing. Several farmsteads sell produce such as milk and cheese, produced locally. Granted, it can be a bit off-putting to think that you're about to get a comestible which literally squirted out of that bovine shitting machine on the other side of the fence not that long ago but it's actually good stuff. My point is that they leave the stuff in an easily accessible fridge with prices shown and let everyone simply use an honesty box principle to put the right cash in place. Some of them even have electronic payment terminals too. What's nice, in my view, is that everybody up there knows the code of behaviour, they stick to it and they're all happy. Try finding that in the average, Spanish beach resort/colony for the Anglo-German crowd.

All of this is not to say that you don't have tourist traps. Of course, there are your Zermatts and Interlakens, mainly places surrounded by stunning scenery where virtually everything is in English. This basically means that the target audience is generally from the United Kingdom, the United States or the wealthier parts of Asia (India, South Korea and China being particular favourites) and the assumption is that they speak about as much German as the average wallaby. Everybody knows that Switzerland is a pricey country but trust me, it doesn't have to be as pricey as what people pay for things in these dives. Sure, it costs more than Benidorm but that doesn't mean that every Swiss person thinks that it's normal to pay twenty francs for a cheese sandwich. In case you don't know, the Swiss franc is worth a small shade more than the US dollar. Go figure. The way out, as with most tourist traps, is to work out where the locals go and in Switzerland, this is pretty easy. Just find a hotel or restaurant where the signs and menus are in German. You only need to learn enough to ask, "Sprechen Sie Englisch?" (do you speak English, for the one or two who hadn't realised) because they will anyway. They just can't be bothered in the first instance.

Please don't imagine that I'm being mean to the Swiss here. They're certainly no worse than the rest of the world and anyone who's ever taken in the sights in New York, Paris, Rome, London etc etc will know the gig. They even run this show in Liverpool. Boosted by the fact that, as most people know, the Beatles originated in Liverpool, the tourist business was handed a golden spoon in the 1960s which it has never let go of since.

Ringo Starr took a dump here in 1967? You can get a Beatles toilet seat for just fifty quid, don't worry. Fifty quid? Kind of pricey, isn't it? Just be glad that it wasn't John Lennon or you'd be paying a hundred.

"All You Need is Love". Provided you can afford the merch too.

As I've tried to make clear though, the best bit about Switzerland is that it does provide the opportunity to escape all this and get into a really nice bit of mountainous scenery instead. It's unsullied by rip-offs, enough booze to get you drunk by breathing in the surrounding air, and your fellow tourists. Just a lot of cowpats but I can live with that. What a great country.

Chapter 2
THE FOOD OF LOVE

Harris

I can't be late. I really can't be late. Why are there so many cars in front of us? I wouldn't have bothered to get a ruddy taxi if I'd known that half the town would be sitting around like this. Why won't a single one move? What if Isabel gets there ahead of me? What if she thinks I've let her down? Not tonight of all nights, please not tonight. Not when I can finally promise her the most perfect of plans. Not when I've gambled everything.

Who would ever have imagined that there could be so much traffic in Bristol? It's hardly London for crying out loud. A lively and bustling town, I would certainly say but hardly the sort of metropolis to be seeing traffic jams like this one. This is frankly obscene. I just can't believe it. But why tonight? Why?

Oh come on, I must get a grip. Take a breath, you silly man. Let something sooth your soul. Perhaps a piece by Elgar. Just lean back and listen to it play across your mind. They say that music emanates from the cortex, that the soundwaves coming from instruments actually just stimulate the reflexes which produce it. If you can stir those with your imagination, then it will flow.

That may be the case, but I seem to have a cascade of reflexes surging through me right now and it's not helping a lot. I simply must reach that club. There's too much hanging on this moment. I'll just have to brave the rain, I suppose.

Yet finally we're moving. My goodness. After such a long time. What on earth has been happening?

Ten minutes later and I find out. Oh dear. I am rather taken aback. It appears that some sort of street-cleaning truck has crashed into the side of a grocery store. That can't have been a good thing. I don't know if anybody is hurt but there are several emergency services vehicles nearby. How ghastly.

Once past the police barrier, we finally get going and I reflect on what I have planned.

I have to make Isabel feel comfortable and confident of my love for her, which she certainly should be. I have never loved another as dearly as I love her. I would even go so far as to say that I adore her. Her beauty is reminiscent of a particularly fine van Gogh and she has the most delicate yet strong, modest yet determined character I have ever encountered. I can only be enchanted.

Following that, I have to demonstrate real confidence that I now have the key to our life together, not through any sort of compromise but with all which she desires. I do so wish her father was not an obstacle, but I have the answer. I really do. If she believes that and accepts what I have to offer, this may be one of the richest evenings I have ever enjoyed. We may even have time left to make the second half of that wonderful performance of "Tosca" at the Bristol Opera House. Who knows what the evening may hold?

The taxi comes to an abrupt halt. The Knights Club. Let's hope Isabel hasn't made it yet,

"That's twenty-three quid, mate."

Twenty-three pounds? For a trip of some five miles? I do not believe it, but I suppose it must come from that accident. It's nobody's fault but it still rankles. Still, nothing for it. I pull out a twenty-pound note and search for a fiver in my other pocket.

"I can take cards as well, you know," says the driver in a rather annoyed tone as I try to find that wretched bank note.

I give him a supercilious look. Those awful card machines. Paper money and coins have worked perfectly well for hundreds of years. I see no good reason to replace them with some dreadful piece of electronic tat simply because we can.

My fingers wrap around the five-pound note and I hand over the two notes to the driver, asking him to keep the change. That seems to mollify him, and he pulls away, finally leaving me to reach my destination.

"Good evening, sir. Do you have a reservation?"

I don't know why she's asking me this as it's hardly the sort of place I would have come to without a reservation, but I suppose we have to stick to the protocol.

"Yes," I respond as graciously as I can manage after dealing with the taxi driver. "I have a reservation for two under Beadlesby."

She checks her list and finds my name.

"Welcome to the Knights Club, Mr Beadlesby. You have a companion with you?"

She looks around curiously. This is good news since I suppose nobody else can have come in already, looking for me. I check the surroundings for any sign of Isabel just in case.

The reception area is quite sumptuous really, though in good taste. It has a 1920s feel to it with light beige colours and a lot of fine wood. A small number of ridged pillars mark the various doorways leading off towards the lounges and the dining room. The dark green carpet offsets them neatly and the marble of the reception desk itself is also a contrasting element though in a well-measured way. The lights are tidied away in the upper crevices of the ceiling and are complemented by a couple of lamps standing by the pillars at the far end.

There's no sign of Isabel, however. That's a very good thing. I would like to take control of the evening and being first in place is an important part of that. I just wish I wasn't so nervous. I tell the receptionist that I'll wait here until my dining companion arrives.

A pair of slightly elderly gentlemen pass me by. Tweed suits and brown leather shoes, I notice. They seem a fine example of the clientele although I'm rather taken aback when I catch their conversation.

"He looked like he was trying to eat a packet of prawn cocktail crisps which he'd forgotten to open first!" one of them intones.

The other cackles rather vulgarly.

Dear me. Standards really are dropping in this benighted country these days.

Thankfully, that doesn't apply to everyone. After five minutes of examining some of the back copies of, "Game and Country" which lie scattered around the low-slung tables in the waiting area of reception, I hear Isabel's delightful voice.

"Harris, darling! I'm so sorry I'm late."

I couldn't care less. She walks up to me and kisses me on the left cheek. I respond with a light kiss but fully on her mouth.

She looks askance, then tilts her head to one side with a knowing smile.

"Please, darling, there are people here who may be wondering what we're doing!"

There are people who are discussing rather revolting ways of eating prawn cocktail crisps so I rather doubt that a loving kiss will be too scandalous, but I play along.

"I'm sorry, Love of my Life. You're just too beautiful for me."

That is undeniably true. She is, as always, absolutely stunning. Isabel is not one to put herself on display but her understated outfit simply emphasizes how gorgeous she is. She certainly puts my light grey three-piece suit in a clear second place. A close-cut dress in deep blue stretches from her shoulders down to her knees, an only barely visible floral pattern stretching from the high neckline to the waist where a thin belt of black leather holds the clothing in place above her hips. Below the dress, lightweight tights of a burgundy hue make their way down to the flat loafers adorning her feet. Her arms are covered to just below the elbow, below which a pair of bracelets hang from her wrists. Bracelets which, it thrills me to say, I gave her as her birthday present last month.

Her red hair bounces in the bob she has, which stirs my passions so. It may not be to everyone's taste, but I don't want everyone trying to marry her either. That, I very much hope, is my job.

"I wasn't too early myself actually," I add. "There was some awful accident a couple of miles back and the traffic was backed up terribly."

"Oh is that what happened?" she asks. "I thought it was the roadworks they've put up around the Hippodrome. They're simply dreadful."

"Well, let's move to happier things, shall we?" I ask. "I believe we have a fine serving of dinner awaiting us."

The dining room is somewhat darker but a lot more intimate. The purple-red walls give an almost claustrophobic feel to the room, but this is offset by the multiple windows which let in enough light to make it homely rather than oppressive. The leather, high-backed chairs are of a similar hue to the walls, and the effect lends itself to one of respectful welcome. The tables are well-spaced, and each has its own set of candles. I see some idiot on the far side has managed to set fire to his menu with one, but you can't account for all tastes and the waiting staff douse it quickly with a pitcher of water anyway.

We start with the small talk. This is good. Have to be relaxed so that I don't rush things when I get to the important moment.

"How was the gallery today?" I ask. I'm not just being polite either. The gallery where Isabel works is simply enchanting. It's also where I first met her, so it holds a significant meaning for me. A copy of that painting of an African vista now hangs in my office at school, something which keeps me going each day.

"It was a quiet day for the most part and really quite relaxing," she begins. That sounds nice but there's a slight hesitancy which warns me that not everything was necessarily so relaxing.

"There was one downside though, early in the afternoon. An elderly, American gentleman came in, complaining that we had delivered him an incorrect print. He was quite forthright about it too and you know that I do not appreciate bad manners."

"Quite right too," I sympathize. As a teacher in a secondary school, I see more than enough of those, let me tell you.

"He insisted that we had made an error with the print he had ordered from us," she continues. "When I enquired what he had ordered, he said that he had requested a print of a hurricane coming in from the sea. It was a strange request as I believed that we had never had a painting, original or print, of quite such a description.

"When I looked up his original order, I saw that it was indeed the name he had given and that we did not have anything by that artist. However, we had found the sole print in our collection which represented a hurricane of sorts. Somebody had suggested that this must be what he wanted and so we had dispatched it. Apparently that was not the case and since he was now over here on a visit to England, he had decided to come and sort things out in person. That I don't mind but I was very much wishing that he would use some more refined terms to express himself."

You should hear what I have to put up with sometimes, I grimace to myself mentally, but I keep the thought to myself. Isabel doesn't like to have her stories interrupted and I'm happy just to gaze at her face while she tells them. I like to think of myself as someone who can at least listen sensitively. It's not a widespread skill these days, I fear.

"Anyway, to get to the point, it turns out that the mistake had been all his. Eventually he said something which indicated that he had been wanting a picture of an aeroplane. This was extremely confusing since, as you know, we don't really have that sort of thing. Nature and historical paintings are much more our realm. Some expressionist and a bit of reflective art too but not mechanical and modern representations. However, he was insisting that he had seen whatever it was he had been searching for on our website. We asked to see it and finally figured out the answer.

"The silly old man had confused us with the Ledger Gallery across the road. As you know, they cover more modern themes than we do. This includes some pictures of the Second World War when, if I recall, the Battle of Britain included an aircraft called a Hurricane. It seems that this was what he had been wanting but he had confused the two galleries when he placed his order."

I chuckle sympathetically.

"Daft, old thing. I'm surprised he found his way into the right country to make a complaint in the first place."

"Oh, Harris, don't be so beastly," she chides gently. It sounds outdated how she speaks but I find it delightfully charming myself. It's as though she represents a type of lady you simply don't encounter anymore, even though you would long to do so. "Anyone can make a mistake. We cleared up with the Ledger people and got him what he wanted. He was actually very apologetic about it afterwards and bought a print of an 1800s Berkshire mansion from us to make things up. I suppose it turned out all right in the end.

"How was your own day?"

I sigh slightly. I do enjoy my work but it's rarely easy.

"I keep fighting the good fight," I start, slightly ruefully. "Persuading today's teens that Puccini might enrich their lives or that Bach did not just compose to impress but to speak to the listener is always an uphill struggle."

"So you tell me, and I believe you, don't worry. You do a fantastic job, Harris, really."

That's the wonderful thing about Isabel. She will always recognize the effort, not just the achievement. I just wish her father might as well.

"Did you hear anything about that piano competition you were putting those pupils in for?"

"Well, no," I confess. "But next week is half-term and I doubt anyone in the West Country Music Board will be trying to set up the Young Pianists Finals until after that. The logistics will be near impossible to organize in any sort of meaningful way until that's over.

"At least for the potential winners," I add with a knowing smile. "I understand that several of the no-hopers have been informed of their status as such already but there's no indication yet with regard to any of my three."

"Do you really think one of them could make it?" asks Isabel.

I consider the situation. The three pupils are all very fine musicians but there's one who stands out. That being the case, I really doubt the other two could qualify.

"It's a good question, Isabel," I respond at last. "Alice Morrison and Robert Fletcher have real talent and a lot of it but there's something about Katie Porter which just sets her apart. I would love to see any of them selected but it's hard to see how Alice or Robert could really make it in place of Katie."

At this point, I decide that it may be time to move to more important matters.

"Isabel," I begin. "There is something else though, which I would like to talk to you about."

I lean back slightly in my seat, making an active effort to relax my shoulders and to fix a half-smile on my face which shows confidence but not arrogance, knowing a secret but without being smug. It's not easy to do and I'm also trying to calm myself with deep breaths.

The whole effect is rather undermined by the waiter arriving to clear away our starters and refill the wine glasses. I may have misjudged my timing a shade. In my nervousness, I think I have maybe come across as sneering at the choice of wine being poured, which given that it was my choice, is at least more just bizarre than offensive. In any case though, it's hardly helping the mood, and the dratted waiter seems to be taking forever.

When he's finally bustled away, I forget the posture and just concentrate on trying to be relaxed and not to speak too quickly.

"Isabel, I have something important to tell you. It's about the life we will have together and how we can make it happen."

"Oh, Harris, please. Could we just keep things simple for once? I understand that the situation is frustrating but simply re-hashing it over and over again just doesn't solve anything. You know that I love you and that I want you forever in my life. It's just that I need to make sure that my life and you can be compatible with each other.

"You both matter and you know that," she finishes with a slightly apologetic yet determined tone. "It just makes me sad to hear about the conflict."

"Well perhaps I can cheer you up a smidgeon," I beam. "I have something very important to share with you."

"Really?" She seems more perplexed than anything. I do hope I can soothe her worries. I do so.

"I have something to confess," I begin. "Nothing untoward, trust me, but something which I have not been wanting to share until I could be sure that it would, that it will, work."

She seems unconvinced but curious.

"As we know, the main reason why we cannot make public our engagement or even our love for each other is your father."

"Please, Harris, not again."

"No, no, wait," I cut her off, "I'm not going to lecture or pontificate. I actually have a plan. A plan to persuade him that I am worthy of you."

She raises her eyebrows.

"I've told you several times already. My family does not exist in the 1700s. It's not as though you have to win my hand and gain my father's accord in order to marry me. It's simply that I can't bring myself to enter a situation where I would be married to someone who is simply nothing more than a grudgingly accepted house guest in the family. I want a husband who is accepted, who is welcomed, who is loved by my family. I don't want to have a second family which is only tolerated by my first. I keep telling you and myself that I love you equally and I happily accept, welcome and love you, my darling. And I mean it, absolutely.

"But I can't, and I won't live in a world where I'm part of two halves who won't love the other. And that, as you know, is that."

She stares at me with a mixture of pity, empathy and defiance. Only she can mix so many emotions and still have me adore her equally for each.

I have, needless to say, heard all of this several times before.

"The thing is, Isabel, that I do listen to you very sincerely."

"I know you do, darling, it's just that –"

"No, wait." I see her look rather taken aback for an instant. "I mean that I actually have something to propose."

She looks on expectantly. Progress at last, I think.

"My understanding is that to your father's way of thinking, I am a decent enough sort of chap but just not much of an over-achiever. I work hard and I enjoy what I do. I believe in the value of the music I hold so dearly and try to share with the next generation.

"As we know, this is my saving grace in terms of being at least tolerated as a romantic acquaintance, thanks to your father's own refined tastes and praiseworthy appreciation of the arts. For that I applaud him.

"At the same time, if I were to ask for your hand, whether literally or metaphorically, I know that this is more than he would be pleased to see, mainly because I am not exactly an over-achiever in a professional, financial, political or even" – I breathe for an instant –"an artistic sense."

I pause for a moment. All I've done so far is recap the problem. I think I may need to move a little faster with the proposed solution at this point.

"So I would like to achieve something, or more precisely to show that when something really matters to me, that I can and I will make all the effort possible.

"You matter more than life itself to me, Isabel, and so does your family by extension. However, I can't demonstrate this, can I? At least, not in a practical sense."

A quick pause for effect. She looks more confused than ever, so I continue again.

"Except that now I can. I will be presenting your father with a gift from me to the family, at the same time as I formalize my engagement to you by getting down on one knee in front of all your family at your mother's seventieth birthday party next month."

She looks sceptical.

"What do you mean, a gift? Are you trying to buy yourself some goodwill? You don't have to present a dowry. This is the twenty-first century, you know."

"No, no," I reply hurriedly. "The purpose of this gift is to capture the importance which I attach to your family, at the point where I ask to join it. Not just to show that importance in an absolute sense but to show the effort which I'm prepared to make to be part of it. In presenting my gift, I want to show that I am also welcoming your father, and of course the rest of your family, into my world."

She still looks dubious. I don't blame her but I'm going for the dramatic effect here. I lean back in my chair again, this time checking carefully for any waiting staff first.

"So what is this gift, darling?" She cocks her head quizzically.

I wait a moment.

"It's a clarinet."

"A clarinet?"

"Not just any clarinet. Karl Givret's clarinet. The very one and only clarinet which he played."

Her eyes widen, as they well should. It's not every day that somebody promises you the original instrument of the finest player of the clarinet in musical history. It's not something you would just take on board as though somebody had informed you that they were merely going to take you on holiday to the Côte d'Azur or Gstaad. There's nothing wrong with those, but this is well out of even their league.

"Harris," she stutters. "What can you possibly mean by this?"

I lean towards her, my eyes fixated on hers. I adore that offset azure tone they have. It's striking when she's genuinely surprised.

"I'm going to lay it all out here. I've been casting about in my mind for months as to how I could demonstrate my love for you in a way which would really resonate with your family, mainly your father. What could I do to show some sort of achievement? What could I do to prove that I can make something happen?

"Then a couple of weeks ago, I saw something. I was reading, 'Classicals Weekly', when I noticed that there was an auction coming up in Milan, where a range of musical pieces would be sold. This was being hyped because they were no mere mementoes. I was looking at original instruments played by some of the most exquisite musicians who have ever been known to the human race. They even also had original manuscripts by Beethoven and a lock of Mozart's hair. It was like the Aladdin's cave of musical history.

"That was when it occurred to me. Here was something I could achieve, I mean actually make happen. I wanted so badly to do something which would serve as a symbol of my love for you, my darling, and also of my dedication to your family, where I know I will belong. But how to make this happen?

"I went through the list carefully and finally settled on a couple of options where I might find the funds. One was an original Amati violin. The other was Karl Givret's clarinet."

"Hold on, Harris," she cuts in. "What do you mean, where you might find the funds? Those things must be extortionate."

"Oh yes, they are," I agree knowingly. "That's why I am now a mortgage-holder on my house."

She examines me carefully.

"You mean that you took a loan, using your own house as collateral? The same house which your parents left you?"

"I have no other."

"How much was the clarinet?"

I look slightly askance for a moment.

"About a quarter of a million pounds," I reply as casually as I can.

She gapes.

"But why?"

"Because," I stare at her as intensely as I can, "that's what you mean to me. That's how special you are."

I think the message is finally getting through. She blushes profusely and takes a menu to fan herself.

At this point, the waiter has to reappear, damn the man. The drama of the conversation takes a brief hiatus while he serves up two plates of lamb tagine with a light inflection of oregano and garlic. Quite an exquisite dish, in my view but I do wish it could have arrived five minutes later.

The vegetables having been served from a side platter and the wine glasses refilled, we're finally left on our own again. The intimacy returns.

"But, Harris, when was this auction? You've been busy at work since at least Easter."

"Of course, you're right, but it wasn't easy to get a ticket to the auction either, which was actually two days ago."

"Two days?"

"Yes. I obviously couldn't get there myself, but Charles could."

My good friend Charles is a musician himself, an extraordinary flautist and clarinetist with the Somerset Symphonic Orchestra in fact. I know that sounds a shade parochial and perhaps it is, but it is one of the best county symphonics there are, and Charles often has the chance to tour with national level ensembles as well.

This is where he is at present, on tour in northern Italy. This was extremely lucky for me since he was in Florence at the time of the auction. Being a good friend, he agreed to take a day off and go over to Milan on my behalf, where he registered for a place in the auction as a professional musician. Admitted as such and equipped with the largesse I had temporarily bestowed on him, so to speak, he went full throttle into the bidding and acquired the precious clarinet.

When he reported back to me on his success, I was ecstatic. Finally, finally, the loves of my life were coming together, and they still are. It's a wonderful feeling, truly wonderful.

I explain all this to Isabel. She seems frankly astonished.

"But that's incredible, Harris. I just need a little time to take it all in. You've done all this, you've done so much, you've gone to so much trouble for, for… me?"

"For us, my darling, for us and our love."

She looks as though she's about to burst into tears.

Which is a shade unfortunate since it happens to be precisely when the waiter re-appears to refill our wine glasses. Does the man imagine that we're alcoholics or something? Can't he appreciate what really matters to us both here?

Still, it's a minor inconvenience at worst.

Isabel eventually takes a couple of deep breaths and wraps her hands around mine on the table. She looks into my face, lets her eyes wander a moment and then looks up into my gaze again. Her eyes are moist, but her voice holds fast.

"Harris, darling, I don't think I've ever loved anyone as deeply as I feel I love you now. I can't imagine how I ever will except that I think this feeling will continue forever."

A moment of silence ensues. The rest of the room has ceased to exist. Nothing else intrudes on us. I can't hear anything apart from her breathing and my own.

"I think I'll have the prawn cocktail!"

Very well, I can't hear anything else apart from her breathing and my own plus some dreadful loudmouth who's just arrived at the next table and seems unable to express himself at any level of volume which doesn't put a ship's foghorn to shame. I know I should probably have planned this moment in a more intimate location, but I also wanted to show that I was prepared to bring Isabel to somewhere more sophisticated than my own home.

The intervention from our neighbour appears to have shaken her out of her contemplation now.

"Tell me, darling, how do you propose to retrieve this clarinet? Doesn't it have to be registered with customs and the like? Will you actually have it by Mother's birthday?"

"Absolutely, my darling, absolutely," I assure her. "It's all taken care of."

I do rather wish she hadn't brought up this technicality though. Bringing an instrument worth around a quarter of a million pounds over a national border is not actually as simple or inexpensive as some might imagine. Nonetheless, this is where Charles comes in again. As a professional musician, few people are likely to question his carrying a flute, a clarinet or the like with him. He should attract minimum attention. This is possibly not the most salubrious aspect of my masterplan, but it was Charles' idea, and I do agree that it was not a bad one at all, when you stop to consider it.

All of this is swept away for me by Isabel's next movement, however. She gets out of her seat and adjusts her dress, sweeping a slender hand from her midriff to her upper leg to smooth the fabric. She looks around carefully then comes to my side of the table. Her two hands nestle into the sides of my face and grip my beard lightly.

Her lips brush against mine, then fix on them for what feels like an eternity. I have lost track of time at this point and do not know anything except for the embrace of her emotion.

She draws back.

"Harris, you are the most delightful man I could ever hope to love," she says. "There is nobody else who could possibly achieve what you have just achieved. I have no doubt."

I know that in the most important respect, my life's work is now already complete.

Chapter 3

KEEPING IT IN THE FAMILY

Jessica

Zürich Airport. What can I say? A great place? Not really. A complete dump? Certainly not. It's just a big airport. Heathrow, Charles de Gaulle, JFK and so forth. They all have a slightly samey feel to them. They're a bit like cathedrals. Nothing wrong with them either and they're impressive pieces of architecture, even if not to everyone's taste. The strange thing about them though, is that they're all that similar no matter where you are in the world but not only that. They all have the same, musty smell to them. It's not just that they're all of a certain age but for some reason, old cathedrals all have their own, particular cathedral smell to them. It's not one shared by medieval castles, old palaces or even those ancient pubs you sometimes see out in the countryside where the only things which appear to be preventing the whole building falling on your head are an old mop and a slot machine.

Like cathedrals, most airports are much the same, at least the really big ones. You do get a bit of variety with the smaller jobs, to be fair. I like London City, for example. It looks like an extended bit of grass stuck out in the middle of the Thames River. You come charging down the flightpath, skimming over the sights of central London (oh all right, the East End if you want to be pedantic) with only this tiny bit of tarmac on the horizon. It feels like you're heading for an aircraft carrier landing. It's "Top Gun" and you're Maverick. Actually, the pilot is upfront ahead of you so you're more like Goose. Didn't Goose get killed when the ejection sequence went wrong in the film? Oh yeah. Maybe it's not quite such a great analogy but never mind. You still have Kenny

Loggins' "Highway to the Danger Zone" going on in your head and you're feeling cool.

Then there's Luton, another of Greater London's airports next to the town of the same name. "Highway to the Danger Zone" indeed, if your idea of the danger zone is getting beaten up by the locals should you ask too loudly if the source of that kebab was once somebody's cat. Come the school summer holidays and the departure lounge is like a holding zone for Ibiza, Malaga and Benidorm with enough booze on sale to ensure that most of those flying out won't know which one they actually land in anyway. They won't care either so long as they can spend their life savings to date on maintaining a state of semi-consciousness for the next fortnight.

Still, Zürich is not in that class. It may not be quite on the same scale as Heathrow or Frankfurt but it's still a significant transport hub and therefore pretty boring. True, it's in Switzerland but Switzerland is only 70% mountainous. The majority of the other 30% stretches in a sort of arc just north of the Alps, along which are located Geneva, Lausanne, Fribourg, Basel, Bern and Zürich, plus a few others which nobody outside the country has heard of unless they got a lucky guess on "Who Wants to be a Millionaire?". Right now, waiting at the airport arrivals, I'm right in the middle of that 30%. No, it's not ugly. It's just boring and it's frustrating to be in the largest city of what is probably my favourite country but with scenery which is about as mountainous as the harbourside in Liverpool. It's like winning a ticket to a rock concert, only to find yourself in the local bingo hall in front of an Elvis impersonator with false teeth and a bunch of octogenarians having hot flushes while they stick ten-pound notes into the waist band of his incontinence briefs; all to the sound of "Jailhouse Rock" performed by a jackdaw with terminal tuberculosis. Well, maybe not quite that bad but still a bit of a disappointment.

So what am I doing here when I could be scaling the heights of a ridge overlooking a gorgeous blue lake or at least dodging some cowpats as I descend through the quiet vista of mountainside pastures?

What I'm doing here is waiting for my niece to exit the arrivals hall, accompanied by her father, also known as my brother-in-law.

Alice is wonderful. I really mean that, and I love her dearly. Fifteen years old with the wit and wisdom of someone twice her age but the innocence of her own, give or take. An excellent pianist, I understand, although I confess to not knowing the difference between Franz Schubert and Elton John except that one's dead while the other looks as though he should be too, now that David Bowie has passed to the other side as well. Oh dear, Jessica, steady on with the ageism here. Still, all that aside, I believe Alice is damn good.

Of more interest to me is that Alice and I bonded when she was around two years old and continue to do so. While piano music may not be quite my forte and Timothy Dalton may not be her idea of one of the world's fittest dudes, we share a genuine love of mountain hikes, witty sarcasm and a free spirit. Put another way, we like to go out for a good time and somehow find one, ideally in an Alpine setting. Liverpool works as well though.

Of virtually no interest to me is my brother-in-law, now accompanying her. Colin has to be one of the most unattractive idiots I have ever encountered, and I've even encountered some dude attending a rally for homophobes' rights who looked like he'd blocked up his rear entry passage with his elbow (long story). I'm pretty sure Colin hates me even more than I dislike him. He's highly opinionated, has something to say on every topic and is never, in his mind, wrong about anything. He's very good-looking, has an awesomely paid job in international finance of some sort and wears outfits which probably cost more than I make in a year. He's also boring as hell and completely full of himself which is why I find him so unattractive.

This is a true story from the day of Bethany's wedding. At the reception Colin was, predictably enough, prancing around in some morning suit outfit which had no doubt been passed up on by Elon Musk because it was a bit too pricey. His thick, black locks were billowing in the gentle breeze, his high cheek bones had a sheen reflecting the bronze glow of the sun and there was a general air of complete bollocks about him which you know is the case when you read that sort of poetic crap in the description.

I was milling around, trying to see if the buffet had any of those bacon sausage roll things to which I'm quite partial. I finally saw some just at the back of the table, right behind some hummus stuff with artichokes and lettuce. Or something like that. I don't know. I'm always suspicious of anything which looks too green. But I know I'm safe with bacon sausage roll things. The question was how to reach far enough back since they were clearly meant for later consumption, presumably once the guests had cleaned up on the posh stuff at the front and were generally too wasted to notice that they were on to the three-for-the-price-of-two deal garbage further back. Something like that at least. I'm not a wedding planner myself.

So I'm leaning over on a garden chair which I found by the fountain next to the buffet. Talk about bougie. The freaking fountain had a naked cherub in the middle of it, spouting water out of his mouth and privates back into the fountain. And they say that I'm vulgar. Somehow or other, Colin manages to ponce up behind me and "accidentally" kicks away one leg of the chair I'm on. I crash into the fountain, managing to catch the front of my spring jacket and underlying bra on the statue's over-sized knob so that both pass up to the level of my chin and I'm left hanging there like a caught porno-trout with my boobs hanging out the bottom of my jacket and my skirt floating around my waist. I give Colin my most evil eye.

"Would you look at that harlot?" squawks some ageing relative of this worthless addition to my family. "Trying like that to steal Bethany's lovely, new husband! It's frankly disgusting!"

Steal him? Him? Are you out of your mind? If I were to steal him, Bethany's biggest worry should be that I'd likely give him straight back.

In case you're wondering, I finally escaped when my bra and jacket both snapped. I covered up my modesty by applying what was left of the jacket over my top half and tying the sleeves behind my back. Unsurprisingly enough, you won't see me in any of the wedding photos. I never got a bacon sausage roll thing either. That was the biggest disappointment of the day.

Colin on the other hand no doubt regards me as a hopeless bum. He thinks I'm someone who drifts through life without any purpose, believes that giving to charity constitutes a moral code and for whom a retirement plan is something you start considering around the age of sixty-five, assuming you remember by then that you might be needing one. And he's probably right.

One thing really, really pisses me off, however. His name is Morrison. Not Morriston. Morrison. So by getting married and adopting his name, Bethany finally got rid of that stupid surname by one letter, which has always been one of my main life ambitions. True, she paid a very high price in my personal opinion. Nonetheless, I'm jealous.

Still, got to act the part. You'll find out why in a moment, as I get back to what's going on at the airport.

I toss my packet of salt 'n' vinegar crisps into the bin. Oh all right, so I toss them at the bin, miss as usual and head over to put the bag into the bin myself. I get a snotty look from some elderly Swiss German dame who regards this as a piece of bad behaviour equivalent to getting my rear end stuck in a set of railings while mooning the president of the country. Still, I know that I should respect the culture of other people's countries. Pity I missed though. I doubt I would have been in such trouble if I'd hit the target. Only equivalent to mooning a member of parliament and no more.

Despite all that, I feel quite cheerful. Salt 'n' vinegar. Lovely. One of Switzerland's few weaknesses is the limited range of crisp flavours. They just don't have what you can get in a proper, British supermarket. Admittedly, it maybe doesn't reflect that badly on the rest of the world that they don't bother with flavours such as pickled onion and garlic, cheesy mayo, or ketchup and hot dog but you have to give us Brits credit for innovation. Nonetheless, the airport does have a bit more of the international outlook you need, including decent crisp flavours.

It's also raised my spirits which were flagging after hanging around for forty minutes after the flight from Heathrow supposedly landed. They couldn't fly directly from Bristol so just took the train to London. I know, Zürich is a huge airport, and the Swiss do like to cross-check your passport against your tax declarations for the last three decades (even if you're only twenty), your Interpol file and whether you ever associated with Gary Glitter, either before or after he went to prison. Still, how long can these two take? Are they bum-sliding along the corridor floor or something? Could be in the case of Alice. Colin would no doubt refrain in case he stains his Calvin Klein slacks.

Ah right, a couple of hot chocolates later, there they are at last. I know, you're expecting Alice to come running up with her arms wide open and a huge grin on her face, yelling, "Auntie Jess! You're the best!" Well, I'm afraid not. Alice is fifteen and considers herself quite cool. She's looking the wrong way too, which is probably not so bad, as I'm standing in front of a Victoria's Secret outlet and I would hate for her to go running in there with her arms wide open and a huge grin on her face. Most important though, she and I have our special parts to play right now.

Colin is strolling along beside her, keeping watch to ensure that she doesn't get exposed to too many UV rays coming in the window. The biggest risk there is probably due to the reflections from his Gucci Homme sunglasses but never mind. Calvin Klein slacks – what did I tell you? A dashing Ted Baker shirt under a Polo Ralph Lauren jacket and a pair of Santoni loafers. No socks mind you. That's the look of a guy who knows what's chic these days and he certainly does. Every inch of his frame is decked in a style which proclaims in an understated but confident way that this is a man who is defined by the highest standards of today's culture, and he knows it.

Twat.

Alice on the other hand is dressed like a dark blue Michelin Man. Covered in a puffy jacket of the type worn only by Arctic explorers and guys who've been fishing for too long to be aware of the world beyond that tree on the other side of the stream, she's stomping around in a pair of wellington boots for good measure. The fact that outside it's about thirty-two degrees doesn't seem to have bothered the one who dressed her up in this combined assault on clothing style and common sense. I mean, wellington boots? On a fifteen year-old?

For some reason, Bethany was always regarded as the brains of the family, but I have no idea why. Fair enough, she has degrees in African archaeology and ancient Norse poetry (someone's got to do it although I would have thought they'd live in Norway), but she has zero common sense and switches off her brain as soon as her over-protective instincts cut in. If you ask me, she must have switched it off permanently when she decided to marry Colin, but I can't prove that.

Bethany, you see, is the one responsible for the awful state in which Alice finds herself. She is hardly convinced that a week's walking trip in the mountains of Switzerland with her stupid aunt is such a great plan but amazingly enough, she's been agreeing to it each year since Alice was thirteen. However, she then has to ensure that her darling daughter will be perfectly safe. This is why Alice is struggling under the weight of a rucksack which your average paratrooper would wince at if issued as standard equipment for a route march. Also a wheelie case almost a metre high. As you may have guessed, Bethany herself has never been near an Alp. Her idea of a mountain is the slope up to the tea shop in the village of East Dawlings where this delightful family lives. Must be an altitude differential of at least ten metres, maybe even eleven. Someone get that woman a respirator.

The icing on the cake is that our hike will be restricted to a series of pre-planned walks which Bethany has most likely downloaded from www.frightened-wusses.com, each of which consists of no more than three clicks and covers part of the lakefront of Lake Constance or Lake Lucerne. The only thing I've been entrusted with is booking the accommodation since I can speak German and Bethany can't. Lucky we're not going on holiday in fifth century Norway, I guess.

Colin is probably less concerned about the finer points of Alice's safety, but he knows that he needs to take all this palaver very seriously. He himself is concerned for Alice's wellbeing and has also contributed his expertise to the standard operating procedures to prevent her possibly grazing her knee. However, I'm pretty certain that the real reason why he's agreed to this expedition is because he wants to spend a week boffing my sister senseless. If Colin displays one weakness apart from his character in general, it's that he suffers from a case of horniness verging on sex addiction.

You can somehow just see this in some people. Usually men, although it can affect females as well, even human ones. In Colin's case, anyone passing in a skirt has to get checked out with a careful curve of the head. The guy must be able to twist his neck by about two hundred and seventy degrees by now. The faintest hint of cleavage on a woman has him gazing downwards like a gold prospector in the Old West. He never goes to a swimming pool, probably because his constant, raging hard-on would get caught on the ladder on the way out of the pool. I've even seen him touch himself in a restaurant when a lady slipped on a burrito someone had left on the floor and ripped her tights as she fell against a radiator. And that was when her grandson was helping her up again.

The guy is simply insatiable. I don't even know if his little stunt at the wedding was because he hated me or because he just wanted to see enough female flesh to keep him going until Bethany had finished thanking all the well-wishers and could get down to the business of the day where she no longer needed her wedding dress. Probably both. Whether he's been faithful to Bethany or not over the years or just made sure that she has trouble sitting down comfortably every weekend, I don't know but I don't frankly care either. What I do know is that when I need to report on Alice's wellbeing every night at seven o'clock promptly, I'm to call Bethany's mobile and not the house. So they must be going away somewhere.

Right now, Colin is here to pass Alice into my care. Obviously, she couldn't possibly catch the flight on her own. She's hardly allowed to use the zebra crossing on her own back in East Dawlings. So now, I have to have lunch with this pillock before he releases Alice and me and gets his flight back to London. Good luck to any air hostesses making their way up or down the aisle in anything less than a bullet-proof pair of undies, I say.

"Alice! You look great!"

I've finally got their attention.

"Auntie Jess! How's life?"

She does give me a modest hug. Alice and I are close, but we don't go in for all that over-exaggerated hugging like a couple of bears who've lacked any company for the past decade, which you tend to see in American films. I've nothing against Americans but you can live with a bit of under-statement too, you know.

Colin is certainly not going to hug me. I'm most grateful.

"Oh hello, Jessica. I hope you're well," he almost sneers, with all the warmth of someone trying to be friendly to a dog turd.

"How nice to see you too, Colin," I beam. We both know we're lying completely but for whatever reason, we keep up the charade. "How was the flight?"

"It was reasonable," he sighs without much enthusiasm. "Business class isn't always what it used to be, mind you."

I refuse to be drawn. He knows as well as anyone that I never fly with anything other than an economy airline unless I accidentally find myself base-jumping.

"So where would you like to go for lunch?" I ask as I reach down to take the wheelie case and relieve Alice of some of her burden.

"Oh dear." Colin's eyes roll a couple of times. "I really can't be doing with all this heavy, Germanic dairy and meat. They just have no subtlety."

Nor do you, matey, and right now we're outside a McDonald's so I don't know what you're talking about but then again, most people don't so I'm hardly alone.

"Look, Dad, there's a French restaurant up there. It looks as though it might have some salads and seafood quiches."

At least Alice has some idea how to handle this guy.

"I suppose it might do," he intones in an exaggeratedly wearisome tone. "Your aunt certainly won't have any better suggestions. Her mind is something of a desert of taste."

Well, screw you too, arsehole.

We head up a series of escalators and moving walkways of the sort you only find in over-sized airports. Colin strides ahead with a masculine sense of purpose. Alice and I struggle behind with slightly more luggage than the average house-mover.

When we finally reach the restaurant, Colin is seated at a large table, overlooking the main carpark. I do love Swiss scenery, but I've seen better. However, it doesn't really bother him as he has both a menu and a twenty-something waitress to check out.

The restaurant itself is clearly meant to look like something upmarket out of Paris. Given that it's called, "Le Parisien", and each item on the menu costs at least fifty Swiss francs, that's not too hard to figure out. What is hard to figure out is how the hell I'm going to eat here without needing a second mortgage unless Colin coughs up the cash for this one. He might but I'm not relying on it as he may realise that it's another way to screw me over.

Right now though, he seems more intent on screwing the waitress, at least in his imagination. Annelise should really find something other than her breasts on which to rest her notepad, so she doesn't need a push-up bra, if you ask me.

His brow is contorting in some form of concentration. Let's leave him to it. I turn to Alice, who is trying to decipher the menu for herself.

"Seen anything you fancy, Alice?"

"No, Auntie Jess. I'm afraid that guy Dan went out with someone in the year above in the end," she intones flatly. The reference is to some kid she considered quite hot in her class at school. Puppy love doesn't do much for me but I'm enjoying the sarcasm.

"More fool him, I suppose, although he probably gets a better view of her cleavage than yours if you're dressed up to go Christmas carolling in Siberia."

Colin raises an evil eyebrow in my direction at that remark. The implicit criticism of Bethany's maternal instincts is not to be tolerated, at least not when coming from me. For him, Bethany is everything I'm not: conventionally beautiful, polite in her conversation, a real home-maker and dedicated mother, a first-rate trophy wife all round. She gives first-rate blowjobs too, according to an ex-boyfriend of hers I once met, but that's not a detail I've cross-checked with Colin.

Alice also eyes me suspiciously, but the look is more pointed. We're meant to be in character here. I acknowledge my mistake with a quick shrug and apologetic look and move on to safer territory.

"What I meant, Alice, was whether you've seen anything on the menu which we could get you for lunch."

"You mean what I'll be getting her for lunch, Jessica," Colin interrupts. "I rather doubt your holiday budget can cover much beyond a cheese sandwich."

"They do have some nice cheese in Switzerland, Colin."

He grimaces.

"So I smelt on the way up here. Was that smelting pot we passed what they call a fun do or something?"

"Fondue," I correct him although I don't know why I bother.

"Well whatever it is, it was an awful stench. I think we'll stick with some proper, French finery."

How about a guillotine? If this goes on much longer, I'd welcome it for either him or me.

"Auntie Jess, I don't really know what half of this is," Alice intervenes. "Can you translate it for me?"

"Please, Alice, I think I know my French dining," snorts Colin. "There's no need to bring in your aunt."

No need at all. I'm just a professional translator. However, I look on serenely while Colin goes through the various culinary options with a naff pronunciation which he's picked up either from back episodes of "Agatha Christie's Poirot" or some Pixar movie with a character who has a cod French accent. He has to explain where each one originates from in France and how it reflects the local characteristics. How he thinks he knows any of this is beyond me but since he already missed that two dishes are Belgian, I don't have much confidence in his sources. Alice nonetheless listens intently and asks some intelligent questions which he is actually able to answer. She's doing well.

After ten minutes or so of this dreary grandstanding, he's decided to take a lightly roasted veal steak with seasoned and sauteed potatoes finely sliced, and a side of fennel with diced radish. Alice has gone for the seafood quiche. I'm sticking with the closest-looking thing to macaroni cheese.

Annelise shows up to take the order. Colin launches into some dire version of what may be French in an attempt to demonstrate his cultural prowess.

Annelise doesn't catch a word of it. Whether that's because his French sounds more like a Hindi speaker suffering from a bout of diarrhoea or because we're deep into German-speaking Switzerland isn't obvious, but it may be a combination of both.

Annelise goes for the immediate default option for idiot tourists and launches into fluent English. Switzerland is one of the most pitifully easy countries in the world to get around if you can only speak English. Probably easier than America.

This doesn't go down well with Colin though. How can his linguistic skills be outshone by those of a mere waitress? A woman whose breasts and child-bearing regions may be exquisite but whose brain capacity is of no interest to him? So he tries again in French.

I'm tempted to relieve the pain by simply putting it all into fluent German for poor Annelise but that would just humiliate Colin even more than he's managing himself. So I keep quiet while he massacres the language of Voltaire, Dumas and Sartre in an attempt to order some steak and chips from a German-speaking waitress. When this clown show eventually comes to a close, Alice and I look on approvingly while he moves to consider the wine menu. Alice merely points on the original menu to what she would like, and I mutter my choice in German when he coughs to himself in criticism of the limited choice of booze.

Colin does not define what he drinks as booze, of course. Only a delicate bouquet or a precious liqueur can grace his palate. So we wait another five minutes while he chooses some glorified grape juice. At this rate, we'll be lucky to complete the order in time for dinner. I just hope he's booked a return flight which leaves before dark.

And the whole while, he has to keep talking. About anything and everything since he's always the expert on whatever it is. Usually, I think he picks an elevated topic for no better reason than that he thinks I won't know anything about it and will therefore feel even more inadequate than I usually do. Bethany may be a lot bougier than I am, but I still don't know how she puts up with all this. I can't imagine what a dirty weekend with this walking ego-cum-erection must be like. All the romance of intimate relations with a piledriver followed by a lecture on the exchange rate fluctuations between the Canadian dollar and the Swedish Krone, while you have five minutes to slap some Vagisil round your crotch before round two gets underway. There's marital bliss for you.

In case you're wondering, no, I don't usually enjoy family Christmases very much either.

What I do like, though, is spending time with Alice. I just wish Colin would leave more than five seconds between endless lectures for us to have a conversation on something other than working out where the nearest toilet is.

Eventually though, the torture does come to an end as Colin looks at his Rolex and breathes sharply.

"Goodness, is that the time? I suppose we really should wrap up here even though it is always a delight to converse with you."

And I thought the Alpine farmsteads were full of bullshit.

Thankfully, the bit about having to head off is actually true and so we quit "Le Parisien", no doubt much to Annelise's relief. I even tip her out of pity and because Colin never bothered to do so himself. At least he was in too much of a hurry to remember to try to find a way to make me pay for myself.

We make our way to Departures, Alice and I hauling along the wardrobe's worth of junk which Bethany has so kindly sent over with her beloved daughter. Colin advances in front of us with a disapproving look at the various designer shops we pass, which are no doubt the equivalent of a knocked-off Salvation Army end of season sale by his standards.

Since he has no hold luggage to check in, we get to the security gates fairly soon, which is a minor relief. Colin launches into a check of everything Alice must do to ensure that she can stay alive in the wilds of eastern Switzerland. Apparently these are on a par with the mountain passes of Afghanistan in terms of the risk they pose to life and limb, especially when I'm nominally in charge.

"So you have your allergy pills in case of animals dropping too many hairs on the paths? You won't go out in the sun between eleven o'clock and four o'clock? You'll make sure you call as soon as you reach the hotel each evening and that won't be after seven?"

And so on. And on. And on. If I wasn't trying to be polite and avoid antagonizing Colin, I'd have gone for a coffee break by now. At least one.

Luckily enough, a woman with breasts bigger than her head passes by into security. Not being a tourist to miss out on the scenery, Colin decides that this a good time to go and get checked in so he can check her out and he finally leaves us in peace.

"Bye, Dad! Love you!" calls Alice dutifully. She's such a good actress.

"OK, he's definitely gone round the corner so we're good to go."

I turn round to check on Alice. She's already ditched the puffy jacket and has it strapped onto the side of the wheelie case.

"It was like a microwave in there, Auntie Jess," she exclaims. Poor girl. She's probably better done than her father's steak was.

"Never mind, Alice. You up for a proper holiday now?"

"Hell yeah!" she responds. It's time to get out of character and into what we both know is coming.

Like many airports in Switzerland, Zürich has a very convenient arrangement of a giant rail terminus directly underneath the terminal. We descend straight down on the escalators, still lugging what feels like three times Alice's body weight in complete crap behind us. Then we head for the left luggage area.

Another excellent feature of the public transport network in Switzerland is the widespread availability of luggage lockers everywhere. They cost very little to use and you can deposit serious amounts of baggage over significant periods of time. That's about to come in very handy.

I go straight to 423B and insert my key. The locker, a pretty big one, falls open to reveal my hiking rucksack together with another similar but slightly smaller one, currently empty except for a set of hiking clothes and a couple of sensible accessories. There's also a second pile of hiking clothes and a pair of boots in Alice's size next to it.

Alice has few inhibitions. She's already out of the Eskimo survival suit her mother put her in and is getting down to her underwear pretty quickly. I don't want to look like some sort of lesbian paedophile who took her to "Le Parisien" to wine her more than dine her so I pass her a T-shirt and a pair of cargo trousers as fast as she'll take them. Alice slips in quickly and starts to look more convincingly like she's just my niece again. She ties her hair up into a neat bun like the one I have, changes her socks for some proper hiking ones and gets her boots on.

"Nice outfit!' she beams. "Thanks for this. What do I owe you for all this?"

I wave her away.

"Less than your dad spent on my mac 'n' cheese at lunchtime. Forget it."

She snorts in mild derision at her father's spending habits then turns to the considerably larger rucksack and wheelie case with which she arrived.

"There are a few useful things in here and we need to open up the bags to make it look as though I actually used their contents while I was here."

She doesn't have to tell me. I know how this gig works. We get down to business.

Where on earth does Bethany shop? I didn't know you could find outdoor sports stores this bougie. There are about eight sports cardigans (don't ask), a camping shower bag with compartments for fingernail and toenail polish, and a survival blanket with an inbuilt diary. All this despite the fact that Bethany thinks we'll be strolling around Lake Constance on paths suitable for every age up to ninety-eight and staying in a local hotel there every night.

"I'm surprised you weren't given a six-pack of extra strength condoms in case you fell over in all this bullshit and didn't get up fast enough to stop the bull coming up behind your rump with an evil glint in his eye!"

Alice laughs out loud at this one, vulgar though it is. I do love my niece. How she was spawned from two such complete dorks as my sister and her husband I will never know but then again, how anyone could consider having sex with either my sister or her husband I will never understand either. Even a piss-drunk sex addict who'd gone cold turkey for two years might have to think twice if that was all which was on offer.

In the end, we take a useful-looking water bottle, the basics for personal hygiene and a book called, "Get Yer Hand In!" Alice swears this is a hilariously funny novel about teenage romance although I have my doubts. Still, she managed to pack it without Bethany noticing so it can't be all bad.

We re-pack everything else back into the huge rucksack and the wheelie case, stash them in locker 423B and lock up.

"All set?" I ask. "Have you deactivated the tracker on your phone?"

"Thanks. Almost forgot," she grins, slightly embarrassed and reaches for the phone to make the necessary adjustments.

"Good going. I've two tickets to Chur and we can catch a bus from there to Flims-Waldhaus. The train leaves in fifteen minutes so we can get a couple of ice-creams first if we're quick."

"Let's head, Auntie Jess."

Chapter 4
WE LOVE TO GO A-WANDERING

Jessica

"Careful there. Don't use your sticks on the bridge. If you get the end caught in the latticework, you can do a lot worse than just trip over."

Alice nods in agreement and picks up her hiking sticks. They're good for slopes and even for flatter areas of grassland or woods, although you should bear in mind that they make you look like a complete pratt if you use them to go round public parks in Britain. Just saying. In the Alps, however, they keep your upper body working out, reduce the pressure shocks to the legs and generally prevent you from falling flat onto your face or your bum, depending on which way you're leaning when you slip. If there's a cow turd directly underneath, you'll be damn glad you had them at that point too.

Where they're less useful is on a latticework suspension bridge. These are impressive pieces of engineering which serve to get you from one side of a gorge to the other where it would otherwise take forever to get to the bottom and then back up again. They generally cross waterfalls and similar passages. It's actually very helpful and thoughtful of the Swiss to put these things up, thus making nature that bit more convenient and accessible in a purely artificial manner. I like it. At least, I like it as a thoughtful concept. The bridges themselves are another matter.

These bridges are typically constructed from four, huge steel poles anchored into the ground, two on each side of the gorge. A steel latticework bridge extends between each pair and is attached by steel cables on either side. There's a lot of steel involved, you'll have gathered. This forms a remarkably robust and reliable passageway across. You can get spectacular views both upwards and downwards and the Swiss, being thoughtful and prudent, even add things like safety rails so that it's pretty hard to commit suicide by jumping off one. Short of posting a psychiatric therapist on either side, they offer a level of public service which most countries would struggle to meet. Nonetheless, there are two drawbacks to these otherwise impressive constructions, which are quickly apparent if you suffer in the slightest from vertigo.

The first is the latticework itself. The bridges can only ever have been intended for those with zero fear of heights because a latticework floor, if crossed at speed, becomes almost transparent. So if you're walking over a one hundred metre drop directly beneath you and you look down, you appear to be literally one step only from plummeting to a messy demise. At least the waterfall might wash away the muck so there won't be a public littering fine related to the remains of your ribcage but that's little consolation at the time of crossing.

Still, you can always just force yourself not to look down but simply straight ahead when you're crossing. However, there's no such simple solution to the second issue. This is the fact that despite the tautness of the cables and the strength of the poles to which they're anchored, this is still a suspension bridge and that means it can sway. And if there's any sort of disturbed air current, excitable children or dogs, or just a somewhat overweight individual taking a long gaze over one side of the bridge, it will sway. Not just a little but quite a bit. The worst thing is when you get some moronic tourist who imagines that it's funny to stand in the middle and sway it deliberately. By the time you reach him or her, you're really wishing that safety rail just wasn't there for the "accident" you'd otherwise like to cause.

If truth be told, I'm actually slightly scared of these things. I go over them when I have to because I don't want to admit to myself that I'm scared of something in the mountains, and I certainly don't want to tell that to Alice. In her eyes, I put James Bond to shame in "On Her Majesty's Secret Service" because he escaped from the Berner Oberland, aka Bernese Highlands, in a car, not on foot. So I stare fixedly ahead and get across when necessary. What Alice doesn't know because I haven't told her yet, is the story of what was probably my scariest moment in the Alps. It took place on a suspension bridge.

I was west of the Thunersee (Lake Thun in English), near Weissenburg, and making my way to a hotel stop quite late. It had been a hot day but that had generated an incoming thunderstorm, and it was a lot darker than usual for the time of year. I figured I could probably make it to the hotel just about in time before the storm set in, if I pushed myself. The plan was touch and go as the wind was getting up quite seriously although no rain was falling yet.

Pushing myself at the end of the day too, of course, I was generating a somewhat pungent aroma, notably coming from the region of my armpits. I was therefore also in a hurry to reach somewhere with a decent shower before I passed out from my own emanations. Ironically, this of course meant that I was making myself sweat even more.

I reached a huge gorge which must have been at least a hundred metres deep, perhaps more. I'm not sure but I wasn't going to hang about with the utility apps on my phone to get an accurate measure at this point. The suspension bridge stretched across it and was already flapping in the wind. There was an alternative route down the side of the gorge but there was no way I was going to make it in under an hour down there, round and back up again. In view of the sky at that point, the lack of streetlights at the bottom was likely going to be problematic too. So I looked straight ahead, gulped a couple of times and set off across the bridge.

I really don't quite know what happened next but somehow what had been a mild gale seemed to turn into a raging hurricane coming down the gorge from above. That might be an exaggeration in meteorological terms, but it certainly felt like it where I was crawling over. There was no way I was going to stand up at that point.

That was when the swaying got going. I mean serious swaying, a bit like the deck of a ship in similar weather or a hammock when somebody trips over while climbing in. I was crawling at a reasonable pace but feeling increasingly concerned that this was not my greatest ever day of mountain adventuring. Possibly my last but certainly not my greatest.

Of course, the bridge did actually hold. Swiss construction is very reliable. But it was quite a small one without the gigantic beams which anchor the larger ones elsewhere, and I was feeling pretty nauseous by the time I reached the middle. That's actually putting it lightly. Imagine a combination of the worst menstrual period ever, downing fourteen shots of whisky and eating a jellied eel sandwich. Well, imagine it if you're female. If you're a bloke, just imagine feeling as drunk as possible, but without any of the good bits. However you picture it, it was very, very bad.

I'm ashamed to admit it but in the end, a huge gust knocked into the bridge and as it swayed considerably to the left, I threw up. Given the angle of my head at that precise moment, five francs fifty worth of egg mayo sandwich re-emerged from the top half of my alimentary canal and launched itself skywards. Unfortunately, it hung there for a second and then started to descend just as the bridge swung back on itself, which was where I ran into my lunch for the second time that day. I did finally get across the bridge but suffice to say that when I managed to check in to the hotel, it wasn't just my body odour which made the receptionist look for a gas mask. She probably thought I'd escaped from the nearby Spiez Laboratory, which is where the Swiss Federal Institute for Nuclear, Biological and Chemical Protection is located.

Anyway, entertaining anecdotes about my previous adventures in the Alps aside, I manage to shepherd Alice across today's bridge, together with myself, more or less retaining an outwardly confident composure. We don't take photos because there's no way in hell that Bethany would retain a similar composure if she knew we were up here.

Once over the bridge, we set off along a forest path which isn't too steep and indulge in a bit of conversation. You need to take the opportunities when you can since you'll be too busy trying to inhale half the oxygen in the valley once you reach the steep, uphill sections.

Alice decides to come out of left field on this one.

"I'm interested to know," she starts, "did you go through a lot of boyfriends when you were in school?"

I don't know if this is really a path I want to go down but a bit like the forest here, I don't think I'm being offered much of a choice.

"You mean mine or other girls'?" I ask, hoping to add at least a degree of amusement value.

Alice looks at me askance.

"You went around taking other girls' boyfriends from them? I don't think that's a good thing to do at all. I've seen other girls doing it, but it just doesn't seem right."

"Chill out, Alice. I was just joking. In answer to your question though, no, not a lot of them. I didn't have anything against going out with boys and it's not as though I was into girls either, but I found that the whole relationship business was kind of over-rated in my opinion."

"What do you mean?"

"I mean," I pause and consider for a moment. "I mean, that when everybody's hormones started streaming round their bodies like some kind of torrent of horniness, it was as if being in a relationship with someone was a goal in itself. Like it was the only thing which mattered. The problem I had with that was that there were other things which mattered too. I could only have got a boyfriend who mattered if I'd been prepared to give up things I liked or, even worse, get into some of the things which the guys in school liked doing. And I had zero interest in playing darts with full ice-cream cones or setting fire to my farts. Nor was I interested in getting banned from the local cinema for performing oral sex too blatantly on my loudmouthed boyfriend as one girl managed to do."

Alice looks rather taken aback.

"She was a bit older than you," I offer, slightly apologetically, slightly embarrassedly.

Not actually a hell of a lot older, I recall with some disdain, but no need to go into that now. I think the cinema will probably have dry-cleaned the seats since then.

"Coming back to the original question," I continue, "what I found was that you just had to prioritize. If being with someone you love is your ultimate goal, then go for it. Just don't expect to get as much leeway as you might want for other things you want to spend your time on. But at least ask yourself why it matters so much. Because it just does? That seems pretty lame to me."

Alice looks a bit dejected at this point.

"Oh right," she says. "So what you're saying is that if I like playing piano, going to films with my best friends or even hanging out with you, then I shouldn't look for a boyfriend just because I want one, since he might stop me doing all those other things?"

What do you mean, "even" hanging out with me? Cheeky, little cow. However, I decide to overlook it.

"No, I didn't say that. I just mean that you want to be sure of why you want any of these things, relationship included but not forgetting all your other ambitions. If you can't figure that out, you'll probably just disappoint yourself."

The incline is getting kind of steep right now, which is making this conversation increasingly hard work. However, I'm inclined to keep going with it since I doubt she receives any insights of this kind from Bethany, poor girl.

Alice is evidently trying to sort something out in her head and struggling to do so. Her brow creases and she mumbles to herself as we take a pause to get over a serious but short climb ahead of us. She puts her thoughts into words once we're past.

"Does this mean that I have to become somebody else just to get a boyfriend? What's the point then?"

It's a fair question and quite possibly one I'm not very well prepared to answer. After all, you're talking to a professional waster with an inability to take most things too seriously. A good example would be my Tinder profile – yes, I do have one – where I fear I may have been too honest about myself. For those not familiar with this dating app, or others like it, you need to post a photo or two, your profile in terms of likes, dislikes, hobbies, appearance, politics, religion or whatever, and also a statement about yourself. Fairly obviously, most people go for classy shots, which have probably taken them hours to set up and make them look like celebrity superstars even though half of them likely had to scrape off half a ton of make-up afterwards or else collapsed with the effort of cranking up their muscles all weekend on boiled eggs and protein shakes. I went for a thumbs-up pose with an Austin Powers smile. For some reason, loads of people list hiking as something they're into. My ass. I bet they walk down to the local Aldi's for a discount vodka bottle and a couple of scratch-cards, then claim that they like to walk half the distance across the Himalayas. However, I maybe shouldn't have said so when I declared that I was into hiking and would do a 25-click route march as a nice warm-up. My other main like being Timothy Dalton probably didn't help me much either in the Daniel Craig era.

The worst bit, though, was probably my personal statement. I put up a photo I'd taken of a mountain next to a lake, where you could see a dark forest stretching upwards with an idyllic scene above it of Alpine meadows just below a pristine snowline. It was supposed to be a metaphor for my vision of love, and I wrote next to it, "We need to get high together to reach the good stuff." Everyone probably thinks I'm a pot dealer now.

Consequently, I suppose I shouldn't complain that the best match which the app found for me was some octogenarian with what looked like a salad bar growing under his left armpit and a tag line on why he would be a perfect match as a life partner because he had, "Just got a new tortoise last week."

So all in all, I can hardly claim that being yourself is necessarily the best way to score. Certainly not if you're me. Let's try something different.

"Look, Alice, the thing is that you're starting with the early stages. You can't let those put you off. It's like climbing these mountains. When you stand at the bottom and look up, you can hardly imagine that you're going to have any chance of getting up there. But you don't keep looking at the top. You look at the path in front of you. You look at the next steps in front of you and you go for it. You don't look back, but you keep heading upwards, one step at a time. Halfway up, you look back and realise that you've made a lot more progress than you ever thought you would. You keep going, one step at a time and eventually you make it and it's beautiful. It's awesome. You did it. The thing is though, that you didn't let the challenge put you off at the start."

"So what are you aiming at? Getting married?"

There's an awkward silence. Neither of us has to say out loud what we're both thinking.

If the relationship between Bethany and Colin is the ultimate goal of the climb, wouldn't it be preferable just to stay at the bottom and drown yourself in the lake instead?

"Assuming you climb the right Alp," I mutter eventually. Then a thought occurs.

"Actually," I breeze a bit, "that's a very good point to consider. You see, marriage is where you can have a state where you can be who you want to be while also having a relationship with someone and it works better than all this dating malarkey in the interim. Unless you're a nymphomaniac, that is."

Alice giggles at that one. It's nice when things take a pleasant direction for sure.

"The great thing about marriage, you see, is that you don't have to worry about all the sex and romance and blah-de-blah which make dating so complicated, mainly because you don't need them."

"People don't want to have sex?" Alice seems horrified. I need to remember that she's still a teenager and so believes that carnal relations are even better than salt 'n' vinegar crisps. The malign influence of Tinder strikes again.

"Yeah, a bit but it's not nearly the big deal it's made out to be. It's just easier to sell things if you hype them up. Condoms, booze, baby wipes, that sort of thing.

"What you have to realize is that sex and romance are like a sort of label. If you've got a boyfriend, you kiss him, you hold hands with him and all that because it says that he's your boyfriend, this is your territory and hands off. Plus any other parts of the anatomy too."

Another snigger at my smutty descriptions. I'm on a roll now.

"But think about it: if you didn't have all the romantic stuff, he would just be your friend, wouldn't he? You can hang out with as many guys, as many people as you like and it doesn't mean you're dating them. You can chat with them, go to concerts with them, even hike with them, and it doesn't mean you're two-timing anybody, right? It's only the intimate actions which define your relationship and all that takes a whole lot of time, effort and adjusting to one another.

"However, it all changes when you're married because then you have something else – a marriage certificate. Problem solved! You have a legally binding bit of paper which declares your relationship to be more or less unique and exclusive. You don't have to do anything special anymore. You can forget their birthday and just get put onto taking out the trash for one week more than usual. You can come to breakfast, eat Frosties and burp loudly. Try doing that when you're trying to impress on your first sleepover with a new boyfriend and see how far you get.

"Even this," I declare grandiosely. "Here's a good example. Imagine a couple on a dinner date. They get home and she suggests that they go upstairs and that he might like to lie down for a little, while she goes into the bathroom to slip into something more comfortable.

"Let's imagine that she comes back into the bedroom now. He isn't lying there, stark naked under a thin sheet, guns hot. He's put on his Spiderman pyjama shorts and his T-shirt which says, 'I'm with Stupid' and he's lying on his back, snoring away. If they're dating, he's screwed, and not in the way you were expecting a moment ago. However, if they're married, she's hardly going to divorce him just for that. She'll probably punch him in the nuts to turn over and reduce the volume of the snores, then kiss him night night on the cheek and go to sleep.

"Same thing applies if she comes back and her idea of something more comfortable is a parachute-sized pair of tighty whities and a Care Bears snuddy."

"You mean like my mum?" asks Alice.

I cough and swallow a moment in surprise. I had no idea what Bethany's nightwear looks like up to now. I haven't seen her go to bed for at least twenty years and don't really relish the thought now. Why do these images of her and Colin keep cropping up in my otherwise jovial reflections on marriage?

"But if being married is so great, Auntie, why aren't you married?"

"I have my hands full finding time to climb the real Alps, Alice. I suppose I don't have the energy left to climb the one I just described."

I'm not sure that any of that really makes sense but as you can see, relationship therapy is another of those areas where I really have no clue as to what I'm talking about.

We exchange some more thoughtful reflections on the state of human relations. Next we have to dodge the attentions of some cattle suffering from excessive hormone levels, presumably without the escape clause of being married or even sticking to trying to bonk just your own species. After these diversions, we make it to our hotel. Nice little gig, really. Chalet style, two floors, on the side of the mountain about halfway up. Quaint and old school on the outside but clearly renovated not too long ago on the inside. Our room is a basic but comfortable twin job with an en suite on your right as you enter and the beds either side once you're past it, leading up to the windows. These include a door out onto a balcony where there's a nice view right down the valley. With free Wi-Fi and breakfast included, this is the sort of place I like.

We're chilling out on the balcony and taking in the view. It's pretty much what we've been seeing all day, but you get a new perspective when you're not face first against the next five steps on the incline and trying to keep the sweat out of your eyes. In fact, one of my eventual ambitions is to spend some serious time paragliding. You see these huge things like parachutes which just seem to float around for ages up there with somebody hanging down below. But it's not as if they're parachuting. There's no clearly fast descent. They can even manoeuvre around and just go with the flow. The view must be simply amazing. And the peace and quiet. One day, I know, one day I'm going to take that up. Not just get a session or two but really do it properly so I can see for miles over all the places where I've walked, sweated, and hiked my butt off to see some of the best of God's green earth.

OK, so I'm exaggerating a bit and hiking is actually worth doing, completely worth doing. My point is that even if it's still not quite comparable to paragliding in terms of the view, both types of view are great, and you get a nice but different one again from your hotel room. This hotel doesn't have a laundry so I'm just sitting in my regular trousers and top since there's no particular reason to get changed and I'm too lazy to do so if I don't have to. As in most things up here, Alice is following my lead. She really is great. I still do wonder if she's actually adopted since the genetic heritage is just so misaligned otherwise.

"Oh no, Auntie! It's past seven already and we haven't called Mum!"

Bugger. I forgot about having to check in with HQ. A whole five minutes? Bethany will probably be thinking that an atomic weapon has just vapourised Switzerland.

Alice is already on her phone, calling up her mother as fast as possible.

"Alice, darling, is that you? Where have you been? You've been away for so long! I've been so worried!" Bethany starts. I'm not holding the phone, but I can hear her irritating voice a mile off. So can half the valley probably. I hope she hasn't already alerted the mountain rescue service. Not least because she thinks we're about thirty clicks away.

"It's OK, Mum, I'm perfectly fine. I'm having a great time, actually."

Bethany sounds almost miffed that Alice might be having a good time with me of all people. She goes on some endless rant about whether or not Alice has been exposed to more sunlight than your average potholer, if there's a serious risk of catching malaria anywhere near Zürich or if she might have tripped over a croissant dropped carelessly by an illegal immigrant. Or if a random dinosaur recently emerged from Lake Constance due to an earth tremor, or whatever other idiocy infests my sister's mind. For someone as educated about other parts of the world, she really seems to have all the savvy of somebody whose only reason for not voting to leave the EU was that they couldn't spell it.

Alice keeps the phone studiously trained on her face while Bethany waffles on and on about whatever drivel is on her mind at the moment. I suppose that if I'd spent all day shagging Colin, I might be feeling a bit brain dead by now as well, to be fair but that's just a theory. If I were in her place, I'd be stuffing a leaky plasma bag into my underpants so as to posit a believable claim to be on my period right now. I still find it hard to believe that she or anybody else could actually be attracted to him.

"So what is Steinach like, dear? Can you show me the lake on your phone?"

Shit. We're meant to be in Steinach beside Lake Constance but of course we're not. The nearest lake to us is also about eight clicks away down the valley and it's not Lake Constance either. Alice looks over at me desperately.

"Just a minute, Mum. My phone's playing up a little."

She's holding up OK but we're going to need a better solution fast. Come on, Jessica, come on. Dodging the bullet is meant to be one of your specialities. Right now it had better be.

Inspiration strikes. Pretty late but it strikes. I go onto my phone and search up Steinach lake views. There aren't a whole lot but there is a nice one of Arbon which is near(ish) to where we're supposed to be. It's not as though Bethany will know the frickin' difference anyway. I bring up the picture on my screen.

"Alice!" I hiss under my breath. "Focus your phone on this picture!"

Alice zooms in dutifully and her own phone picks up the shot.

"Goodness me, Alice! The sun is still shining very brightly there!"

"Well, Mum, it doesn't get dark until quite late up in the mountains and I've also got a special feature on my phone's camera which enhances the daylight so you can see pictures better when it's getting dark. It's really cool!"

Damn, Alice is good. And damn, her mother is stupid. Between the two, we might just get away with this.

"It seems very still somehow," muses Bethany. Honestly, does a university education count for anything these days?

"It's a quiet place, Mum. Very peaceful. Anyway, my arm's getting tired from holding up the phone, so I'll go back to my face if you don't mind."

"Oh, of course, darling. Don't strain yourself too much."

Bloody hell, Bethany, we covered twenty-two clicks and climbed nine hundred metres today. The only greater source of stress anyone in this family has suffered has probably been in the region of your groin but I don't think we'll be discussing that here. I sure as hell do not want to see any photos of your day, thank you all the same.

Alice is now sweeping her phone around the room, pointedly avoiding the window with its view of mountains which might be slightly higher than Bethany is imagining. Presumably, this is so that Bethany can put aside her fears that there might be a rogue yeti hiding under the bed. After all, Switzerland is a foreign country, isn't it? You don't know what horrors it might have which you don't find in East Dawlings.

Unfortunately, not everything escapes her eagle eye.

"Oh my goodness, Alice! Is that a coffee mug next to your headband? Are you drinking coffee over there? That stuff will completely ruin your sleep! You're far too young to be drinking it! What on earth is your aunt letting you get away with?"

I ask you. However, this is a problem. The only other coffee mug is my own which is sitting in my hands and full of coffee at the moment. Still, my quick-thinking comes back to the fore.

"Alice," I whisper. "Tell her it's my coffee mug. I'll be back in a moment."

"Oh no, Mum," Alice stutters. "That's Auntie Jess' coffee mug. She's just nipped out for a moment…"

This had better be quick. I dive into the bathroom and head for the sink, emptying the fresh coffee into the toilet as a I pass. Talk about a hot flush.

I fill up the now empty mug with cold water and race back to Alice.

"Here you are, Alice," I say more loudly than I would really need to. "I got you your water in the mug which-. Hang on! That's my coffee mug, you silly girl! You're meant to have this one with the water in it! What on earth are you thinking? Dear me!"

This is generally how people talk in East Dawlings. At least you know why I don't live there anymore and have no intention of ever doing so again. Nonetheless, it seems to have calmed down Bethany who is now lecturing Alice on the importance of not getting her left big toe caught in the shower curtain or some such risk to life and limb. I zone out for a bit.

"Anyway, Mum, I think I might have to sign off at this point."

"Of course, darling, you need your rest," Bethany responds.

Needs her rest? It's still only quarter past seven in the evening and she's fifteen years old, not fifteen months. It's frightening to remember that I'm related to this imbecile.

"Could I just have a word with your aunt first, please?"

Oh no.

I steel myself and take the phone from Alice. Bethany's beautiful features fill the screen, together with her air-headed smile.

"Now, Jessica, can you promise me that Alice is as well as she says she is? We both know how she imagines that she's able to do more than she really can."

"Hello, Bethany," I start, at least remembering to acknowledge her presence before launching in which is more than she's done for me. "I can assure you that Alice is staying well within her own capabilities."

"Oh, that's so nice. And you are feeding her properly, aren't you?"

As in, am I force-feeding her with all those protein shakes, fat-free, gluten-free, reality-free, atomically cleansed snack packs you sent her with? Well no, because we dropped them off in a food bank in Chur, but I have been giving her some food which actually stops you feeling hungry. It's a major scientific advance. Of course, I don't say that.

At this point, there's a noise from behind Bethany and she turns around. That's when I can see that in fact she's wearing a very thin, silk nightdress. At what is half past six in the evening where she is? Oh yes, my suspicions about what she and her orc husband are up to while I'm keeping their daughter out of the way are entirely true. This becomes undeniably clear when her smooth nightie somehow slides on the seat, and she drops right off it onto the floor. Always one for a comedy moment, I start to chortle but my laughter is brought to an abrupt halt by the sight of Colin lying stretched out on a bed behind her. Absolutely butt naked. As in nothing on whatsoever. As in I can see part of him which I never wanted to see in the totality of my existence.

Until now. All of a sudden, I'm glad that I've rested my eyes on what I would have thought would be a truly revolting sight. No way! No frickin' way! I do not believe this! Colin is so under-equipped that it looks as though he simply has a small clothes peg hanging out of his pubes! This is unbelievable!

And it's true! I take a quick screenshot just to have the evidence (not for private prurience and thrills, I hasten to add; no way in hell).

Finally, I have something I can use to hit back against all the snide insults and general abuse I have to take in his presence. No wonder he pounds Bethany so hard. Unless she has a miniature vacuum operating on full suction mode when he tries it on, she probably doesn't even notice that he's there. I tell you, for the first time since I was about twelve years old, I'm really looking forward to Christmas now. I've always thought that Christmas jokes based on sexual doubles entendres were pretty boring. Stuffing your bird, pulling your cracker and so forth. People have been telling these corny gags since somewhere around AD 1. The main reason none of them is in the Bible is probably because by the time He was thirty, Jesus had heard them all about twenty-nine times already and they were too hackneyed to recount.

Now, I can see why they might be funny after all. Because now they can be about Colin and about nothing at all, by which I mean the nothing at all in his unnecessarily expensive designer underwear. Hark the herald angels sing. There's going to be a new song coming this Christmas. Which is more than Colin will be doing unless Bethany is feeling generous, I imagine.

There's an almighty kerfuffle on Bethany's end of the phone and she springs up from somewhere or other with her hair a shade less tidy than it was twenty seconds ago. Colin is nowhere to be seen but then again, there's not as much of him to see as I once imagined, is there?

"Er, right," she stammers. "I'm glad everything is all right. You and Alice just keep enjoying yourselves and let me know if everything is OK? I'll see you tomorrow."

She hangs up. I hand the phone back to Alice, sit back, admire the view and smile. This is turning into a truly great holiday.

Chapter 5

PRATTS AND DOGS

Harris

Love is an amazing feeling. It somehow frees your mind. It brings a fresh perspective that nothing can really hurt you so long as your loved one is safe in your embrace, be that actual or metaphorical.

I don't know if I would really have believed that before, at least not in quite such open terms. I've been in love with Isabel for some time, of course. Every day of it has been wonderful when I have thought of her but all the same, it hasn't stopped me feeling quite worried, concerned, upset or even angry sometimes. Not with her, I hasten to add. She remains my angel. What I mean is that the rest of the world and the rest of life have kept going on and they have still been able to cause me bother. Isabel has been part of my reality all along, but the rest of that reality has still been happening at the same time. And of course, my inability to reach the level of a recognized engagement to Isabel and of an eventual marriage has been such a source of pain, even anguish. It has been one of the worst sensations ever. I never did anything wrong, but I felt excruciatingly guilty for not being good enough. The problem was not of my making, but I felt so inadequate at not finding a solution. I wanted to reach the goal but every day, the frustration of seeing it so close but always out of reach just got worse. They say that parting is such sweet sorrow in the context of love and they're right. I know. But the sorrow of never quite being good enough for the one you love and just never managing to deliver on your promise is not one I would wish on anyone. It has tempered the sweetness of love for far too long.

Yet no longer. Finally, the solution is at hand. My love will be rewarded, and I will make Isabel as happy as she can be and as she deserves to be. She means so much and I want to be worthy of her love. I don't want to be loved out of pity or just for trying hard. I want to be loved as I love her: for the sheer value which she represents. And now I have managed to earn that value and am going to be demonstrating it for all to see, something which not even her father will be able to deny. It's a wonderful feeling.

All of a sudden, I feel the real joy of love. Now that I have reached the end of the tunnel and can see the light, it is as though I'm a in new world. I see things differently. I know what matters and I don't let the less important things bother me so much. The same things happen which have always irritated me. The same worries occur at work. The same concerns leap out when I read the newspapers and hear about wars, about the destruction of our environment, about terrible diseases and about all the other horrors which plague our world. Still, they simply don't matter as much, not because logically they are any less important but because they sit next to an immediate reality which is bringing a colour and shade to my life which I never realized until now was possible.

And this is not just romanticized rambling. It is entirely true as I am discovering now because I'm in trouble. I'm on my way to the office of Mrs Bodega, headmistress of the school. I'm not stupid and I know what it's about. I can't say I'm looking forward to the interview for one moment. At the same time, I simply don't feel the nerves I would normally. That terrible anticipation when you're facing disaster but don't know how bad or not it will be: it's simply not so important. Of course, all this matters. It just matters less than what I'm feeling otherwise.

Besides which, it wasn't really my fault. I was only following the highway code but fell foul of bad luck.

Mrs Bodega is not in a good mood, but I would not have expected her to be. Having knocked on the door, I am called in and find myself standing in front of her desk, behind which she is sitting. It's a weathered old thing, a wooden construction with a worn, red leather top. It seems rather out of place in an otherwise more modern room with light grey walls and a large window offset to one side of that wall which is behind her. The rest of the furniture seems to date from around the mid-1950s and the whole ensemble would seem quite functional were it not for the plush, dark blue carpet which somehow prevents the place seeming too utilitarian.

Mrs Bodega must be in her mid to late-fifties, I would imagine. Her worn features and grey hair put her at an advanced middle age, but she has a reasonably well-kept physique, perhaps a little plump but well-adjusted beneath the elegant, purple sari she wears. I do appreciate how she manages to wear make-up at all times but without ever going overboard. I find it gives her a certain serenity, at least it does most of the time. Today, however, she looks decidedly displeased.

The same is true of the man seated to the left of the desk, a tall, thin man in a dark suit with a white shirt and dark grey tie. He eyes me quite menacingly.

I can't help feeling that as a teacher rather than a pupil, I should not be made to stand here in front of the headmistress' desk, as if called in to apologize for some playground misdemeanour. At least a seated interview would be nice. Unfortunately, I am not in much of a position to dictate terms.

Mrs Bodega eyes me malevolently for a few seconds, then breathes out audibly.

"Harris," she begins, "this is Mr Plummer of our Board of Governors. He is here to find out just what happened yesterday afternoon."

"Harris Beadlesby. Pleased to meet you." I do my best to beam and extend my hand. He stands briefly and grasps my hand in a very limp manner. His handshake is neither firm, not friendly but nor is his gaze. He sits down again. He has not said one word.

Mrs Bodega breathes loudly again before continuing.

"Perhaps, Harris, you could outline for us in your own words what happened after you left the school gates yesterday afternoon."

There is an ominous pause. A small bird flits by the open window, it's high-pitched twitter seemingly quite careless and very out of line with the atmosphere inside the room. I think for a moment of Isabel and of how life as a whole cannot overcome the happiness I'm anticipating whenever my thoughts turn to her. Love really does have a calming effect because right now, I honestly do feel at peace inside myself, notwithstanding what lies immediately ahead.

"As I recall," I start, trying to sound both in control and also unruffled but without being arrogant, "it was somewhere in the region of half past four –"

"More like ten past," Mrs Bodega interrupts. Damn the woman. I don't need her nasty friend from the Board thinking that I head off out of the door in advance of the finishing hour every time I have a free period.

"Well, be that as it may," I resume, "I was on my bicycle, and I turned right out of the school gates and cycled up to the crossroads. Normally, I would have gone straight across on my way home, but I needed to run an errand or two down at the post office and supermarket, so I was going to turn left instead. I pulled up to the left-hand side of the road and indicated that I intended to go left by extending my arm in that direction.

"Unfortunately, and I fully admit this, I had not taken full account of the presence of an elderly lady who was there and with whom my hand collided. So of course, I immediately got off my bicycle and went over to help her. She was quite distressed, I learned, because she had also been taking out her dog for a walk on some strange, wheeled contraption, which had gone astray. Since I couldn't see it, I concentrated on trying to help her, but she got quite agitated and seemed to be on the verge of passing out. So I did my best to administer the kiss of life by holding her nose and blowing into her mouth. I believe I succeeded in my efforts since an ambulance arrived and took her to hospital where she is now making a full recovery.

"Given the nature of the incident, I did have to accompany a couple of police officers to the local station and answer a series of questions, but I was released without charge later that same evening. If anything, I found the officers to be in a state of some merriment, which I imagine was a good thing."

I stop for a moment and gaze around the room, trying to remember if I've missed anything significant. The small bird flies past again but nothing else stirs.

"I believe that sums it up," I conclude.

It appears that Mrs Bodega does not entirely agree with that. She fixes me with a very quizzical stare which lasts rather too long. I would look elsewhere except that that ghastly Mr Plummer also seems to be looking at me with considerable distaste as well. This awkward moment lasts what feels like at least half a minute before Mrs Bodega eventually raises her eyes to the ceiling and breathes loudly before rising from her chair. She comes right up in front of me and fixes me with a very menacing stare.

She hisses, "I do believe, Harris, that you may be overlooking some of the more pertinent facts surrounding what happened yesterday."

I open my mouth to protest but she silences me with a wave of the hand.

"You cycled out of the school gates, that much is true. You then took a right up to the crossroads. So far, we're on the same page."

She turns away momentarily then swings back.

"They tell me you were singing at the time. Why?"

I'm quite taken aback. What has that got to do with anything?

"Well," I stammer, "I'm a music teacher. I appreciate the great classics, and I feel that they bring a certain joy to the occasion."

I have the distinct impression that adding in my current state of euphoria at the prospect of starting a new chapter of life together with Isabel may not be the best direction to take right now. I'm spared anything further by a new question from Mrs Bodega.

"And could you explain why this should have been such a distraction that you did not notice the old lady at the side of the crossroads?"

"You can't just sing music," I start, explaining patiently as I do to the more culturally devoid of my pupils. "You have to draw in the music and make an active attempt to express it inside yourself, for yourself. And I should explain that was very much the case here since I was performing a particularly intense piece from, 'Tosca'– "

"Shut up!" she screams out of nowhere, losing her temper completely and in my view at least, quite inexplicably. "I couldn't care less if you were singing, 'Tosca' or on your way to bloody Tesco's!"

Tesco's? Oh for goodness' sake. I'm very much a Waitrose man myself. Or at least Marks and Spencer. You certainly shouldn't expect to find me ferreting around in the likes of Tesco.

I'm not left with a lot of time to reflect on my shopping preferences.

"You, you clueless wonder, cycled up to the crossroads and promptly stuck out your arm, literally punching a senior citizen in the face! Since you had knocked her to the ground, she dropped the lead she had been holding which was attached to her pet bulldog. For whatever reason – I'm not quite sure at the moment – she was one of those people who take their dogs out on these little wheeled skateboard things. Seems kind of stupid to me but regardless, the dog immediately rolled away, down York Gardens.

"In the meantime, you somehow failed to notice the existence and hence departure of the dog although at least you did cotton on to the fact that there was an old lady lying on the ground in front of you. This should have been some sort of relief, but it seems that it prompted you to try to administer something presumably intended to be first aid."

"I believed she was having a heart attack," I explain.

"Oh you did, did you? I suppose it never occurred to you that having been punched in the face and knocked to the ground, and having lost her precious dog, she might have been a shade perturbed and breathing heavily?"

"She was passed out." I state emphatically. "I had to administer chronic pulmonary revival."

"CPR is cardiopulmonary resuscitation, you moron!" she glares. "What's more, you don't normally administer it – or attempt to administer it – when someone is still fully conscious! She wasn't passed out, as you claim, until you shoved her back onto the ground and started pounding her upper chest. On the right side where the heart isn't even located!"

That might explain why she didn't seem to revive much at the time, I suppose.

"So after beating her up and unfortunately losing much of her upper body clothing, you then decided to, as you put it, administer the kiss of life. Which presumably means that you thought you were resuscitating her by blowing air into her mouth while holding her nose shut?"

"I do believe so, yes," I state in slightly downbeat manner. I don't think I like where this is going.

"Well she certainly recovered consciousness. After a good while of what most onlookers thought equated to you trying to suffocate her with a French kiss, it seems that one of your fingers slipped some way up her nostril. Given that you had consumed a ham and mustard sandwich for lunch and, I assume, forgotten to wash your hands subsequently, she sneezed violently. This must have reversed the process of you sticking your tongue into her mouth because hers appeared in yours, just as your teeth clamped shut. At least the ensuing pain made sure that she woke up."

Mrs Bodega stops for a moment to pierce me with an increasingly malign stare. The woman certainly knows how to intimidate. Images of Isabel's smile are still sustaining me although keeping love on top of everything is proving a little harder to manage than I had been imagining earlier today.

"In the meantime, and a minor detail which you omitted to mention earlier, the dog had set off on its way down York Gardens. Reaching the end of the road, it quickly crossed Hotwell Road, accelerating all the way until it reached the edge of the Cheddar Gorge."

Oh dear. I do know about this aspect of the story, but I don't need it spelled out for me. Cheddar Gorge, with its majestic sides and the Avon River running through it have always been a dear part of the mystic welcome which Bristol extends. I feel as if there is something almost eternally special there which sets my mind at ease when I see or think of it. Nothing has ever changed that since first I saw it.

At least, not until yesterday.

"It seems that the speed of the dog and its board was far too great for them to stop at the edge of the gorge, and they went straight over. That you were directly responsible for the inevitable demise of the dog was bad enough. Given how most of reality seems to flow by your existence though, I'd like to remind you of what happened next.

"The dog descended the hundred or so metres down to the bottom of the gorge. At that point, a small river cruise boat was passing, on which a reception was being held with drinks and a buffet of refreshments, notably including a hot dog stand. Whether ironically or not, the dog crashed into that stand, splitting it into two and spraying the ensemble in pork sausages, not least I understand, across the vegan counter."

I suppose it's a vaguely amusing fact although I can't for the life of me imagine how she would know that.

"Rather more importantly, the other half of the stand contained the cooking fuel and heating elements which fell from the upper deck onto the outer engine deck below and ignited the main fuel pipe. Thankfully, the resulting explosion somehow channelled itself downwards and so nobody was caught in it. But it did blow a hole in the bottom of the boat which sank in about three minutes flat."

That was a shade unfortunate, yes, but I daresay somebody's insurance will cover it. It's not as though anybody died in the end. I don't suppose the police would have let me go so quickly if that had been the case.

Mrs Bodega seems to be challenging me to reply but I don't respond. I have a feeling that there's more to come.

"Do you know why Mr Plummer is here, Harris?" she asks. It's not quite what I was expecting.

"I suppose this is a matter of some concern to the Governors," I reply. That would make sense.

"Oh very much so," she starts with a sinister air. "Something you may not have gathered – and you're pretty good at missing out on relevant details – is that the cruise boat had been hired by the Board of Governors of this school for a social evening event."

Oh dear, I admit that I had not quite taken that detail on board. It would explain how come Mrs Bodega is so well-informed as to what happened on the boat, but this certainly is not looking too good.

"It didn't help matters much that the woman who swam to the shore naked, along with the captain, with whom she'd been making love in his private cabin at the time of the explosion, happened to be the wife of the Deputy Chief Governor either."

I cough markedly. I really don't see how I can be blamed for this element, but it is a rather startling revelation. If only people would behave themselves in a decent fashion. I really can't imagine Isabel or myself ever even dreaming of carrying on in such a way.

"Exactly," Mrs Bodega adds, cutting into my thoughts with the icy touch of a razor-sharp knife.

She walks away from me and returns behind her desk. She picks up a pile of newspapers and looks at the cover of the first.

"It seems that a combination of violence, sex, exploding boats and dogs on skateboards falling out of the sky, all stemming from what is supposed to be a respectable, private school, does not escape the attention of the local press. In fact, given the lack of too much else happening right now in the world, it hasn't escaped the attention of the national press either. I haven't seen the American newspapers yet but given how much the British press has been enjoying the event, I would not be entirely surprised if this becomes an equally entertaining distraction from whatever the United States Congress happens to be debating at the moment."

She starts to read through the headlines.

"It's Raining Pratts and Dogs."

"OAP-dophile in Horrific Gran Bang Incident."

"That's One Hot Dog!"

"Bristol's Poshest School Dogged by Disaster."

"Snogs, Dogs and a Bit of Pooch-ini!"

She pauses and looks straight at me.

"The journalistic corps may find this very entertaining, and I understand that one of the main reasons why the police did not press charges was that the officers detaining you were finding it too hard to stop laughing in order to do so.

"However, the Board of Governors, represented by Mr Plummer here, and I do not find this quite such a cause for hilarity."

She drops the papers. Her eyes bore into mine and everything is suddenly deadly serious. It is as though nobody exists except for her and myself. Even the image of Isabel feels forced in my mind for a moment.

"Harris," she starts in a very measured tone. Neither rapid nor slow, it just continues in a steady direction, directed, pointed and self-determined. The menace is under-stated but in a way, all the more fearsome because it's still very much there. Very much.

"I ought to sack you right now. You have embarrassed this school and turned it into a laughing-stock across the country. You have caused the Board of Governors, quite rightly, to ask if we have any idea of what we are doing when we hire teachers. You hurt a perfectly innocent, old lady, killed her dog, endangered a few dozen lives and destroyed an entire boat. All of this because of your total ineptitude and lack of any common sense.

"In case you're wondering, Mr Plummer is here today simply to discover if there is any reason at all why your employment with us should not be terminated as of the end of this meeting."

I look away from Mrs Bodega's eyes for a moment to where Mr Plummer remains sitting, completely silent. The menace coming from him is no less than what is coming from Mrs Bodega. I do not know what to say. I simply stand here. I hate to admit that right now, the thought of Isabel is not really stopping me from feeling quite afraid. I would be more upset about that probably, if I had the time to think through what it actually meant but that is not a luxury I have at present.

Mrs Bodega suddenly stops. She turns her back on me and sighs very loudly before continuing to speak. Now though, she is adopting a rather sad tone.

"I really don't know, Harris. As I said, I should have sacked you before you even returned to the school this morning. It would be the logical and probably the right thing to do. At the same time, for reasons I cannot fully understand myself, I find that a small part of me somehow likes you. Believe me, right now that is a very, very small part and most of me would like to have the chance to smack you in the face and throw your unemployed carcass out of the school gates in the next two minutes. But I find that I just don't want to.

"What I suppose I'm trying to say is that the one factor in your defence is that you never acted with any malice or malintent. You are an utter buffoon, a nitwit and a fool. Yet you did try, however uselessly, to put the situation right and you never blamed anybody else for anything. You did everything wrong, but you never tried to do anything which you shouldn't have done. That's why I've called you in now rather than simply terminating your employment. I would like to hear from you in no more than two minutes why you think you should keep your job."

I stop for a moment. Mental images of Isabel are beautiful, but I need something a little more concrete to go on. Not being able to pay the mortgage I've just incurred so as to acquire Karl Givret's clarinet is unlikely to convince Mrs Bodega as to why I should still be employed, and certainly not Mr Plummer. This is not my forte. So I decide to go with what I know. Why does music matter.

"Thank you, Mrs Bodega. I appreciate having the chance and let me start with the most predictable but necessary and, if you will allow me, genuinely heartfelt apology for all which happened yesterday. I recognize fully that I was not paying adequate attention to my surroundings and that I did not exercise proper judgment. I am genuinely ashamed of what happened and would like to offer my most sincere and genuine apologies to the school, to the Board of Governors and to yourself for what occurred. I will, of course, be looking to make a public apology and also due amends to the lady who suffered so much.

"If I may move from there to the question of my continued employment, I think I will need to explain why it is that I believe that the teaching of music is so important. If I can show you this, then I believe that the commitment which I hold will answer your question."

I take a breath and draw myself upright. At six foot two, this does at least have an imposing effect.

"There is only one organ in the human body which responds automatically to external stimuli," I begin. "That is the heart. The brain will respond to such stimuli, of course, but it has to process them. The heart, however, will actually beat in time to a musical rhythm which is detected by the body. This is the reason why music has such a powerful effect on us. It genuinely speaks to one of the core functions which keeps our lives going. This is why we feel music and why it can speak to us. Of course the brain detects it and processes it as well but there is an underlying emotion built in.

"For this reason, music is often combined with other art forms. With drama, for example, in the case of opera. It is why film soundtracks are so carefully designed and engineered. Even art exhibitions are often accompanied by music. The marketing industry worked all this out a long time ago."

This may take more than two minutes, but I can see that for better or worse, I seem to have their attention. I press on.

"Like all art forms, however, there is only so much which music can do if it is not understood or appreciated fully. We need some awareness of what we are feeling when we hear music in order to listen to it and realise what it can mean. Some of us are blessed in this way and have a natural affinity. Others less so but I genuinely believe that we can all find benefit from the musical genre if we are shown the way. The same is true of painting, literature and other arts.

"The arts themselves have been shown to be very useful media for ensuring wellbeing. Both performing and creating art forms release several chemicals within the brain which have great effects in terms of growing, sustaining and healing. Science is starting to show us how we do not simply enjoy these things but that we can use them to enhance ourselves and to become more than just who we may think we are.

"That is why I believe that I have something to offer. The appreciation of music is something amazing and can open our minds in a way which nothing else can do. I possess such an appreciation and teaching lets me share it with others, especially with children whose growth and potential can really be enriched by what music has to offer if it is employed correctly. That is what I have always seen as my mission here and why I would respectfully like to ask that I continue to perform my work."

I stop here. I think it is quite an articulate piece which comes naturally enough. I have said all this before, of course, but it never becomes pure rote since I believe every word. I hope Mrs Bodega does as well.

"Fair enough, Harris," she intones after another pause. "You continue to impress me with your sincerity, your genuine belief in what you do, and in your basic decency. This is my decision and not Mr Plummer's. He is here to listen and to report back on my decision which, I hope, the Board will accept, even if it does not necessarily like it."

That is quite a relief since he continues to regard me quite ominously.

"At the same time, I would ask that when it comes to opening the mind, that you yourself might also try to open yours a little further to concepts such as common sense and paying some sort of attention to what is going on in the world around you!"

I suppose that is a fair point.

"In the meantime," she seems to be concluding, "you will make all of the apologies which you promised, both personal and public. I'm afraid your pay will need to be docked by an amount deemed fair by the Board to contribute towards all the various damages caused although this can be taken on a staggered basis rather than all at once. And also, you will stay on the school premises between working hours for the next six months. Is that understood?"

It certainly is but then a thought occurs.

"Excuse me please, Mrs Bodega, but there is one issue. The Young Pianists Finals of the West Country will be taking place in two weeks' time. We have three entrants under consideration at the moment. If one were to be selected, they would need to be accompanied to the four days of the competition by a teacher. As the one who has coached them all, this is something which my colleagues have been expecting me to do."

I tail off a bit. It's starting to sound a little insignificant. Mrs Bodega raises an eyebrow.

"But none of our pupils has yet been selected?"

"Katie Porter, Alice Morrison and Robert Fletcher are all under consideration."

"There could be three of them going?"

"I rather doubt it," I explain. "It's unheard of for the West Country Music Board to select more than one pupil from a single school and I still don't think that the other two can outclass Katie. They're all talented pupils but I sincerely doubt that anyone other than she can make it. She's just one small cut above."

"And if none is selected?"

"Then of course there's no need for any of us to go anywhere."

Mrs Bodega rolls her eyes.

"Let me think about it, Harris, if and when it happens. Now please leave. And do not do or say anything stupid for at least six months."

"Thank you for your consideration, Mrs Bodega. I really do appreciate it," I say with genuine meaning and even warmth before I turn to Mr Plummer.

"It's been very nice to meet you," I add, before extending my hand to bid him goodbye.

He doesn't extend his hand one inch. He still hasn't said a single word, and he does not start now.

Chapter 6

SCOUSELAND

Jessica

You can never have too much of some things. Many others you can, for sure. Think political discourse, flights to Luton or boy bands. Enough is enough. But the really good stuff is what never quite satisfies but only in the sense that it's so good that you have to have a bit more.

The vista of the Eiger, Mönch and Jungfrau mountains before me now, is one of those things. It's so painfully beautiful that you simply don't want to take your eyes off it because whatever you go on to look at next just won't be as good. At half past eight in the morning, the sun having risen a couple of hours back already, you can stand in Beatenberg and look straight down the Lauterbrünnen Valley with a perfectly uniform blue sky behind the mountain range in front you. The Mönch is right ahead of you, with the slightly lower Eiger to its left. The two are wrapped in a grey-blue sheen while the Jungfrau sits behind them and to the right. As the tallest of the three, the grey is minimal and the peak shines white, even in mid-summer. A snow-covered range starts on a shoulder to the mountain's right and continues away behind it until dipping behind the peak of some nearer Alps. Looking straight ahead towards the Mönch, about halfway to the top, my view is obscured by a row of closer, dark green trees, passing across in a near horizontal line. They're on the other side of a crevasse between their ridge and the one I'm looking from, so there is an interchanging pattern of darker treelines and lighter meadows. It's not something I want to look away from. It sounds almost pathetic, but I just want it to last like that.

The bummer is that it probably will but mainly because it's a print of a photo I took, which now hangs in a large frame beside my desk. My desk being the one at home in Liverpool. It's a great souvenir but it doesn't make up for the real thing.

I reflect a moment longer. I do wonder, when I look at this, who came up with the names and legend of the Eiger, the Mönch and the Jungfrau. Apparently the Eiger, or Ogre, is seen to be prevented from molesting the Jungfrau by the intervention of the Mönch, or Monk, which lies between the two. Jungfrau is a term used for either a maiden or more specifically a virgin though it could be both – check with her gyno if you want the inside scoop. The Eiger, in case you're interested, is the one whose north face is notoriously difficult to scale, hence the description of something extremely hard being like trying to climb the north face of the Eiger. Not that the other two would be something to knock off on an otherwise boring Sunday afternoon either. They're absolutely immense, majestic and, to my mind, almost passive threatening, as if they're daring you even to think about trying to get up there. I'm a hiker, not a climber, so you won't catch me trying that stunt. Mountain-hiking is for people looking to stay healthy, enjoy real beauty and find a unique sense of tranquillity in nature. Climbing is for those slightly lacking their full, mental capacity.

What I fail to get anyway, is why these three, immovable towers of rock and ice somehow reminded anybody of an attempted rape being prevented by a heroic Churchgoer. I feel a lot of different thoughts and even emotions when up on an Alpine path somewhere, but nothing of a particularly sexual or violent nature. Hiking is a healthy pastime, you understand. None of that sex and violence stuff we hear moaned about so much. This isn't Netflix, you know. Not even Channel 4.

It's probably a good thing that whoever came up with the legend wasn't hanging out in Zermatt next to the decidedly phallic Matterhorn Alp, which towers above an otherwise uninterrupted ridge. I hate to think what that would have suggested to them, but I daresay his horn would have mattered quite a bit.

Oh dear, Jessica. Your sense of humour does you proud, doesn't it? I thought that was funny, even if nobody else did but since nobody else lives here, who cares? Entertaining though I'm finding my contemplation of Alpine scenery, however, it's time to tear my gaze away and return to Liverpool, specifically Huyton and my own residence within it.

Reasonably pleasant, reasonably safe and reasonably affordable, while well-connected to central Liverpool and hence much of the UK, Huyton is a good place to live and work, especially when you more or less do so from home. My own little one-bedroom place more than fits the bill. It may be nothing special but it's my nothing special and I like it this way. The front door opens straight into the relatively spacious living room, from where three doors lead to the kitchenette, the shower room and my little bedroom. It's compact but as roomy as I need myself. It also sits on the corner of the first floor (or second floor if you're American) so it's nice and light with windows on two sides.

As you may have guessed, Alpine scenery does grace the walls to quite a degree, photographed by both myself and others. Glaciers, lakes, Alpine pastures, forest pathways plus strangely hungover-looking cows adorn many a space. At the same time, there is also my collection of planets and astronomical phenomena. I really can't say why but I like the night sky. I'm not a science fiction fan. "Star Wars" doesn't really do much for me. I have no exceptional interest in NASA rockets and space shuttles. I just like the stars out there and found at school that I really liked the way things such as the solar system and the Milky Way are put together. One of my prized possessions is a very expensive model of the aforementioned solar system. A scale model, or so the box said, it holds the sun at the centre and moves the series of revolving planets around it thanks to a cable which attaches its power source. It works in the dark with lights inside the various globes and can even be configured to reflect different seasons. Quite how anyone knows what the difference is between summer and winter on Mercury, never mind how to model them, I don't honestly know but it looks great. It's also the single most expensive item in my house but it's not that pricey really. It demonstrates less how I splash out on unnecessary things, so much as how cheap I am in most other respects.

And of course, there are then my two James Bond posters: "The Living Daylights" in my bedroom and "License to Kill" in the bathroom. I hasten to remind you that I'm not a 007 nerd but those were the two films with Tim as Bond and dear me, he was one handsome guy in those. I mean, that bit in "License to Kill" where he gets his shirt off.... I'm not some sort of sex addict, not a bit. People even tell me that I don't seem all that interested in men at all sometimes. To my way of thinking, the problem is more that when you get to see prime rump steak on a daily basis when you step out of the shower, you're less likely to be that bothered when confronted by a veggie burger later in the day. I'm not frigid. I just have high standards.

Anyway, I'm back and I've finished unpacking. Alice and I completed a fantastic holiday of hiking, and pigging out on Alpine cuisine, the two of which offset each other very well so you can get away with two of the things you like the most at once. The few days when the weather sucked, we just paid for an extra day in the hotel and hung around, playing cards, bouncing peanuts off the ceiling to catch in our mouths, and trying to find the worst possible profiles entered by people on dating apps. It's the sort of stuff you can get away with when you're supposed to be acting like a parent, but you aren't actually one.

Talking of whom, the only hard work was keeping Bethany off our case. I think she was possibly just starting to get wise to the fact that we might have strayed slightly off course from Lake Lucerne, once we supposedly got there. Not the eighty odd clicks we'd actually strayed off it, of course, but she did keep asking to see what the lake looked like, almost as if she knew that there wasn't really a lake all that close by at all. Stock shots from Google as a background worked for a bit and we also managed one evening to show Alice up to her knees in what was actually a duck pond next to a mountain farm, just without showing the other side of the pond which was a lot closer than the other side of Lake Lucerne really would have been in reality. Most of the effort in setting up such a shot went to waste anyhow since Bethany went berserk over the fact that Alice might have caught some combination of cholera, typhoid and HIV which apparently inhabits Swiss lakes, might have trapped her foot in a random beer can and drowned, or might have fallen victim to a species of alligator unknown to infest Swiss waterways up to now. I don't really know what her problem was but all I can say is that if she got that excited during the times when Colin was trying to raise his flagging pole, then I would have to credit the guy with being one of the top lovers of all time, his personal chipolata notwithstanding.

Eventually, we just got on with filming video sequences of Alice next to any random waterways we passed during the day and then intertwining those with live discussions from whichever hotel room we happened to be in when it came time to report in most evenings. I guess it worked. When we arrived back in Heathrow, Bethany was there (with Colin, sadly) to pick up her poor princess who had been at such risk of harm in the lonely, awful wilds of one of the world's richest nations with the best mapped hiking trails of virtually any country with height differentials above five metres. We had picked up all the crap left in locker 423B in the railway station underneath Zürich Airport and ruffled it about a bit before re-packing most of it. The consumable items such as factor three million sun cream we ditched and replaced the space with some lovely souvenirs for mum and dad: a battery-operated teasmaid in the shape of a chalet in the winter, and a cuckoo clock which every two hours would play something sounding vaguely like the William Tell overture performed on a kazoo full of cowpats. How Alpine. All made in China, of course. I didn't know whether to laugh or cry when we shelled out fifty francs for this garbage. Fifty francs? Fifty freaking francs? I know the holiday was basically being bankrolled by Bethany and Colin, but I could have found something a lot better to do with that sort of cash than splash out some of the random expenses slush fund on the equivalent of what I could have pulled out of a cow's bum for free.

So I said goodbye to Alice with my words and my eyes. I bade farewell to Bethany and Colin with my words and basically told them to piss off with my eyes. They drove all the way here from Somerset to pick up their darling daughter when I could have brought her on the train to Bristol in under half the time it took them. From there, the train ride up to Liverpool would not have been that dramatic. But did they want to offer me a ride as well in the empty back seat, at least as far as Bristol? Not a chance. Off you go, Jessica. Get yourself back to that northern dump you call home.

I don't think Bethany has ever forgiven me for leaving Somerset. Sorry, if you're not from the posher parts such as East Dawlings, perhaps I should be referring to it as Zoomerzet, the English county where the letter s is pronounced as z, and nobody declines the verb to be. "I am", "you are," "she is" are all unknown. You just use, "be". "He be a roight foine fahrming lad, me boy." "We be of zound ztock round here, you be mahrking moy wordz." You get the idea. They probably think that "The Combine Harvester Song" by the Wurzels is the national anthem.

The only other place where they don't sound more rural than the livestock is the naval air station at Yeovilton since most of the navy people aren't originally from Somerset themselves. The farming community inevitably whines away about the effect on their sheep, goats, pigs and so forth caused by the noise of helicopter rotors and jet engines but what I wonder is why would the Royal Navy put its closest equivalent to Top Gun in a place like Somerset? Don't tell me it's because it's near the sea. So is everywhere in Britain, relatively speaking and the Americans would never have put Tom Cruise in Blackpool or Margate either. With the exception of James Bond, we Brits just seem to keep missing out on every other chance to be genuinely cool.

The idea that Bethany actually misses me is ridiculous but my temerity in choosing somewhere other than East Dawlings to live and work in must have beggared her belief. The fact that I went to somewhere as downmarket as Liverpool is, I'm sure, simply unforgiveable to someone of her social standing. I just hope that Alice has enough of my genetics to get out before she turns into a wannabe upper class zombie like her parents.

So where was I? Ah yes, unpacking finished so load the washing machine with most of what came out of it, then stop for a quick breather. I haven't been to the supermarket yet, so the supplies are a bit thin on the ground, but I do believe I have a bottle of white wine somewhere and, equally importantly, a family size bag of salt 'n' vinegar crisps to go with it.

Despite what you may have read in the popular press, those of us who live alone are not all a bunch of hopeless alcoholics. I might be having a glass or two of white wine, but I do not intend to wake up with a hellish headache and my hair full of what used to be my crisps. I'm no puritan. My alcohol consumption back in the days of my studies in particular was perhaps a shade higher than it should have been but it wasn't really a pleasant experience either. Perhaps it is for some, but when I somehow ended up in a situation one Sunday morning where it looked like I'd got lucky with a goldfish the previous night, I decided that I would just drink what tasted nice without going overboard. You do what you like. What I do works for me.

Unlike my brother-in-law, I do not have a particular taste for fine wine. I like white wine because it tastes nice and that's about it. I really don't care if it comes from a French chateau, an Australian vineyard or one of those DIY grape-gigs which they run down in Kent. At least so long as they've washed the grapes off after removing the used condoms which were probably left hanging on the branches. Fine by me. Actually, I doubt I should even run down the Brits so much. Who knows what the Australians get up to as well? Billa-ma-bong with me didgeridoo, mate. Whatever that means. I only ever studied French and German plus a certain level of Spanish. I never learned Aussie. Understanding Scouse when I reached Liverpool was perhaps the closest I got to picking up another anglophone pronunciation.

So Tesco's finest in white wine for the princely sum of four pounds ninety-nine is quite OK. It keeps me going until I'm halfway through the crisps and then I turn to the messages which have arrived during my absence by mail, both physical and electronic. It's not exactly the highlight of the evening but somebody has to pay the bills for all the hiking, astronomical effects and general living so I do have to do a bit of work now and again. I try to minimize it over the course of the summer so as to have more time for the outdoors but that doesn't mean I can take four or five months off at a time. My boss at the agency does also like to check that I'm still alive, putting in sufficient effort and not moonlighting as a people trafficker, lunchtime prostitute, British Nazi Party activist or whatever other wholesome, alternative employment prospects he imagines we agency contractors occupy our time with.

Being a contractor is actually quite a sweet deal, all things considered. It means that I can work at home most of the time and also choose to accept or reject contracts, within reason. A linguistic professional can be reduced to the role of nothing more than a glorified translator if she or he is not careful. Even with the advent of some serious AI (Artificial Intelligence for those less up to date with modern tech terms), there's still a role for translators although it can nowadays be reduced to reading through what the AI is spitting out. I have a lot of respect for the capabilities of AI, but I do know that it can't be entirely trusted with anything which is or might become a sarcastic remark or a double entendre. This is probably because I can't be trusted with them either, except that in my case it's intentional while I believe the AI does it by accident. Be that as it may, it does mean that an unthinking translator can end up spending half a week reading through a report on the proofing of a new steel alloy against high pressure atmospheric humidity, with little remit other than to make sure that a reference to, "salvage in a steam process" doesn't show up as an attempt to, "sell vagina's team proceeds."

The interesting work lies in marketing campaigns. These can be what you'd normally associate with marketing, namely private sector gubbins, flogging everything from sports cars to novelty false teeth. On the other hand, it can also include public sector publicity for things like health campaigns or giving up smoking, charitable causes or even politics, although you want to be wary of the last one. Politicians, for reasons which escape me, seem to be invulnerable to law, meaning that if you're a politician, you can say the most blatantly untrue things you like, and nobody will ever sue you. I really do not know how they get away with it. In the world which the rest of us inhabit though, if you even insinuate publicly that the sky is blue when in fact there's a vague hint of azure just to the left and a possibility of a gunmetal tone on the opposite horizon, then that's false advertising, the use of disingenuous claims or basically just lying your face off. Any reasonably minded intern in a law firm will be up your ass with a claim for at least half a million by bedtime. Working for politicians does not mean that you get their bulletproof protection conferred upon you, so it's best not to have to take the fall, especially if they end up losing the election.

Politics aside, the thing about marketing campaigns is that you need a really good grasp of a language if you're going to put together messages which will sell in them. You also need a reasonable level of cultural awareness. For example, you can't sell cheese sandwiches across Britain, France and Germany just by translating a cheesy slogan from English into French and German. You can see that already – a "cheesy slogan"? It's a crap joke in Britain, means nothing in Germany and is likely to have French people wondering if your IQ is lower than your shoe size if you're thick enough to try it in their country. As for the sandwich itself, it's a functional item in Germany where you eat to live. In France, as they say, you live to eat and so the gourmet qualities, the fresh preparation and the superiority in quality to any culinary alternatives are what matter. In Britain, it's more multi-faceted. You eat it to keep you going on the way to the chippy, then halfway through, you chuck what's left at your neighbour's dog to stop it pissing on the back door of your car. A good marketing campaign will adjust and use both language and culture to sell.

The downside of contractor work is that it's not very predictable and since your pay is indexed to it, you can face quiet times without earning too much. The agency helps by trying to plan things out in advance, but a steady income stream can be a challenge. Looking on the bright side, however, it does mean that you can plan to be absent without too much hassle so long as you can afford it. It works for my lifestyle.

So, let's see what gives. I want to manage at least another two hiking gigs before the autumn sets in and that means I need around two and a half weeks off between now and September but I'd better have some decent jobs otherwise so I can afford them. Last week was awesome since Alice was there, the weather mainly held, Bethany was too busy having sex with Colin to notice how far off course we'd actually gone, and thanks to the two of them, I basically didn't have to pay for any of it. Unless I can persuade Bethany to release her beloved daughter into my care for another week abroad, I'm going to have start earning a bit now. Bummer.

Eight translating jobs are available. Six of them for universities so no thanks. If the work of the science department is so boring that the university's own language department won't take the work and they have to pay someone like me instead, it can't be good. One pornographic novel – sorry, a work of literary eroticism. Sounds like it's been translated into bougie already. Someone else can handle that. Diverse Franco-German terms for genitalia are not something on which I've spent a lot of time.

The final translating gig might be OK. Some zoo in the Midlands wants to hype the fact that it's aiming to be bear central with black bears, brown bears, polar bears, pandas and who knows what, all housed in the same place. It looks a bit over the top and I'm wondering if they're planning to get in a couple of Care Bears while they're at it, but you can't fault their enthusiasm. They want the materials in a variety of languages so if the agency can get somebody else to handle the Spanish and Italian, I can take the French and German. Works for me so I put it to one side.

The marketing looks a bit more thin on the ground. Somebody wants to sell, "law enforcement gear" to various Francophone countries outside Europe? Sorry, matey. My moral and ethical standards may not be those of the Pope, but flogging pepper spray and ill-fitting handcuffs to the local constabulary in some low-income country where the customer is the one in power with ninety per cent of the national wealth in his Seychelles bank account? That's just not my thing. Flogging ill-fitting handcuffs to the local gentlemen's club is something I can live with, especially after some off-duty pole dancer once kicked me in the face while practising outside around a bus stop timetable. But I stop short of some things.

A couple of boarding schools want to sell their curricula to upper class French and German families looking for a solid, British education. Not sure what we have which they don't, apart from cheese sandwiches which you can throw at dogs, but I'll give it a go. And then there's one for a new movement aiming to sell outdoor birthing clinics to, "give mothers the chance to divest their offspring into the oneness and wellness of nature". I don't like the look of this thing at all. The marketing materials already designed give the impression that they intend to carry out this rubbish at high altitudes, so I'd better get involved, if only to make sure that they stay away from the mountain ranges where I like to hang out. It's bad enough dodging the cowpats. I don't need to add flying foetuses, used placentas and newborn spew into the equation. I want to hear the birds singing, not birthing mothers screaming their uteruses out and aiming every expletive they know at their husbands who are trying and failing to provide any sort of useful support. Keep all that in the hospitals and out of my hiking areas, thank you very much.

Otherwise, there's a reminder that I've missed my last smear test by about a year and a half and ought to hurry up to fix an appointment before I die of cervical cancer without realising it. Credit to the health services, it's a fair point. Two utility bills which I'd better remember to pay by the end of the week. Yawn. And then there's something from the food bank. A strategy committee meeting next Wednesday? I suppose I'd better go. The strategy to target teenagers was actually my idea so it would be a bit much to skive off. Then there's another meeting two days later on premises security. Oh great. I know it has to be done but when I signed up to help people a bit, I wish I'd realised how much bureaucracy there seems to be to charity work.

I actually feel slightly hard done by. Helping people out is fine. I appreciate that I live alone but it doesn't make me a selfish person, at least not totally self-centred. I don't like to see other people suffer. Well OK, maybe Colin now and again, but not most people. Colin doesn't actually suffer enough, at least not in my opinion, but I'm not a vindictive person so I leave him alone. My energy is better applied to lessening the suffering of nice people.

So you'd think that a bit of charity volunteering would be what I need, wouldn't you? There are certainly enough poor souls in Liverpool to give it a meaningful shot. More than you'll find in East Dawlings at any rate. However, it seems that I have a talent for critical thought and problem-solving. As a result, while I can spend my time on a bit of genuine work with those who require sustenance and nutrition, I've also somehow got myself roped into a whole series of management and planning committees. I undertake enough behind the scenes activities to keep me busy for weeks on end without ever actually seeing a hungry person. It's not that it isn't needed. I'm not that stupid or idealistic. It just kind of takes the shine off things.

I suppose the problem with charity is that it's always been romanticized. It's never been portrayed as what it should be: not simply a question of showing pity for others but of organizing something which can have a meaningful impact and actually make people's lives better. It's not just about the better off showing a small act of kindness to some poor wretches who don't know any better but who gratefully accept the morsels cast their way, before heading off to be just as poor after a quick snack. Maybe that worked in Victorian Britain but it's a shade outmoded these days.

That said, you can't blame the Victorians. They didn't start it. Even the Bible doesn't make it entirely obvious that meaningful charity might require some sort of social movement and organization. The Biblical concept of selling all you have and giving the proceeds to the poor is hardly an enlightened discourse on effective resource management. True, that's taking it out of context, and it isn't quite as superficial as that, but the immediate line does seem to take the backstory for granted while it hypes the need simply to give and be done with it.

Let me give an example of where I feel short-changed by superficial charity. Jesus taught that, "The poor are always with us." So one day, I'm hauling myself along the city centre in Liverpool and I see some homeless dude asking for cash. I go up to him and ask, well do you need cash or are you hungry? He tells me that he would really like to eat but if I provide the means, he can get something. Given the wad of cigarettes in his pocket, I don't really trust this, but I nip into the Gregg's round the corner and buy him a chicken slice. Nothing too special but it'll keep you going. I get back to where I was a moment ago and he's gone. I look around and, guess what? There's not a single homeless person or beggar to be seen between where I am and the waterfront. The poor are always with us? Not in bloody Liverpool, they're not. They've pissed off for a coffee break or something. I don't even want the chicken slice myself but it's going cold, and the local cop shop will not be too impressed if I feed it to the seagulls, so I end up having a snack I didn't want in the first place. I may not be the most dedicated scholar of the Bible, but I don't recall Jesus ever having this problem.

Still, whatever. It keeps me going. It keeps my world functioning. I like it. It might not be for everyone, but it works for me and since I'm the only one here, that must be good enough. There's a certain value to being alone which the world at large doesn't get. So much is made of people being lonely that it almost becomes something like the equivalent of worshipping Satan, sacrificing infants or being a Karen. It's to be avoided at all costs. The only difference between that and being a Karen (less so the other two) is that it's recognized as being not entirely your fault. However, being lonely is not the same thing as being alone. Loneliness is, I'm sure, awful if you suffer from it but being alone doesn't have to make you a sufferer. In fact, it can be quite the opposite. I can decorate my place as I feel like. I can do the chores when I want and how I want. I can watch anything on TV, listen to whatever music I like or eat ghastly food without anyone complaining. I can also do so without having to worry about offending anyone. I never fight with anyone else. I don't have to sit with my legs crossed tightly and thinking about quantum mathematics while somebody else finishes off a serious session in the bathroom during a moment of temporary crisis in waiting for a turn on the toilet. Nor does anyone else. My only real fear is getting bored but that rarely happens. Such being the case, I can quite happily enjoy this fascinating lifestyle which eludes so many frustrated wives, husbands, daughters and sons, who spend countless hours complaining on TV shows and in magazines about the challenges of living with others and without "their" space. Go and get some, if it matters that much to you. Or go and climb a mountain. Actually, on second thoughts, don't. I'm not sure I really want to run into you and all that moaning up there.

The only other downside to living on your own is that you do develop a tendency to ramble on a bit. But you probably figured that much out already.

Chapter 7

PLAN A GOES SOUTH

Harris

I think that I am starting to feel the elation of love once more. The earlier conversation with Mrs Bodega had me very concerned indeed. I actually believed at one point that I might cease to be employed and the loss of income, even if temporary, would have left me high and dry for sure. I did also have to appreciate that a little more awareness of the world around me might be no bad thing. I do suppose that on occasion, I may be overly tempted to view the rest of the world as just being full of people who simply don't realise that the wonders of music are as powerful as they are and that they are there for them. Yet you only have to reach out and grasp them. How anybody could ever hear the haunting call of a duet sung by an alto and a tenor in a minor key or the sheer rush and energy of a full symphony is simply beyond me. These things bring actual joy to me. I cannot for the life of me understand how anybody else can exist without being touched by them. It's impossible to be fully unaware of their awesome sound. Even the most borderline television channels still employ classical music in their productions from time to time. Once you hear just a few notes, how can you not be touched by the awareness they bring of your need for the cultural, even natural yearnings you have, which only they can meet? Perhaps I'm becoming a shade poetic but when I think about this to myself, I really do become quite eloquent in my own mind.

My own experience today has shown the power of music as evidenced in emotion and being. After the horrible session in Mrs Bodega's office with that awful Mr Plummer, my mood was rather soured. I admit that I may have been a touch stupid and that while all which happened was by no means entirely my fault, my own contribution to those events was still notable. This feeling of inadequacy took hold, and I began to question myself and how much I could really mean as a man and, as I still very much hope to become, as a husband.

There is not and never will be any question of how much Isabel is worth to me. I cannot conceive of being able to love another as much as I love her. My greatest fear is not even that of losing her. It is the fear of simply not being good enough myself for her. She is so precious to me that I know I have put her on a pedestal. Even so, she deserves the best there is and what if I cannot become that? This is a fear which drives me to a terrible extent.

I'm very grateful in fact to Mrs Bodega for her acknowledgement of what she referred to as my overall decency. I certainly do not consider myself a bad person. I do not hold grudges. I do not have a short temper. I try not to be lazy or to fail in my duties. What I do find myself lacking is a degree of savoir-faire of the world, perhaps even just common sense, although I hate to admit that. This has been troubling me for the basic reason that I am afraid that I may not be able to provide Isabel with some of the basics which she simply has to have as a human being. There is more to life than cultural and spiritual awareness, I suppose.

However, that feeling was again tempered after I returned to my little office in the back of the school. I turned on some Schubert and felt the music sweep over me once more. I could bask in that all day. The music itself reminded me of why this matters. It speaks to me, perhaps to that inner decency which Mrs Bodega referred to, because it seems to capture something about me which can't be quantified or even properly described. Decency is something which cannot be captured. You can't extract it from a person. You can't set it on a table and look at it. You can't measure it according to a scale. From a purely rational and scientific standpoint, I don't know that it even exists. However, we know that it is absolutely very real. And most of what Mrs Bodega so kindly noted were my good points, are ones which fall into much the same category.

If music can also have such a powerful yet elusive quality, perhaps its true value is in speaking to that part of me which cannot otherwise be reached or even communicated properly. It lets me recognize some actual worth and we know that self-worth is a crucial feeling for wellbeing. If I can leverage that with music, then I think that I must be achieving something worthwhile and my mission to share that with others is one worth having.

As a consequence, I know that I have real worth as an individual attuned to this channel into our souls. Maybe I don't know as much as I should about serving Isabel's material needs but I do believe that that is something I can learn. I have the intelligence and the will to do so, I know. I am starting to feel that bit more confident again. The power of music, combined with the strange mixture of soothing serenity and excited longing, which is love, lets me feel strangely at peace with my surroundings while also straining to transform them further with the goodness which I feel. Music and love. They are all I need to be the best I can be.

My reflections continue for a while. I really am in a delightful place in my mind.

The telephone on my desk rings and draws me back into the rest of the world. I don't resent this. I am well aware that the rest of the world remains out there and that I have a role to play in it. So let's see what this is.

"Harris," a breathless voice intones. "It's me, Charles."

Ah, Charles. I've been expecting to hear from him. I wonder why he sounds quite so flustered though.

"Hello, Charles," I begin. "It's good to hear from you. I trust all is well. How is our masterplan working out?"

He doesn't reply. There's silence for a moment. It's very odd.

"Charles," I ask, "is there something wrong there?"

Again there is a silence, but I can hear Charles breathing. I look around my office in a slightly confused manner while I wait for him to speak. It's quite a brown place, I reflect absently. I really don't know why I'm suddenly taking this into account but it's as though I'm being put on hold while Charles gets his thoughts in order. Why that should be taking him so long I simply do not understand but it seems wrong to pressure the poor man.

Eventually his voice returns.

"Harris, something terrible has happened."

I can't say why but my blood has frozen in my veins. It's bizarre. Somehow, I already know that something has gone wrong with the plan, but I have no idea whatsoever what that might be. Then the situation reverses itself in my mind. The clarinet might have been seized at customs. It might have been stolen. Perhaps a key part of it has somehow been broken. I just don't know but possibilities are coursing through my mind. I can't keep track of them. If I tried to write them down, I wouldn't finish describing one on paper before the next one flew into my mind and made me forget the last as it asserted itself over it. Until another one did the same and so on. It feels as though I'm drowning in nightmares. I wish fervently that Charles would just get to the point. There seems to be an eternity stretching in front of me with something awful at the end of it which I cannot avoid but in the meantime, Fate is playing with my anticipation in the most perverse and cruel way imaginable. Perhaps this is how condemned prisoners feel on their way to execution. Still, at least they vaguely know what to expect. In a certain way this is worse.

"Perhaps I should just describe what has happened as simply as I can," Charles finally says, in a markedly dull and toneless manner, actually quite slowly after the breathless introduction.

That would be best, and I encourage him gently to explain what he has to say in straightforward terms. It seems the least I can do for both of us. Charles exhales loudly, pauses briefly and then continues.

"You remember, Harris, that I acquired the clarinet during a short downtime with the Somerset Symphonic Orchestra?"

"How could I forget? Your tour with them was a key part of the plan."

"Yes, Harris," he continues. "The thing is that when we played in Milan, there was a promoter there who heard us play and liked our rendition of the Haydn."

"You mean the London Symphony?" I know the repertoire they were playing.

"Yes, of course," he replies hurriedly before returning to his more laborious monotone. "He heard us play and asked if we could take on a special job for one of his clients."

"One of his clients?" I ask. What on earth is Charles talking about?

"Yes. You see, the man was something of what some refer to as a talent scout. Very high class, you understand, of course."

"Well, of course," I repeat. I cannot imagine the Somerset Symphony Orchestra performing for some dreadful nightclub or drinking den.

"It turned out that he was seeking someone to help with an unusual advertisement to be made for an international perfume brand. He said that he just had not heard the right sound from the right musicians until he happened to chance upon our recital. We also appeared physically to be what he was looking for."

I do so wish he would get to the point. The feeling of dreadful anticipation in my stomach is physically painful.

"It was a very strange set-up," Charles goes on. "The producer of the advertisement, a television commercial, wanted to film an orchestra playing high in the mountains. It was supposed to be a very unusual and fantastic scene. Apparently the Somerset Symphonic playing Haydn's London Symphony was just what would be needed.

"As you know, funds are a little tight for the orchestra, so we agreed to take it on. It would be all expenses paid, naturally, with a group fee amounting to a few tens of thousands. Of course we agreed."

This is turning into a very strange story indeed. One thing is for certain and that's that my own feeling of dread is not being assuaged one bit. It just keeps growing. That brown colour of my office is starting to swirl, and I do not genuinely know if it would even be safe to try to stand up at this moment in time.

"The actual filming location was in Switzerland. We spent a couple of days in Italy, waiting for the paperwork to be fixed with the authorities there for a commercial performance to be made. Then they shipped us on a first-class train carriage all the way over the border and high up into the Swiss Alps. We received accommodation in a delightful, little village which was, if I recall correctly, somewhere south of Bern in the middle of the country.

"When we got up in the morning, we were asked to put on our black tie outfits and be ready to perform. On top of that, they gave us some very heavy coats to wear with hats, scarves and gloves. The plan was that we would reach the very top of a mountain by helicopter, disembark and remove the outer layers. Everything at the top of a mountain that high is just snow and ice. We would then be able to perform briefly in our black tie for the cameras before we froze to death. Then we could quickly get back into the protective gear and return in the helicopter. Most of us had never been in a helicopter before so it was quite intriguing and definitely a novelty. A production crew had already set up all of the orchestral furniture, together with the lights, sound systems, cameras and what-not which the filming crew required. That part of the operation took a bit longer but those carrying it out could keep on their winter gear."

Some of this is perhaps a shade obvious but I don't want to distract him from his train of thought.

"The production crew also took all of our instruments up there," he says, then pauses.

He just mentioned instruments explicitly. Something is very wrong here. I can feel it. I cannot explain it, but I know it. Oh please, Charles, just tell me. It won't change the facts, whatever they should be. If anything, the waiting is the worst piece of the torture.

"As you know," he resumes, "the plan was to bring back Givret's clarinet as part of the orchestra's collection of instruments. I had placed it among the wind section where it was unlikely to be noticed."

He stops once more. I feel as though I am ageing a couple of years every time he does so. Please, please, let this end soon. Just exercise the blow.

Charles continues. Very slowly, excruciatingly slowly. But he is getting there. My own body is actually shaking, and I feel so weak that it is all I can do to hold onto the telephone.

"When we arrived on the summit, we disembarked from the helicopter and proceeded to our places. Once we had found our seats in the ensemble, we were signalled to strip down to the black tie. This was coordinated so that nobody would remain unclad for longer than was strictly necessary.

"I was struggling with the dratted coat I had received, which had a wrist opening which was frankly too small to accommodate my hand in the quite thick glove I was wearing. The production crew was meanwhile bringing over our instruments. My own was, of course, my usual clarinet, which I had labelled as such and called, 'Clarinet – principal.' Givret's was in its box, which was labelled, 'Clarinet – reserve.'

"For some reason, the new production crew from the filming company had assigned someone to me who decided to assemble the wrong clarinet, namely Givret's. He cannot have been anybody who was faintly aware of classical instruments because he pulled it out of its box and put together the pieces before handing it to me.

"Of course, I was flabbergasted and aghast at the site of Givret's clarinet being offered to me in such a way. I was also struggling to get my gloved hand out of the sleeve of that coat. And then…."

His voice tails off. I feel as though I want to be sick and at the same time, I just want to scream at him from the top of my lungs to get to the impending finale of this most horrific of dramas. My chest is contracting, and I am having to force myself to take conscious breaths.

Charles still cannot continue. I breathe deeply myself several times.

"Charles," I finally break in, "please just tell me."

His voice returns. It is even more of a monotone than before and absolutely, perfectly flat.

"My hand sprang out of the sleeve unexpectedly and in being released like that, I lost control for an instant. It flew into the clarinet and knocked it out of the grip of the production crew member. It slid across the ice on the ground until it reached the edge. It kept going there and simply disappeared over the side.

"Below that edge was a sheer drop down an almost vertical slope of, I don't know, a couple of hundred feet at least. The peaks around us were shaped like the top of some sort of bowl and there was a vast mass of ice at the bottom of it, forming a glacier, if I can call it that. I did not see the clarinet come to rest there but when I reached the edge and looked over, I could just make out what may have been the bell a long way off. I couldn't see any other parts.

"The ice bowl was unreachable from above. As far as I could tell, it might just have been possible to climb up from below, at least for a skilled climber but it was still a very long way up into the mountains."

I feel as though I can no longer see. Only a mass of brown floats before my eyes. It is as though I have just been hit so hard in the stomach that I am totally winded and incapable of moving in any direction, even downwards.

"So what happened next?" I don't know how I was able to ask that.

"Well, they apologized profusely but clearly didn't seem that concerned since there was another clarinet, namely my regular one, which they carefully extracted from its case, put together and handed to me so I could play. I felt truly awful, Harris, truly awful. More awful than I've ever felt before. But I had no choice. We would literally have died if we had spent too long without adequate clothing and we still had to perform. Since nobody else knew what that first clarinet had been or why I should have had it, there was literally nothing I could do. I did wonder if the helicopter could have made it down there but there were a lot of freezing cold people needing transport. Also, nobody would have understood why it merited so much trouble to chase after a single clarinet which was probably lost and broken to all intents and purposes. I know nothing about helicopters, but I understand from what I was told that piloting them around Alpine mountaintops is not the easiest job.

"I doubt anyone could retrieve it, even if they could reach the glacier.

"I'm sorry, Harris." The monotone has disappeared suddenly. He sounds as though he's now in tears. Sobs are rending what he's telling me. "I am so, so sorry. So sorry."

The loss is immense but somehow, I can still feel for my friend. It's the only thing I can do just now in any case.

"Please, Charles, do not blame yourself. This is a disaster, but I do not need you to," I pause. I just don't know what to say next. After a few seconds, I conclude, "to take it all on yourself.

"What I need just now is a friend I can talk to. You're the only one with whom I can share any of this. You're all I have. Please don't go to pieces."

There's an even longer pause than before. It drags on for what feels like hours but may have actually been around two minutes.

"Thank you, Harris," he replies at last. "You're more generous than I could possibly deserve."

I suddenly want to end this conversation right now. I don't know why but I've simply heard enough and talking just feels like too much pain.

"When will you be back?" I enquire.

"Another couple of days. The tour will finish tomorrow."

"Please let me know when you reach Bristol again, Charles. We can talk then. But please do not worry. Accidents happen, even dreadful ones. Blaming people does none of us any good but I'm going to need your help. Please let me know."

"I will, Harris, I assure you I will."

"Thank you, Charles," I manage. "I'll see you in a couple of days then. Goodbye."

I hang up before he responds. Maybe a little sharp but there's only so much I can manage.

I have never been truly bereaved before. I lost two grandparents as a child but never had a chance to get to know them properly. It wasn't a great loss. Even when my parents died, it felt terrible but proved relatively easy to recover from. My father's work in multiple locations across southern Africa meant that I spent most of my childhood being cared for by my uncle and aunt or else in boarding school. When my parents were lost in that air crash, they weren't the people I'd spent the most time in my life with. Of course, I've known enough people who have been genuinely bereaved of their closest relatives and friends, and it seems horrible. I've attended funerals and I've always dreaded encountering a loss like that myself. Now I think that suddenly I know what it is. It grips me physically. I feel as though some gigantic serpent has wrapped itself around my torso and is drawing itself in. It's not a sudden feeling, just an inevitable crushing which will not stop and from which there is no escape. I cannot see or feel anything else.

Everything has gone. It's all in ruins. Why did I even try? I've lost it all and gained absolutely nothing. I could take the loss if I still had Isabel but how can I keep her now? Truly, I really am unable to provide her with anything, even when I try my hardest. She deserves better than I am, truly better. That clarinet has disappeared over the edge of an Alpine precipice, and all my life has descended with it. My dreams are in that frozen tomb and there is no way to rescue them. Why? No music can answer that. Love has deserted me. What I have just lost, nothing can replace.

My inertia is replaced by an incontrollable shaking. I don't want to cry. I just do. It comes in fits and bursts until I let it flow without any attempt to control it. I can't do otherwise. My face sinks onto my arms on the desk and I stop trying to think. I simply cry.

Chapter 8

FROM THE MOUTHS OF BABES AND PIANO STUDENTS

Harris

You often seem to hear about those in a state of shock losing track of time and the reality all around them. This may be true in many cases. I have no idea. What I do know is that in my case, it isn't true. I sit and I watch the hands crawl round on the face of the nineteenth century grandfather clock which stands to the left of the office door. I'm facing that door, offset a little to the right. I've been here for two and a half hours.

Why I'm noting all this, I really do not know. I have no particular interest in it, nor any distaste for it. I note it all, but it means everything and nothing at the same time. It is everything which I can see, which I can hear – the clock ticks regularly enough – or which I can smell. The mustiness of the fine but elderly Afghan rug on the floor has always been a reassurance to me. At least it was up until now.

It is all nothing in that although it is physically there, it's not the reality which matters. At least, it was part of the reality which mattered but I now see that that reality depended on another part. I thought that other part was genuine. I could see it before me. I could feel it whenever I thought about what was about to happen. It was so real in my mind that I could touch the clarinet, I could see the delight in Isabel's eyes when I presented it to her father, I could feel myself acknowledged as the man whose love meant something. It wasn't just a dream, or it never felt like a dream. I could hear the conversations in my mind, I could see the light as it fell on the different settings. I was actually planning what would happen next. It wasn't just a dream because they were all sounds and light from my world right here. The old clock was still there. The Afghan rug still shared its scent across the room. I was never living in some fantasy world straight out of a fairy tale.

Only now I may as well have been. So many of the trappings of that world remain but the element which gave them any meaning has simply evaporated. My whole experience just seems so devoid of meaning all of a sudden and the worst thing is that nothing I can see, hear or smell has changed. What I'm looking at, what I'm experiencing is no different to what I was looking at or experiencing before I received that horrible call from Charles. The world outside my office door was never going to look any different and it doesn't. The schoolyard and the street beyond were always and still will be the same.

I've never seen Karl Givret's clarinet with my own eyes. I've never touched it. I've certainly never heard it play music except as a recording. I did once try to attend a live performance when it was being played in New York's Carnegie Hall but never managed. A slight misunderstanding with the United States Immigration Service did not help but that isn't the point. The point is that in terms of what I perceive, my world hasn't changed one iota. Yet something which just took place hundreds of miles away on a mountaintop has changed it all. I'm not weeping because I want to change something. I don't even know what I could change. I think I'm mourning a change which almost happened but then never did. Accepting that it never was real in the first place is the greatest challenge of all when I believed so fervently in its reality.

These are the thoughts careering round my mind and I can see the passage of time. It isn't fast. It isn't slow. I don't have to be anywhere else. I could be. There's a rehearsal of the Church Choir at St Raymond's where I could be singing my heart out in the bass chorus of Mozart's Ave Verum. A truly wonderful piece, I know but I just can't find it within myself to give as I should. It's a pleasure evening in any case. We're not rehearsing for anything in particular, merely practising fine compositions which we will be ready to use quickly whenever called to do so. I don't have to be there, even though I would have wanted very much to have been until about three hours ago. I remain here.

Likewise, I could just go home. But why? I know that I will simply sit and pine mournfully to myself there. What is the point? I suppose that really is the question? What on earth is the point? The only changes I think I will have accomplished are going to be to disappoint Isabel dramatically and to leave myself with a huge debt repayment to carry. Why was I so stupid as to tell her before I had the instrument in my hands? What will she think of me now? I admit quite openly that common sense may not be my forte but now I can only appear to be a spendthrift fool with great ambitions and no worldly hope of ever realising them. However, what if I hadn't told her? Could I keep such a thing from her? I do not like to hide anything from Isabel. She is too important for that. The question of Charles bringing back the clarinet in a roundabout way was bad enough. Is this my punishment for that lack of integrity? If so, it's a very harsh one. I never intended any harm, any malice, any ill will. Yet the invisible scales of justice seem to regard this as fit for me.

If only there were a way forward. If only. I have no qualms about trying. I can work hard. I can do my utmost and especially for Isabel, I will. Right now though, I just don't see where to go. I simply do not know what I can do, what I can even try to do. I tried to give all I had for Isabel, and I failed. It wasn't good enough. Something could have gone wrong. My imagination never foresaw that, but it did go wrong, badly wrong. And now I'm living with it.

Love and music. They were supposed to be enough to carry me onwards. They were my spiritual support in all this. I suppose I even considered Isabel to be the one who personified them. I never imagined that they would not be enough. It wasn't conceivable. Perhaps it is still the case except that the basis for both in what was my worldview up to now has taken a terrible setback. It was never really all about the clarinet itself, was it? It was to reveal to all, with total certainty, that my love was good enough, strong enough, persevering enough to achieve something which it would never have done had it been any weaker. The presentation of that clarinet was going to be the barometer of the state of health of my passion for Isabel. You can't measure passion or adoration, but the clarinet was going to be what could be seen, felt, known and measured.

Except now it isn't because I failed. What my love was supposed to achieve has failed. What does that say about my love? That it simply isn't good enough? That it cannot live up to my ambitions?

I sigh deeply and breathe audibly a few times, stopping to clear some of the tears from my glasses. Why I'm wearing them still at this moment, I can't tell. I just want to know that the world around me is still there, even in its much reduced state.

I suppose I maybe was fooling myself. I really am just not good enough. I know what I would like to do. I thought up to this point, that I was who I would like to be although I'm starting to wonder how true that really is. Do I even deserve to be loved by Isabel? I love her so but is that even enough to deserve her love in return? I have nothing left to give except empty promises and boasts which I can't keep. Is that a husband any sane woman would want to have?

I lift my arms in front of me. They fall to the red leather cover of the desk, and my head follows them down. The glasses have fallen somewhere beyond them, but I can't tell. My tears follow.

There's a knock on the door. It should have been startling as it's quite late in the evening but I'm not in a mood to be worried right now. I suppose it could be a janitor or some such.

I start responding to ask them to leave but my voice is slurred, and the door opens anyway. Alice Morrison looks around the door.

What is Alice Morrison doing here? School pupils should be long gone at this hour. Usually, the answer to that question would be of some concern to me but not this evening. I just wish she would depart.

"Sorry to bother you, Mr Beadlesby. I was staying late to practise on the grand piano and just wanted to come by and –"

She stops and takes a breath.

"I'm sorry, Mr Beadlesby. I didn't realize you were a bit upset. Is something wrong?"

There are some, I know, who would regard that as a rather stupid question under the circumstances but cutting sarcasm is not something I find very attractive. Alice herself is a kind-hearted girl who I suppose only means good. A somewhat free-spirited, forthright and independent thinker, I suppose, but not unkind. Again, I don't know why I should be thinking of all this except that considering what lies before me seems about all I can do.

I do wish she would leave me in peace, however. Instead, she comes in through the doorway and presents herself before my desk. Alice is shorter than I am by some way but standing over me, she would be more imposing if she weren't a few feet back. From there, she looks down at me with a mixture of curiosity and, I suppose, compassion. Either way, I can tell that I won't be left in peace before providing an explanation.

"Mr Beadlesby," she begins. She has a less refined tone than I do but she knows her social graces. I find it reassuring, given how some of her fellow students might be talking to me at this time. A small mercy finally. "I can tell that you're very unhappy. Your eyes are bright red, your beard is wet and even your desktop is covered in tears.

"It's not for me to pry, of course, but if something really isn't right, maybe somebody could help you. You don't have to tell me what the problem is but what can I do? Or can I get someone else who can do something? You just don't look right."

I imagine this is normally what you would expect the teacher to be asking the pupil rather than the other way round but this not a normal setting. Alice is certainly a mature and sensible girl, and for that I'm admittedly grateful, even if I do still wish that she would leave me in peace. I sit up and look her in the eye. At least I do, once I've fumbled around to locate my glasses and put them on again.

"Certainly, Alice," I reply, "you've caught me at rather a bad moment. Something quite bad has happened to me and to my….my…family."

It's all I can manage for a moment. She steps forward a couple of paces.

"Oh my goodness, you mean a bereavement? I'm so sorry. I didn't mean to intrude or anything."

"No, not quite a bereavement," I sigh and pause. "More a financial disaster of sorts which could ruin everything."

I don't know why I bothered with all that. I just believe in inherent honesty as far as possible. I'm not sure how much it has really helped me to date, however.

She draws herself up a little.

"Please, Mr Beadlesby, hear me out. I don't know what your problem is, and you do not need to tell me. But I will not just leave you like this if I'm not sure that you are going to be all right. And I'm not. I may only be a school pupil, but I know something about what's right and what's wrong and going out of your way to hurt somebody is wrong and so is completely ignoring someone who needs you. I'm not a perfect person but I believe in doing what's right."

I'm impressed. She may be young, but she can set out her principles and that is to be encouraged.

"I have to say, Alice, that if that's your position in life, you're a very well brought up, young lady. Your parents must be quite proud of you."

I certainly did not foresee her reaction to that. She snorts derisively.

"My parents are two of the most self-centred and shallow individuals you could ever be unfortunate enough to meet," she sneers. "They wear their wealth on their sleeves, provided the wrist is decked in a Rolex or Cartier watch.

"Luckily for me, there are other influences in my life."

She isn't forthcoming with further details but changes tack back to me.

"So please tell me, Mr Beadlesby, will you get home this evening and look after yourself or do you need someone to bring you?"

The quick focus on practical aspects is not something I can manage and indeed, I have not even thought about actually going out of the school except in conceptual terms.

I reply, "Thank you, Alice, I do appreciate your kindness. I genuinely do. As you can see, I am not happy just now. That said, I do believe that given a little more time, I will find it within me to muster the strength I need to resume my life. I'm truly grateful to you for your concern. It means a lot that somebody would try to be so kind to me."

"Please, Mr Beadlesby," she cuts me off quickly. "I'm not trying to show special charity or anything. It's the decent thing to do when you run into somebody who so clearly needs a bit of help. Being a decent person shouldn't be enough to win you a special award."

I suppose she's right. I can't fault anything about her, except possibly for how she seems to be standing over me so much which I find a little intimidating. All of this does make it harder to ask her to go away. I lean back in my chair for the first time, both to gain a little distance and to make her smaller in my view.

"Alice, please. You are being every bit as good a person as anybody should be. The only thing is that I've had a shock. I can't do a thing about it except learn to live with it. You don't need to know what it is. I can assure that it isn't a fatal disease. I haven't committed a crime. I just haven't done... I haven't... Actually, I haven't done anything at all."

The tears return. I can feel my face running with them.

Alice takes a step back and looks quite humbled.

"I'm really sorry, Mr Beadlesby. It's just that you look so upset. Are you sure that there's nothing anyone can do to help you? Not even a little bit?"

She's such a kind girl but I do so wish she would quit at this point. It's simply too much. I don't know what to say so I say nothing.

"Really," she starts again, "is there absolutely nothing at all? Not even something which somebody could do to make it feel a tiny bit less painful?"

I find myself ignoring her at this point. There's only so much I can take. I remove my glasses and let my head fall onto my outstretched arms again, then mutter briefly, "Alice, please just leave me."

I'm not sobbing. I can hear perfectly well, and I hear nothing from her direction. The door always creaks so she must still be there. I look up to repeat myself, but she just stares at me. She stares sternly but without any sense of threat.

"In a purely practical sense, Mr Beadlesby, what can somebody do? Even if it's just to get you a cup of tea, call you a taxi or something like that? Of course, I'd be very happy to help you with the actual problem too if you would let me know whatever I can do."

I've reached a new depth when a tone of hopeless sarcasm colours my next reply.

"Honestly, Alice, there's nothing you can do. Nothing at all. Not unless you should happen to know somebody who can magically get me all the way up a mountain in the Alps where an extremely valuable, musical instrument has been lost with no hope of recovery. Please just give me a little room now."

I lower my head again and wait for her to depart. How clear do I have to make myself?

It feels as though at least a whole minute has passed although it may be longer than that. It occurs to me that I still haven't heard that door creak. Is she still here?

I look up to see that Alice is standing back towards the doorway but with her arms crossed in front of her and with her head to one side.

Why is she giving me that quizzical look?

Chapter 9

TELEPHONE SEX PEST

Jessica

The end of another long day at the office, or rather another long day sitting in front of my desk at home, working on some marketing materials. I'm not complaining. Professional linguistics is my career of choice and it's not as if I've been forced into it. It's always just a bit of a downer for the first few days back from hiking but when it's still summer. For all my arguably gung-ho attitude towards roaming around Alpine tracks and forests, I have to confess to being a summer hiker. Winter hiking is really not for me. Which is why I feel like I'm missing out when it's summer outside but I'm stuck, doing my job, which is using French and German, only not to order train tickets, book into cheap hotels or talk my way out of spilling my ice-cream on some cranky pensioner at a Swiss bus stop. These things happen.

Don't get me wrong. The winter scenery in the Alps is gorgeous. Snow-covered mountain ranges, gleaming before you up to the horizon with the sun rising behind them are like nature's work of art. I have been up there on occasion, and I know. On a good day, the air is incredibly dry, and you can feel the chill though unless it's several tens of degrees below zero, it doesn't hurt. It just strokes your cheek. The trees are white on top with their evergreen branches a deep shade underneath and they appear like some kind of cheerleaders for the peaks behind and above them.

Of course, that's when you get a good day. Failing that, the whole world is white, the sleet dribbles down your neck despite your best effort to acquire a waterproof scarf at great expense, and you feel as though you're trudging through the world's largest slushie machine. If you're super unlucky, you can even end up with your foot caught in a frozen cowpat left over from last summer. Or possibly the one before if the flies were taking it easy that year.

However, all that is par for the course. The scenery still makes it all worthwhile and as I know full well, only an idiot or the truly ignorant go to the Alps expecting perfect weather all day, every day. More to the point mind you, the Alps are notoriously prone to avalanches in winter. For the most part, the dangerous areas are properly mapped out and people herded out of them, but it goes to show that you really shouldn't be up there on your own. You also need quite expensive equipment. The worst bit, for me at least, is that in the summer, it doesn't matter all that much if you chill out a bit to enjoy the view or even just lose your way slightly. If you arrive at your hotel an hour or two later than planned in the evening, big deal. You can normally check in up to about ten at night and it won't be properly dark up there in June or July until about then either.

Not so in January or February. If you're not down by four in the afternoon, you face a solid sixteen hours in darkness, in the middle of a forest with temperatures falling down faster than the attendees at a hen night in Newcastle. Winter hiking takes discipline, planning and organization on a serious scale. I accept that. It's just not for me.

Hence the summer season is when you'll find me out there. Regrettably, I still do have to work and even if I do, I can't afford to live full-time in Switzerland, so I'm back in Liverpool and trying to remember how to speak High German. Technically "Hochdeutsch" in the original language, High German is basically the German you get taught in school and university if you're not a native Germanophone. Very crudely, it's the German of Germany itself and most noticeable round the north of the country in places such as Hamburg, Bonn, Cologne and Berlin. It's vaguely equivalent to Queen's English in Britain or California English in the United States. Reasonably refined, not heavily accented, understood by native speakers anywhere and with a consistent grammar and vocabulary.

The German language itself is a bit like English in the United States.

Leaving aside the oddities of New York City, the English spoken in the US gradually but surely becomes less and less standardized and more heavily accented the further south you go. Boston English and Houston English are hardly alike. The United Kingdom is the opposite. English gets more and more incomprehensible to foreigners the further north you go. I don't know how any poor sod manages who has studiously learned the English of middle-class London, only to end up in Newcastle, Blackpool or Glasgow. Your best bet is probably to eat up your Britified curry as quickly as possible, smile sweetly and say, "Yes, thank you!" as often as you can while paying, then run for the door. Still, enough people seem to manage. Credit to them, I say.

In the case of German, the change develops as you go south. Munich speaks a very different variant to what you'll hear in Kiel. However, the real difference kicks in when you cross the border and hit the deep south in the next country down, namely Switzerland. I need to be quite careful in how I describe this next as it's quite sensitive to a lot of people, but I'll try to stick to the facts. First of all, Swiss German, as it's generally known, is basically incomprehensible to anyone not Swiss, unless spoken quite mildly. Despite this, Germans still claim that it is only an accented version of the mother language. Many Swiss, on the other hand, insist that it is another language entirely and claim certain linguistic similarities to the likes of Flemish and Dutch to be evidence of this. What undermines their case is that there isn't much of a written version of Swiss German, only a few transcriptions of what anyone actually speaks in the Germanophone Cantons. So, across the German-speaking world, the jury is basically out.

What is not in doubt, is that it's bloody hard for a foreigner to work out what the hell is going on south of the Swiss border if she or he is trying to use the native language. Switching to my own perceptions and to paraphrase "Star Trek", it's German but not as we know it. If you want to speak Swiss German, I would suggest that you learn High German, then swallow half your syllables and gargle a lot. To give a practical example, in High German, when arriving at a hotel, I would say, "Mein Name ist Morriston. Ich habe hier eine Reservierung." This means that my name is Morriston and I have a reservation.

This gets reduced in Swiss German to something sounding akin to, "Miennam ischt Morriston. Isch habne Reschervierng." It's hard to transcribe since you can't swallow in print.

They also seem to be exceptionally keen on using consonants too, particularly S, W, Y and Z and why stick with two syllables when six will do? I guess the Village People must have been a big hit in Switzerland since "YMCA" sounds very Swiss German if you just drop the last letter.

Finally, there's the actual phrasing. In Germany, you typically use the greeting, "Guten Tag!" meaning good day. Perhaps a little archaic as a direct translation but perfectly acceptable. You say thank you with the phrase, "Danke schön."

To hell with that in Switzerland. The standard greeting is, "Grüzi wohl!" while the standard thank you is a Germanicized corruption of the French, "Merci beaucoup", which translates as, "Merci vielmals". Par for the course in Bern or Luzern but try using those phrases in Germany or Austria and they'll look at you as though you missed evolution. Chances are you can't use the internet because you still rely on drawing on the side of your cave to prepare your shopping list.

Despite all that, I like it. I can't understand full-on Swiss German, but I can speak with a local inflection, and I can certainly use the phrases. I get a kind of rush from everything sounding vaguely exotic and the locals are usually really nice to me because, unlike most foreigners and especially anglophones, at least I've made the effort to learn their language. Most of the time, they couldn't be nicer. It went south one time when I tried to ask a receptionist for a spare towel and accidentally requested a vulvic massage but that was probably my fault in the first place for booking into a joint called, "The Scarlet Loincloth". The leather dressing gown in the bathroom really should have been a bit of a giveaway too.

Now I'm back at work though, and I need to revert to using proper Hochdeutsch again. French isn't so tricky to adjust to. The Swiss do have their own variants on the otherwise strictly enforced, linguistic regime of the Académie Française in Paris but they're not extensive and half of Paris just grunts anyway. Pretty much all of them if you're talking about the waiters and hospitality staff. Reaching the gold standard hardly requires you to be Descartes or Sartre.

Today has actually been quite reasonable. I do like the marketing work most of the time although I've had my fill of anatomical products for a bit now. An urgent load came in from the agency this morning and for some reason, there seems to be a huge push among British companies to flog health foods and hygiene products or nappies across Austria, Belgium and Luxembourg. Don't ask me why. I didn't ask myself. Everything seemed to be about getting something into you or stopping it erupting out again. I can only turn down so many temptations to insert a double entendre or a crap joke about somebody slipping on something more comfortable while they go skating across the bathroom floor on a discarded sanitary pad. But I'm a genuinely hard worker and I get the job done. I've knocked out the wording for three campaigns and the agency has had a solid day's work from me. I'm done.

After half an hour's jog round the local neighbourhood, I'm back home and ready for a shower and a break. Or perhaps a break and a shower, then another break. It's quite a nice evening in fact, mild weather which is fine for shorts and a T-shirt but not so warm as to have you sweating it out where your body is resting on the furniture. Yes, I'm a hiker, I think in terms like that, sorry.

So maybe I'll grab another fine white with a packet of salt 'n' vinegar crisps while I sit by the window and admire the passing scenery. Mainly supermarket delivery vans and boy racers by this point in the day but it's still scenery and it's still passing. I don't want to concentrate, just drift mentally. I'll take my shower once I've cooled down slowly a bit after the run. Going straight in only cools me down temporarily.

Unfortunately, it seems that not everyone is cooling down. Certainly not right now.

I'm hardly the first person to complain about the disturbance to my peace and tranquillity caused by the sounds of human intimacy and the sharing of passionate moments. To be less poetic, I wish the neighbours wouldn't shag so noisily. However, what makes it worse in my case is the pre- and post-soundtrack. Sure, the main event is not something you ever really want to hear although it's nigh on impossible unless you're clinically deaf or you have time to wedge half a kilo's worth of cotton wool into your ears. But the before and after, that's what really puts me off sex. And eating. And drinking. And pretty much anything vaguely anatomical.

Summertime is the worst. You simply have to leave the windows open. As does everyone else, including Mr and Mrs Montague. Their bedroom is right above my living room. The English is quite accented but it's the context which is the killer.

"So, dearie, good day at the garden centre?"

"Ooh, not bad, precious. I did get a nice coriander set."

"Really? That's right nice, that is."

OK, so far, so mind-numbingly tedious but I'm soon wishing it would stay that way.

"Do you think you might like to get your plant rising this evening? All that fresh air does woonders for me energy, you know."

"Oh, you are a naughty girl sometimes!"

She's at least 78 but fair enough. I don't want to be ageist again.

"But what did the doctor say about that there problem of yours? Do you think it'll be mended enough to cook me books?"

Cook her books? Since when did accounting slang become a double entendre? Or are they actually planning a passionate night involving a spreadsheet?

"I think one of them tablets should give me the throost and jab I need."

No, they're planning something involving spread legs on top of a sheet.

"The thing is, if I stick to raw eggs and that there hoomoos stuff, then I take a cold bath just after so as not to get me gases exploding too mooch, then if I munch that pill half an hour later on, I should be ready to launch after all that."

Honestly, it's one thing to hear somebody discussing a night of passionate lust in some detail. But when it starts with a review of male impotence, its bizarre treatment and the flatulence associated therewith, you can be pretty sure that you've found the soundtrack cure to over-population right there.

"Well then, me lad – let's peel off those sheets and slam in the lamb!"

And they say romance is dead. It's been more like extinct for a couple of million years upstairs.

The cacophony which follows is like listening to someone making a porno in a retired pigs' shelter. Grunts, squeals and a quick break in the middle to use the toilet. Yes, seriously. I don't understand it either.

Eventually, it all ends after the part of my brain responsible for processing sound has been begging for euthanasia for the last ten minutes.

"Ooh my goodness. I think I've just coom!"

"Oh that's nice, shall I go and get you a coop of tea then, love?"

"Ooh that would be nice. Two sugars mind. I'm right worn out now."

The state of my mind feels like the world's most effective chastity belt ever. I'm telling you, Timothy Dalton could walk through the door right now, fresh from 1987 and entering through that gun barrel logo you see at the start of Bond films. He could turn round and pull his shirt straight off, stare at me with that piercing gaze he has halfway through, "License to Kill", and say in his most throaty voice, "Just drop that top, Jessica and get ready for a night full of non-stop, orgasmic ecstasy. I am going to shag the living daylights out of you!"

I'd still only be capable of responding, "Cheers, Tim, I do appreciate the thought but I'm due my period in about two weeks and have a bad case of earwax cohesion so what do you say we just share a bottle of Vimto and talk about your Aston Martin's gearbox?"

Somehow or other, I manage to rise from the inertia of mental shock to which I've just been subjected and head to the bathroom. I do so wish I'd gone for the shower straightaway now and not tried to finish my wine before the Montagues got going. Sure, it's not the first time when I've been subjected to the noise of their pornographic acrobatics but the combination of raw eggs, houmous and peeling off the sheets was a new low. You wonder why I'm single? Consider that the last man I've seen naked to date was Colin on a WhatsApp call with Bethany, and the last time I heard someone have an orgasm was my elderly neighbour slamming in the lamb. You still wonder?

In fact, it takes a little time to get into the shower because I stand in front of the mirror for a couple of minutes, looking into my harrowed face and wondering if removing my clothes is too sexualized a move, even in the company of nobody other than myself. Anything vaguely related to sex feels as attractive as sticking an electric eel into my underpants. Or watching, "Strictly Come Dancing" without being blind drunk. Tough call.

Eventually I do manage to ditch the running gear into the laundry basket after glancing over at my poster from, "License to Kill" and reminding myself that if it's only Tim seeing me naked, then that's actually quite OK. I wish he would have returned the favour but sadly, I don't think he ever did that sort of movie. Time to get into the shower and stop dwelling on such things.

Of course, I'm finally getting into my stride and genuinely relaxing under the flow of warm water when the phone rings, as it always seems to do when I'm in the bathroom. Not just that but usually when I'm not well disposed to answer it, such as today while I'm halfway through washing my hair.

Dammit, where have the taps gone? Got it. Hot or cold, which is which again? Aiiyyyeee! At least I know that's the hot one. Where the hell's the cold again? OK, water off. Where's the towel so I can get the soap out of my eyes and see where everything is once more? Where's that freaking towel? Oh, hold on, got the face cloth. That feels right, quick wipe and let's see. Holy crap! That wasn't the face cloth, it was... oh no. Oh no, no, no! Suffice to say that I really have to stop leaving the laundry basket next to the shower.

I stagger into the living room, wrapped snugly in my She-Ra T-shirt, which is somehow lodged between my left armpit and my right knee. I possibly have the world's first case of optical jock itch as well. Amazingly the phone is still ringing, although for the sake of whoever's calling, this had better be worth my time, effort and, probably, health.

"Hi, Auntie Jess?"

Alice? What's she calling me out of nowhere on Thursday night for?

"Er, yeah, hi, Alice, what's up?"

"I need to ask, do you have anything on, Auntie Jess?"

What the frickin' hell is this? My niece just turned into a telephone sex pest?

"Well, Alice, I just got out of the shower so I'm maybe a little under-dressed right now but –"

"No, no, Auntie. I mean, are you very busy for the next few days?"

Well, that's a minor relief. My niece is very special to me. One of the last things I want to do is to take the witness stand when some public prosecutor asks why she was hanging around the local primary school playground with nothing on but a brown raincoat and with a bottle of WKD Blue in her hand. I check that I'm not generally dripping water in minor torrents wherever I go, then park myself on the edge of the sofa and gather myself together.

"OK, Alice," I say in a more measured tone. "What can I do to help you?"

"Well, Auntie, it's a very weird request," she starts, "but I'll explain as best I can. I have a music teacher who's, well, a bit strange but he's actually a very nice guy and he's the one who coaches me with my piano playing."

"So he knows what he's talking about at least?" I ask her. If the guy is developing that sort of talent, he must have some clue. Alice is extremely good on the piano and I won't argue with that.

"Well, he does with respect to playing the piano," she comes back, a little hesitantly.

"Meaning what?" I enquire.

"He's a bit, sort of, clueless otherwise," she says before speeding up. "Like I said, a very nice guy, only he doesn't really know what's going on."

"Well, what do you want me to do about it?" I ask her. "Teach him how to tie his shoelaces and look both ways before crossing the road?"

The Swiss apply their accent and phrases to German. I apply sarcasm to English. It's all just about communicating effectively as human beings.

Alice responds, "No, Auntie Jess. It's a bit more specific.

"The thing is, he's lost a clarinet, and he needs some help to get it back."

If I had a shorter temper, I'd ask her what the frickin' hell she's talking about, but I figure that I'll find out in due course and the best thing is just to let her get on with it. Indeed she does.

"This clarinet is worth some insane amount of money, like a quarter of a million pounds. He says the world's best ever clarinet player used it or something like that. He wanted to get it as a present for his fiancée and her father so that he could get married."

"Why?" I finally ask. "I didn't think parental permission was legally necessary to marry someone these days, at least not if they're eighteen or over. Please don't tell me he's trying to get it on with one of your classmates in the school orchestra."

"I don't really understand it at all either, Auntie. But I just found him in floods of tears because apparently he needs this clarinet to convince the fiancée and her father that he truly, genuinely loves her and that they should welcome him into their family.

"I think she's about your age anyway," she adds as some sort of afterthought.

Frankly, this sounds like something coming from a bunch of total headcases, but her school is within striking range of East Dawlings so that maybe shouldn't come as a complete surprise.

"Be that as it may, Alice, why are you coming to me? So this guy has somehow lost this ludicrously over-priced piece of musical history. I'm in Liverpool, not Bristol. What do you want me to do about it?"

"The clarinet wasn't lost in Bristol. It was lost in the Alps."

OK, this is finally starting to make a modicum of sense, at least insofar as I can understand why Alice might be coming to yours truly as opposed to anyone else who could go scouring the charity shops of Bristol to ask if anyone had handed in a ridiculously expensive wind instrument of late. And I don't mean a piece of proctological flatulence relief equipment worth a couple of hundred grand. The rest of the story still sounds completely whacked though.

"How the hell did he lose it in the Alps? I know not everyone sticks to the basic rule of only packing what you're really going to need when you're hiking. Your mother would be a prime example. Even she, however, is yet to add an orchestral instrument to the packing list."

"He wasn't hiking," Alice replies. "One of his friends was part of some sort of orchestra filming an event way up in the mountains and he managed to lose the clarinet over a glacier. The clarinet landed down there but he doesn't know how to get to it.

"I wondered if maybe you might be able to help him get up there."

There's a moment's hiatus before Alice continues, "Obviously, he would pay for all the tickets and costs. But he needs somebody who knows the Alps and how to find their way around the mountains. So I thought of you and wondered if you might be interested in spending a few days there with him."

She's tailed off and is clearly waiting for me to provide a response. I consider whether it would be wise to rub my itchy eye before I start talking again.

"OK, Alice, I might have the time but first things first, can you be a bit more precise? Switzerland may not be the world's biggest country, but it does still cover a lot of space and while global warming may be reducing their total mass, the proportion of that space covered by glaciers remains quite considerable."

"Yeah, sure, Auntie. I don't have the actual name right now but it's somewhere in Bern Canton. I'm sure Mr Beadlesby will have more details if I ask him."

"What's his name?" I ask.

"Mr Beadlesby, Mr Harris Beadlesby."

"Harris Beadlesby?" I repeat in a somewhat incredulous fashion. "Who the hell is this guy? Some reject from a Harry Potter book who sounded a bit too much like an upper-class twit for J K Rowling to keep in the final cut?"

"Look, Auntie," Alice sighs, "I really don't think he's your type."

"Alice," I intone slightly more gruffly than is my wont. All the same, after a day of sanitary pad commercials, the Montagues shagging, and now an optical infection which I may have to get a gyno to fix, I really don't need this sort of thing. "I am not, I repeat not, trying to score!"

"No, no," Alice comes back hurriedly, "I just mean that I don't think you and he will really hit it off. But I'm not asking you to be his friend, just to help

143

him out because deep down, he's a decent guy and he really needs help, and I think you're the only person I know who can help him. You always say that a few more people helping each other now and again would make the world less dominated by twats."

"So, I get a warm, fuzzy feeling out of it?"

"Plus a free hiking trip to Switzerland."

Good point. Altruism and self-centredness in a two for one deal. This might be worthwhile.

"If we want to take this forward, then what next?"

"If you can come down to East Dawlings this Saturday, we can meet up with him and he can explain the details. Then you can see if you can come up with a plan for him."

"That could work," I tell her, "but why East Dawlings? The last thing I want to do is run into my sister or her husband, not only because your parents are a pain in the ass but also because I assume that they will be horrified if they find out that you're involved in any sort of plan involving your dreadful aunt, even if your own role is just to set up the meeting."

"Well, it has to be East Dawlings," Alice responds testily. "Mum won't let me go any further without being dropped off, so we'll just have to keep a low profile and try not to be noticed."

"That's quite ambitious," I retort. "The place is so inbred and inward-looking that if they built a brothel, it'd offer a family discount. Where specifically do you propose we meet?"

"I've told her that I'm meeting a friend from school, which is almost true, and that we'll be getting a milkshake in a café."

"There only are two cafés in East Dawlings," I remind her. "That hardly lets us lose ourselves too discreetly."

"Yes, but I didn't say which one. Since I said I'm meeting a friend from school, she'll assume that I'll be in Daisy's. So we'll meet Mr Beadlesby in The Georgina Café. Nobody else under seventy ever goes in there anyway.

"Besides which," she adds with a sudden tone of fake innocence, "when I said that I might be out all afternoon, Dad's eyes lit up and he said that it sounded like a good plan because he had a brand new putter extension and he'd like Mum to help him try it out."

I can imagine her face as she says that. Funny. What's not so funny is the idea of what Colin presumably meant in practice. Then again, he's going to need quite an extension by some way to make it worth Bethany trying it out. It is a funny thought after all.

"OK, Alice. Saturday afternoon it is."

Chapter 10
HIKING ISN'T A TEAM SPORT

Harris

It's a pleasing day in East Dawlings. So I try to convince myself anyway. After all, this is a delightful part of the world. That nobody could deny. I do like the nineteenth-century style of cottages as you approach the high street, offset by the more impressive stonework of the mansion houses which itself is just that bit colder. The two play against each other quite nicely. There's a lot of greenery around: trimmed bushes, manicured lawns, cropped trees and the like. It all fits nicely together with a day of clear sunshine but a brisk wind off the Irish Sea a few miles away. It's warm but fresh. I do admit that the whole place looks a shade old-fashioned and like a Britain from a different point in time almost, but I would immediately question if that were at all a bad thing in any case? Is this not the Britain which we have all been striving to find again ever since? Now that I can hear some Purcell in the background too, I am near convinced that this is so.

The problem is that while I find all this very uplifting, it is still not quite enough to lift me from my fears and concerns. On the one hand, I suppose I should be grateful to have the chance to consult with someone who could maybe help me. I don't mean to denigrate anybody's offer but on the other hand, I do wonder if this attempt simply demonstrates the hopelessness of my situation. I've been instructed to keep a low profile so as to reach a less frequented café set back a couple of streets from the village centre. There, I'm to meet with the aunt of one of my music pupils who works as a translator but also happens to go hiking a lot in Switzerland. Apparently her combined knowledge of walking in mountains and the German language might just be enough to help us come up with an idea to retrieve Karl Givret's clarinet. It sounds ridiculous but I have no better plan. The latter assertion is what's depressing me so much.

My thoughts are interrupted by something suddenly rushing by in the sky just beyond the village but set against the hillside on the horizon. About two seconds later comes the immense sound of aircraft engines which were presumably driving that thing along. It certainly distracts me from the Purcell, and I do not appreciate it. I believe it's from some military base a little further away, but I really don't know much about those sorts of things. I daresay they're necessary but I do wish they would keep themselves to themselves.

I turn off the high street and head down the second side street which leans around a curve where a yew tree is leaning out over the road. On the other side of the tree, I see a small cul-de-sac with a sandwich board on the pavement in front of it. This informs me that a few steps further I will find The Georgina Café. Moving in this direction, a door appears with the same name above it, and I enter, as per Alice's instructions.

In fairness, the Georgina Café is somewhere I could see myself spending time in. Alice may have picked it as a less prominent meeting point but it's hardly some sort of clandestine bolt-hole for the more untoward elements of society. It's relatively dark away from the windows but the tables are arranged neatly with four places at each and dark green tablecloths to match the upholstery. The walls are painted in a beige and pink pattern, but the ceiling is quite low which prevents the place becoming too open to the light otherwise streaming in from the windows at the far end. The overall effect is to make it something like a sufficiently lit cave. That said, the comfortable settings make it quite acceptable.

A young waitress approaches and asks if I would like a seat. I explain that I would and that I'm waiting to be joined by two friends. She responds pleasantly enough and finds me a table halfway down the café although I get the impression that her interest in an in-depth conversation is limited. I can hardly hold that against her. So is mine. I order a camomile tea and sit down to wait.

My goodness but this is frustrating. I'm reflecting once more on the hopelessness I feel. It just seems as though there are walls all around me. I know where I am, and I know where I would like to be. But I just cannot envisage in my mind how there can be a route from the former to the latter. I do appreciate Alice's effort to help me. I'm genuinely touched that she would do that. It restores my faith in the concept that not everything around me is locked against me. There is a goodness out there which counts for something and that matters. It matters very much. What risks overwhelming me right now is that despite that goodness, I am quite unable to imagine a practical solution and what it would look like. I should have more faith, I suppose. After all, faith in a certainty is simply knowledge. It's just difficult to stick to an uncertain faith when you want to see it in your mind's eye but all you can make out is the brick wall you know.

Two cups of camomile tea later and the door finally opens to reveal Alice, dressed a little more casually than she would be at school. But I suppose it is the weekend. That said, I do wish girls that age would consider wearing something a little less high above the knee. I daresay Alice can find a good husband all in due time without having to put her wares on display right now. It's not a marital cattle market, for goodness' sake.

She's accompanied by a woman of a similar height. Alice is a tall girl for her age and so no doubt has a stature not unlike that of her aunt who, I'm assuming, is the woman accompanying her. A little nondescript, I would say. Functionally dressed in somewhat masculine attire although I suppose that's typical of the outdoor type. All these outfits you see in sports shops and the like are basically unisex and this mountaineering business seems to be verging on the military which is hardly known for the feminine delicacy of its uniforms. In any case, I'm not here for the aesthetics.

Alice spots me and leads her aunt over. It's quite clear who's the senior and who's the junior in this twosome although her aunt does still have quite a youthful quality to her appearance and movements.

And also her attitude, as I quickly find out. The two are talking between themselves as they approach.

"So basically," the aunt is explaining to Alice, "the woman jumps out of bed and just stands there, stock still, like it's happy hour at Madame Tussaud's or something. Her boyfriend must have had something wedged in an unfortunate cavity since he tried to walk over but could only stagger from one leg to the other every few seconds. He looked like C-3PO with a hernia!"

They both chortle over this witticism. I sigh inwardly. I anticipate that this may be hard work. Alice has always come across as a quite cultured girl, yet I have also suspected that there might be some less refined elements at work in her psyche too. There's a slight tendency to sarcasm and just a touch of a sneer when something cannot be explained in fully scientific terms. I have a feeling that I may be about to find out where this comes from.

They reach the table, and Alice turns around so as to have me on her left and her aunt on her right.

"Good afternoon, Mr Beadlesby. This is my aunt, Jessica Morriston."

"You mean Morrison?" I ask, slightly confused. The aunt herself looks rather put out by this introduction, but I can't understand how Alice would have got her own family name slightly wrong.

"No, no," Alice continues. "Morrison is my family name, but my mother's maiden name was Morriston, and this is my mother's sister."

She giggles slightly nervously. The aunt looks decidedly unimpressed. I decide to move in on the exchange and extend my right hand.

"Beadlesby. Harris Beadlesby."

I understand that this is the routine used in some series of lowbrow spy films, but I hope it makes me look sophisticated enough. If nothing else, the aunt, or perhaps I should now say Miss Morriston, takes my hand and shakes it.

"Pleased to meet you," she says in a neutral tone. "Please call me Jessica. Formality isn't really my strongpoint."

Not to be put out, I ask, "Won't you take a seat? I'll see if I can order us some tea. Would you like anything to eat?"

She and Alice glance round at the cake counter just as the waitress approaches. Jessica, as I suppose I'm now calling her, and Alice order a cream tea and a rock bun, respectively. There's evidently nothing too dainty about these two together. I know plenty of ladies who would blanche at the thought of a heavy, sugared refreshment and end up taking a couple of wafers with their tea, remarking that they must take care of their figures. Jessica is certainly not overweight, however, so I suppose that it must be all part of the rather rough and ready approach. This is no doubt a good thing if I want to get up a mountainside, I have to confess.

At this point, the air is split asunder by another roar of jet engines passing overhead. Jessica raises her eyebrows and looks at Alice.

"Oh shut up, Maveruk," she says pointedly before grinning. "Get it? Maverick with a UK? Clever line, huh?"

Alice rolls her eyeballs but smirks.

"Suit yourself," Jessica retorts. "I'm allowed one per show."

I have no idea what they're talking about.

Jessica turns around from whatever she and her niece were discussing and looks at me questioningly.

"So, Alice has told me a bit about you, but I'd be interested to hear it from the man himself. Let me see if I've got this straight. You're a music teacher, working in her school. About my age, give or take. Dedicated to your profession and in love with the classics. Personally adept at playing viola, French horn, oboe and piano with reasonable skills on various other, similar instruments as well, but not including the harmonica for which you have a strong, personal dislike. Pretty clueless with regard to the rest of real life as in near to zero common sense but not badly intentioned or unpleasant."

I can only guess that she got all this from Alice. Such an assessment, especially coming from someone I only met a couple of minutes ago, is a shade off-putting and I wish Alice might have been a bit more discreet. I would have objected to the bit about zero common sense except that after the incident with the old lady, the skateboarding dog and Cheddar Gorge, it might be a little tricky.

"On a personal level," she continues, "I understand that you've fallen in love and are planning to get married, which is very nice for you.

Congratulations. The only problem is that for reasons I don't quite fully understand, all this somehow depends on some incredibly expensive clarinet which a friend of yours has helpfully managed to lose somewhere in the Swiss Alps. And now you need someone to retrieve it for you."

She pauses and looks straight at me.

"Which is where I come in, correct?"

In terms of character and style, I already would have preferred to be relying on someone a little more refined. At the same time, I do get the feeling that she might just be what I need. She seems to have no inhibitions about the mountains and is simply trying to size up the nature and scale of the challenge. Nor does she seem suspiciously over-confident or arrogant, going by her tone. Brash perhaps and probably quite disinclined towards the finer things in life but still capable. If Alice is correct about her experience and knowledge of mountains, as well as her fluency in German and French, then no doubt a certain lack of refinery is tolerable.

It's not as if beggars can be choosers either.

That said, I do need to set her straight on one thing.

"Thank you, Jessica," I start, quickly regretting that I've used the same tone as I would have employed to address a secondary school pupil, but I carry on as fast as I can. "I do have to correct you on just one thing, though. I don't need someone to retrieve the clarinet for me. I need someone who can help me to retrieve it. Do you know precisely what has been lost?"

"I know what a clarinet is, yes."

"I'm sure you do but this is no ordinary clarinet. It is Karl Givret's clarinet."

She looks at me blankly. I don't believe this.

"Are you seriously telling me," I ask in disbelief, "that you do not know who Karl Givret was?"

She casts around blankly with seemingly no idea.

"I dunno," she replies eventually. "Maybe he played for Queens Park Rangers or something."

I suspect she's trying to antagonize me and has enough idea that this simply cannot be true but I'm not going to rise to the bait. Instead I adopt the look I normally reserve for school pupils who are simply too unaware of something to realize how truly marvellous it actually is. Regrettably, this is needed much more often than I would like but that does at least mean that I'm rather good at it.

"Karl Givret," I begin, probably sounding quite supercilious even if not intending to do so, "is generally recognized as having been the finest clarinet player whom the world has ever known. The man could cover six octaves in a heartbeat, he never used sheet music but played for hours from memory, and he could play any genre possible."

"Even gangsta rap?"

I ignore this obvious piece of idiocy. I don't know what she's referring to, but I've heard pupils discussing it in school, so I assume it's something modern which never overlapped with Givret.

"He lived during the mid-nineteenth century and stayed mainly in his native France where he was much sought after by royalty and nobility for his exquisite skills. However, he also set time aside to perform where people from all of Paris would be welcome to hear him play for an hour or two. He believed, as I do, that real music, played with passion and a belief in what it represents, really does have an impact for the good of its listeners. He made time to experiment too and worked with top musicians and scientists to devise ways, both artistic and scientific, to elevate the artform of classical music and enable its delivery in bold, new and accessible ways. In short, the man was a legend.

"He passed away in 1884 at the sadly young age of forty-six. All of his possessions concerning music, he left to the researchers with whom he had worked with the sole exception of his clarinet. That he left to his father's sister, who had brought him up as a child after his parents passed away from tuberculosis. It was an understandable but not wholly wise choice since the lady herself outlived him by only five years, at which point the clarinet entered the private collectors' circuit, despite the best efforts of several museums and musical establishments to get their hands on it. It spent a lot of time in the collection of a certain millionaire in San Francisco during the first half of the twentieth century, which was perhaps a good thing since it ensured that it survived both World Wars perfectly intact. This Californian collector was no doubt quite a vulgar piece of work since he only kept the clarinet in a box and presumably only wanted the prestige of having it, as opposed to any genuine appreciation for what it actually was and what had been achieved with it.

"Anyway," I conclude, "following the death of the San Francisco collector, the clarinet ended up back on the private collectors' circuit and re-entered Europe through a couple of auctions somewhere in Asia, I believe. To cut a long story short, it eventually came to be on sale in Milan a couple of weeks ago, which is where I acquired it, or rather my friend did on my behalf."

"Before he promptly lost it in the Alps?"

"That's right," I sigh. "That's right."

Jessica eyes me curiously before asking, "So how come you have to retrieve it? This background is quite fascinating in its own way, but it doesn't explain why you have to go to Switzerland and get it yourself. I mean, you only need someone to go and pick it up, not play a concert on it. What does it matter?"

I would have thought that was obvious, but I pause for a moment. Perhaps not. If you stop to think about the stupid questions which other people ask, just sometimes you realize that they might not be quite so stupid at all. At least not when you consider what they know and what they don't know.

"A clarinet," I explain, "is made up of five parts. From top to bottom you have the mouthpiece, the barrel, the upper joint, the lower joint and the bell. The mouthpiece and the two joints are each encased in a ligature and keys as well, when the instrument is fully assembled. When Givret's clarinet was lost, it was fully assembled and most likely broke apart to some degree when it landed on the glacier where it is just now."

I pause for a moment. I hate to think about that, and I find the mental image disturbing. Jessica and Alice glance at each other, shrug and then dig into their cream tea and rock bun while I recover myself.

I continue, "It is crucial that when the clarinet is recovered, there is somebody there who will be able to re-constitute it fully and assess any damage so that we can be sure that it is truly Karl Givret's clarinet which is brought back in its full condition."

Jessica looks back at me bemusedly.

"As opposed to what? How many random wind instruments are there sitting up in the Alps? Trust me, I've hiked a fair number of paths up there, I've crossed numerous passes, I've been through the forests, around the lakes, over the bridges and even fallen face-first into a cowpat once.

"Don't worry," she adds hastily as Alice starts to snigger, "that was some time ago and I had a very thorough shower afterwards.

"My point is this: in all that time, I have never once encountered a flute, a horn, an oboe, a bassoon or even a harmonica lying around at random. You can see a lot of things in the mountains, but wind instruments are in pretty short supply. If I find what I think is Givret's clarinet up there, I doubt there's much risk that I'm actually going to have found one which belonged to some dude called Freddie who also managed to lose his when he was taking a piss-break during orchestra practice on the Jungfrau. Why do you need to be there?"

I sense that this is going to be rather hard work, but she deserves an explanation.

"My own point is, that ensuring the structural integrity of the clarinet, in order to bring it back in as near to its original condition as possible, will take the oversight of somebody familiar with musical instruments. Would you be able to guarantee that all of the keys were in place and attached correctly to the upper and lower joints? Would you know how to assess the structural integrity of the ligature on extracting it from the ice? If not, there is a high risk that the clarinet, if recovered, would only be recovered in a massively damaged and incomplete state which would mean the loss of its historical value and would also reduce its worth quite considerably. That is why I myself need to be right there when the pieces are found."

Jessica stares at me incredulously. I feel like an atheist in the Vatican.

"You want to get up to the glacier line of an Alp yourself, in order to carry out a professional assessment of an antique?" she asks in deliberately measured tones before moving back into the much faster pace which seems to be her normal mode of speech. "Do you have any idea what that would take?"

Well, actually, I think I do, and I'm prepared to tell her.

"If you'd excuse me," I start, "I don't need my physical prowess questioned here, thank you. I'm simply looking for a guide, not a personal trainer. I myself cycle to and from work each day. I walk up to three miles at a time on both a Saturday and a Sunday and when time from work allows, I even permit myself a swim or two at the local baths where I can manage ten lengths without a pause."

I daresay that should boost my credibility. She sits up straight and leans over the table.

"Look, Haggis –"

"Harris."

"Harris, Haggis, Halitosis, whatever, they have a saying in Switzerland: the mountains are not your friend. If you want to get up there, you need to know what you're doing. Glaciers do not sit next to towns. They're miles out of town and they're very high up. Three miles in the park? How do you fancy your chances on twenty clicks in a couple of hours with a thousand-metre plus altitude differential?"

"What does that mean?"

She sighs for a moment.

"It means walking twenty kilometres over terrain which includes climbing the vertical equivalent of one kilometre. All under your own steam. And to get to a glacier, it's going to be more than that.

"Hiking is not a team sport. You can't rely on someone else to pick up the bits which you're not so good at. You yourself have got to be able to get up there, get around and get back again because nobody else is going to pick you up. At least, not unless you want to count the mountain rescue helicopter service, but you have to be in some deep schtuck before they'll haul your ass off the mountainside. That's one stunt I haven't managed to date and have no intention of ever doing so. They'll also ask why you're there.

"What I'm saying is, without any disrespect, I don't think you've got what

155

it takes. I thought you were only going to stay at the bottom of the slopes for quality control purposes on my return. Maybe I don't have what it takes to identify all the clarinet parts, but I suspect that's easier to learn quickly than for you to turn into Chuck Norris."

I wish I knew who Chuck Norris was, but I can guess the point she's making.

"Anyway," she concludes, "what's your timeline?"

"I need to recover it the week after next."

Her eyes almost bulge out of their sockets.

"You mean in just over a week's time? Are you nuts? You think you can go for a jog round the park, listening to, 'Eye of the Tiger' and somehow be ready to scale an altitude which is only possible to reach in this country by air travel? What's the big hurry?"

"The big hurry," I explain, "is that first, that clarinet is unlikely to survive for too long, stuck in a glacier."

"Who knows?" she counters. "It didn't seem to cause Ötzi the Ice Man any problems."

"Who?"

"Some guy called Ötzi whom they dug out of the ice in Austria a few years back. It turned out that he was a very well-preserved specimen of someone who died about 3,700 years ago. It was a great archaeological find apparently."

"Interesting," I muse. "I'm surprised I didn't hear about it myself."

"Well, he wasn't carrying a wind instrument, so you maybe weren't that interested," she cuts in, somewhat snidely. I think it's time to move on.

"More to the point, I myself am currently constrained to staying on school premises between working hours for the next six months, owing to a slight…well…mishap a couple of weeks back."

"You're on parole?" she asks.

"Well, not legally, just professionally," I explain before adding hurriedly, "I don't mean I'm a sex offender or fraudster or violent criminal or anything."

"That's a relief. I never really wanted to go hiking with Jack the Ripper."

"But the thing is," I come back, "I do have some leeway to leave the premises the week after next to take the school's candidate to the Young Pianists Finals of the West Country. Since this takes three days which back onto a weekend, I wondered if it might be possible for me to excuse myself after the first day and make a very fast trip to Switzerland between the Thursday and the Sunday. You see, highly talented though Katie Porter is, I can't honestly see her getting beyond the first day. However, we're all supposed to wait until the contest finishes so if a friend of mine would take care of Katie, I could be gone."

"Hang on!" Alice interrupts. "Why Katie? It could be me!"

Oh dear, I forgot about that.

"Listen, Alice," I try to be as reasonably sounding as possible, "at the moment we're waiting to hear if anybody from the school will make it. I know that you, Katie and Robert are all in the final selection but without any disrespect to anyone, you and Robert are both truly excellent pianists, but Katie is in a class of her own. If anyone gets through she will, and the event organizers will never permit two entrants from the same school.

"I don't mean for a moment that you shouldn't try. You may well get there next year and indeed you deserve to do so. It's just that this year, well…"

Alice sits back and looks down at her shoes.

"I see," she intones, a stony look spreading across her face.

Her aunt looks none too pleased at this either.

"Look, I'm sorry. I don't make these decisions. I'm just going with what I have."

Jessica leans over and murmurs some words of encouragement to Alice who looks up a little less angrily. Jessica then turns back to me, her expression more one of pained concentration than anything else.

"OK, so you need to get up there to recover this thing, but you need me to guide you round the mountainsides, and it has to be done in about three or four days at most? That's a big ask.

"Next, you need to reach a part of the mountains where most hikers never go because it's too dangerous. That's a big ask.

"Then you want to find the individual pieces of a musical instrument scattered somewhere over a glacier which is likely the source of freshwater in summer for a few hundred thousand people thanks to its inherent size. That's a big ask.

"And finally, this isn't going to come cheap. Directly from me to you, that's a big ask."

I don't know how to respond to most of these questions. I start with the one I do.

"I had to take a mortgage against my home to acquire the clarinet," I explain. "In the end, the auction came in at a few thousand less than I'd been anticipating so I still have a reasonable amount of cash in terms of what a trip like this would cost. Travel, accommodation and equipment, I am obviously prepared to pay for. I would not be asking you to pay for the privilege of helping me. I don't even know how much you charge for your services, but I'm obviously prepared to –"

She waves me away before I can finish that sentence. What an odd woman. Snide and crude on the one hand but far from mean-spirited on the other.

That seems to have mollified her a little. But the other questions still remain. We look at each other blankly, knowing what we want to ask but also knowing that neither of us has an answer.

There's another clatter of noise from above us outside. It's not as loud as the jet engines but still kicks up a fearful racket.

Jessica's eyes suddenly light up. A knowing smile spreads across her lips.

"You know what, Harris? I think the Royal Navy may have just provided the answer we need."

I do so wish she would stop saying things which make absolutely no sense to me.

"If you can spare the cash, here's what I propose. Alice has told me that the glacier we need to reach is a few clicks south of Interlaken. While the thought of going to Interlaken is about as appealing a prospect as sharing an Uber with a drunk orangutang with a bowel problem, I suppose needs must. If you go to Interlaken and you can afford it, something you can do is rent a helicopter for a scenic trip of the Alps. In the winter, they can even drop off skiers at predesignated points but in the summer it's just a sight-seeing tour. It doesn't come cheap but it's not totally extortionate. So, we could hire one, pay them a bit extra, and then get them to land us on the glacier. We pick up the clarinet and then get the ride back. From Interlaken, you can make it to either Geneva or Zürich in around three to three and a half hours and those two places are where the main airports for the country are. Problem solved."

She looks up questioningly. On the surface at least, it's not such a bad idea at all. And I wouldn't ultimately have to have this excruciating level of fitness which she keeps going on about.

'And I have an idea," pipes up Alice out of nowhere, raising her head from her mobile telephone. "You still need to find the clarinet, right? Well, going by what I can see in Google images, all the different bits have metal attached to them at some point. If you get a couple of metal detectors to cover the glacier between you, you might have a reasonable shot at it. You'd just have to stay away from the helicopter, of course, but there should be no other metal nearby."

"Not unless Ötzi's cousin was up there playing a flute sonata," adds Jessica. What an unnecessary comment.

A moment's relaxation sweeps the table. Does this mean that we might finally have some idea of what to do? Jessica makes a point of finishing her cream tea while she thinks and then looks up with a quite determined look on her face.

"I still think this is one of the stupidest ideas of all time, but I also believe that it has an outside chance of working. If somebody else is paying, then I'm happy to give it a go.

"I will make out an itinerary for us, covering air travel and then rail and bus travel within Switzerland. I will also determine an inventory of the equipment we're going to need. I will buy everything except for the personal equipment on your side, Harris, which you can get yourself. Given your connection to the clarinet, it's probably best to minimize the air tickets bought in your name so you can pay me back for whatever is bought. I don't think this is illegal itself but since it's a little questionable round the edges, let's just be discreet. I suppose there are customs issues or something. We can get rooms in a hotel by simply turning up as and when. It's easy enough if you can speak German. Actually, it's easy enough if you can speak English, just even easier in German.

"Harris, you get ready to travel. Alice, I hope you don't mind staying at home and playing a supporting role."

Alice doesn't look wholly pleased but her aunt seems to have this in hand. She really is quite a vulgar woman in many ways, but I will acknowledge her capabilities here. For some reason, I feel a degree of peace which I haven't felt for some days now.

At this point, two jet engines roar across the sky above us.

Chapter 11
PLAN B GOES SOUTH

Jessica

Why exactly am I doing this? The question plagued me all the way back to Liverpool a couple of days ago and hasn't stopped since. The party line, if you will, is that Alice asked me and I always like to help out my niece. Harris may be the sort of insufferable, bougie twerp who would drive me insane after more than a week in his company, but I do feel sort of sorry for him. I mean, sure, the guy demonstrates about as much common sense as a crisp packet (and I mean not even smoky bacon, let alone salt 'n' vinegar) and he probably couldn't organize his way out of an emergency exit but he did give up everything, or at least risk giving up everything, for the love of his life. Which is more than anyone's ever done for me, I reflect ruefully. Not that I've really tried doing it myself either so fair's fair. Clearly the man is principled and prepared to act for what he cherishes and what he believes in. It's just a pity that he's a total pratt.

Of course, there's also the enticement of a free trip to Switzerland for a few days. The hiking may be limited under the plan envisaged but I can probably fit something in along the lines of running a reconnaissance of the target area. It's a shame we have to go to Interlaken of all places but what can I do? Ask for my money back? At least the decent scenery starts right on its doorstep, so you don't have to go too far.

All of these are valid reasons for taking on this daft adventure, but I can't help feeling that there's more to it than that. After all, I'm not convinced that Harris' proposed marriage is definitely heading down the toilet without that clarinet, regardless of whatever lunacy is going on inside his head. If this Isabel girl is really so shallow that a musical instrument makes such a difference in terms of her choice of course and partner in life, I'd be tempted to trade her in for an improved model if I were in his place. She should be overwhelmed by his dedication, as evidenced by the attempt he's making, at least if she really cares about him. She can hardly have got to know him without realising that the guy's a couple of cellos short of an orchestra. She's reached the stage of almost marrying him. I only spent a couple of hours in some café in bloody East Dawlings, and I could tell that. So a lapse in practical competence can hardly be a deal-breaker.

Perhaps she doesn't give a damn and she's just some kind of harpy sex-demon who's got him ensnared in a web of orgasmic evil which is completely doing in his head, good sense and judgment. Let's just assume he has some of the latter somewhere. It's something to consider. However, he did also mention that her favourite piece of music was Mozart's Piano Sonata Number 13. I've no idea what that sounds like myself, but it seems a bit inconsistent with a rampant sex-demon's tastes. Why a rampant sex-demon would be so keen to ensnare a now penniless school music teacher who wears a tweed jacket and has some of the most dubious facial hair I've seen in some time is also open to question. Harris might be kind of a nice guy, even if hugely irritating, but from the perspective of a vicious sex-demon, couldn't she do just a bit better?

Overall, as far as I'm concerned, the jury is out as to whether or not this really is critical for Harris' marriage plans or not, but nobody seems to have the heart to ask that out loud.

Nor, incidentally, am I doing this simply to avoid him getting himself killed. True, there's a risk that if he were to venture alone into the Berner Oberland and try to shift his candy-barrel all the way up to that glacier, the chances are that he would come back down permanently paralyzed for life if he were lucky. However, I really can't see him getting very far beyond where the exotic dancing bar in the southwest corner of town is. The path leading up to the Rotenegg Alp in front of him would probably give him an apoplexy. Even he, I think, is not stupid enough to try this on his own.

So what do I see in it all? I suppose it's kind of funny in a way, if you're one step removed from the emotional turmoil which is afflicting him. I can see a certain amusement value in it. Perhaps, just maybe, it looks as though I could do someone a vaguely good turn even. I wouldn't say I'm the most selfish person alive, but I doubt I've done much with my life, for which anyone will remember me fondly. Maybe at the food bank but I'm so far into the management there that when I turn up of an evening, I risk getting a free meal since they don't recognize me as a volunteer and therefore assume I'm turning up to get fed. I hadn't realized that I dress so cheaply but it's something I need to look into for sure.

Maybe that's it. I can make something happen for once. How noble of me. My shining armour gig is perhaps slightly diminished when you consider that the one being rescued is the one bankrolling the trip but it's a modern take. I just don't know, to be honest. I keep thinking to myself that it must be one reason or another but every time I do, it's like another one crops up, challenging me to claim that it had nothing to do with it either.

Still, why do I really care? I'm getting the logistics in place, I've told the agency when I won't be free and that I'm doing some additional, "background research" for a special client project over the days in question. I doubt they care anyway. Whatever my motivation may be, let's just roll, track down this clarinet and head home again. Finding the clarinet may be tricky but the rest looks straightforward enough. Harris seems petrified about customs busting his ass over the clarinet itself, but I think he's getting a bit overly worked up. Domestic flights and flights from mainland, western Europe all arrive at the same areas in Britain's airports, and they attract about as much attention from the UK Border Force (customs and excise as were) as a seagull does in a beach resort. Unless you're literally shitting cocaine down your inner thigh or trying to cover up three million dollars in notes stuffed up your nose, they probably see you as posing as much threat to the security of the realm as a rat-arsed Teletubby. The idea that some musical instrument is going to stir their interest is nothing but a pipe dream. Apologies if that's a crap pun.

I feel a bit humbled in front of Tim though, looking down at me sternly from my, "License to Kill" poster. You wouldn't have found James Bond getting involved in this sort of malarkey. Don't worry, Tim, we've all got to start somewhere. I may be in the minor league now, well OK, the tiny, microscopic league well down the bottom, but one day, I'll be doing something really cool. One day, every Bond girl is going to be rushing off to get a serious, hormonal booster shot so as to compete with Jessica Morriston, but it won't make a bit of difference against my innate, lethal, cool and calculating sexiness.

Nice idea but it does rather ram home the point that I need to change out of the striped orange and green, fluffy bunny shorts with a rip down the crack, which I've been wearing to clean the bathroom in. What? It's not as if anyone else is going to see them.

Predictably enough, said shorts are halfway round my ankles when the phone goes off in the living room. I trip across the bathroom doorway and find myself lying with a randomly discarded Pizza Hut discount voucher entering my mouth. I hope it's still legible as I was wondering where I'd put that. Standing up, I manage to get one ankle out of the shorts and kick them with the other as hard as I can.

The shorts fly out of the open window and a moment later, there's an angry shout of, "What the hell?"

I'm running for the phone but take a quick glance out of the window to see a random pizza delivery dude with some orange and green shorts wrapped around his head. Maybe I'll leave off trying to use that voucher, at least until I get back from Switzerland.

Amazingly enough, I reach the phone in time and pick it up.

"Hello, Jessica?" It sounds like Harris of all people. "Do you have a moment?"

I think it was time to get rid of those shorts for good really, so I don't desperately need to leave the house. Since my lower half isn't on display only so long as I remain indoors, I suppose going out can wait as well.

"Oh, hi, Harris. How's life?"

There's a pause, possibly a pregnant one but I'm not very good at those sorts of diagnostics.

Harris resumes, "I'm afraid the plan is off. Katie Porter didn't get through."

"Nor did Alice or the other kid?" I ask, completely forgetting what the other kid's name was.

"I'm afraid not. Katie was always the best so it was something of a certainty that if anyone got through, she would.

"I'm sorry to have bothered you with this, Jessica, but there really is no possibility now. I can't leave Bristol for long enough and you can't retrieve that clarinet on your own. I'm afraid it's all off. I will, of course, reimburse you for any outlays you may have made to date."

I'm a bit taken aback by all this. Everything is off suddenly? One minute we're about to launch for Switzerland, the next it's a complete non-starter? This isn't how you do things. You encounter a problem, and you find a solution. Goodness knows it's happened to me often enough. I'm so disorganized half the time that my main plan is to find a solution from one disaster to the next until somehow or other I pitch up at the other end. I admit that I don't have a solution right here and right now but give me a few minutes.

"Look, Harris," I begin, "that's a bit of a bummer for sure but let's just think a minute."

"Please," he says very heavily. "I just cannot face it. This is the second disaster to happen, and I feel as though Fate is against me. I don't need any more disappointment. I just need to find a new way forward."

I'm tempted to say that he could start with a good shave but I'm not that mean and I appreciate that he's in a delicate situation. Besides which, I would actually like to help.

"Well, give me a moment or two, and –"

"Jessica," he says boldly and rather more loudly than I'd expected, "I do not want to drag this out."

He pauses to collect himself then continues in a slightly quieter but just as determined tone, "I genuinely appreciate you taking the time and making the

165

effort to help me. Really, I do. However, unless you have a real idea, I don't see how sharing our thoughts and reflections will do anything for me.

"I would like to thank you sincerely for your consideration. I daresay we will speak again but for now, goodnight."

And he hangs up. Anyone would think he was a translation client.

Well, I didn't see that coming. His vibe must be infectious because I'm suddenly feeling quite low myself. I wasn't earlier. Definitely confused a bit and unsure quite what I was doing. But I was feeling kind of buoyant about the prospect. Now I don't really know why I was going to be doing something which I'm not going to be doing anymore. And I feel quite empty.

Frustratingly, I still reckon I could pull it off myself. I'm not sure that I buy this spiel about how only he can retrieve the clarinet in all its parts. With a bit of background knowledge and a print-out from Google, I reckon I could do it. What I can't do, however, is afford everything needed to undertake this on my own. So if he's not joining in, all I can do is try to climb the glacier and I know full well, that you don't undertake that without being an experienced professional or somewhat imbalanced in the head. Or both. They may go together in several cases.

Still, why do I care? It's not my life which has gone to hell. No free mini-trip to the Berner Oberland? It's hardly the end of the world. We were going to have to stay in Interlaken of all places in any case. That would be a bit like getting told that you had a special science event ticket which would let you snog one actor who had been James Bond, genetically re-engineered as he was at that time. And then getting George Lazenby. Yeah, I know.

I feel sorry for Harris, but I hardly know the guy. We all know that we have an innate sympathy for our fellow humans which is quite genuine. However, it's difficult to feel it for someone you don't know all that well at the same level of anguish as you do when it's somebody really close to you. I don't mean that you don't feel sorry for the others. We see war victims and famine sufferers on the news and our hearts go out to them. We hear about a friend of a friend with a terrible cancer condition. We hear about someone else we know who just lost their job. It's not like we don't care because we do but at the same time, it's hard to retain the full force of shock and grief when it's not somebody in the inner circle. If it happens to your brother or sister (well, maybe not my sister since she would have to generate a hell of a lot of sympathy first), to your best friend or someone who once really cared for you, then it feels infinitely worse. It's more than feeling a generated sympathy, it's like bereavement.

So when it comes to Harris, I shouldn't be that bothered, should I? He may even yet solve his problem. Then great, all's well which ends well. And if he doesn't? If nothing else, he can learn from the experience, I suppose. That's not really very good, is it? Well, OK, it isn't a good thing. I do feel sorry for him. I never said I didn't. It's just, well, something else.

It's what, exactly? Hell, I don't know. I flop onto my couch instead and stare out of the window, part wondering why I feel like this, part hoping that a manky pair of orange and green shorts doesn't come shooting back in through said window, loaded with a fresh dog poo or the like.

Why have I taken on such ownership? I suppose that's the question. I'm disappointed a bit like I was when I worked particularly hard on some marketing project for an earwax removal system and then the parent company went broke two days before launch. I still got paid so it wasn't my problem. It was more just that it felt as though there had never been any point to what I'd been doing. It wasn't going to make a blind bit of difference to anyone. Perhaps that's the issue now. Maybe I let myself get too caught up in what looked like quite a funky project. And I was going to be the lead heroine. Not that there was a lot of competition since Harris never had any more chance of getting up an Alp then he did of getting a date with a Komodo dragon but that's not the point. The point is that in some way, I'd let myself become part of it. The project didn't need me as much I liked to think. I can see that now because it was never about me.

Oh well, I'll no doubt get over it.

I get some clean shorts to wear, grab a drink and place myself back on the couch, across from the TV. I don't know what's on but I'm not that bothered.

So long as it isn't about getting off with ridiculously good-looking but ridiculously brainless twenty-somethings, home décor or ballroom dancing, then how bad can it be?

Pretty bad, is the answer. Cookery shows seem to be flowing out of the system like a stream of garbage which nobody bothered literally to digest before it turned into what I'm seeing now. I don't want to buy any of the antiques or designer clothes which appear to be the basis of several other shows. Even the game shows are about people scoring points according to how much they look like a certain Premier League footballer, with bonuses for every IQ point you can show lower than his. Not a lot of prizes are being won, funnily enough.

I flick through, getting increasingly bored, until some show crops up with a young lad playing a piano. Oh, thank you, just what I needed to see. I don't know if Fate is a real being but if so, I could do without having this loaded in my face. Now we all know that Katie Porter, or whatever her name was, won't be doing this. Nor, of course, will Alice or the other kid whose name I really can't remember. No disrespect to him – I can remember that it was a he at least – but I don't feel guilty either.

Something pricks my consciousness.

"Now we all know."

That's what you thought to yourself, wasn't it Jessica? But do we? Yet?

I turn off the TV as my thoughts assemble and run slightly wild. What if nobody does know yet that Katie isn't going? Couldn't she and Harris go anyway? Well, what would you do with Katie then? Kidnap her and lock her up for a couple of days while you were off in Switzerland? No, that doesn't work. Bit too illegal, dammit. You can hardly bring Katie along for the ride to Interlaken. She's not Alice.

But Alice was also in the running for that competition, wasn't she? And if nobody yet knows…

Oh come on, Jessica, the original idea was stupid enough, but this is getting into the realms of a "Carry On" film. Besides, there are national borders involved. You mean to cross at least two, accompanied by a minor, in an attempt to recover a musical instrument worth a quarter of million, and see if you can dodge the import charge on the way back in? You'll also be technically kidnapping Alice in a legal sense. What if the cops find out? What if the school finds out? What if the agency finds out? What if Bethany finds out?

What if Bethany finds out? She'll go frickin' off-the-scale ballistic.

I smile to myself. That's clinched it. Where's the phone gone to?

"Hi, Harris. It's Jessica again. Listen, I've just had an idea."

Chapter 12

FIVE DAYS FLAT

Harris

I really feel as though I'm becoming a criminal these days. Those who like to moralize are clearly quite correct. It is a slippery slope. I started off with a minor question of import duties on Givret's clarinet. Now I'm sitting in The Georgina Café again, opposite Alice and her Aunt Jessica. I should be giving Alice her piano lesson back in school, but we headed out the back door instead and straight for East Dawlings. According to Alice, this gives us enough time for us to meet up with her aunt and then for her to get home again before her parents realize that she's been absent. Since nobody else polices her movements in the school, there's a window of opportunity.

Technically, I've absconded with a minor although I trust nobody who matters will notice. Alice and her aunt are happily devouring another rock bun and cream tea at my expense although thankfully, the armed forces appear to have ceased flying for the day now. I've heard it claimed that the music of Mahler is akin to a roar like no other but it's a roar I certainly prefer over a modern, military jet engine.

Not only all that but I'm being presented with a plan which involves lying to my employer and to a teenager's parents, absconding with said minor a second time, this time across national borders, taking a dubiously legal flight around the Swiss Alps, and then getting back into the country with the initial intention repeated of avoiding import duties. I should be grateful that all this is only envisaged to take no more than five days. Extended to a week, I'd probably find myself guilty of grand larceny and murder.

The whole idea is utterly insane, but this aspect doesn't seem to be bothering Jessica too much any longer. As far as I can tell, she's thriving on the challenge and where the aunt leads, it appears that the niece will follow. Apparently my take on the whole prospect counts for much less because it's for my benefit and I should be grateful, and because I've never been to Switzerland myself and can't speak German. Hence my questioning the common sense of the whole endeavour is of no real consequence to these two. The one reason why my opinion does count for something is that I'm paying for this trip.

"So, if you'll let me check, perhaps I can see if I understand this fully?"

Both Jessica and Alice grunt. It seems that I've picked a moment when their mouths are too full of pieces of bakery to argue the point.

"The plan, if I can call it that, is as follows. At present, I have yet to inform Mrs Bodega and the respective children's parents that neither Katie Porter, nor Robert Fletcher, nor Alice Morrison has ultimately qualified for the Young Pianists Finals of the West Country. Quite why I called you with this news before then is something I do not really understand but I did. And that is the basis of your plan.

"If we take this forward, my next move will be to inform Mrs Bodega along with Mr and Mrs Morrison," I pause as the two of them suddenly appear a shade less enthused by their mouthfuls for some reason I don't know. I continue, "I will inform them, quite untruthfully, that Alice has actually been selected for the finals and that I will therefore need to accompany her to Taunton between Wednesday and Sunday next week. When we leave for Taunton, we will immediately double back to Bristol, where we will meet you, Jessica, and then get on a train towards London and Heathrow Airport.

"In the meantime, you will have booked us on a flight to Geneva, from where we will catch a train to Basel –"

"Bern."

"Sorry, Bern. You'll have to forgive my limited grasp of where places are in Switzerland. I'm a music teacher, not a geography teacher and these Germanic names all sound much the same to me!"

I grin sheepishly at this attempt at humour and am met by two expressions which seem to indicate that my intelligence, my wit or more likely both are open to question. One tries.

"In Bern," I continue, "we will take a train to some place called, if I recall, Interlaken –"

I've pronounced the name with a long a sound, as in the English lake. However, I'm cut off again.

"Interlaken."

It appears that the a is pronounced more along the lines of the word ah. Honestly, am I supposed to learn a new language in the space of a week? I thought one of the reasons Alice recommended her aunt was precisely because she could handle the linguistic elements. There's no need to rub my nose in the fact that I'm more at home ordering a fine Merlot in a bar on the Côte d'Azur in my finest French. While I would never diminish the language of Beethoven, Mozart or Schubert, the rather throaty and grating sound of the Germanic realm has never really been something I would consider refined enough to appeal.

I press on.

"Having arrived on Wednesday evening in Interlaken," I intone with my best pronunciation applied, "we will find a helicopter tour on Thursday with a crew willing to set down on the glacier in question –"

"The Upper Grindelwald Glacier. I determined it from your friend's description and cross-referenced various coordinates. Knowing which glacier it is might be important."

I do wish she would continue to demolish her cream tea scone with the same gusto she was showing earlier. I could so do without these interruptions.

"Ideally, we will make the trip on Thursday but if needs be, mainly by virtue of the helicopter timing, we can make the trip on Friday. Once there, we will use metal detectors to recover the pieces of the clarinet, check their integrity and re-constitute the clarinet.

"Either way, we will remain in Interlaken," I get the pronunciation right a second time, greatly impressing myself, "until Saturday morning when we will return to Geneva, or else Zürich in the event that it should be a preferable option for whatever reason. From there, we will return as discreetly as possible to a London airport, buying our tickets as close to departure as we can. We will spend the night next to London, then return by train to Bristol where we will meet Alice's parents."

Once more a brief look of distaste sweeps both of their faces. I really cannot fathom it.

"We will inform them that although Alice gave a stunning performance, she did not manage to win the competition."

Jessica intervenes, "And on the train journey back, you need to remember to call up somebody who's actually been at the competition so that we do know who's actually won."

"That's a good point. I will certainly need to make a note of it."

"Just memorize it. The less of a paper trail the better on this one."

"Point taken," I note stiffly. I really am being made to feel like the junior partner here and I can't say I'm enjoying it.

"And finally, I will return to Isabel with the clarinet before showing up again for work on Monday morning. You, Jessica, will be able to take the train from Bristol back to Liverpool without your presence being noticed further."

"And I will, of course, be immensely grateful."

I feel it only right to accord some respect, regardless of how little I may be receiving myself. It at least shows the benefit of treating others as you would have them treat you since Jessica's attitude seems to relax a little at this juncture. She leans back slightly, whether to regard me with a knowing gaze or to swallow a particularly awkward piece of scone, I can't say for sure, but at least her expression softens. She takes her time to reflect and then starts talking.

"Fair enough, Harris. I think you've got the basic idea. But we're going to have to be flexible. There are quite a lot of variables in this plan which could go wrong but we're just going to have to handle whatever problems come our way as best we can. All I'm saying in this regard, is be ready to react fast and improvise. It's something Alice and I have to do quite a bit of in the mountains and relying on a fixed plan will get you nowhere. You need a broad plan, and you work within it. A bit like if you're trying to score at a night club but I suppose that may not be quite your thing."

She smirks slightly but I ignore her obvious provocation. It doesn't seem to bother her. If anything, the witticism, if I can call it that, was intended for the benefit of Alice who appears somewhat amused by it. They do make a strange pair but there's an undeniable chemistry of sorts between them.

"There are a few other things we need to take care of in advance though," she continues. "First of all, you're going to have to work out a bit. The critical thing, if we need to cover distance, is that you can keep going. We're not going to go mountaineering, don't worry. I don't need you to be ready to climb. Nor do you have to be able to move extremely quickly. What you do have to have is the ability to keep going. A bit of stamina. Take some long walks or, even better, jogs. Just make sure that if we have to cover distance, you can do it. And don't forget, in such a case, it probably won't be over any terrain which is all that flat."

I make a mental note to increase the number of times I walk round the park each day. It'll be important to include a few of the hillier bits too.

"Next, you're going to need some gear. Get in some hard-wearing shirts and trousers. Trousers, not shorts. If we end up on a path through grassland, you risk catching ticks from the longer grass. It's not guaranteed but you certainly don't want it to happen. It won't last that long but you will have a bit of a job explaining why you're scratching away at your legs after spending a few days at a piano competition if you do get tick trouble. So suit up. Add some decent boots to the equation. You'll need a proper, medium-size rucksack, a cagoule and a water bottle. Hiking sticks are also worthwhile though be sure to get ones with rubber tips, not metal since we'll be wanting to travel with hand luggage only and metal-tipped sticks won't get past airport security. The sticks make people look like total idiots when they stroll around the local park in Britain as if they're heading off up Mount Everest after twenty minutes passing The Trout and Haddock chippy bar. But on actual mountainsides, they let your upper body take some of the strain in ascending and can save your knees from hell on the steeper descents. They're also good if somebody's dog decides to annoy you and you need to give it a reason to sod off."

I have no intention of doing anything at all harmful to canines after my recent experiences, but I don't want to labour the point.

"And then," she concludes, "get yourself a few things which might come in handy. A compass, a first-aid kit, a set of high-sugar snacks, a spare toilet roll."

I look up in surprise at this.

"What am I going to do with a toilet roll?"

The look which greets me in response is even worse than the one I received on confusing Basel with Bern.

"What the hell do you think? Signal to any passing helicopters that you need them to pick you up because you have to reach a public toilet as a matter of emergency in the next ten minutes? It's because when you have to go, you have to go. So you nip behind a tree or bush, do your business and clean up. If the toilet roll is bio-degradable, it's not as if you even have to feel guilty either. You're simply fertilizing the next generation of fir trees."

I'm quite flabbergasted. What sort of behaviour goes on up there?

"You mean to say," I ask, "that people go out into public spaces to urinate and defecate?"

"Look, Harris," she starts with a patient but patronizing tone, "you can be miles away from any sort of civilization. You leave the path, find a convenient spot set back from it and do your business. It's all part of the code. You see, there's a code people are supposed to follow up there. You always say hello when you pass somebody on a pathway. That's, "Grüzi," in German Switzerland, "Bonjour," in the French-speaking part. You never drop litter, no matter how small a piece. Farmers can leave fridges full of produce on sale, with a small honesty box for people to pay for whatever cheese or drinks they take. Nobody ever cheats anyone else. Regarding bodily functions, it's perfectly OK to relieve yourself discreetly, you just don't expose yourself on a hiking path. It's not the done thing.

"Mind you," she looks up almost wistfully, "if you're not fully au fait with the code, you don't always even need to worry about that. I was once walking along a path in the woods, and I went round a corner. There was some guy standing on the edge of the path with his dick in his hands, spraying the bushes without a care in the world. That, I should add, is not an acceptable way to behave. This guy was pissing uphill but imagine if he'd been on the other side of the path and letting it go downwards. Someone passing underneath might have got a lovely, golden shower. What's more, it wasn't even anything much worth looking at. His girlfriend was a short distance along the path, looking distinctly bored. I can't say I blame her."

I do not like these sorts of conversations, especially not with people I don't know all that well. They're called private lives for a reason, as far as I'm concerned. I try to get off the topic of human anatomy.

"But even if you follow the code and go to a less frequented spot, isn't it awful for the mountains to be full of human waste?"

Again, I'm regarded as being intellectually deficient by a long way.

"These mountains are over a kilometre high and tens of kilometres in girth," she explains in the same, patronizing tone. "A single turd is hardly going to make them the epicentre of global pollution. After all, there are cows producing way more crap than you or I can, with hundreds of them doing so on a half-hourly basis. The mountains are not reduced to being composed predominantly of dung as a result.

"To come back to my original point, however, although you can do your business peacefully enough, you might still want to bring a toilet roll and enjoy the benefit of not having to wipe your bum on a spare leaf or an old crisp packet afterwards."

I suppose it's a fair point, even if made very crudely. What a vulgar woman she is at times.

This isn't a concern for her. She keeps going.

"We're also going to need to get hold of a full set of hiking gear for Alice. Bethany –"

I look up blankly. Who's Bethany?

"I mean her mother, also known as my elder sister, Bethany," she goes on. "Bethany is bound to send Alice off with half a ton of survival gear to Taunton in case the locals there have forgotten to stop fighting the Wars of the Roses or there happens to be a radiation leak from a nearby power plant or a random navy jet crashes into the local Sainsbury's. Whatever goes on in Bethany's head."

She rolls her eyebrows before continuing, "I doubt Bethany's had a straight thought for at least a decade. In fact, I suspect the only straight things to have gone in or out of her head at all have been her toothbrush and what sticks out of her husband's pubes. Although the toothbrush is no doubt more substantial."

She and Alice both laugh uproariously at this. I have to confess that I'm absolutely horrified. How can a fifteen-year-old be finding this sort of smut amusing? How can any sort of responsible relative dream of articulating it in front of someone below the legal age of consent? How can she find it entertaining to impugn her own family's dignity in this way? I simply cannot respond, which is perhaps why she proceeds to carry on as if nothing all that significant has taken place at all.

"As a result, Alice will have around two suitcases full of unnecessary garbage, which will have to be deposited in a locker in a station somewhere or else at the airport. She'll need to be re-equipped before we leave. I can get in the gear, but I'll need you to pick up the tab."

I nod. It's all I can do for the moment.

"The question remains," she turns to Alice, "how do we extract your passport from that stupid safe where your parents insist on keeping anything more important than their Netflix subscription? Do you have the access code?"

Alice looks pensive for a moment before replying to her aunt.

"Officially, no, I don't. But I've watched my dad open it enough times and I know what the code is. The problem is that even if the safe is opened properly, it can only stay open for two minutes before an alarm kicks in. I don't know what all is in there or if I can find my passport in under two minutes."

Alice sits back, clearly perplexed. Jessica looks more thoughtful. I wish I could contribute but I'm still too shell-shocked by the exchange of a minute ago to gather my thoughts properly.

A sly smile creeps over Jessica's face, and she turns back to Alice.

"Do you think your dad – or your mum for that matter – could be persuaded to give you your passport for a few minutes so you could examine its watermarks, layout and security measures, or something like that, supposedly as part of a school project to do with something you're studying for geography?"

Alice grimaces before replying, "My geography studies at the moment are about the historic movement of glaciers and the effects they have had on undersea topography."

"Yeah, yeah, who cares?" breezes her aunt. "Do your parents really pay that much attention to the course content from one week to the next?"

"I suppose not," Alice says neutrally, "but so what?"

"Here's why." Jessica seems impressed by the brilliance of her thought now. "You tell your parents that you need to examine your passport for a few minutes for some school project. When you're supposedly done with it, you take an old one of mine, which I'll send down to you by courier, and you place that back in the safe. Your mum and dad will have no reason to open it to look inside, so they'll just stick it in where it should be. One passport looks like another on the outside, so they'll never work out that you actually have the original.

"In the end of the day, you can travel with me as an accompanying adult and since they probably won't pay enough attention to spot the difference between Morriston and Morrison, they may even assume that I'm your mother at passport control anyway."

"And who will they think he is?" Alice indicates me. "Your boyfriend?"

I don't know if Jessica or I blanche more at that thought.

"We're not going to be travelling as if in a group with him," she answers stiffly. "We don't want to draw attention to ourselves as such. He can sit elsewhere on the plane. Nobody will connect us with him when we enter Switzerland that way."

I have to admit that it's an ingenious plan. I can't criticize Jessica for stupidity. Her brain is clearly up to the job. I just do wish she wouldn't employ it in such a lowbrow manner concerning what she apparently thinks is funny. However, she can solve problems. I'll give her that. And right now, it's probably what I need most.

Chapter 13
DRESS TO IMPRESS

Jessica

This is going to be hard work. I cannot recall ever being in quite such a sour mood on touching down in a Swiss airport. In fact, what do I mean, this is going to be hard work? It sounds as though I'm taking my first, tentative steps up a mountain face. In practice, this has been hard work since early this morning, it still is, and it shows no sign of slackening up. I'm not at the bottom of the mountain face. I'm several hours into one hell of a slog up a sheer rock face and I still can't even see the top for all the endless height above me.

Alice and I are standing at the luggage carousel in Geneva Airport. Number six, I think it is although they all look alike. So long as we get Harris' ridiculous backpack, it'll all be much of a muchness to me. Where Harris has got to between passport control and here I do not know but I assume he's going to show up eventually. The last I saw of him, he appeared to be trying to convince the Swiss border guard service that admitting him over their border would not present a serious threat to national security. If they count the maintenance of the average IQ level within their border above a single digit as a security requirement, he may have an uphill struggle. It's not that he's inherently stupid, I reflect. It's just that something had to give when God endowed him with his encyclopaedic knowledge and appreciation of classical music, and that something was a minimum level of common sense.

He and Alice arrived late in Bristol this morning, apparently because they missed the first connection back from the direction of Taunton. According to Alice, this was because he knocked over his cappuccino on standing up and got a lovely coffee stain all down his crotch. Having washed this kind of clean in the men's toilet, he seems to have then tried to dry himself with the hand dryer and somehow got his fly caught in it. I was inclined not to believe this story until Alice swore blind that two maintenance guys had staggered out of the men's toilet, laughing away to each other about, "that total dickhead who was humping the air dryer." And this guy is a professional teacher? If the only thing preventing him from abusing pupils in the sanitary facilities is a predilection for the electrical appliances, the whole concept of safeguarding the vulnerable in the United Kingdom is probably a few lightyears behind its equivalent in Haiti.

Following on from that, Alice and I somehow steered him onto an express train to Birmingham and from there onto a train to London which was fortunately, for us, running about fifteen minutes late. This meant that we didn't end up on a later train which would have necessitated a change at High Wycombe in order to arrive at Heathrow Airport with only about thirty minutes tops to check in before the flight departed. Instead, we made it to Heathrow with an hour and a quarter to check in and get through security on a summer's day. Lucky us. Less pressure is a very good thing since it means less running around and less chance of looking conspicuous. Not that we have a great deal of chance in that regard, thanks to that berk, Harris.

As you can no doubt imagine, he wasn't – and still isn't – dressed as most people would be who are off to indulge in mountain sports. I concede that Harris has never been to the Alps before but even so, I did provide a reasonable indication of what to wear. Alice and I are dressed in our usual military surplus attire, outfitted in loose-fitting cargo trousers, lightweight camo shirts over sturdy sports bras, cotton waistcoats with multiple carrying capacity, neck smocks and wraparound shades. Plus, of course, thick socks and sturdy boots. Nothing too skimpy, hardly seductive or reeking of feminine allure, but practical and fairly much attuned to summertime at high altitudes in reasonably dry air. In our backpacks we also have cagoules in case of rain, and additional layers for the glacier bit.

Harris, however, seems to think that outdoor sports haven't seen any fashion developments since the 1920s at the latest. He's wearing satin white jodhpurs with knee-high, leather boots. His (still coffee-stained) crotch is bulging because he couldn't even find a pair which fitted him. His top half is kitted out in an off-green safari shirt and a pair of binoculars round his neck. These are hanging from a strap so short that he probably can't even raise them to his eyes without undoing them first. And, for some reason I haven't bothered to try to fathom, he has a kind of bright, almost neon orange Che Guevara beret on his head.

What the hell is he telling the Swiss that he's come to their country to do? Play a game of polo with some colour-blind revolutionaries? Set up a mountain-signalling service for light aircraft, using a combination of his dick and his hat? Simply retrieving an inordinately expensive wind instrument from a high altitude in the Berner Oberland is at least going to sound far too normal and boring for them to take the truth seriously.

Finally, he's also carrying a walking stick. I mean the sort of walking stick which is made of wood with a curved handle and is rarely seen being carried these days by anyone born after 1950. I told the pratt to get a pair of hiking sticks, not a single item which he probably had to mug somebody's great-grandfather just to get his hands on. The only concession to what I said was that it has what looks like a rubber doorstop on the end of it, but what I actually said was to avoid metal tips on hiking sticks since that can turn them into potentially offensive weapons. Harris' 1920s fashion accessory, with or without the doorstop, could only be considered an offensive instrument of sorts if accompanied by an industrial strength personal lubricant.

All this and more, I got to consider on our trip down to the southeast and Heathrow. Harris had lost his train ticket, predictably enough but when he pulled at the already taut fabric covering his groin to see if he'd left it there, the female ticket inspector decided to leave us in peace and head on to the next passengers in line. I feel sorry for serious feminists myself. Their real problem isn't male chauvinism in my view. Slowly but surely, that's dying out. What isn't anywhere on the decline is rank, male stupidity and overcoming that is going to take generations yet. It's the ones who act like morons but don't even realize it who are the worst. And Harris is clearly some sort of Top Gun of idiocy – he's the worst of the worst.

Anyway, we finally made it to Heathrow. The original plan had been to proceed through Terminal 2 security separately, with Alice and me going through the North deck and Harris through the South. The less we appeared together, the less we'd be considered an item in the event that anything should go wrong later, and law enforcement agents might be looking at CCTV and the like. I ought to make clear that I'm not expecting such a thing to take place, but accidents happen. We're hardly inveterate criminals on a major heist but the question of import duties remains hanging plus we don't technically have any legal right to be removing Alice, no matter how willingly, from the United Kingdom. Travelling reasonably incognito seemed like a good idea.

For whatever reason, it struck me that leaving Harris to his own devices in security just wasn't the best way to stay incognito and it turned out that I was entirely correct. Despite my initial apprehensions, Alice and I followed along a few punters behind Harris in the line. He already had his ticket in his hand but that didn't stop him trying to get through the electronic security gates by scanning a discount coupon from Marks and Spencer which he also had in his pocket. Alice managed to rescue that one before well-meaning security personnel, whose attentions we could nevertheless do without, came to his aid. Following along to the security gates themselves, we stood in line with two old ladies and some hippy dude between us and Harris.

In case you're unfamiliar with Heathrow Airport Terminal 2, the security decks are divided into two rows of gates which stretch alongside each other. A gate is an electronic gizmo which scans you for metal items or chemicals which you shouldn't have on you. If you fail that, there's then an MRI scanner on the other side which can check you out more thoroughly although you can opt for a manual search instead. Before the gate, are two sets of small trays on either side, into which you offload your bag, coat, phone and basically all your belongings. These go on a conveyor belt through a scanner where various guards check that you don't have a cigarette lighter or a combat-capable assault rifle as part of your essential travel gear. If you do, you get called to one side and given a time whose hardness is proportional to what they found in your bag. Especially if it's the cigarette lighter.

Most normal people can navigate this without too much hassle. Somebody wearing jodhpurs and a safari shirt cannot be considered normal though.

Alice and I had offloaded our gubbins into the trays and were about to head for the gate itself when we looked over to where Harris was on the tray set opposite ours. He was struggling with something around his neck and looked almost as if he was trying to throttle himself to death. It was hard to make out. The security staff were trying to wave us through so Alice pretended to have a coughing fit and I bent over to help her. This was so that we could stay on the tray side of the gate and work out what the hell was going on with Harris.

It turned out that the strap of his binoculars had got twisted and entwined in the oddly shaped collar of his safari shirt. They were looping through some straps which were there for a purpose about as clear as that of condom machines in a nunnery. When I offered to ask the security staff for a pair of scissors so we could cut through the strap, he turned bright red and started shrieking that these were his grandfather's binoculars which he'd used on board the fishing boat he sailed in the Second World War, and there was no way he would let them be defiled as such. It was the first time I'd heard of a World War Two fishing veteran, but I suppose somebody must have been keeping the nation in fish 'n' chips despite the best efforts of the Third Reich, so credit to him. Quite why Harris felt it necessary to strangle himself with the binoculars eight decades later was less obvious.

In the end, Alice and I helped him to remove his shirt altogether, with the binoculars still entwined. You should have seen the looks on the faces of those two old ladies who had been in front of us in the queue. What with his pelvic bulge and now his pecs on full display, I was waiting for them to stick a couple of ten-pound notes in the waistband of his jodhpurs. It was a bit like a classical music version of, "Magic Mike", just with a bit more flab and a manky beard. I had warned him to wear a vest or T-shirt underneath in order to soak up the sweat, but I might as well have been providing all my instructions to a brick wall.

Alice cleared the electronic gate without a problem. I set it off thanks to the metal buttons on my cargo trousers – Alice has plastic so avoided this – but the MRI cleared me fast. Harris, of course, had to trip the sensor because he forgot to take off his glasses and their frames are made of sufficient metal to repair a hole in a sinking ship. He was advised to take them off before getting into the MRI scanner but he's clearly blind as a short-sighted bat without them and walked into the side of it. At which point, he requested a manual search instead. Manual searches in Heathrow need a manager's approval and take about ten minutes to get going so I was increasingly glad of that connection we'd managed to make in Birmingham. If we'd only had thirty minutes to make the flight now, we'd have been praying for that to have been delayed instead.

The guard who was eventually delegated the job of manual search didn't seem very happy. I'm guessing he was straight, which would explain why the prospect of searching a semi-naked, sweating schoolteacher, with a pair of jodhpurs so skin-tight that you could just about tell apart the different elements of his genitalia, did not appeal at all. However, the guy was a professional and knew his job. He informed Harris that he would need to put his gloved fingers inside Harris' waistband and asked for his consent to the procedure.

"My goodness, I do hope you're not going to finger my glory organs!" Harris told him.

"Glory organs"? The prospect of fingering Harris' "glory organs" at that particular juncture would have driven me to lesbianism as a preferred option, assuming I had had any inclination towards sexual relations at all, which I did not. Since then, and still now, I think I would prefer to remove my earwax quietly on my own with an old toothbrush. And that's if Timothy Dalton were asking. Anyone else, even Sean Connery, and I'd consider a lengthy swim inside an active volcano a better way to spend my time in a state of undress.

Getting back to the sequence of events, the poor security guard slid his fingers into the back of Harris' waistband and proceeded to feel around for whatever they look for there. A penknife wedged up your crack or something, I suppose. Unfortunately, at that moment in time, Harris coughed violently. The guard lost his grip on the elastic waistband which launched itself into Harris' back and propelled him forwards, with his glory organs heading right for the guard's face where his jaw was dropping in horror. As were mine and Alice's except that we were more fortunate because there weren't any glory organs approaching the gaps between our teeth at an accelerated speed. You can guess what happened next and the shock caused the guard to shut his mouth a shade too quickly. How to put it? Let's say that if you're looking for something to occupy the muscles in your mouth, you might want to stick to chewing gum over glory organs, particularly Harris'. At least the security guard would have come away with the taste of a nice cappuccino from a railway coffee shop afterwards. That's about the most positive spin I can put on it.

The rest of the security team having stepped in to prise apart what was probably the least erotic instance of oral sex in human history, Harris was finally cleared as not possessing anything of danger to the flight other than his complete lack of functional brainpower. In the meantime, I had succeeded in disentangling his binoculars from his shirt, so he was able to get back into costume and cover up his – in my opinion – distinctly unattractive chest. What this Isabel girl sees in him I have no idea. Perhaps it's incredibly beautiful how true love can blossom even for those who are completely blind, deaf and unable to process any information about the world around them. If she had any inkling of what this guy is really like, I would have thought it'd take more than Karl bloody Givret's clarinet to float her boat.

With all this finally behind us, we headed across the concourse overlooking the departure gates, identified ours and set off downstairs to find it. We passed the usual set of astronomically expensive designer watch and accessories shops, which probably only need two sales a year to turn a handsome profit. They even employ security guards to keep out the riff-raff. This no doubt equates to about ninety-nine per cent of the people who travel through Heathrow and certainly applies to Alice and me who are considered some kind of scum which only recently evolved from single-cell organisms. Harris was equally unwelcome but that's probably because by that point, every employee in the airport had been warned that he was a complete psycho.

We'd taken a fair bit of time at security, so the gate was already boarding the passengers when we pitched up. It was at this point where Harris' failure to follow instructions led to yet another hiccup.

Especially with regard to our return trip, I considered it wise to travel with only hand luggage. Of course, Alice had come equipped with so much crap from Bethany that I was surprised she hadn't needed her own removal van to reach Taunton, but we were prepared for that. We simply offloaded the entire lot into a timeshare storage bin and replaced it all with the ready-packed hiking rucksack I'd prepared in advance for her. She only had to transfer across her current novel, "The Three-Balled Boyfriend." Where Alice gets her reading material I dread to think.

Harris had been instructed to come with a medium-size rucksack which would contain one change of clothes and the other, basic necessities which I had outlined back in The Georgina Café the last time we'd met up in East Dawlings. Obviously, the guy has an inability to comprehend anything not written by Beethoven because he pitched up with a backpack which would have made Sherpa Tensing blanche at the prospect when he tackled Mount Everest with Sir Edmund Hillary back in 1953. US Special Forces carrying out HALO drops into occupied territory from 40,000 feet probably take less than half of what Harris thinks he needs for a couple of days in what is a highly developed country. Apparently, he thinks he might need a change of outfit for his evening dinner after a hard day in the mountains.

To get to the point, if your supposed hand luggage is over a certain limit in terms of size and/or weight, both of which Harris' was exceeding by a phenomenal amount, you have to surrender it for transport in the hold of the aircraft, as if it were checked luggage. If you wait until they call you out on it, you have to pay for the privilege too. Harris, of course, had to argue this out with the check-in staff, assuring them that this example of modern-day piracy would not go unregistered with the forces of law and order as soon as the aircraft touched down. They pointed out that even if they were committing a crime, which they weren't, they would have been doing so on UK territory, but the plane would land in Switzerland which has a different, legal code. He would therefore have to persuade the British authorities to issue an extradition request to the Swiss, who would then have to persuade the aircrew to extradite themselves back to Britain in order to face arrest and possible incarceration, at least according to Harris' legal viewpoint, for the serious misdemeanour of legally charging him an extra thirty quid to check in his gigantic backpack. We were in serious danger of being stuck on the wrong side of a withdrawing airbridge at this point so I intervened and told him that he should either shut his mouth of his own, free will or I'd do it for him with a set of spare jodhpurs which were taking up some of the black hole he'd been carting around on his back. That finally shut him up.

Having just got on board before the doors closed, Alice and I grabbed our seats about halfway down the aisle and got strapped in. Harris was meant to be sitting about five rows behind us, in the aisle seat next to a mother and her small child. On the opposite side of the aisle was the father with another infant. It seemed that this child wanted to be with the mother and so had crossed over to sit in the seat allocated to Harris. Presumably, the family was intending to ask Harris if he would mind effectively swapping seats with the junior passenger. No big deal.

You'd have thought.

But no, disaster seems to follow Harris like flies follow Swiss cows. For whatever reason, the two parents failed to clock Harris' approach. He somehow imagined that the kid on "his" seat was a double booking and that he would need to put her on his lap. If you're wondering how he could think that all I can say is that I don't know either. Harris swung her up without asking and deposited himself into the seat, crushing her doll and depositing her onto his upper legs. This probably meant that she got a nice poke from his cappuccino-flavoured glory organs trapped in those godawful jodhpurs, but I can't be sure of that. What I do know is that she immediately bricked herself and whatever protection she may have been wearing wasn't sufficient to hold it all in. A rank stench and a sheet of brown goo emerged as if from an inverted geyser and she burst into howls of tears. She also grabbed his beard with a small fist encrusted in some sort of green toddler food emanating from a jar of gluten-free nutrition options. Never trust green stuff. The crushed doll must have been one of those revolting toys which they sell to kids these days, which are configured to exercise bodily functions such as, in this case, vomiting. Why children want to play with something which can randomly produce what may at one point have been a gerbil tikka masala no doubt takes a more professional understanding of young individuals' psychology than I possess. The net effect was to eliminate any remaining traces of satin white which still showed on Harris' jodhpurs. That and to ensure that the plane's toilets would be a better place to spend the flight unless you lacked any sense of smell whatsoever.

Having heroically sorted out these passengers into their originally allocated seats despite not having hazmat suits, the flight crew got the aircraft off the ground only twenty-five minutes late and we progressed over the English Channel and down over Paris. Harris pontificated loudly to I don't know whom about the state of the classical music scene in what he called Gay Paris, pronouncing Paris as in English and not French. I thought he said that he had some idea how to speak bloody French too but clearly not very much. "Gay Paree" may sound like an artistic flourish, taking into account the flair of the French capital. "Gay Paris", quite obviously to anyone who isn't Harris, sounds like a nightclub near Notre Dame where you hear "YMCA" being played quite frequently and the best way to get a boyfriend is to bend over to pick up your dropped change next to the condom machine in the men's toilet. Or wear skintight, white jodhpurs perhaps. I don't really know as I've never tried to pick up any guys, straight or gay, using either technique.

Finally stopping for a bit of oxygen, Harris decided that he needed to use the facilities. There was actually the sound of a squelch and two sodden materials stuck to each other being pulled apart as he stood up. The smell was so bad that the oxygen masks above the seats almost dropped in the two or three rows next to where Harris was sitting.

"I say, my good man," Harris asked one of the flight attendants, "whereabouts can I find the facilities round here?"

Where do you think, you moron? They can only physically be located at the end of the aisle. Well maybe not where you're sitting where the seat itself seems to do the job but for most passengers, at the end of the aisle. I was surprised that the flight crew didn't take the chance to direct him to the emergency exit and help him out of it but as I mentioned already, they were true professionals. They all now deserve a promotion to the classier routes in my opinion, at least once they've completed a course of serious psychotherapy to counter the PTSD no doubt endured by virtue of having Harris on their flight.

"What the hell?" I rounded on Alice. This was perhaps a little unfair, but my nerves were a shade strained and there was no better option. "You didn't tell me that this guy was a walking disaster who probably failed his audition to get into a 'Carry On' film by being too unbelievably idiotic."

"Seriously, Auntie Jess," Alice started apologetically, "he's basically OK when he's teaching piano. And you can tell how he really loves music when he explains it to people. He's actually quite inspirational in his own, weird way. I just didn't realise that he was a bit of a berk."

"A bit of a berk?" I retorted incredulously. "That's putting it mildly. You might as well say that the Second World War was a bit of a bust-up. That guy is a walking disaster zone."

I lowered my voice a bit and added, "And we're supposed to get him up a freaking glacier and back to Britain in three days max with a clarinet worth about the same as a small house? This is going to make, 'The Eiger Sanction' look like an episode of 'The Teletubbies'. Clint Eastwood had no idea how easy he was having it."

I do like the 1975 movie, "The Eiger Sanction". Good-looking guys and adventurous derring-do in an Alpine setting – the Berner Oberland no less, in fact. I admit to having a penchant for Alpine films although I draw the line at the more schmaltzy, sentimental ones. I've stepped in too many cowpats to take that crap seriously. By crap, I mean the films, not the cowpats. Whether I like it or not, I have to take those seriously.

But enough culture. Where the hell had Harris got to? The longer I couldn't see him, the more frightened I got. Images of every air disaster movie I'd ever seen came floating through my mind, interspersed with Harris causing whatever had gone wrong. Even, "Sharknado 2" where a random tornado full of hungry sharks crashes into an airliner. It just shows how accident-prone Harris is as a person that I considered for a moment how he might cause something like that to happen.

Come on, Jessica, come on, I thought to myself. You can't do anything just now. Just relax back in your non-stinky seat and think about Timothy Dalton. Imagine what it would have been like to have been at the after party when they wrapped the sequence from, "License to Kill" which was shot in Miami. Swaying palm trees, a dusky breeze, a cool, light white in your hand and you look round to see Tim approaching in a loose-fitting but sensibly modest, Hawaiian shirt. All those tarts from the make-up department and post-production music editing have gone off to bonk Benicio del Toro – he was the villain Dario, for those unaware – and Tim's left feeling a bit lonely. Except now his eye has fallen on me and he's never seen a Bond girl so pretty and so smart. He moves forward to take me in a truly manly embrace, such as only he and occasionally Sean Connery managed to pull off. A whiff of expensive cologne graces my nostrils, and I sway slightly as he looks into my eyes and says –

"C'est quoi ce bordel? On ne va jamais rien vendre avec ce tas de merde qui dégouline juste derrière nous."

You what? Somebody just said something in French which would translate roughly as, "What the hell? We're never going to sell anything with this dripping pile of shit right behind us." That isn't what I would envisage Tim whispering in my ear as he moves to clamp my lips passionately in his. What is it with romantic fantasies? You always get interrupted just before the really good bit. Well, maybe you don't. I don't know as I haven't asked around too broadly and there are some things you just don't ask. But it's certainly what always happens to me.

Needless to say, it wasn't too hard to figure out who was behind all this. The flight crew's professionalism had finally been pushed over the limit as they worked their way up the aisle with the trolley carrying snacks and drinks for sale, followed by Harris. Quite what he had been doing in the toilet was hard to tell but he must have been trying to clean himself off in one way or another. He was completely sodden from head to foot and his bloody jodhpurs were now so skin-tight that you could just about make out individual pubes underneath them. His modesty was being more or less held solely by virtue of his neon orange beret which was somehow hanging in place over his glory organs. I do not want to imagine how that was physically possible.

What was not in dispute was that whatever he had been doing had been a total failure in erasing the smell. Hence the remark of the poor flight attendant with the trolley who was being followed by Harris on his way back to his seat. Understandably enough, few people have the appetite to buy a packet of crisps – not even salt 'n' vinegar – for the equivalent of about five pounds at the best of times. Still, that's inflight catering for you. If you add in the catering trolley being followed by someone who smells like a sewage-processing plant which has just been hit by a cruise missile, then your sales are unlikely to be as sky-high as your jet. In fact, they won't be as sky-high as any of the buses beneath you on the streets of Paris either.

Harris reached his seat again where he was now point-blank ignored by the surrounding family. The parents were pointedly looking out of the windows and holding their children close to them. I felt sorry for the mother who now had the one who'd crapped herself, but I guess this is what you're signing up for when you embark on pregnancy. Sounds like a good ad for condom companies in my view but I'm not really a family girl so what do I know?

At this point, I decided to abandon the whole charade of travelling in two separate groups of Alice plus me on one side, and Harris on the other. I got out of my seat, took a very deep breath of the relatively fresh air where Alice and I were sitting, and headed determinedly for Harris.

"Oh, hello," he grinned up at me. "Fancy meeting you here!"

Even Harris must have some modicum of emotional intelligence because the sheer venom on my face wiped the goofy look from his and he started cowering before me. Despite the plea of my nasal senses to run like hell, I bent over him and looked him straight in the eyes. Or at least as straight as I could, given that there was what looked like a piece of human waste smeared on the left-hand side of one of his glasses' lenses.

"Just shut up and listen to me," I began in equally spaced, equally weighted syllables at a steady pace, neither fast nor slow, just moving constantly forward. It's a style used by Bond villains quite often in fact. "We are trying to get to Switzerland in a discreet manner with as few problems as possible. That will help us considerably with the hiking trip we've planned."

That would not have made much, logical sense to any uninformed listener of course, but the von Crapp family sitting next to us didn't seem all that interested. Amazingly enough, Harris seemed to twig to what I was talking about.

"Counter to that," I hissed, "you have ignored virtually all of my instructions on what to bring with you and how to dress. You have antagonized every other person we've encountered and given that we're using public transportation, that's quite a lot of people. You can't keep your mouth shut for longer than a chihuahua with indigestion. You feel obliged to comment on anything which doesn't make sense to you and since you seem to understand virtually nothing of reality, that means you're like some sort of encyclopaedia of the universe's most moronic content."

I looked away momentarily before whirling back towards him with my nose about two centimetres from his. It was hard to believe that less than two minutes previously, I had been on the verge of snogging Tim in my dreams and now here I was in reality, no doubt poised in the uninformed view of the horror-stricken dad on the other side of the aisle, to get some romance on with my foul-smelling boyfriend here. It just shows how wrong you can be when you take things at face value. Not that I cared.

"I am warning you now," I intoned in a low, quiet voice which still dripped with serious threat, "from here on in, you will not speak a single word unless someone asks you a question and even then you will reply with as little as possible. You will not move a muscle other than your heart and lungs and whatever else is necessary to get from this aircraft to the luggage carousel in Geneva Airport where we will recover your ridiculous backpack. You can sit and meditate or pray but if you do anything which involves a greater degree of movement or social interaction, for example picking your nose, then I will physically punch you in the face. Hard, very hard. If you manage to get us arrested for violating the international laws regulating the conduct of air travellers, I will claim not to know you but advise that I believe that the otherwise unaccompanied minor sitting next to me is in your care but meant to be in Taunton, Somerset and certainly not outside the United Kingdom.

"In short, if you screw this up any more, I will happily take a hiking vacation in the Swiss Alps with your credit card while you spend a couple of nights in a police cell in Geneva becoming best friends with some crack dealer called Jean-Pierre who just landed on a flight from Bogota and pushed out half a kilo of purest cocaine after they served up a bad chicken tikka masala. I daresay his alimentary upsets won't be enough to cool off his libido though.

"Is all this clear?"

He looked at me curiously.

"I'm not sure I quite got the bit about the chicken tikka masala. I believe that's an Asian speciality, but you were referencing a flight from Latin America and –"

"Just shut up!" I all but managed to restrain myself from screaming in his ear. "Say nothing! Do nothing! Just get to the luggage carousel after passport control and meet Alice and me there! Nothing, I repeat nothing, else! Do you understand?"

Finally, I seemed to be getting through. He nodded sheepishly and looked down at his crotch. At least he could spend the rest of the flight working out how he had even managed to get crap on his neon orange Che Guevara hat. I stormed off back to my seat and what passed for fresh air again.

By the time we reached Geneva half an hour later, I had admittedly calmed down again. I like to think of myself as someone with a fairly even temper and normally willing to give people the benefit of the doubt. Perhaps not so much in terms of what I think to myself. I can be a bit of a bitch in my own head when I'm in a bad mood. But I don't usually voice these frustrations. Getting into a fight with people just doesn't produce results. Certainly not for me. Talking my way out of things is more my style. Maybe that's why I like languages as it improves my chances of successfully doing so. The way I spoke to Harris was something of an exception. Imagination, adhocracy and opportunism would be my usual operating procedures, which maybe doesn't make me the world's most admirable character but at least I don't spend a lot of time and energy scrapping with people., And if I do, there's a good reason for it.

Still, it did the job since we neither saw nor heard anything more from him for the rest of the flight. The sense of smell was still bothersome but there wasn't much anyone could have done about it at that point.

Things were still on a more or less even keel when we reached passport control. Thanks to the foresight of Brexit voters, those of us with UK passports can no longer enter through the Schengen Area control, which covers most of the EU plus Norway, Liechtenstein and Switzerland with free travel across borders. Those not from the Schengen Area need to have a visa or at least get a stamp on entry with another on exit, demonstrating that we haven't outstayed our welcome, which is a limit of up to ninety days in every one-hundred-and-eighty-day period. When it comes to Harris, there's a chance that this might be reduced to something more in the range of ninety minutes if they have any sense, but I don't think they revised it today.

I did think about staying with Harris to help him out but reckoned that this was one area where we really did not want to look like we were traveling together in case anything should go wrong later. Besides, not being part of an obvious family group, there wouldn't have been much I could have done as my presence at the control desk would not have been welcomed. Unless you're married to someone or a blood relation, you're on your own at passport control. It's somewhere I love to be if ever Colin is around.

Alice and I were slightly behind Harris in the line to start with, mainly because it wasn't downwind of him. He strolled up gamely enough to the control desk when it was his turn and presented his passport. The officer on duty wrinkled his nose and looked as though his wife had just left him for the binman this morning, and he was trying to work out whether that or having to deal with Harris was the worst thing to have occurred since he got up.

In fairness, Harris did try to speak a modicum of French. He has only a basic grasp of the language and his pronunciation sucks, but I do admire people who make the effort. It's just somehow more polite than the attitude of non-French or non-German speakers who simply assume that the rest of the world has to speak English because they do. This is most obvious among British and American tourists, but you can see a similar phenomenon with the increasing numbers from Asian countries as well.

As usual, the Swiss official adopted a very bored expression and replied in fluent English. One thing which I will confess that I do not like about the Swiss is their constant demonstration of how much better they are at English than you are at their languages, even when you're trying. I can sometimes manage to hold my own in French or German but I'm a professional. Even then, I can still get myself patronized merely by missing a pronoun or swallowing the wrong consonant, the latter being more of a problem in Germanophone Switzerland.

Harris, meanwhile, broadcast himself in as French an accent as you'd expect to find an Ascot commentator using, and the discourse switched into English faster than you could say, "Bonjour." The officer noted that he had entered the Schengen Area quite a few times in the past, though mainly France, Italy or Austria. I'd have hoped that he might have picked up a tiny bit of German in the latter but evidently the sound of Mozart must have been ringing in his ears too loudly for him to hear someone asking if he wanted fries with that.

Such being the case, the next question was why he wanted to visit Switzerland now. Can you name a famous, Swiss composer? Me neither so it's not an easy sell as a particular reason for visiting their country. The problem, of course, is that Harris' knowledge of the world beyond classical music is about the square root of zero.

Still, he made an effort although I was starting to wish that he hadn't.

"Well, my man," he started, "I've come to see your beautiful mountains."

Nice one, Harris. If you'd wanted to keep our true purpose on the down low, you could at least have claimed to be visiting Geneva and Lausanne for their architectural beauty or something.

The passport officer looked at him dubiously. True, the mountains have taken all sorts lately. Thanks to the likes of Interlaken, Zermatt and Lauterbrünnen, there's plenty to do for those with no appetite to hike up more than a flight of stairs and you hardly have to be ready to take on the next best thing to a military fitness exercise. Nonetheless, it does help if you don't look, sound and smell like the world's poshest sanitary engineer who got very drunk and fell into the sewage vat on his arrival at work this morning. And who also looks like he just rode a horse home from a very tacky, Che Guevara-themed nightclub.

It was at this point when Alice and I got called up to another desk along from the one where Harris was being interviewed. The control officer here was probably near the end of her shift and barely paid any attention to our passports, thereby missing the fact that the surnames were not quite identical and presumably assuming that I was Alice's mother. She was too bored to lapse into English despite our passports indicating that it was likely our mother tongue and whisked us through in the sort of French normally monopolized by Parisian waiters. If only all three of us could have managed that.

There was no point in hanging around by passport control to wait for Harris which is why we are now at the luggage carousel, hoping that we'll see him in what passes for his dreadful outdoor gear, and not in an orange jumpsuit with a pair of handcuffs on and a couple of cops on either side of him. As far as I can tell, he hasn't actually done anything illegal on this trip, but you never know what this guy is capable of. I certainly don't.

His ridiculously over-sized rucksack appears before he does, and Alice grabs it off the carousel. We can't lug all this stuff up and down the Berner Oberland, so I use the spare time to take a look inside. What I find makes Bethany look like a normal human being.

I thought we were trying to stay more or less anonymous. So why has he brought all the kids' homework which he has to mark? There are names, class numbers and even postal addresses all over it. I suppose he takes his work seriously but where's he planning to do all this? Does he think that in those little hiking huts up the Alps, for the total loony-tunes who stay out overnight, that they also include a desk or two where said loony-tunes can catch up on their paperwork? And why the frickin' bloody hell does this bozo have what appears to be the collected works of Bach printed out sheet by sheet in some gigantic volume of musical scores about the size of at least two telephone directories? Then there's a formal suit with a couple of shirts and ties. Is he worried that there's a dress code on glaciers or something? I daresay our biggest problem on this trip is not going to be getting KB'd by some Alpine bouncer because our names aren't on the list. He even has a small, fold-out, plastic sledge. Talk about stereotyping. This is borderline racist. It would be like a guy going to Australia in a hat with corks hanging off the brim and broadcasting in Harris' accent that he was there to billa-me-bong with a didgeridoo and a wallaby on the bairbie plus a couple of sheilas round me lunchbox.

He has a couple of elements worth keeping, notably some trainers-cum-boots which might actually replace those stupid knee-high leather jobs he has on at the moment. The water bottle is a vague concession to common sense and amazingly enough, he does seem to have taken on board the need for a cagoule in case of rain. The vague softening of my attitude is abruptly halted though by the discovery of a spare pair of jodhpurs. How is this guy even alive? I'm surprised he could find the correct exit out of his mother's womb.

Alice interrupts my thoughts with a heads-up that she's just seen Harris. I look up to see that he's approaching with a slightly downcast expression.

"Everything OK, Harris?"

He winces but replies, "I suppose so. I just don't recall being quite so insulted before. That horrible border guard made me feel as welcome in this country as a war criminal."

There are some who claim that the Swiss have historically been a shade too accommodating vis-à-vis war criminals, provided they leave a significant deposit of gold in an anonymous holding in a Zürich bank. However, this may not be the time to bring up politics.

Harris looks up across the hallway and a look of surprise envelops his face. A disbelieving smile follows, and he starts waving at someone.

"I don't believe it! That's Sammy Tuffnall over there! Hey, Sammy, over here, my man!"

It's lucky I have fast reactions. I throw myself onto Harris, knocking him to the ground and hold him down below the level of the carousel belt.

"My goodness, Ms Morriston!" he explains in a self-righteously injured tone. "I do not believe that we have this sort of relationship at all, nor that this of all places is where such a discussion should be held!"

My mood has soured considerably in the last second and a half. It isn't helped by the fact that every time I move a muscle, something squelches between Harris and me.

"Shut up, you brainless buffoon!" I hiss quietly through gritted teeth. "Just tell me, who the bloody hell is Sammy Tuffnall and what's he doing here? And keep your voice down!"

I move slightly to the left, mainly to avoid my entire hiking waistcoat turning into what looks like a used nappy.

"Sammy is a good friend of mine from school," explains Harris, still in a rather hurt tone. "I haven't seen him for a few months now, but I would suppose he's taking in the culture and sights round here."

I look up at Alice and ask quickly, "Does it look like that guy noticed us before we landed on the ground?"

"I don't think so," Alice tells me, "although that bunch of drunk lads over there sure as hell did. I heard one of them asking his friend if he thought you needed any condoms."

Ha bloody ha. I have worse concerns and turn back to Harris.

"Do you have any idea where Sammy is going next?"

"No," he says. "I just told you, I have no idea why he's here. I only wanted to say hello and see if maybe we were going the same way."

"The same way? As far as the rest of the world is concerned, Harris, you and Alice are in Taunton right now! If you start broadcasting your illegal, little venture here, it only takes Sammy to mention one word in a bar or post a photo on social media and our faces will be all over the next editions of both 'Bristol's Most Wanted' and 'Switzerland: Crims Caught on Alpine Tape!' We have got to put as much distance between ourselves and Geneva as fast as we can."

I whisk out my phone and look up the necessary.

"According to the SBB app, there's a train heading to Bern in twenty minutes. If we move, we can just about get everything done here which we need to do and still make it."

"SBB app?" he asks. This makes as much sense to him as a North Korean parking ticket.

"SBB is the Swiss federal rail service," I explain as I start to move off. "It also covers other public transport in the country, notably buses, trams and even boats. So it may come in quite handy on this trip. Now let's get going. Don't look hurried or furtive but just follow me and keep yourself to yourself."

Harris follows us in a rather subdued manner. Alice and I know the way after all, which of course he doesn't. Left out of the luggage area and straight along the corridor to where you exit the airport building. Next you enter the train station which is on the lower level where the airport arrivals come out. Harris looks a shade unimpressed as we press ahead.

"I thought this was supposed to be a beautiful, mountainous country," he complains.

Oh for frig's sake.

"Look, Harris," I reply over my shoulder, "first I don't really care what your initial impressions are but inasmuch as I have a shade of sympathy, we just arrived in the airport of the second largest city in Switzerland. Like most airports in urbanized areas, it's a glorified dump. Do you think Heathrow Airport looks much like Buckingham Palace, the Palace of Westminster or Windsor Castle? Exactly. Now stop whining and get moving."

Perhaps a little harsh but we have work to do.

Our first stop is the luggage lockers. Harris looks aghast as I chuck his extensive garbage into one and slam it shut, depositing my five francs to keep it all safe until we get back. I don't tell him that if everything goes tits up, we may be departing from Zürich instead and so he may not get back his precious sheet music until the autumn, but I don't need him worrying and complaining even more. If that happens, he can tell the school kids that the dog ate their homework in a neat reversal of stereotypes.

From there, we head to the ticket machines. I could, of course, use my SBB app to buy our tickets but that would leave an electronic trail which I do not want, especially since I would have to register each individual and that would include Alice. Her presence being the most legally dubious here, keeping our noses clean as far as possible is a very good plan. We've had to suck it up where the airline was concerned since you can't get anonymous tickets but that's too bad. Now that we're in Switzerland, at least we can make some progress by getting three tickets to Interlaken, paid for in cash.

I turn to Harris for the cash. He's the one bankrolling this trip. He dips into his wallet and pulls out a fifty-dollar bill in United States currency.

"What the hell is this?"

"Fifty dollars," he replies defensively.

"Where do you think we've come to? Colorado? Pretty impressive for a flight which only took one hour and fifteen minutes from London but I'm afraid we weren't actually in a hypersonic scramjet, and this isn't the USA."

"But they say that American dollars are a universal currency, and you can use them anywhere," he explains in an abashed tone.

"Well, yeah, if you've got time to exchange them into the local currency when you get there. That's the main point – you can exchange them pretty much anywhere, not necessarily spend them. And we've only come to a country two stops down from ours, if you like. Did it not occur to you just to get Swiss francs?"

"I did think about it," he sniffs, "but they were very expensive, you know."

It's not often that my jaw literally drops thanks to what somebody has said but it does now. How mind-blowingly dumb is this man? Does he really believe that each unit of national currency equals another in worth, such that one dollar buys the same as one franc, buys the same as one Euro and so on but that you can buy more of one than another with a single British pound? If so, we should have arrived with Indian rupees or Japanese yen. We'd be so rolling in it that we could forget about Karl Givret's clarinet and Switzerland and just take the next flight to Salzburg so we could buy Mozart's original harpsichord.

Anyway, think, Jessica, think. Swiss railway ticket machines do not accept US dollars in payment. That much we know, or at least I do. The train we want leaves in about six minutes which is not enough time to get to the currency exchange stand back in the airport and get ripped off for our US dollars. I never trust the exchange places in airports, and we also run an increased risk of running into Sammy Tuffnall in there. Furthermore, I do not want to hang around Geneva where we arrived and got our passports checked, nor do I want to show up, memorably swapping a couple of thousand dollars into Swiss francs like a DIY money launderer. So now what? I have about one hundred francs on me in total which is not going to be enough to get all three of us to Interlaken, even allowing for my annual half-price pass. Harris' idea that fifty dollars would have covered it was also based on total ignorance, in case you're wondering. It would have taken about three times that.

I glance up at the timetable board which looms large over the main hallway. Incredibly, inspiration strikes. The train we want is not an express. It stops at the bigger cities of Lausanne and Fribourg as well as a range of smaller towns and villages en route. Not a huge number but enough to make it slower than an express to Lausanne which is leaving in three minutes and stops nowhere before then. One hundred francs is more than enough to get the three of us to Lausanne. There we should just about have enough time to swap a few hundred dollars into francs before the train turns up which we wanted to get originally. I slam my hundred franc note into the machine and get three tickets out in a minute and a half. Both Alice and Harris look on bemusedly as I haven't had time to explain the plan, but I can bring them up to date on the train. That appears to be leaving from Platform 4 in one minute, so I propel the two of them towards it. We race across the concourse, Harris with a degree of prodding, and down the stairs leading to Platform 4. There's a train sitting there, the sound of the klaxon just beginning to announce its imminent departure. Alice throws herself through the doors which are just starting to slide closed but Harris, like the dork he is, freezes in front of the doorway. What's scaring him? Has he never used a train before? Doesn't he know that even if you block an automatic door, it will still open again in a few seconds? Well, he's about to find out. I take aim at his rear passageway and direct the sole of my heel straight into it with all the force I can. That makes me feel a whole lot better about quite a lot of things actually. Harris literally flies through the doorway, and the doors draw back for an instant. That provides enough of a window for me to leap through, accidentally clipping Harris' ribcage with my boot on landing but otherwise staying upright. He's lying on the floor and probably feeling like he's just been mugged but at least we've made it. The doors finally slide shut behind me and the train starts to move off.

We're on our way into the heart of Switzerland now.

Chapter 14

ANOTHER WORLD

Harris

My goodness, what a day I'm having. I don't recall when I've ever been so bombarded by shocks to the system, curt orders and physical assault. There have been other, truly memorable occasions for sure. The day when I proposed to Isabel and she accepted remains the happiest moment in my life. I still recall when I first performed solo at the age of seven and sung the whole of the Bach/Gounod "Ave Maria" during the Evening Service at the start of Advent. I remember winning the secondary school musician's trophy when I was eighteen and the Somerset County Young Music Teacher Award six years later.

Other memories pertain as well, some more pleasant than others. Family vacations to the Devon coast were always a highlight and I can well remember some of the more pleasant guesthouses where my uncle and aunt found accommodation for themselves, my brother and me. I am also forced to remember some of the less pleasant encounters with school bullies which have stuck in my mind but which, I hope, made me stronger by forcing me to keep up my dedication to music which mattered so much to me, even if not to them. And of course, my darling Isabel. I remember meeting her, courting her and every step in the plans I have for our life together, which go through my mind each day.

Such was the theory, at least, until this awful episode of Karl Givret's clarinet. That I had not planned although initially, it was such a wonderful scheme that I willingly embraced it into my canon of plans to provide Isabel with the best husband and partner she could ever wish for. And then it fell off the side of a mountain onto a glacier. That was never part of what I saw coming.

And now this. The difference between today and all those other days which make up my memories is that those days were essentially defined by signature events or particular locations. Today has been different. It has simply been one, never-ending cascade of what I can only describe as extreme unpleasantness, almost all of which has been directed at me. Perhaps in mainly a passive manner but it's hardly been enjoyable.

I still have to admit that Alice and her aunt are helping me at a dire point in my life when neither of them necessarily has to. For that, I can only be grateful. Logically, I cannot deny any of that. What I am finding increasingly hard to take is this endless barrage of disdain, contempt and even physical violence which has been directed at me over the course of our journey together. I never claimed to be the most experienced traveller or to have a full understanding of the ways of the world. All the same, I have tried to act as an honourable gentleman, exercising decorum and a sense of dignity which should generate and impart polite respect across all those whom I encounter. Instead, I have spent the day being shepherded around by a couple of the most unladylike females I could have imagined talking to who have sneered at what they term my lack of common sense. This in turn has provided the basis for my being treated like a mentally deficient toddler.

Alice is the one I find more shocking. I have known her for a couple of years now. A strong-willed but polite pupil and very talented in her piano skills, she could go a long way. She always struck me as being a shade independent-minded but that is not necessarily a bad thing, at least in moderation. But under the influence of this cultural vagabond who is, incredibly enough, a blood relation, it is as though she has become another girl entirely. The clear rapport between the two of them exceeds understanding but it is very suspicious. It strikes me that this can hardly be the first time when the two of them have engaged in disappearing into the wilds without leaving a trace and I cannot tell how they both seem so immediately au fait with the ins and outs of navigating Switzerland in particular. Worse than that, though, is how their logic, their sense of humour, their modes of expression and even their way of working are near identical. They dress the same way, carry the same sort of luggage and equipment, and take the same food and drink in most instances. The aunt – I suppose I should continue referring to her as Jessica – is the clear leader but Alice is a very willing and very capable sidekick. She has also assumed a certain parity with me, even a sense of superiority, which I find quite distressing. I am her teacher after all. However, Jessica has no inhibitions about putting me down and as the de facto number two around here, neither does Alice.

Nonetheless, I am an honest man, and I will not pretend that I would have made it onto this train, heading to Lausanne, without their guidance, however painful that may have been. Thanks to the leakages from that nasty, little piece of work on the aircraft, I am sitting on my own on a bench of two seats on the right side of the train. Alice and Jessica are sitting opposite me, conferring between themselves about various topics, some of which make sense to me and some not. I gather that quite a few concern mountain sports. They also seem very disparaging of Alice's parents which I find rather strange and quite inappropriate as a topic of discussion between them. By this stage though, I've learnt not to intervene in such matters. Instead, I take the chance to relax for a moment and regard the scenery. It seems the sensible choice. For some reason, Switzerland appears to be having a calming effect of sorts on the two of them. Their hitherto state of constant alert is diminished and the general feeling of irascibility, while hardly gone, feels a little more in the background. If I perhaps just hold my peace and admire the local sights, it might even be that we can spend a few moments of calm in each other's company.

We're heading along the edge of Lake Geneva. I believe it has another name in French, but I don't recall it. It certainly is a huge body of water, running from Geneva at one end to the southern intersection of France and Switzerland at the other. The day is a pleasant one, very warm and with a clear, blue sky. Given all I've heard about Switzerland, it doesn't look all that mountainous, but I can see some more impressive peaks in the distance. When I ask, however, Jessica informs me that those are the French Alps, including the famous Mont Blanc, the highest mountain in Europe. These peaks are set well back from the other side of the lake, sitting behind a range of smaller hills and mountains. On this side of the lake are mainly houses and gardens. I understand that the bulk of these serve as effective suburbs for some of the better off employees in Geneva itself, loosely equivalent to the huge area of suburbia known as Greater London in the South-East of England. It seems somewhat prettier than its English equivalent, mind you.

The overall effect is very pleasing on the eye. It just seems rather like other parts of France which I have visited on occasion. To the left of the train are mainly fields as well as a few vineyards, stretching back to another, lower range of mountains. I'm told that these are the Jura mountains, and are also located in France, at least for now. Further east, they enter what is legally Switzerland. The only issue I have with all this is that it doesn't strike me as looking at all like the place which Charles described to me where he lost the clarinet. It feels as though we've somehow come to the wrong country. Mustering my courage to brave whatever belittling riposte may be thrown back at me, I put this to Jessica and Alice. They look at me slightly curiously, but Jessica then answers in a surprisingly reconciliatory tone.

"The thing is, Harris, that right now we are on the lower level of Switzerland which essentially runs from Geneva in the west though to Lake Constance in the east. I may have mentioned this before but it's easy to forget until you see it. This arc curves around the north of the country and covers most of the 30% thereof which is not considered mountainous. South of it are the Alps. You've seen the French ones already on the horizon but that's because Geneva sticks out into France like a kind of political peninsula. Once we clear Lausanne and go behind the first set of hills on the Swiss side, we'll be properly in Switzerland. Then you can see how things develop."

"Thank you," I reply. I think she almost smiled although her eyes are focused on a packet of crisps in her hand.

As we approach Lausanne some forty minutes after leaving Geneva, Jessica briefs Alice and me. Mainly Alice since it seems she's being left to shepherd me while her aunt does the tricky stuff. Either way, we're back into high alert status so I had better be paying attention and doing what I'm told.

"Right, we jump off as soon as the train stops. We'll have eleven minutes until the next one comes in which is going to Bern. We could stay here in Lausanne, as we're probably far enough away from Geneva but I want to minimize our risks and get to Bern as soon as possible.

"We'll arrive on Platform 1 but we're going to need to switch to Platform 4. The passage connecting all platforms is a tunnel underneath them."

This remark is clearly directed at me. For whatever reason, it doesn't appear to be news to Alice.

"You two go straight to Platform 4 and head to where the front of the Bern train will be. I will run like hell to convert a thousand dollars into francs and then buy three tickets to Interlaken in cash. Then I'll make for Platform 4.

"As soon as you see me reach Platform 4, get onto the train. It doesn't matter if I reach you or not. Just get on board. I'll make my way up inside the train to join you at the front. If for some reason, you make it on board, but I don't or I fail to meet up with you inside the train for whatever reason, get out at Palézieux and wait for me there. I will reach it as soon as I can and if I'm not with you, I will be sure to get out there. It's the rendezvous point if we're not together after leaving Lausanne. You're at the front of the train so with any luck, the ticket inspector will have passed by before Lausanne and won't be back until after Palézieux. If he or she does show up, hide in the toilet and if you still get found, pretend you can only speak Spanish, act dumb as hell and get out at Palézieux because you've heard that there's a good burrito shop nearby."

"Like we did in Lenzburg?" Alice grins. "It didn't work all that well there, did it?"

"Well," her aunt retorts slightly impatiently, "it would have done if that random, Mexican dude hadn't shown up who actually lived there for some reason and told us all that there was no burrito shop anywhere nearby. I mean, how unlucky can you get? But that was hardly my fault, and it still worked more or less. OK, so that was mainly because the ticket inspector spoke no Spanish and was too confused to bother arguing the toss between a valid train ticket and an Emmental burrito. But it wasn't a complete disaster, for frig's sake."

Alice grins again. What on earth have these two been doing previously? It may be best not to dwell on the topic. It seems that there's no time anyway as we slow down, heading into Lausanne. A pleasant town, it seems, full of eighteenth and nineteenth century architecture although it's noticeably more modern and uglier nearer to the station itself.

The train draws to a halt and Jessica is out of the door like a bat out of hell. The woman has no class in my view, but I will grant that she can take decisive action. I suppose we all have some strong points.

Alice nudges my elbow and guides me along the platform to a series of steps leading downwards. I would have liked to admire the handsome building of the main station which has a spacious entrance hall topped by a very high yet reasonably modest ceiling. From the small amount I've seen so far, the Swiss appear to go for a pleasing aesthetic based on functionality offset by a confidence in scale which hints at an unrealised grandeur. It may be considerably less grandiose than what you might find among their southern neighbours in Italy but also less ostentatious.

Such are my basic impressions although I may have to leave it at that since Alice reminds me rather sharply that we're not here as tourists and that we need to move on. Very quickly. Like aunt, like niece, I suppose, at least when you get the two of them together. We descend the stairs into the tunnel described by Jessica and progress through it until a sign indicates another stairway leading up to Platform 4. We take that and emerge back into the sunlight. Further away from the main building of the station, the individual platforms are much more functional and almost like their equivalents in England except that the graffiti is in French. There's also less of it, to be fair. There are computer screens at regular intervals along the platform. As far as I can tell, they map out the next train expected according to its carriages, but I can't tell for the life of me what any of it actually means.

Again, it seems that Alice has no problem in finding her way around, in this instance deciphering whatever those screens are telling us.

"Sector A, Coach B," she says to nobody in particular, then to me directly, "which is up there. Let's move!"

She leads on to the far end of the platform. Sector A seems so far away to me that we might as well be walking to Bern and it's all I can do to keep up with her. We make it eventually and I look for somewhere to sit down for a moment. This is exhausting. Alice continues to stand, watching back to the exit from the stairway coming up from the tunnel.

At this point, a gigantic train approaches. It has two decks, and I cannot see the end of it. Presumably, this is the train to Bern, but I just do not understand. This is a regular service and nothing special, I believe. How can there be so many people travelling around this country that they need such massive contraptions running every other hour? I start to phrase this question but get cut off by Alice in a way which I would certainly not tolerate in school.

"Mr Beadlesby, just shut your cakehole! I don't give a rat's ass what you make of Swiss trains! Where's Auntie Jess?" she comes out with in a rather steely tone. Her gaze is fixed on that stairwell.

The train itself stands still for a couple of minutes while a considerable crowd of people move onboard. Few exit. There is still no sign of Jessica.

The sound of the engines revving up becomes louder and Alice grows more agitated. She starts scanning the far platforms next to the main station building but she sees no trace of her aunt. Clearly she's worried and she hops from one foot to the next.

The guard on the platform is standing with whistle and flag ready when Jessica seems to fly up the stairs and emerge from them at a run, somehow making a ninety-degree turn without slowing down. Alice sprints across to the train door next to us and slams her fist into the button to open it. The guard gives us an evil stare but declines to react further as we jump on board. I glance over my shoulder just in time to note that Jessica has likewise made it on board although she did appear to be both horizontal and airborne at the moment of entering.

Alice and I proceed upstairs and take seats by the window on the right-hand side again. I do believe that the stench of my clothing has diminished by now, but she nonetheless continues to sit opposite rather than next to me.

Five minutes later, there's still no sign of Jessica, but the scenery does become quite majestic. The train climbs out of Lausanne and ascends through hilly countryside next to us. It is mainly covered in neat rows of vineyards, which lead down to a series of villages running along the side of the lake below us. Immediately on the other side of the lake is an imposing range of mountains which certainly justify that term, even if I cannot see any snow or ice on top of them. Their sides stand almost sheer above a tiny slither of land running along the base, next to the lake. However, I can make out trees and a few houses along the mountainsides at various points so there must be a way up there.

Another range of mountains immediately above us reaches to the blue sky on our left, which Alice tells me are the start of the Swiss Alps on the western end. However, my attention is drawn back to our right and the lake as the track curves around it and the view is frankly breathtaking. It looks as though a gigantic semi-horseshoe of land, covered in green vineyards, fields and trees, is stretching down to the road and houses next to the lake, at which point it stretches back for miles towards Geneva. Geneva itself is no longer visible by some way, but the lake disappears into a fine haze which is arising from that direction though a long way off. The other side of the water is framed by those impressive mountains, and the sunlight pours through and covers us in a golden sheen. This light envelops us from outside where the sun is shining brightly from about halfway up the sheer blue of the sky. I can see for miles, and it is like nothing I've seen before, almost like a painting.

I suppose nothing lasts forever. The train curves back around to the left, leaving the lake behind us. I can see the land at the other end of the lake briefly. A flat surface of green fields spreads out for quite a distance before running into the two sides of a large valley, which rise sharply upwards. The stretch of fields narrows progressively but quickly, snaking into a much narrower passage between the two, closing walls around it. I suppose that is the way into the main body of the Swiss Alps, but I only see it briefly before the train enters an extended tunnel to the left and comes out shortly afterwards with the mountain ranges a little way off to the right and receding while we continue into a set of woodlands. These don't last for long before we emerge into what looks like a series of rolling hillsides.

It's all really quite charming. I'm even starting to relax a shade. Alice is proving very helpful too, explaining things to me and pointing out various intricacies of Switzerland. One example she stresses are these odd arrows showing the direction of various hiking paths, even at the lower levels where we are finding ourselves just now. These have placenames accompanied by what looks like a series of numbers and letters. Alice outlines how these are times and indicate approximately how long it should take to reach the destination referred to if you walk at a regular pace. For example, "Montreux 2h 20min" shows that if you follow the route, you should reach Montreux in around two hours and twenty minutes. I'm not quite sure what constitutes a regular pace although I have a nasty suspicion that it may be faster than I can manage. I do hope we don't end up having to walk too far.

Alice is still talking to me more like an equal than a pupil addressing a teacher, but her tone is no longer as short-tempered as it was earlier in the day. I'm increasingly certain that her aunt is not a good influence. And there really is more going on where she is concerned than I know. Alice mentioned that her aunt was allowed to take her on some gentle hikes around the Swiss lakes now and again during the summer months when Alice's parents were otherwise engaged. However, she was very vague about the details. It does make me wonder how come she knows the country so well and is such an expert on its mountains and hiking routes. I daresay she talks with her aunt a lot but much of what she says sounds as though it stems more from first-hand than second-hand information. I do not want to upset things by asking. I would rather have a quiet life and on a certain level, I suppose it's not really my business.

The quiet life suddenly vanishes even more quickly than the scenery of Lake Geneva as Jessica returns.

"Bloody hell!" she intones as she drops down on the seat next to Alice. I assume whatever she's saying is intended for her niece rather than me. She also appears somewhat damp.

"Where have you been, Auntie Jess?" asks Alice, slightly annoyed but also quite clearly relieved at the same time. "It's ages since we left Lausanne!"

"Well, I didn't realise that I was going to have to hike inside the train," retorts Jessica. "This is Coach B, right? Well, I only managed to get on at Coach I. So there was some way to come.

"When I jumped on, I caught myself on the fire extinguisher and ended up lying on the floor with my head stuck somewhere between my armpit and my belly button. That was when I realised that wrestling our pal over there to the ground in the airport," she indicates me, "had left me with enough of that toddler's ready-digested couscous impression spread over my own clothes to give me a somewhat unpleasant aroma."

Alice looks at her uncertainly and sniffs a couple of times before adding cautiously, "Well, I don't think it's that bad."

"I damn well hope not," Jessica tells her, "because I just spent fifteen minutes in the toilet, trying to wash it out and I do believe I got somewhere with it.

"However," she opens up and then pauses momentarily for what I suppose is dramatic effect, "I didn't realise that my legs also had some of the stench on them. This became clear when I reached Coach E."

"Isn't that where the restaurant and snack bar are?" Alice asks.

"No, that's Coach D and trust me, I know. I know very well for reasons you'll understand in a moment.

"So anyway," she continues at a suddenly faster pace, "I'm passing through Coach E when some nasty, little runt of a dog comes running up to me. I think it was some sort of small terrier. I don't know. I don't do dogs. They shed too many hairs, craps and everything in-between for my liking."

"Yes, Auntie Jess, I know. It's not like I've never heard this before. What happened?"

"The stupid thing must have smelled my trousers and decided that I was the next best thing to a popular tree because it straightaway leant against me and raised its hind leg!"

"No way!" gawps Alice. "We're in Switzerland, aren't we? You have to train your dog properly here!"

"Yes, so I thought as well," sniffs Jessica. "Maybe these owners were British or something. As far as I can tell, you can get a license to own a dog in Liverpool for few more qualifications than being able to spell D-O-G and even that's optional. But over here, that sort of thing is a nigh-on capital offence. Or so I thought. Clearly not in this instance.

"I wasn't going to stand around for this," she continues, "so I drop-kicked the little bastard down the corridor before it could get going. At least, that was the plan. Yeah, I know, there were a million and one reasons why I shouldn't have done that, but it just really got to me, being used like some sort of public convenience by some lazy yobbo's dog."

She stops for a moment and glances around nervously before continuing the story.

"The thing was, it must have been desperate to go or something because it was already starting to spray when I booted it, so it flew down the passageway, giving everyone on the left-hand side a golden shower as it passed. I also must have applied a bit more force than I'd meant to because it shot through the opening at the end of the carriage and carried straight on into Coach D."

Alice is staring at her in wide-eyed wonder.

"How did you get out of that one?" she asks excitedly.

"Well," explains Jessica, "first of all I swore loudly and profusely in German, then legged it through after the dog into Coach D. That was where I saw that it had flown into the snack bar and got its head stuck in the freezer."

"Awesome!" Alice chuckles.

I don't see anything humorous in any of this but that seems to be entirely beside the point as far as these two are concerned.

"It took them about twenty seconds to pull it out," Jessica continues, "and you should have seen it then. Its eyes were wide, wide open and it was covered in ice. Do you know what a terrier which has had its head stuck in a freezer for twenty seconds looks like? A bit like Nigel Farage if he'd got drunk and then sat on an electric fence, that's what!"

Her earlier inhibitions about broadcasting this story have clearly evaporated as she labours the point further and remarks, "If he tries licking his balls any time soon, it'll be more like having a salty choc ice!

"As soon as this happened, I switched into French and expressed my shock and horror at the terrible thing which had happened to the poor dog and how I hoped they would find that horrible, German lady who had done this. Then I got the hell out and shoved my way through Coach C as annoyingly as I could, saying, 'Scuse me, love, I fink I've 'ad a bit much to drink' and burping loudly as I went. Everyone will have noticed me, but they'll all think I'm English."

"Well, you are," Alice points out.

"Of course, but the drop-kicking dog assailant, whom nobody physically saw except in Coach E, was speaking German. So with any luck, if anyone's bothering to follow up on this, they'll be looking for someone else called Heidi, Kerstin or Gretchen, not Jessica. They won't have any leads on me!"

The two of them cackle away over this one. Frankly, I find it revolting. What would the RSPCA make of this? Jessica would be up on a criminal charge in a heartbeat. Except, I'm forced to reflect, they probably don't have any jurisdiction in Switzerland. What on earth am I doing with people like this? Would I ever treat a poor animal like that?

Oh dear. A horrible thought occurs to me. There does seem to be something of a trend with airborne dogs and the disastrous route my life is taking right now. Really though? I never touched that bulldog. Jessica deliberately propelled the terrier down the train. Then again, I did accidentally – I stress, accidentally – punch the bulldog's owner. And the bulldog is, sadly, dead. The terrier, I understand, is still alive despite Jessica's best efforts. Am I somehow becoming like her without ever intending to do so? Do her aura of casual indifference and her distinctly cavalier moral code infect those around her by some kind of osmosis? Is that what happens to Alice in her presence?

I cannot say but I shall take a moment of silence in which to reflect upon the suffering of those unfortunate dogs. It feels like the decent thing to do.

The ambience changes almost imperceptibly but definitely, nonetheless. My two companions finally take a break from regaling each other with lowbrow jokes and a mix of observations which seem to range from coarse to faux intellectual for no better reason than that they can each understand both French and German. Alice is probably not fluent yet, but her aunt seems to be perfectly adept in both languages, at least as far as I can tell. Alice pulls her reading material out of her bag and proceeds with it. All I can say is that I'm confused. Her aunt actually looks rather bewildered by it, but I would have assumed that it would have been her influence which was most likely to have inspired Alice to indulge in such smut in the first place. Please don't let there be two such influences in her life.

Still, a relative calm has descended, and I take the opportunity to enjoy it. The scenery since the tunnel is markedly different to what it was sooner. Where before was a range of pastureland to the left with a lake to the right, shadowed by mountains behind it, we're now in the middle of a series of rolling hillsides. I can only say that it really is very picturesque. The overall effect is a mixture of farmlands and woodlands, with various villages and farms interspersed among them. Many of these buildings in fact are of the chalet style, which is associated with Switzerland and so, I suppose, not simply a stereotype. The landscape rolls away to the horizon on either side. It shines in various shades of green, lighter across the fields and darker across the woods. There are still some yellows in some of the fields, and the sky is a brilliant blue with a shining sun and only a handful of clouds dotted around it.

In some ways, it reminds me of the landscape of a fairy tale, such as children read. Those stories, supposedly set in a sanitized version of medieval times, where the heroes and heroines go on a long quest or even just a journey, are ones which I always pictured in what would be a Teutonic landscape. Hardly surprising, I suppose, given the influence of the Brothers Grimm in bringing them together. That said, I don't recall actually seeing such a landscape before me until now, but it really is very much what I was imagining. You can see the spires of Churches and towers of castles set on top of hills or sticking up from little hollows behind them. Walking paths twist across and between the fields, disappearing into forests and then emerging a short while later. The train passes along a ridge or two and you can see down to a medium-sized river, surrounded by rows of dense trees climbing up the steep banks next to them. However, there is no sense of threat there since there is always some form of bridge or crossing in place. Sometimes the train also passes along the top of a steep slope, and you can look down the length of the hillside, seeing it descend to the bottom of a gentle valley, which rises to the same level across from you but with some woodland or a small chalet at the same height opposite.

It also feels like something of a relief. These hillsides do not look as intimidating as what I've been expecting. I daresay there are some higher ones somewhere but that feels like another world away. Jessica is also looking at the scenery as we pass by. A light smile of contentment sits below her eyes, and the hitherto almost constant sense of sarcasm seems strangely removed. I decide that it might be time to try some friendlier conversation.

"So, Jessica," I begin, "I understand this part of the world is quite special for you."

She looks round briefly and eyes me curiously. I don't know why. Perhaps she's trying to assess whether I'm genuinely interested in her love of the mountains or if I'm trying to find out something else. I hold her gaze and stare back firmly but without any sense of confrontation. You do learn one or two useful tricks as a schoolteacher.

She turns her head back slightly towards the window as another wood flashes by.

"Well, it's not for everyone," she says, almost apologetically for whatever rationale she has. "I think you'll find that the Costa del Sol is way more full of Brits at this time of year. Actually, it's probably way more full of Swiss at this time of year."

She chuckles sardonically at that line before continuing, "But I like it here. I don't really know why but you can see partly why out of this window. At least on a good day, it's simply beautiful in a way which doesn't change. It's peaceful as well. You can see how the countryside expands to the horizon. You could walk for miles in that and never reach the end but there's no reason to hurry if you don't want to. It'll all still be there. So long as you don't just want to sit on your butt and wait for something to happen, you can make of it what you want, and it'll always look good."

Allowing for a momentary lapse into vulgarity, that's actually quite a thoughtful description.

"At the same time, like I mentioned before we left, the mountains are not your friend. The weather can change fast, and it can be scorchingly hot or numbingly cold. You can be happily trotting along a gentle ridgeway and then turn a corner to find there's a climb the height of a skyscraper in front of you. You have to treat this place with respect. But if you do, then there's a real sense of achievement.

"You see all these postcard tourists sitting around in tourist trap towns conveniently located at a major rail intersection," she remarks snidely before adding in a somewhat surprised tone, "but I really don't know why they bother. They pay a fortune to come to what's basically a highly artificial impression of something real which is just above them and absolutely stunning, except that they would need to make an effort to get up there, to navigate a bit and to find their way to a real vantage point which isn't just a manufactured café. There is so much real space but hardly anybody seems to go there. It's amazing. The trains can be crowded on a weekend if you're going to somewhere in the Berner Oberland. You think to yourself that it would be quieter on the London Underground. You get out at the station and find yourself just about tripping over a sea of designer handbags, last season's polo shirts and cameras which are probably better than what most professional journos use. You almost wonder if this vast crowd is going to leave enough oxygen for you to breathe before you have an aneurysm. Then you find your way to the next hiking path going upwards and within literally five minutes, it's as though there's nobody there.

"You see, that's what I mean. You have to put in the effort here. You have to be prepared for everything which might happen, and you also have to be prepared for days of disappointment, not least when you can't see anything because there's mist and rain everywhere or you've hiked into the cloud line. But when it does go right, it's just so rewarding.

"And you get swallowed up into this massive world where all the work schedules, the rent payments, the utility bills, the endless e-mails and even your in-laws basically don't exist. I don't mean that negatively. Of course, they're still out there and I'm not simply trying to get out of my life. Hell, I could just sit at home in Liverpool and smoke pot if leaving the regular life behind was all I wanted."

I'm learning to live with these interjections by now.

"What I do mean is that in addition to the world I inhabit on a regular basis, it feels as though there's another one up there which I can go to, explore and enjoy all I want to, whenever I have the chance. It's a great feeling."

"Does it not get a bit lonely?" I ask. "I take your point about the quality of it all but given the fitness and experience you need, which are clearly not something everyone has, don't you end up spending a lot of time on your own?"

"What's new?" she comes back with, a shade gruffly before changing to a brighter tone. "I don't know. I suppose it can be a shade lonesome but then again, you have to distinguish between being lonely and being alone. The two are not always the same thing, despite what some people think.

"I personally would rather be up there on my own and able to proceed in a combination of beautiful sights and smells, than trying to pick my way along with some whiner who wants to stop for a sandwich every five minutes or blanches at the thought of climbing anything higher than their own garage. Also, I can speak German and even get by, though only to a limited extent, in Swiss German. Still, that's a whole lot better than most Brits can do, and when I pitch up for the evening in a local hotel, they could hardly be nicer most of the time. Sure, they can all speak English, don't worry, but the fact that somebody has gone to the bother of learning their language when they don't strictly have to, seems to count for quite a bit. Maybe that's why I tend to avoid Italophone Switzerland. I believe it's gorgeous to see but I can't speak Italian and don't want to become just another tourist.

"Still, I take your point. It would be nice to share a hike with somebody, provided that they wanted to be there as much as I do, and probably provided that they were at about the same fitness level as I am. Those two things would be very important because without one of them, it would quickly become a chore. Unlike the Costa del Sol though, there aren't that many people who fit into such a category."

Alice looks up briefly from her novel.

"But Auntie Jess, I can - "

"Sshh, Alice!" she cuts her off. "Some day, sure, but we both know that you're not quite there yet, don't we?"

"Would you like Alice to join you?" I ask, genuinely interested. "It sounds like a smashing idea to me if you're both fit enough."

Jessica seems to be taking a moment to consider her next words carefully.

"I suppose so," she responds a shade wistfully, "but it'll have to wait."

She looks out of the window almost dreamily.

"What would be amazing one day would be to get one of those one-month country passes which gives you unlimited access across the whole of Switzerland. It covers everything except air travel, for obvious reasons as the only internal airline routes are Geneva to Zürich and that's an environmentally unfriendly waste of time and money anyway. But trains, buses, cable cars, even boats – you can get anywhere. Well, you can if you can afford it but that's going to take a bit of saving on my part. A year or two down the line at least."

She turns to Alice and smiles.

"One day though, you and I are going to get two of them and have the best holiday ever!"

Alice looks up and beams back at her with real affection. A look of mild consternation then crosses her face.

"I don't know how we'll get Mum's permission for that though," she adds. "Not unless the pass includes a 24-hour bodyguard protection in case a random yodeller tries to mug me with a fondue pot."

"There's always a way, Alice," Jessica replies. "I just haven't thought of it yet."

This is a rather different exchange between the two of them. I can't recall hearing them talk for more than a couple of minutes before without lapsing completely into glib humour, sarcastic commentary or passive aggressive commands, admittedly allowing an exception for the inappropriate remark by Alice about her mother. Then again, this is perhaps the first time when I've been with them and there hasn't been any pressure to achieve an outcome or avoid some unpleasantness. I doubt their kindlier personas will last long once we get into the core business of this trip but I'm enjoying the change while I can. That being the case, it might be a good moment to see if I can get away with returning to a certain point which has been nagging at me for a short while since Jessica mentioned it.

"If you don't mind me asking, Jessica, I'm very grateful for your help and I don't for a moment imagine that I should have any attitude problem, such as you described earlier. I mean the people who would complain about having to take some exercise.

"I do also know, and I'm merely being upfront here, that I'm not as advanced as you are in terms of physical fitness. As you're aware, I'm a music teacher, not a gym teacher. All the same," I add hastily, "I've been looking at these hillsides we're passing, and I do believe that I can give a pretty good account of myself regardless so I'd like to assure you that you shouldn't find me too lacking. Are you prepared to take my word on that much, at least?"

There's a moment's awkward silence. Jessica and Alice stare at me strangely before looking at each other. A raised eyebrow passes briefly across Jessica's face before she reverts to me, leaning forwards slightly. Perhaps that awful child's smell is finally lessening a bit.

"Harris," she sighs briefly, "I'll give you credit for a decent attitude but what you're looking at out there are hillsides. You could walk up and down something similar in the Lake District. If that's all there was to the Alps, do you think I would bother coming to Switzerland?

"Here's another question for you." Her voice lowers to almost a whisper for a moment. "Your friend told you that the clarinet was lost on a glacier, didn't he? Do you see any hills around here which look anywhere near high enough to have a full glacier on top of them in summertime?"

She sits back again and then looks out of the window.

"Do you see the far horizon?" she asks and nods towards what appear to be a series of jagged teeth reaching up into the sky.

"Yes," I reply stiffly. I'm not that stupid. "I do appreciate that there are mountains over there, but it looks as though they're another world away. Are we going that far?"

"Absolutely," she sniffs. "Those mountains are a lot closer than they might appear from here. That's where we're going."

She looks around again to check that nobody else other than Alice will be overhearing us.

"The reason I'm not too concerned is that the overall plan does not involve any hiking. If we can get air transport onto the glacier, grab the instrument and then get back again, the only real hiking we'll have to do will be round Interlaken, looking for an amenable helicopter business.

"If we do have to hit a serious hiking trail, you'd better be ready for the time of your life, and not in a way which you'll enjoy."

I gulp a little and ask, "Is that why we have the equipment with us?"

"Yes, that's why. We can hardly rely on everything going totally to plan and it seems to me that there's a good chance that we could still end up having to find our way around in what is a very mountainous part of the world. For example, what if part of the precious clarinet somehow rolled over the edge of the glacier and down the slope below it? A helicopter won't go down there but it'll still be high enough that we'll have to walk up some way to get it. Just one possibility for you to consider. If that happens, I suggest you just keep putting one foot in front of the other and think about a Bach opera."

"Bach never wrote an opera," I inform her with a slight degree of satisfaction at finally knowing something which she doesn't.

"Fair enough," she acknowledges with a small shade of humility before brightening up. "Mind you, Ian Fleming never wrote a scene where James Bond parachutes out of the back of a burning jeep crashing over the Rock of Gibraltar, just in time to score with a fit bird on a yacht below. But that didn't stop Tim doing it in, 'The Living Daylights'. That's something I could think about if I wanted to distract myself."

I presume she's referring to one of those James Bond films she seems so keen on but really have no clue what she's talking about beyond that. Things crashing over the sides of cliffs and catching fire, however, are not really to my taste. Let's just enjoy the moment of relative balm, I reckon.

After passing through various stops, notably the city of Fribourg, we're now approaching Bern. I have to say, I'm not entirely impressed by Switzerland's capital. There's concrete and graffiti everywhere and the scenery has quickly given way to an industrial wasteland. Electric wires obscure the sky at multiple points and if this is where we're supposed to be going, then I don't know what all this talk about hiking has been in aid of.

"Oh, get a grip, Harris," Jessica responds when I voice my concerns. "Have you never travelled by train before? This is what stations look like the world over in cities. London, Liverpool, Bern, Rome, New York, Hamburg, probably everywhere except maybe Pyongyang, it's the same thing. Some idiot with a spray can turns up to decorate the walls on the way in every time. It's such a common feature that nobody even bothers trying to make the stations look nice. They just stick a load of concrete and train depot crap to lie around so that nobody cares whether it gets spray-painted or not. How come the supposed artists haven't twigged to this yet, I don't know.

"As to your question as to whether this is what Bern looks like, the swift answer is no. We're going to Bern the Canton, not the city, which we're only passing through. There are several Cantons with the same name as the principal city so it's hardly a big deal. We already passed through two of them in the shapes of Geneva and Fribourg, in case you didn't notice. In fairness to Bern the city too, beyond this crappy bit round the station, it's actually quite a pleasant place. Its main negative feature is more just that it's a bit boring."

The train starts to slow down, and she rouses Alice from her novel, then looks at me.

"OK, so when we arrive, we'll have eight minutes to get the next train to Interlaken. It's right across the platform so shouldn't be difficult. Just try not to do anything which a normal person wouldn't."

That last remark is quite clearly for my benefit rather than Alice's. I suppose we're back to patronizing put-downs and overbearing commands already, I see. Rather than retort, I decide that the best thing will be to maintain that stiff upper lip, for which we British are so renowned, and follow her instructions without question. I shall make myself a demonstrably able follower and maybe even garner a modicum of respect.

That plan falls flat on its face within thirty seconds of exiting our train on Platform 4 and crossing over to Platform 3. Not all Swiss are quite as pristine and tidy in their habits as the stereotype would have you believe. This much I find out as my right foot slips in a pool of bright yellow sludge, and I fall backwards onto my bottom. Given that it still smarts from where Jessica kicked me onto the train in Geneva, this is doubly painful.

I understand from Alice that what I slipped in was probably somebody's vomit. How lovely.

"Get that, Auntie Jess! This isn't Platform One, it's Platform Chum!"

Any consideration of the pain I may be suffering is instantly erased in a cascade of laughter. The original pairing is back in action. There's no doubt of that in my mind.

Jessica proceeds to shepherd us onto the smaller train which is, I believe, heading for Interlaken. There are limited seats, but we find a single one about halfway down the carriage. Jessica tells me to sit down which I do with a notable squelching sound. Something yellow oozes from under my behind. The other passengers seated next to me regard me with a look of disgust and one of them, a slightly elderly lady, even holds her hand to her nose. Jessica says something loudly in German, which I do not understand, and immediately the passenger next to me and the two opposite leap out of their places, grab their bags and move away to find alternative seating.

"What did you say?" I ask her.

"Trust me, you don't want to know," she replies, wrinkling her own nose but still sitting down on one of the seats opposite. "Let's just hope they have laundry facilities when we get there."

The train moves off at this point and we proceed swiftly out of the city and into what I believe is referred to as the Berner Oberland. That said, these so-called Bernese Highlands still look like glorified hills to me. Pleasant enough but hardly the precipices and huge heights I've been told to expect. I decide not to bother asking this time though.

That's maybe just as well as there's a strange transformation. At no point do the hills suddenly turn into mountains. They just seem to grow a little and move closer to the track. When you can see behind them, there now appears to be something even bigger there. I'm facing backwards but when I turn around, the same effect is there, moving forwards. We're just moving on and on into what seem to be increasingly high hills. Except that at a certain point, we seem to be next to what I would myself consider mountains. It's a strange effect but a very impressive one. There remain hills next to us, but they are quite clearly only foothills in front of a much higher range which starts immediately behind them.

My previous confidence is a little shaken, I admit. It would not be easy to go scaling these heights. It would certainly take a bit more effort on my part than a stroll around the hilly vales of Somerset. That said, they don't look all that severe, do they? They're not the sky-high peaks which Jessica was spending so much time lecturing me on. That's reassuring. Isn't it?

Then again…

Jessica remains transfixed to the window, looking forwards. I twist myself around to look in the same direction and that's when I see what she's gazing at in almost wide-eyed wonder. There are the Alps. The hilly and less mountainous country currently around us has by no means finished its ascent and development. In fact, it's only just started. Looking round, I can see that it continues on as far as the eye can see, throwing up ever higher ridges and peaks. There are the treelines which Jessica described earlier, with Alpine meadows on top of them. Still further but becoming increasingly clear are vast heights with clear lines of snow at the top. The temperature is quite intense down here but up there, something must be keeping it cool, and I understand that's the height. I know from colleagues in the geography department that the temperature decreases by one degree for every hundred metres gained in height. Don't ever listen to those who say that we teachers can't learn from each other.

The train stops briefly in some small station. I look for the name and see it on the platform.

"Hhmm," I say to nobody in particular, "Thun."

I've pronounced it as you would, "thumb" in English, just with an n at the end. Jessica looks up immediately and corrects me like an errant schoolchild.

"Toon," she says, "it's pronounced Toon. The h is silent and the letter u in German is always pronounced oo.

"It is important to know," she carries on in a more friendly though still brisk tone, "since we're going to be working around the Thunersee, which means Lake Thun in English."

She has pronounced Thunersee, "Too-ner-zay" which I assume is the correct pronunciation in German.

"Oddly enough, Thun also means tuna in German, so how they ended up with this name, I can't say but it's worth noting that Interlaken itself lies between two lakes, Lake Thun and Lake Brienz, which are west and east of the town, respectively. We'll be operating around the Thunersee side if we can. Thun sits at the head of the lake. From it, you can travel around the lake on the north or the south shore. This train is going to be following the lake around its southern side to get to Interlaken."

"Is that the next stop?" I enquire.

"No," Jessica murmurs, all of a sudden quite wistful almost. "There's one stop in-between which is Spiez."

She pronounces this, "Shpeets". I'm doing my best to learn.

Alice chips in at this point, suddenly smirking up at Jessica and then turning to me with a knowing expression on her face.

"Auntie Jess is in love with Spiez, you see," she informs me in an almost didactic manner. "Aren't you, Auntie Jess?"

Jessica scowls briefly but replies, "I just really like it, that's all. It's a pretty town, right next to half my favourite hiking routes but easy to get to and with plenty of space just to chill out.

"You see," she turns to me, "Spiez is technically a tourist trap but it's nowhere near as bad as Interlaken since it's smaller and it's a tourist trap for mainly Germanophone tourists who are not as easily taken in and overcharged as those from the anglophone world and Asia. As a result, it still has some character and retains the charm of a small town. It has a great marina, a vineyard and a castle which includes a Chapel dating from the tenth century AD."

Goodness me. This is almost like a new Jessica. She sounds like a live tourist brochure but she's selling me this town in a way which indicates a real enthusiasm for cultured charm, and with no obvious sarcasm. What can this place be like?

"Of course, it's also home to the Spiez Laboratory which is the Swiss Federal Institute for Nuclear, Biological and Chemical Protection but at least someone might be able to get your jodhpurs cleaned up there."

Maybe a long-term escape from the sarcasm was too much to hope for. That ceases again at this point, however, as Jessica herself stops talking and looks fixedly out of the window. I turn around again to follow her gaze, raising my arm to shield my eyes from the sun in the process which I see causes Alice to raise her handkerchief to her nose. I admit that I do really need to freshen up a bit, but it has no effect on Jessica who stays glued to the view.

Coming up is a picturesque town, bordering the lake. It appears to be situated above something a little like a half-bowl. Green sides run down from above to form a park at the bottom which joins a small harbour full of sailing boats. It extends into the lake in a horseshoe shape. To the left of the harbour, the tower of a castle stands above the water. On the left-hand side of the horseshoe, coming back towards us from behind the castle is a vineyard which stretches back to a large hill, covered in trees, which borders the lake itself. Behind and above the other two sides of the bowl, opposite the forested hill, stands the town itself, which overlooks the park and harbour and stretches back a short distance. Further back, the town seems pretty enough although more functional than truly picturesque. However, this is probably what makes it a functional town and not simply a beauty spot with no practical application. It's a pity that there doesn't seem to be a concert hall but I daresay the castle courtyard could accommodate a marquee at this time of year.

Presumably, this is Spiez since Jessica seems incapable of taking her eyes off it, at least until we get into the station which is predictably grubby. I don't know if Spiez can be considered a miniature version of Bern, but it certainly has the station for it. Jessica at this stage looks up and sighs.

"I wish I could live here. I mean, if I didn't have to go to the agency every now and then, and if I had a Swiss work permit, and if I could afford the rent, then this would be a big improvement on Liverpool."

"Those are quite of lot of ifs," Alice reminds her. "And besides, what good would you be here? They hardly need somebody who can speak German, and you wouldn't make much cash in a place where ninety per cent of the population can speak English better than your average Scouser either."

"Thanks for the encouragement, Alice," Jessica groans, "but you're right. It's just a dream, not an ambition. I probably wouldn't think so highly of it if I really did live here anyway. The weather would be crap in the autumn and winter, people's dogs would take a dump on my front doorstep or there would be some sex-addicted pervert upstairs from me with a very strange fetish involving salami pizzas. These sorts of things always happen everywhere, don't they?"

Maybe they do in Liverpool, but I think Bristol may be a little more genteel. At least, I hope my pupils and I won't end up sharing Jessica's life experiences to date.

Alice adopts a more reconciliatory tone as the train pulls out.

"Cheer up, Auntie," she smiles. "I'm just telling you it like it is but that doesn't mean it's all so bad. You can still find plenty of times to come here and when you do, they'll still seem that bit better because they're special and not just what you do every other day. And that's not a dream, that's a genuine reality."

Jessica smiles back, slightly ruefully. She doesn't say anything, but she reaches over and ruffles Alice's hair for a moment. The two of them then go back to watching the scenery.

After leaving Spiez, the train makes good time along the south side of the lake. Opposite us on the north side are some vast, densely forested slopes which, I learn, Jessica has been up and down quite a few times already. On foot. My earlier hopes have been dashed now. If we do find ourselves having to make our way without transportation, I will be completely out of my depth now.

The late afternoon sunshine does give a soft glow which is very pleasing. The water laps up to almost just below the train but there are several stretches of grass alongside as well, where people lie sunbathing or are even going swimming. It seems a world away from the land of hardened adventure which my co-travellers seem dressed and equipped for. But the looming slopes on the other side of the lake are a constant reminder that we are not here on holiday and that there is more to this place than some relaxation in the sun. However, for the moment, the world seems to be at peace. If Jessica and Alice are at peace here as well, then there has to be something right with this part of the world.

That may be but it isn't going to stay right for long. A voice in German announces over the interphone system something which I obviously cannot understand but which ends in the word, "Interlaken". Jessica groans again but it isn't a soft groan, tinged with regret or longing as we heard so recently before. This is more akin to the groan of someone forced to go to a rock concert instead of an opera. I know there are some who might not share such a view, but I don't think I mix with any of them on a regular basis.

She gets to her feet and swings her rucksack up and onto her shoulders. The train is coming to a halt in the station of what looks like a pleasant enough, if somewhat anonymous, town. It looks all right to me although I admit that's we've only just arrived. Such is my impression at least but it obviously isn't Jessica's as she heads to the door of the train while Alice and I follow on dutifully. We descend to the platform, and she looks around her with a real sense of disdain before turning back to us.

"Welcome to Switzerland's Luton," she announces.

Chapter 15
PLAN C GOES SOUTH

Jessica

I've said it before, I'll say it again and I'm saying it now. There is no limit which needs to be applied to this. I love Switzerland. The Berner Oberland is one of my top locations on Earth. Spiez is adorable, at least to me. Yet despite all this, despite its position in the heart of the Berner Oberland and despite being just along the Thunersee from Spiez, Interlaken is one of my pet hates.

It's like a true blot on the copy book of the Berner Oberland. A textbook tourist trap. You can tell that immediately because it's so pathetically easy to get anything and everything in English. To be fair to the Swiss, like most non-anglophone countries with strong international, commercial interests and also popular with tourists, they have gone to considerable lengths to welcome the rest of the world. And these days, despite what is still now and again imagined in Paris, the common language by default is English. Stick three people in a room from Japan, Ecuador and Kuwait and ask them for a language in common. It's not going to be French. It sure as hell won't be Japanese, Spanish or Arabic. It'll be the language of Shakespeare, Dickens and David Beckham. So, like everyone else, the Swiss have embraced English as the de facto language of tourism and are keen to welcome visitors in said lingua.

On the tackier side of things, this means that there are places which will consistently draw in those coming from abroad, where it seems that the official language has suddenly become English. Whether you're British, American, Australian, Indian, Korean or a lost saltwater crocodile, you're very welcome.

As long as you can pay.

Fair enough, Switzerland is not a cheap country. Things cost here. They're usually good quality but they're never inexpensive. However, there are places designed for the real tourists, notably those monkeys who have no idea of what the real country is like. I mean the people who just want to enjoy the trappings slathered all over the ubiquitous tourist experience which is basically the same in any country popular with those on a global tour of sightseeing hotspots. Interlaken is one of these. Postcards of the Berner Oberland at five francs a piece, plastic models of Alpine cows with a glazed expression on their faces for twenty francs each, mugs which show a Swiss flag when you pour in a hot drink, at thirty francs each. No problem. To be fair again to the Swiss, it's no worse than the toot on sale with depictions of Buckingham Palace, the Empire State Building, the Eiffel Tower and so on across the world. Someone in Beijing is no doubt making a fortune from all this crap.

Interlaken doesn't stop with the souvenirs though. Hotels with signs in English. Restaurants which might as well be in London or Melbourne. Curry houses modelled ostensibly on chalets in terms of design. Even lap-dance clubs for the discerning gentleman with no questions (or any other discourse) in German, just English. In fact, there's virtually nothing in German.

Interlaken itself lies between the Thunersee lake to the west and the Brienzersee lake to the east. Each is beautiful in its own way, the two being roughly equal stretches of water, each of an approximately kidney shape surrounded by forested mountainside which stretches up to grassy slopes with rockier slopes above, which will turn into snowy slopes in the cooler months of the year. They're the real thing in terms of Alpine and they're gorgeous. They're also steep enough to ensure that beyond a couple of peaks served by funicular railways and cable car connections, you can be guaranteed of not running into the clientele served by Interlaken itself if you can survive ten minutes or more of actual hiking. A very snobby remark, borderline sneering, I admit but also, perhaps sadly, quite true. Interlaken is where it starts and ends for the hoi polloi.

It's tricky truly to describe what Interlaken is like but I'll try. Perhaps you've seen those commercials for women's underwear or swimming gear where some impossibly worked out beauty strides purposefully towards a stretch of water, somehow walking in a straight line despite the fact that her legs are maintaining some sort of corkscrew motion. The centrifugal forces around her crotch are probably enough to service a helicopter's drive shaft. However, the target audience is doubtless not supposed to be considering questions of physics beyond how long it would take for her top to descend below her belly button once unfastened.

Whatever. She turns to give the camera a quick gaze of seduction mixed with passive aggression, presumably indicating that you can have her so long as she doesn't kick your teeth out first. Then she lies down by the water and stretches out her full length from expertly groomed head to perfectly pedicured toes. It's then when your gaze is drawn by the camera to her two, perfectly formed buttocks, a couple of globes of toned wonder.

I myself am no lesbian. Girls' bums just don't cut it for me, sorry. That said, I understand that to some, these two shining orbs are a source of great beauty and attraction. To get to my point here, let's just assume that they are. Well, if the Thunersee and the Brienzersee, with their awesome surroundings are like those two, beautiful buttocks, then Interlaken is basically the bit in-between. Everybody's got one and the Berner Oberland is no exception.

I need to pull myself together. It's a new day. I'm on the verge of being in a decidedly foul mood but I need to remember that I'm not here on holiday, that I'm in Interlaken to help somebody out and that yesterday's debacle with the accommodation was as much my fault as anyone else's.

Back in the day, you used to be able to walk into Swiss towns and villages, rock up at a nice-looking hotel and book yourself a room for the night. I don't even mean that in the context of the sort of hotel where you'd need to be a middle-aged guy on a "business trip", pitching up with a local lady of ill repute and slipping the receptionist an extra twenty francs to say that you'd gone down with a tummy bug if your wife were to call. Not even. I mean pretty much all hotels, including those little more developed than glorified bed and breakfasts.

Technically, you still can do that, only you need to be prepared for the fact that there's nothing left. The increasing popularity of Switzerland as a global tourist destination, combined with online booking apps, means that at least in high season, there's hardly anything going by the time you pitch up and that's if you're two days early. This is especially the case in the tourist traps so why it never occurred to me before we reached Interlaken, I do not know. Anyway, the net effect was that we ended up with a choice between the local youth hostel and a couple of 5-star gigs with a price tag around a couple of thousand francs. Each. If we'd gone for either of them, Harris would have had to consider whether he stood to lose more by booking us in as planned or just forgetting his clarinet and going home again.

As a result, we ended up in the youth hostel. Shared rooms with complete strangers who may or may not have an interest in sharing the contents of your collective underwear. Communal showers which look fine but still make you pray that the last few users didn't have verrucas or treat their genital herpes just before they reached for the soap dispenser which you're now touching. OK, I admit, you don't have to pay much so you can hardly complain, but there are reasons why I like to book slightly more upmarket places when I hit the Alps and am not too concerned about anonymity. I just feel more comfortable with my own space. And that certainly applies in Interlaken.

Harris did seem to calm down a bit during the train journey, which was nice. The guy remains an incorrigible pratt but at least once we got out of Geneva, he seemed to stop antagonizing the world at large which made a pleasant change. However, once into Interlaken, the more common traits showed again at the reception desk of the youth hostel. I had more or less managed to fudge the question of our ages at the reception desk to get us rooms and then he straightaway demanded, in English, to know where the dining facilities were. Luckily, the receptionist looked too bored to care and simply waved out of the window behind us. Harris turned around then turned back again, saying that he couldn't see any sort of dining room or terrace, just a Migros supermarket across the road. I somehow managed to shepherd him away from the desk and explain to him that that was precisely what the receptionist had meant. Our best chance of eating was to get something from the supermarket. This prompted a near tirade of pompous postulating about the dire standards of service in foreign lands. I have never myself lived during Britain's colonial period, but I can imagine that this is the way in which the more obnoxious, imperial types might have behaved themselves in British India before they got beaten up by the natives. And probably by most of the more reasonable Brits who were there as well. I only persuaded Harris to can it by threatening to insert one of my hiking sticks into a gorge where Heidi would have blanched to look and which the average cowherd might have considered a bit stinky. I then let him take Alice and me out to a somewhat tacky but expensive Chinese restaurant down the road so as to satisfy his need for a civilized feed. Opportunistic, I know, but he seemed happy enough, he can afford more than the average youth hostel clientele, and if you don't ask, you don't get.

This morning, we piled out and went straight to the station to deposit the bulk of our belongings in yet another luggage locker. I actually managed to get us a booking for tonight in a vaguely more upmarket hotel which doesn't cost a fortune but will give us two rooms, one for Harris and one for Alice and me. I doubt we'll get a helicopter to take us up to the glacier and back in time to catch a train and flight home again today. In fact, I'm assuming that we'll need until tomorrow to get whatever flight we may book today. Regardless, we'll need that stuff sooner or later but not right now so we can come back for it later when we finally need it. I'm fast losing track of what all we've stored where in left luggage lockers by this point. Between the two of them, Alice and Harris probably have a spare wardrobe in half the airports and railway stations of Europe. It's a pity that they're only stocked with the back end of a Black Friday sale from whichever Planet Unreal store Bethany and Harris must shop at.

Now we're trekking along the touristy areas near to the airfield, checking in on all the places renting out helicopter rides for preposterous amounts. Unfortunately, this part of the plan is looking decidedly trickier than I'd anticipated. It's also quite wearisome. Fair enough, I hadn't expected that hiring a helicopter was going to be like paying for one hour on a crappy mountain bike which somebody was renting out because it was giving them a wedgie, but the seat would cost too much to replace. That said, I wasn't quite expecting that the aerial tourist industry would be subject to so many regulations.

First of all, you have to certify that you're fit to fly. And I mean as a passenger. Aircrew you might expect to have a basic fitness level but why do they care if someone sitting in the backseat for half an hour has ever had a stroke, a heart condition, an aneurysm or a common cold? Are you able to jump out of the door in the event of an emergency landing? Well if not, how do you think I was capable of getting into the helicopter in the first place? Can you see to the other side of the road? Again, if I couldn't, why would I be paying through the nose for a sight-seeing tour which would be one big blur? Did anyone bother to do a health check on the people writing this garbage to see if they had any functioning brain cells in their heads or not?

Next, you have to demonstrate that you don't have a criminal record. Now, I'm not a bank robber but I imagine that if I were and if I were planning a mega-heist, there are three things idiotically wrong here. First, I would be robbing a bank somewhere a bit less tacky than Interlaken. I mean one of those towns where seriously rich people hang out. Roger Moore moved to Switzerland back in the 70s but he went to Gstaad. You sure as hell weren't going to see him hanging out on Interlaken's high street, wiping the remains of a spilt strawberry cornetto off his gaff. Second, I would probably have planned enough in advance to have a reliable and discreet helicopter and pilot lined up. I wouldn't be cruising in the day before robbing the bank to see if that bozo Dietrich would give me a quick whirl in his old-school Jet Ranger 206. Finally, even if I were dumb enough to ignore the first two constraints, the chances are that I wouldn't be so dumb as to go declaring my criminal record openly on a form to be registered with the Cantonal authorities. It would no doubt be a slight giveaway to the local cop squad if they were looking for someone who had knocked off the town bank, and a record flashed up that somebody had rented a helicopter who happened to have served three sentences for armed robbery and was out on parole with a grand larceny charge.

It's not that the Swiss are stupid. Far from it. It's just that, "imaginative" is not a word which translates naturally into German and believe me, I've seen enough Teutonic attempts at marketing campaigns to know what I'm talking about. The problem here, though, is not the paper-pushing. That much we could get around with a bit of patience and grit. Much more of a problem, as we're discovering, are the rigid rules surrounding what you can and can't get away with as a pilot. That includes where you can and can't land and it seems that on commercial sight-seeing trips, you only take off at the start and land at the end. Touching down in the mountains to offload and then pick up passengers is strictly forbidden. I hadn't seen this coming since in winter, you get special services who drop off intrepid, off-piste skiers right at the top of certain peaks, so that these adventurous, highly skilled and quite possibly mentally unstable sportspeople can take a day to descend some of the finest but also riskiest slopes in the Alps. That much I know but what I didn't know until now is that even then, they're still only allowed to set them down on specifically designated peaks and not just wherever said loony tunes point to on the map. I suppose that does make sense, but it isn't helping us much. We've trudged all over half of Interlaken – oh joy unbounded – and checked out five air tourism agencies so far. We've been rejected five times. Even an offer to pay a generous enough fee has never worked. It seems that the local law enforcement penalties would only make it worth the risk for this lot if we were to pay near to the value of that damn clarinet in the first place.

It also hasn't been easy to come up with a convincing reason as to quite why we want to land on the Upper Grindelwald Glacier either. When I tried to explain that Harris had lost something of great importance to him up there, I received the response that he would be better off getting a new wedding ring at the jeweller's shop down the road. There was also some snotty remark about how he might have to look a bit harder to find the common sense and dress sense which he seemed to have lost somewhere or other as well. I couldn't really argue with that one. I told the next couple of places that we'd just converted to Buddhism and needed to go up there to pray at the right moment when the summer solstice touched the spiritual alcove. The first one turned round and said that his brother-in-law was a Buddhist and he'd never heard such crap, while the second directed us down the road to where he said the Moonies were building a new temple behind the place with the arcade machines. So religion's not going to cut it. When I claimed that we needed to get up there to film a nature documentary, it was pointed out to me that professional crews tend to film things with more than just the cameras on their phones. The last time around, I just said, well what's it to you if I pay enough? The answer, as referenced earlier, was that I was unlikely to be paying enough so please go to hell.

In case you're wondering why I'm doing all the talking, it's because I told Harris that it would be better to use German as it would be more discreet and make us stand out less. This, of course, is complete bollocks. The international language of aviation is English and probably at least 80% of the clients for helicopter tourism can't speak a word of German but can all manage English as spoken across western Europe, North America and the bulk of Asia. The reason why I'm insisting on using German is because it means there's much less chance of Harris intervening with some incredibly stupid remark which will quite likely give away a whole lot more about what we're really doing here. Alice, thankfully, is just following dutifully around.

So now for number six and probably the last. There's a real sense of pessimism in the group and I don't blame the other two. It's almost guaranteed what we're going to hear but right now, there doesn't appear to be a better plan so here goes.

I walk through the door and into the little office. A pretty, young woman is sitting behind a desk with a computer in front of her. There's a certain 1980s feel to just about everything here, including her. I mean, get a haircut, girl. You probably weren't even born when Bananarama were in the charts, but you look like a comeback tribute audition. The sound of Wham in the background does nothing to ease the sense of having travelled back in time to 1985. Still, perhaps the rules weren't so tight then so we could be on to a winner.

"Good afternoon," I begin. Always, always stay polite in German Switzerland. Bad manners get you nowhere. "I would like to book a flight for later today or tomorrow, please."

By this time, later today looks about as likely as getting a reservation for yesterday but I'm still trying. After all, they may have a time machine here, going by the haircuts and soundtracks on display.

"Good afternoon," she responds. "I'm terribly sorry but we are all booked until Sunday."

Sunday? Oh no. We have to be back in Bristol by then without fail. Amazingly enough, Bethany didn't call last night but our luck on that front won't last for long.

"Yeeahh," I begin, sounding concerned. "The thing is, we really need to go tomorrow because my friend here is an astrologer, and he has to set up a remote telescope to catch the movement of the stars over a 48-hour period which begins tomorrow afternoon. It's kind of a special request anyway."

"Of course," I switch into a brisker tone, "we are funded by an important research university in the United Kingdom and will be able to pay whatever your costs should require."

The girl continues to be polite but looks disinterested. She simply recites the different, Cantonal regulations which by this point, I pretty much know myself. Eventually though, she looks up and smiles almost sympathetically.

"Look," she says, "I don't want to be unhelpful. I do know that for this sort of thing there are ways to get formal permission for scientific work from the government in Bern. Why don't you ask there?"

"But the problem is, the star pattern will pass overhead tomorrow evening and never again that way for another four hundred and thirty years," I respond, trying to sound both desperate and distressed. This is tough in view of the fact that I also don't want to sound like a completely brainless wonder who calculated the movement of the celestial entities to the nth degree of angle and timing but couldn't figure out that she maybe should have arranged a research permit and a few logistical necessities in advance. Or at least she didn't until the day before this once in a millennium event. Standing next to Harris in his neon orange beret, looking intelligent is a tall order.

The girl's face crumples in thought for a moment before she leans towards me conspiratorially.

"You could try Captain Borisovich," she almost whispers. "He works to a looser set of rules than the rest of us though he charges higher rates."

"Fine by me," I whisper back. Harris' expense account isn't my problem. "Where do I find him?"

"You go round the back of the airfield. Next to the sanitary cleaning equipment shed is a hut in corrugated iron. You'll know he's there if his helicopter's nearby."

"How do I know which helicopter is his?" I ask.

"It's the only Russian one there is," she responds. "It looks ugly as hell like somebody squashed Kermit the Frog and stuck a rotor on his head."

"Thank you," I reply. "You've been extremely helpful."

She smiles sweetly and goes back to fiddling with the perm of her hair.

The girl was right. The Russians really do know how to build some butt-ugly helicopters. This thing looks like a metallic cowpat with a lawn-mower engine attached. It's even still painted in some sort of military camouflage though I figure it's already got an excellent self-defence system. It looks so cheap that an enemy soldier wouldn't want to shoot it down because it probably costs less than the missile they'd have to use in order to do so. Can't miss the shabby, little, corrugated iron hut a short distance away either.

The hut itself smells of bleach for some reason. It's dark inside so I remove my sunglasses and squint down to the far end where a somewhat overweight, quite short guy is sitting with his feet on a desk. He looks to be in his fifties, balding and with an exaggeratedly pointed moustache. It's hard to tell if he escaped from a gay club when the 1970s were ending or if he mixed up the terms for "toothbrush" and "toilet brush" when he was shopping in a foreign supermarket.

Either way, he doesn't seem to care. He looks up and barks in a heavily accented German, "Who are you?"

"We're here to book a helicopter flight," I start.

"Where are you from?" he demands, sitting up straighter. "You don't sound like a Swiss or a German to me."

"Well, Britain actually," I reply in English, a shade taken aback.

"Britain!" he exclaims in English himself, suddenly beaming, though with a clear touch of sarcasm. "God Save the King! And how can I be of service to the Empire?"

Dear me. He really is like a second tier Bond villain. Tim would have kicked his ass in five seconds flat. James Bond, however, knows how to fly a helicopter. I don't so I'm going to have to be nicer.

"You're Russian?" I begin. Might as well know what we're dealing with.

"Russian?" He looks offended and spits against the wall to his left. "Pigs! I am from the country of Bulgaria!"

"Er, right. Lovely place, I've heard." I've been lying all day so one more won't hurt. The only thing I know about Bulgaria is that it might be home to vampires. On a good day. "How come you're out here?"

He laughs drily.

"I was, how do you say, forcibly retired from the Bulgarian Air Force after I ran a few extracurricular business adventures over the border. NATO countries weren't too impressed, but I managed to get here with enough money to convince the Swiss that I could set up a legitimate business and pay a decent tax rate. I had my own helicopter which nobody wanted anymore, so I picked up the slack which the other agencies round here didn't want.

"So how can I be of service? I take it you don't want a simple sightseeing tour of the Eiger?"

How does he know that? Do we look that dodgy? Sure, Harris looks like an escaped patient from some sort of controlled asylum but not like a drug smuggler or money launderer. I ask Captain Borisovich.

"You see," he tells me after a brief silence, "I don't advertise my services. I just let it be known to the other agencies that if they get an unusual client who's happy to pay for the privilege, I can provide a slightly different flight to what they can. They give me their recommendations. My helicopter is too old to have all of the flight tracking devices which theirs do and nobody seems too bothered, provided that I keep myself to myself. Nothing too illegal, mind you. My days of avoiding chats with Interpol are long behind me. I'm just talking about the more adventurous destinations which the other idiots round here are too scared to serve.

"So tell me, where do you want to go?"

This guy may miraculously be just what we want.

"We need to get up the Upper Grindelwald Glacier."

"And how do you propose to get down again?" he asks curtly.

"What do you mean?" I respond. "We need you to get us up there and back."

"Sorry, that's not happening," he retorts. "The Swiss are not stupid. They know that I sometimes come back with fewer people than I left with, but they can live with that. But landing on glaciers, picking people up? That smacks of all sorts of things which they do not like, do not like at all. Dropping off is very fast, very hard to track unless they're trying and just a small fine if you're caught. But touching down, picking up? Those take a lot longer, are much harder to coordinate and get you into way more trouble than I need. No, I'm sorry. I can get you there but then you're not my problem and I don't care how much you want to pay me. You're not going to become my problem.

"And by the way," he adds, "I can only drop you at the end of the day. Not before. At that point, nobody is looking."

"But come on," I begin before I'm cut off.

"You take the ticket up or you get out," he says in a way which brooks no comeback. "Your call."

We're sitting under the shade of the Chilchegg mountain on the edge of town. It's simply depressing. I don't know if I have ever felt this down in Switzerland. It's like hitting a brick wall. I was so sure that the helicopter route would get us what we needed. It just seemed so obvious. Well, congratulations, Jessica, you're clearly not as bright as you thought.

Harris, to his credit, started trying to think of alternatives. They were pretty stupid but at least he was trying. Ice climbing is only for seasoned professionals, true headcases or a combination of both. Going up there and abseiling down would be suicidal though not quite as much as trying to sledge down. All these ideas came into his head, and I had to shoot them all down. They just wouldn't work. At least I was gentle though. I couldn't bring myself to point out how moronic some of those plans were. The guy looked distraught enough already. Why make him suffer further?

Alice is sitting glumly on the bench where we've dumped ourselves, her legs splayed in front of her and her arms hanging limply by her sides. She's between Harris and me. She looks like your archetypal, grumpy teenager but I know full well why she's feeling down. I feel dreadful myself.

Even worse is Harris. I can hardly convince him that there's a way ahead when I can't see one myself. He's just sitting there, rocking very gently. Actually, I think he's sobbing very quietly, which just makes me feel worse. He has a tiny casket open in front of him which seems to have the face of a woman in it. I can't see any of the details but I'm guessing that's Isabel. It's unlikely to be Taylor Swift since he doesn't look like much of a Swiftie and even if he knew who she were – which he probably doesn't – she doesn't do Haydn's back catalogue so he wouldn't rate her much.

But why am I sneering at him? At least he's got someone or something he cares about. At least he's got a reason to be here. Why am I here? What's the point? To get a free holiday? That was an initial attraction, but I will admit that there maybe was more to it than that. I don't know. Maybe I just wanted to achieve something for somebody for once. Did I want to be somebody's hero?

Well, a fine job you made of that, Jessica. You lectured everyone on how much smarter you were than everybody else. The great action heroine, the true linguist, the problem solver sans pareil. The wannabe female James Bond. And all you did was to spend a ton of Harris' cash getting him to somewhere completely unknown to him and where you don't even like being yourself. You didn't just fail to achieve anything. You made it a whole lot worse. You're no James Bond. You're almost like an accidental villain. Except you're too stupid.

Alice has sat up and put her hand on Harris' shoulder, bless her.

"Come on, Mr Beadlesby," she's saying quite gently. "It's nobody's fault, not at all. Why don't we go home and you can tell Isabel about everything you've done for her. You've made a huge effort in all sorts of ways. If she won't take you after all that, she probably doesn't even deserve to have you anyway."

Whether this actually makes things better or worse is debatable but at least she's trying. At least she's got something to do. I wish that were me. I wish I could just do something. But maybe when it comes to doing anything worthwhile, I'm as useless as the next person. Probably even more useless. I can hear Harris keening softly in the background. I feel like I want to cry myself right now.

I sit forward, my elbows on my legs and my face between my hands. Now what? Do we just admit defeat and go home? Come on, Jessica, come on. Admitting defeat is not what you do. Or is it? Maybe I just never had to before but now I've hit the limit. We've all got one.

I look up miserably. There are people everywhere enjoying themselves. Even in Interlaken. I'm about to sneer again to myself when I stop. They're probably better people than I am and just because I can think of some snide remarks based on the snobbery of a high-altitude hiker, does that actually make their vacations and their choice of location so much worse? Are they really so inferior to me simply because they didn't have the chance to study German? All those Koreans, Indians, Chinese, they maybe didn't study German, but they can speak English at least as well as I can. How good is my Korean, Hindi or Mandarin?

There they all are, sunbathing, playing volleyball and badminton, swimming in the river, just enjoying themselves on the land and in the water. Even in the air, I reflect, as a couple of paragliders loom overhead. It must be beautiful up there. Maybe one day I can try.

My brain stops for a moment.

No, no, Jessica, let's not be stupid now.

Oh yeah? Up there?

Don't be a moron. Yes, you've had some crazy ideas in your time and even made a few of them work but not this. No freaking way. This is insanity, girl.

My mind is in turmoil. It looks ridiculous but then again, it might just work.

Stop it, Jessica, stop it. You've already disappointed everyone enough. Now you want to promise them something which really can't work?

Well, what if it can? Give me a moment to think it through.

Let's just back up a second. All right, I grant that it's a nice idea in theory but really, there are too many cons. That stuff has to be regulated too. You can't get up there until the evening. You can't descend in the dark. You'll probably freeze to death before it gets light again. How are you going to find the clarinet in the dark anyway? You don't even know how to use the equipment required. How the hell will Harris manage?

All good points, I admit. But come on, what would James Bond do? Would a million to one shot stop Timothy Dalton? What would he say if he knew you'd backed down? Just because the odds are stacked against you only means that you lay off, "If you play the odds," as Bond put it in, "For Your Eyes Only".

Give it a break, Jessica. Stop living in your silly, little fantasy world of spy films and mountain paths where nobody else goes. There's a real world, full of real people out there. Try living in it and pay some attention to them. And then there's Alice. And bloody Bethany. What happens if she finds out? She'll go ballistic. No, not even ballistic. She'll go nuclear. Actually, that's putting it mildly. She'll go off like a supernova.

The mental debate ceases abruptly.

A wicked grin spreads slowly from the corners of my mouth.

Bethany would go off like a supernova?

Oh, I'm in. Hell yeah!

I spring to my feet and look down at the other two.

"Give me ten minutes, will you? I'm just going to book Captain Borisovich for tomorrow afternoon. Then I'll come back and explain the rest."

Alice gapes up at me.

"You are the coolest, Auntie Jess!" she tells me before turning back to Harris. "You see, Mr Beadlesby? I told you she would find a way. She always does!"

Fifteen minutes and one hyper-expensive booking later, Alice seems slightly less impressed.

"Are you out of your tiny, freaking mind, Auntie Jess?" she almost shrieks. "You want to paraglide off a glacier?"

Harris is simply sitting there, looking like a deer caught in the headlights just after toking a bit too much.

"Yeah, yeah," I try to sound reasonably but not excessively nonchalant. It's about the only chance I have of sounding as though I believe this isn't crazy as hell myself. "I've got it all worked out in my head. You see those paragliders up there? Well, they move very slowly, don't they?"

"I suspect they're moving faster than it looks from down here," Alice tells me.

"Whatever. They're still moving very gently, and you never hear about any fatal accidents. Plus, they wouldn't be allowed to continue if it were all that dangerous. This is Switzerland, not Zoomerzet, you know."

Nobody reacts to that jibe, so I carry on.

"The plan is this: tomorrow morning, we take a lesson in how to paraglide. I mean, how hard can it be? I've seen people doing it who look thick enough to be Premier League football players or reality TV stars. We learn the basics. Then we go into town and buy ourselves our own ones. There are specialist shops where you can get this stuff. We also get some cold weather survival gear.

"Then, we fly up to the glacier with Captain Borisovich. He drops us off and we use the remaining daylight to find the clarinet with our metal detectors. It doesn't get dark for ages up there because the sun has to dip miles below the horizon before it sets properly on the areas at the top of the mountains in summer. You can see the sunset crawling up the sides of mountains from down below and some of the summits are still in daylight around ten at night at this time of year.

"Next, we bed down under a survival blanket to spend the night. It'll be cold but it's only a few hours and with all three of us together, we should stay just about warm enough to get through. When the sun comes up, which will be very early, we just strap on our paragliding chutes and float back down to Interlaken. We could try landing elsewhere but we're going to stand out regardless. Our best chance of not attracting attention will be to look as though we're meant to be there in the first place, and floating down to Interlaken is what most of them do. They even use the Höhematte Park as a landing strip for paragliders, so we'll look like we're actually meant to be there. And the park is next to Interlaken Ost station, so we just fold up our gear and get the train out.

"Great plan or what?"

Alice looks up at me quite dubiously before her expression suddenly changes and she smiles broadly.

"Auntie Jess, you are the greatest! That is the most lunatic plan I've ever heard, and I love it! You always amaze me. Every time you have an insane idea, I think that you'll never manage to top that one but then you always do! And somehow they always work. Plus, Mum's head would explode if she knew about this so let's do it!"

"I was thinking something similar myself," I admit, "though she may have a heavier load on other parts of her anatomy than her head, I would imagine."

"You what?" Alice seems confused.

"I mean that while your dad thinks you're away playing on your piano, he's probably seeing it as a good opportunity to play a bit on his organ with your mum."

Alice wrinkles her nose in mock disgust and says, "That's just revolting! And I was hoping to eat later on today!"

At this point Harris chips in.

"But isn't this very dangerous?" he asks.

"Well, it is a shade risky, Harris, but as the Admiral who won the Falklands War said of the first airstrike he launched off the carrier, 'You don't win the lottery without buying a ticket.'"

I'm not totally sure that the Falklands War is a very apt comparison for this undertaking but these two are meant to live next to Top Gun UK so it might mean something to them.

"What about Alice?" Harris continues. "Does she have to come?"

"It's maybe not essential but there are four reasons for it. First, it gives us an extra seeker for the pieces of the clarinet before it gets dark. Second, it will be warmer if there are three of us sharing the survival blanket than just two. Third, it saves us having to find alternative accommodation for her, and fourth, I don't think she'll agree to any other arrangement whether we like it or not."

Harris still looks decidedly worried. He pauses for a short while before speaking.

"Well," he ends up with, "I don't think I have much option here even though I really can't imagine what anyone else would ever make of this. At the same time, you are making a great effort on my behalf so what else I can do?"

I give him a friendly grin then add, "You're still bankrolling everything so you can let Alice and me choose where you're going to take us for dinner this evening. Cheers."

Chapter 16
THE LANGUAGE OF LOVE

Jessica

Well, that was nice. I enjoy a good plate of spätzli. For those not familiar with Swiss cuisine, spätzli are a sort of egg-based pasta which is not as light as what you get in Italy but also more immediately filling. It's often served with cheesy sauces and pieces of pork. Basically, it's very Teutonic and the sort of thing which hardy farmers would eat up in the mountains, where they work hard all day and need to keep up the bulk to ward off those cold winter nights. Which is also a pretty crap chat-up line still used by some Swiss teenagers these days although mainly by country bumpkins who have somehow managed to get past the bouncer with the invite list at a nightclub in Zürich or Basel. Heidi and Peter never really got down to some serious action in terms of shots and rave music. Either it just wasn't the done thing in those days or else they had a bit of indigestion after too many heavy dinners based around an excessive amount of cheese, eggs, flour and porcine meat. It would be a bit like nightlife in Britain actually, only starting with the kebabs instead of waiting until you're too drunk to notice later on.

Nonetheless, it is tasty stuff and good to go for once in a while. This is very true if you're planning an exceptionally energetic day to come which is due to end in a dinner no more ambitious than a supermarket sandwich while sitting outside at an altitude deliberately avoided by anybody not resident in Dubai's Burj Khalifa or travelling by air. I had no compunctions about letting Harris keep us fed at a reasonable, "traditional Swiss" joint about ten minutes down the road from the hotel where we're staying tonight. Let's not forget though, we're still in Interlaken so "traditional Swiss" is loosely equivalent to having a true experience of, say, Scotland by virtue of eating a deep-fried haggis on Edinburgh High Street because apparently Mel Gibson did something like that when he was filming, "Braveheart" thirty years ago. All the same, it wasn't bad, and it has filled me up. Given how Alice has temporarily turned into some sort of burp machine for the last five minutes, I guess she must have enjoyed it too.

I am, in any case, trying to keep the mood merry. Personally, I'm feeling pretty good about things. There is a gnawing ache at the back of my mind, warning me that I haven't yet actually achieved anything more than I had when everything looked lost earlier this afternoon. The only thing which has changed is that I've got a plan and is that really good enough? Am I simply some kind of action addict and wouldn't it be better to get a result before lapsing into the regular swagger?

Maybe so but on the other hand, someone has to keep Harris together. He's clearly bricking himself completely at the prospect of what lies ahead. To me, the best solution seems to be to act as though it's not that big a deal and that the main point is that we're going to get that clarinet after all, not that we might technically stand a reasonable chance of killing ourselves in the process. Harris, of course, has virtually no idea how the real world functions anyway so I want to give the impression that jumping off a helicopter onto a glacier, spending the night there and then taking a paragliding descent right down again when you've never done it in your life before is what any, normal person would do. If he believes that, then his complete lack of common sense may be what gets him through. Credit to him, his bravery on behalf of this Isabel is still commendable. I would otherwise slam it for being the reason that he's easily led into total loony-tune land but since I'm the one doing the leading, I can only commend it. The underlying point is that this is only going to work if I keep myself as cavalier, over-confident and slightly bossy Jessica. Not too much attitude. I think that can get a little overdone by the more naturally aggressive females in the post-feminist culture. Just enough to make sure that Timothy Dalton would definitely fancy me.

Either way, I have to admit to myself that it does come sort of naturally. At least give me a mission and I'll give you the woman for the job. That's how I see it and right now, I reckon that's what we need.

I think I must be doing something right since Harris has been back on form at least, and not just going on and on about whether he might get altitude sickness and lose some of the hearing in one of his ears which might reduce his ability to pick up the underlying, symphonic accompaniment of sonatas with a particularly Spanish influence. Or something like that. He might as well have been worrying about catching some infectious earwax from an unhygienic mountain goat for all I could care until he finally got over the fact that yes, we will need to be airborne for a little tomorrow. Having finally taken that on board though, he perked up a little in the restaurant and ordered a fine rosé from a local vintage. Again, that didn't mean a great deal to me. It looked a bit like cough medicine and smelt a bit worse. However, he insisted that I share the bottle as he didn't want to get "too tipsy". I tried to get Alice to help but he railed against the terrible crime of permitting an under-18 to drink alcohol. My bad. I thought technically kidnapping her from the UK would be considered a worse offence, such that giving her a glass of crap wine wouldn't add more than an extra day or two to our sentence if we get caught, but Harris' mind works in mysterious ways. I ended up feeding my couple of glasses of the stuff under the table to the restaurant owner's cat which promptly passed out underneath the coffee machine. There was one hell of an uproar when some dude ordered a macchiato twenty minutes later and the machine was switched on but thankfully, nobody realized that it was my fault, not even Harris. My track record with pets on this trip is not promising.

So anyhow, we're now wishing Harris goodnight. The instructions are pretty simple at this stage. Tomorrow morning, we get out of the hotel immediately after breakfast and stash our gear back in the station's luggage lockers. We retrieved it earlier for tonight's stay. Then we get a beginner's class in paragliding before lunch. After lunch, we go shopping for cold weather gear and our own paragliding equipment, and then we head to Captain Borisovich's. My only real plea to Harris is that we have to stay discreet.

"I don't believe I draw a lot of attention to myself," he sniffs rather loudly.

I'm tempted to spend about five minutes straight disabusing him of this notion by listing everything he's done of a prominent nature since we left Somerset yesterday. Was it only yesterday? But I'm tired and I feel marginally guilty about giving him too hard a time until we've got something to show for our efforts here. So I constrain myself to simply asking him to get rid of his hat.

"My hat?" he asks in a very surprised tone. "Whatever's the matter with it? It's supposed to be a good thing for those indulging in outdoor sports!"

I'm not sure that my sarky remarks are that mean after all. The strain this guy can put on your patience would likely make your average yoga instructor want to knee him in the nuts – sorry, in the glory organs.

"Because, Harris," I start through almost gritted teeth, "how many people do you see running around here looking like an inverted traffic cone trying to impersonate Che Guevara? If we want to keep a low profile, it would be best not to wear something which screams, 'Hey, everybody, check out this pratt!' even more effectively than a T-shirt which only bears the slogan, 'Hey, everybody, check out this pratt!'"

I leave it at that, bidding Harris a pleasant sleep and heading off to our room with Alice. It's been a long day.

The next morning, things are starting to look up. Incredibly enough, we were spared a conversation with Bethany for a second night in a row. Alice sent some messages to say how exhausted she was after her tough days. This was probably true, only that Bethany thinks that this refers to a music competition in Taunton, not to some leftover action script sequence in the Swiss Alps. Still, who's counting? No doubt Colin has been working it like it's his job while Alice is out of the house for a couple of nights so Bethany may be a bit exhausted too. I'd want to be in intensive care if I'd been through what I think she has.

So overall, it was a nice rest. The hotel is nothing special but in the sense of not amazingly good but nothing dreadful either. It's your classic hiker gig, in fact. Not over the top but a place where you can sleep peacefully and get your strength back for another day of exercise and excitement. Plus, and this is important as you know, it does a decent, continental breakfast. And this one is good, I see as I come down to the dining room with Alice. A solid spread of hams and cheeses, a wide choice of croissants, brioche buns and freshly baked baguettes. Some nice mueslis and yoghurts, fruit juices with fresh fruit and, which is always important to me, a decent set of jams to choose from. And you can take as much as you like. Yeah, I know, it will never be good enough for your traditional anglophone who needs their bacon and eggs fried and roasted to a crisp with enough fat encrusted into the food to make it slide down the gullet without any real need to chew or taste anything. However, at the risk of being a traitor to my country, I'm definitely with Switzerland on this one.

Harris joins up and is even not wearing any primary colours or bright white jodhpurs. His fairly tight, quasi-safari suit trousers still have a sort of jockey look to them and don't seem to be a massive improvement, but they are olive green, and he is wearing a pair of trainers so it's an improvement overall. There's also no sign of that beret. Perhaps my luck is on the turn.

"Where do you get a spot of tea then?" Harris asks, looking around.

"Just grab yourself something from the buffet and wait a bit," I tell him. "For whatever reason, they insist on having a waiter or waitress or two to bring you the hot drinks. Why they don't depend more on basic coffee machines next to the buffet, I can't tell you but it's something of a tradition."

He looks askance for a moment but does as he's told. He does have a point anyway. I myself do not know why the hot drinks are guarded so carefully in these settings either. Still, who cares? There's a lot to be getting on with in this buffet as it is, and I intend to do it justice.

I get back to the table we've taken for ourselves and set about buttering up my croissant and baguette for the application of a whole load of apricot jam. I want to enjoy this.

At this point, some waiter sidles up. At least, I think he's a waiter. I noticed him hanging around since about ten minutes ago but didn't pay him a whole lot of attention. He appears to be about nineteen years old at most, kind of spotty in the face, and is wearing a white shirt with a red bow tie and a black waistcoat which is clearly about ten sizes two big for his skinny frame. He looks a bit like somebody vacuumed out his internal organs with an attachment stuffed up his bum and then left the skin hanging off the bones because it was a bit too manky. For what it's worth, I once actually had a boyfriend with a similar frame. Trust me, it's not what you'd call high romance when you get literally boned through nothing more than taking the guy's arm.

His name badge indicates that he's called Jöchi. Not all that common, even in this part of the world. He's looked fairly miserable and in need of some motivation up to now, whether through careful personnel management techniques or a good kick up his arse. That said, he suddenly starts beaming as he approaches our table.

"Grüzi wohl! Wie könnte ich Ihnen helfen, mein schönstiges Fräulein?" he opens.

Something isn't right here. He just offered a greeting and asked how he could help but he used a singular and he's looking straight at me, almost as if Alice and Harris didn't exist. He also addressed me as a most beautiful, young woman. I'd like to consider this flattery but it's coming from someone who could probably be my son, at least if I'd had a teenage pregnancy. He's also being way too friendly when you consider his surly attitude until now and the fact that he poured the coffee for the lady at the next table into her cereal bowl because he was so busy looking in this direction. Not that my anatomy is notably on display but I'm starting to get a good idea of what was distracting him so much.

This we could do without.

The best way to ditch a chancer in Switzerland is often to speak a language which they don't understand and then pretend it's the only one you know. German works very well in Geneva, for example, French in Zürich. Fribourg and Bern are trickier since they're in the middle. The former is more Francophone, the latter Germanophone but they're only about twenty minutes to half an hour apart by train so it's a tough call. What you never, ever do is use English. Everyone knows that, including the ones who can't even speak French or German.

In this case, German clearly isn't an option. Jöchi has to be a Swiss German name. Nobody else would go around with a name like that unless they were the offspring of a chronically drunk bison-farming mother in the butt end of Mongolia and born with blood already seventy per cent proof. English no way, as noted a moment ago. French? Could well work but this is the hospitality sector and not a million miles from Cantons which operate almost exclusively in said language.

I go for the option which usually works well in the United States, at least in films with a lot of WASPs and a random Mexican. I'm not fluent in Spanish but it'll probably confuse Jöchi enough that he'll leave us in peace. Go for the classic line, girl.

"Que? No entiendo."

I just said that I don't understand. Perhaps not the greatest impersonation of a Mexican accent but it seems to have done the trick as Jöchi hesitates before heading off.

Or maybe not.

"Oh, Signorita! Sie eres aus Espanien, ja?"

What the hell?

"Sie eres sehr bonitisima!"

I'm very beautiful, am I? Is he trying to be funny here? He's somehow combining Spanish and German then massacring both of them in this dire pot-pourri of the world's worst chat-up lines from Buenos Aires to Berlin. Or is he actually serious?

"Muchas gracias," I reply as fluently as I can. Perhaps if I can remember enough of my basic Spanish to speak reasonably fluently, he'll give up trying to understand and piss off. It's not as though I can't get away with a grammatical error or two. Herr Professor Cervantes here is hardly going to notice.

"Quiero un café normal con leche, por favor, y muy temprano." I want a coffee with milk and make it quick. Nothing fancy but spat out fast enough to confuse him, I hope.

Apparently not.

"Ach, meine liebste, dich quiero tambien!" he announces.

It seems he loves me too. Bloody Spaniards. "Quiero", I've just remembered, can mean, "I want". It can also mean, "I desire", as in, "I love." Honestly. I just want a coffee, not a shag.

Alice, meanwhile, is enjoying this immensely. Little git. Still, I don't suppose she gets much entertainment like this at home. Nor do I usually, mind you.

"Look, Mr Beadlesby," she nudges Harris, "Auntie Jess is so nice. She's helping us to get up a glacier. And now she's helping this guy to get it up too!"

Ha bloody ha. At least Harris only looks slightly uncomfortable and doesn't try to add to Alice's back catalogue of crap, Alpine double entendres and cougar jokes.

Jöchi must be pretty thick as well as horny. How else has he failed to recognize that this woman, who apparently can only speak Spanish, is being talked at by the girl across the table from her in English? Or maybe he can't understand a posh Somerset accent. He continues undeterred in any case.

"Sie eres verheiratata?" he asks.

I think he may be asking if I'm married but it's quite hard to tell.

"Que? No entiendo," I repeat. It's pretty much true.

"Ich meine, podemos lieben?" he enquires.

He's asking if we could be in love? Dude, I would seriously advise you never try to score with anyone called Maria-Elena or Alarcos on Tinder. They'll probably think you mistook it for an Alcoholics Anonymous app.

I fix him with as intimidating a stare as I can and snap, "Un café con leche, por favor. Ahora!"

Somehow this demand for a milky coffee right now gets him to push off. I breathe a sigh of relief but when I look up, I see Alice rolling around with unbridled delight at what just happened to me.

"You go, Auntie Jess! You nearly scored! And you didn't even have to speak German!"

"I'm glad someone enjoyed it," I respond darkly. "I was hoping the Spanish would get rid of him, but I must have been out of luck on that one."

"What was he actually speaking anyway?" asks Harris, looking no more than curious at this display of attempted seduction. I wish my life was as easy as his. He's only lost a clarinet worth a quarter of a million quid.

"It was a crude mixture of German and piss-poor Spanish," I explain.

"Oh?" he asks. "You mean like what they call Spanglish when tourists try to mix Spanish and English?"

"I suppose so," I begin but am cut off as Alice suddenly hoots with laughter.

"He was trying to chat you up in Sperman, Auntie Jess! That's great!"

Oh for frig's sake. I don't think I've ever enjoyed a breakfast in a Swiss hotel less than I am this one.

"Let's just call it Germanish, shall we?"

"No, Auntie. I think Sperman is much better," she intones smugly. "Anyhow, maybe you've finally found your true love. You should be grateful. You like the Alps after all. He could be your soulmate up in a remote chalet, surrounded by mountain beauty and harvesting the goodness of the cycle of life as you reap the seed of your pastoral life together."

This is not normal Alice-speak. There's also a sneaky look in her eye.

"You see," she continues, "when you've got your cow-farming family on the go, you can squeeze out the milky goodness for the young while he goes up the mountainside with his stick in his hand to ensure that everything's properly fertilized!"

I raise my eyebrows. This may be hysterical humour in a posh secondary school but for those of us who've sat through more than one "Carry On" film, it's all been done before.

She then gives me a rather disapproving look.

"You're being quite mean you know, Auntie Jess," she chides. "He seems a nice boy and he's not that bad-looking either."

"Are you joking? Even if I were into teenagers and I'm not – I stress not – this one has all the sex appeal of a runover hamburger which was originally roadkill before somebody got it into a burger bun."

"Oh, come on," she chides before grinning evilly. "He's actually quite good-looking. I'm sure all those pimples will have cleared up by the time he's twenty!"

I am really being put off my jam baguette here, even if it's an apricot jam one, which is usually my favourite. I turn to Harris to change the topic of conversation but before I can say anything, a cup of milky coffee is plonked down in front of me.

"Grüzi, Signorita! Das es el besto Kaffee was es gibt's!"

He seems to think this cup of what looks like pigeon vom is the world's best coffee. Mind you, he also thinks he has some sort of incredible sex appeal so I suppose his brain must be a little divorced from reality at the best of times.

"Ah, Signorita. Ist der denn Ihr mannrido?"

He's indicating Harris and is, I think, asking if he's my husband. I know you could do worse than Harris, Colin being a prime example, but being married to him is not a very attractive proposition either. Besides, since he probably doesn't speak a word of Spanish, it's not going to be an easy act with which to convince anyone, even someone as dumb as Jöchi.

"Mi marido?" I enquire, correcting his crappy grasp of vocabulary in both languages. "Ah no, es mi hermano."

I've just told Jöchi that Harris is my brother although that leaves him blank for a moment. Chances are that Jöchi doesn't know what the word means. However, I did say no so that's good enough for him.

"Ach so!" he picks up, "Sie brauchen el amor!"

According to him, and it's not a question, I need some love. I only told him that Harris was my brother, not my husband. I never said that I didn't have a husband. So that's a bit of a logical stretch but then again, logic doesn't seem to be Jöchi's forte. No more than good looks or seductive chat-up lines.

"Hmmmm," he mumbles, running his eyes up and down me.

It's about the first thing he's said which makes sense, but I'm not impressed. He's blatantly checking me out! Is the little bastard even using his notepad to take coffee orders or just to write down my critical dimensions? I'm on the verge of flinging a teapot in the direction of his groin when he looks up with a very weird expression on his face.

"Signorita," he starts again. "Ich liebe tu. Sie eres muy muy bonita und schön."

You've probably got the idea up to this point, but he continues.

"Tengo un Zimmer oben wo wir rumpito pumpito machen können!"

He's just told me that he has a room upstairs where we can make rumpito pumpito. You can translate that one for yourself. It's too much for Alice though, who simply can't hold back her hysterics and explodes in laughter, neatly spraying Jöchi, me and most of the people at the next table in a shower of half-eaten ham and cheese croissant.

I'm a shade less inclined to find this quite so funny. By this stage, I'm sorely tempted to switch to fluent German and tell Jöchi to go screw himself because there's zero chance that I'm going to. However, thinking clearly instead of losing my temper at the first post, at least most of the time, is something I consider to be one of my positive qualities. There may not be that many of them but those which do exist are often quite useful.

"Hey, Jöchi," I start, trying to fix him suddenly with my most seductive look. I doubt it's anything you're going to see in an Yves Saint Laurent ad any time soon or even a Tinder profile. In fact, you'll be lucky if something like it makes it onto an ad for a genital herpes cream but it's good enough for Jöchi.

"Tu eres guapo," I tell him. He's handsome. I don't know if he understood that, but I continue by raising my eyebrows upwards as if in the direction of the room he just mentioned.

"Vamos en zehn minutos, ja?" I ask. Let's go in ten minutes. If he were brighter, he might have noticed that I used the German "zehn" for ten, not the Spanish "diez" but I want to make sure of the envelope I have and I figure there's little chance of this spare-time nuclear physicist working it out too quickly.

Clearly translating numbers is not his main concern. You can actually see the hard-on growing in his trousers. It's as horrifying as the scene in "Jaws" where the shark's fin closes in on the victim and the huge, hungry fish emerges slowly but surely and steadily. I pray that Jöchi has his fly done up or I'm going to get an eyeful in more than one sense. I'd rather be facing the shark, thank you.

I'm spared that torture at least. A look of incredulity on Jöchi's face is quickly replaced by a huge grin. He turns to the people at the next table, still busily picking the remains of Alice's croissant out of their hair and now asking if they can expect any coffee before the next ice age. Jöchi informs them in a very vulgar turn of German phrase that this is unlikely for at least half an hour since he has an extremely important client to take care of. He then winks at me, strokes his crotch – I think I'm genuinely cursed – and strides off up the stairs at the back of the restaurant.

Alice is still rolling around in fits of laughter while Harris just sits there looking bemused. It's all right for some perhaps, but not much longer.

I spring up, look at my watch and down the milky coffee in one gulp.

"Right, you two!" I order sternly in my most authoritarian tone. "We have ten minutes to check out! Forget your food and get upstairs. Throw everything of yours into your bag and get out of the front door. It's a pre-paid arrangement so we just need to leave the keys on the desk."

They look up at me in surprise.

"What the hell are you waiting for? You've got nine and a half minutes left! Get straight up to your rooms, get packed and get the hell out! Move!"

Maybe if professional linguistics hadn't worked, I could have made it in the army.

Chapter 17

ECONOMY AIR TRAVEL

Harris

I really ought to have a very deep appreciation now of what appeals so much to Jessica in these mountains. I'm what feels like halfway into the sky, on a grassy meadow at the foot of a cliff of rock which towers above me. Only a short distance away is an effective cliff edge at the end of the grass, which looks out across the lake, lying a lot lower beneath us. On the other side of the lake from where I'm standing is another ridge of peaks, glimmering in the sun as they rise high above the water.

And I'm afraid that's about it. There's a lot more to describe but I can't take any of it in, essentially because I'm terrified. Not just scared. Not simply frightened. Those things I have been before, and I would have said then that I was terrified. Angry dogs, failed choir auditions, swimming out of my depth off the coast of Devon. Those things, I thought, terrified me at the time. Even proposing marriage to Isabel was one of the most exciting things I've ever done but when I considered the mere possibility of her turning me down, I imagined that I could never be so petrified at another thought.

Now, though, I know the meaning of fear. I suppose I just never considered it before, mainly because until late yesterday afternoon, the idea of jumping off the side of a mountain, attached to a piece of canvas was simply something I never had any intention of doing and which I had never once considered doing. Half an hour later, and it seems that Jessica had signed me up to do it the following day after breakfast. It feels as though I've been sentenced to death while only briefly considering the crime.

Following our rather ignominious departure from the hotel, Jessica marched us through the streets of Interlaken to what termed itself a flight school. We had to wait a while since we had arrived slightly earlier than expected, again because we had left the hotel in such a hurry. I daresay I can't really blame Jessica for what happened there with that frightful waiter, but it did seem to be the sort of thing which always occurs whenever she's around. I wonder if vulgarity spreads out invisibly to its surroundings.

Whatever the case, after half an hour or so, we were herded into a small classroom of sorts where a pleasant, young man called Daniel proceeded to brief us on the basics of paragliding. I wouldn't have thought that Daniel was necessarily a very Germanic name, but I suppose they can't all be called Hans or Heinz. Daniel did prove to be something of a comfort at that point. His delivery was friendly but knowledgeable, firm but confident and he gave the distinct impression that this was not really a very dangerous sport at all. As a professional teacher myself, I would say that he did a very good job. We learnt that simply sitting in the paraglider will cause us to drift and that sitting back will slow us down while leaning forward will accelerate us. These movements are enhanced by pulling back on the control cords when leaning back and pulling them forwards with our arms when leaning in that direction. Pulling back slows a descent and even helps to climb briefly if the speed is already up. Leaning forwards lets us descend. Pulling just one cord or the other will let us turn.

The basic idea, according to Daniel, is to keep a steady descent with just enough speed to enable a decent level of control. Changing speed or direction when paragliding is, he said, somewhat like doing so in a boat. You don't get an immediate reaction, and you should not keep turning, for example, until you're facing the direction you want because you will just keep going. Rather you should cut the turn a few moments before you face that direction because you will more or less swing into it. He said that it's easy to get the hang of after a little bit. I didn't find that accidental pun quite as amusing as Jessica and Alice did. At higher speeds, the control is more responsive, but he stressed that there would be no real reason on our flight today to try much beyond a controlled, steady descent and to enjoy the scenery. He looked out of the window and remarked that we really did have fantastic weather, and we would be able to see for miles. This at least seemed to put Alice and her aunt in quite a sunny mood.

What finally made me think that this might not be such a bad idea was when Daniel told us that this was such a safe sport that Jessica and I could fly solo, even as beginners. As a minor, Alice would legally have to fly in a dual-seat harness with him. We would each have a radio earpiece and microphone which we could use as we saw fit, but it should be mainly Daniel who would do the talking and guide us all down. Jessica and I should only talk when we had to and only to him, not to each other. That much I quite liked since I'm fairly sure I would be getting a torrent of sarcasm otherwise.

So overall, the basic training helped to settle the butterflies in my stomach. Then we were taken outside and loaded into a minivan with a lot of equipment in it. Daniel was joined by a colleague with a very German-sounding name which I never caught. The minivan left Interlaken and headed into the hills which quickly became mountains. That trip was scary enough, in fact. The way up followed a road which spiralled upwards, allowing vehicles to climb by providing a sufficient slope for them to engage without toppling over. Cut into the side of the mountain, at every other turn, the window I was next to suddenly appeared to be looking straight down into an ever deepening gorge of trees with a river at the bottom which was fed by a waterfall. That waterfall came ever closer with each turn, growing more menacing every time until it somehow fell underneath our path as well. I have to give credit to our driver for managing the road so expertly and even overtaking a small car at one point although I do not know how he did that. I had my eyes closed at the time as I was feeling physically ill. There was at least one benefit to having been ejected so presumptuously from the hotel by Jessica which was that I hadn't eaten very much. At the time, this hadn't seemed such a good thing, but I was starting to see the benefit.

Finally, we emerged from the forest into a sort of meadow which spread out above the treeline. This was a real relief as the minivan veered away from the side of the mountain and progressed upwards but on less of an incline and with fewer turns. The meadow extended for miles, but we were not on it for long before the driver swerved to the left and stopped. We disembarked into the sunshine. For a moment, this was quite pleasant. It was much cooler up here than in Interlaken, even with the sun burning brightly above us. Very fresh, in fact. But that was when the true terror started to set in.

We were right by what I can only describe as some sort of runway, a stretch of grass where I'm now standing, which points down and reaches out over the side of the meadow and over the lake below. Daniel's colleague promptly set about stretching out the paragliders while Daniel himself kitted us out in harnesses and helmets. We were then marched over to the base of the paragliders where his colleague strapped us in and placed the cords in our hands. He reached around the back of my helmet and turned on my earpiece and microphone. And that was when the sheer, absolute terror set in. The only part of the world around me of which I'm still conscious is a void of air in front of me, set over a huge lake which looks disturbingly small from up here.

"OK, every-vun," Daniel announces in his pronounced though understandable accent. "Vee vill now take off into ze vunderful skies around Interlaken, ja?

"I vill go first vit Alice here, and zen vun of you vill follow after thirty seconds, and ze uzzer thirty zeconds later, ja?

"Who vants to go first, ja?"

That habit of putting, "ja" at the end of almost every sentence when giving orders would be getting on my nerves by now if I weren't so worried about literally losing control of my bowels. Jessica would probably find that funny but for me, it's an expression of a level of fear I have never conceived of before.

"OK, sure, I vill, I mean will," responds Jessica, presumably losing patience at my mental inertia.

"Good," says Daniel. "My colleague vill vave you both off at ze correct times, ja? Let's go."

With that, he picks up Alice – he's a surprisingly burly man for this sport, I think – and jogs steadily down the slope, the paraglider trailing behind them until they both leap off the edge. They disappear instantly in a heart-stopping moment which seems to last forever but I've been told that their paraglider only has to catch up with them and open above for it to blossom outwards and arrest their descent. Looking downwards, I can now see a bright blue canopy above them as they drift out from the edge.

The only thing is, I'm not certain that that provides a very accurate description of how I'm feeling. There is a massive contrast between the almost gentle way in which their paraglider caught them and the gut-churning illness I am suddenly feeling at the prospect of leaving the ground where I'm currently standing. Or swaying uncertainly. I can't be very sure.

Of course, I have been trying to muster some courage since yesterday and predictably enough, my thoughts have been centred on Isabel. I have to be brave for her. I need to demonstrate my courage to give all I can to love her. The logical problem is that I can't see how it really solves the situation to die for her since our marriage will hardly be going very far. I've never really feared the prospect of death before but, I now realize, mainly because it never really seemed quite so real. I look at my watch which indicates that it's around half past eleven in the morning. The thought that I'll never see the minute hand reach a quarter to twelve because I may physically cease to exist within that short period of time puts things into a perspective I've never considered previously. Am I even doing the right thing for Isabel here?

I breathe deeply. I don't have time to reflect and I'm falling back onto logic alone. Isabel deserves only the best and she deserves everything I can give her. If I cannot show that, I do not deserve her love myself and that is not something I am prepared to accept. Therefore, I must go.

The colleague whose name eludes me shoots his arm forward, waving Jessica off. Predictably enough, she seems almost casual as she jogs to the end of the runway and leaps into the sky.

Thirty seconds. Half a minute. I glance at my watch. It was bad enough when I was counting out my life expectancy with the minute hand. Now I'm watching the second hand counting down. My legs are growing weak, and my vision seems blurred. I think I see the man to my side waving me off, but I can't be sure.

"Harris, vere are you?" Daniel's voice sounds in my ear.

"Errm, er," is the best I can do to reply.

"Come on, Harris," Daniel comes back, sternly but not angrily. He's doing his best. "It really vill be OK, ja?"

I suppose that's true, but my legs are just not responding.

"Harris, get your fat arse over that cliff edge now!" Jessica bawls in my ear.

"Please, Jezzica," Daniel comes back immediately. "I vill do the talking on zis trip, ja? Harris must listen to me, not you."

"Oh sorry," mumbles Jessica, almost ashamedly.

That's it. I will do what is right for Isabel and I will not be put down by Jessica for failing to do it. I breathe deeply and trot down towards the end of the cliff. At the end, it's all I can do to keep going and I simply close my eyes as I approach the end and leap forwards.

The next few seconds are simply unreal. I feel as though I'm falling into some sort of abyss. All of a sudden, it feels as though a massive hand has gripped my groin and my shoulders and I'm suspended in that abyss. I have no idea if there is anything right next to me or if I'm all alone. There is a distinct pain in my back and I lean forward to relieve it.

That is something I clearly should not have done. I finally open my eyes and can only see the landscape of what appears to be half of Switzerland appear before me. At this point, I simply can't help but vomit. I do hope it doesn't land on somebody down there.

"Harris!" comes Daniel's voice, somewhat harshly. "You must not lean forvards like zat. You are going too fast and descending. Zit backwards, ja?"

I'm no rebel and he's the only hope I have so I do what I'm told and lean back. The orange paraglider slows quickly, and I find myself simply floating. It's a dramatic change. I can look down and see my body as well the cords and harness holding me in place. In a certain way, it's almost like being in some sort of hammock on a summer's day in the garden back in Somerset. Except that the hammock doesn't have a mile or two of sky between itself and the ground underneath. Nonetheless, my brain has registered that I am not actually careering downwards to my doom.

I look around carefully and all of a sudden it hits me. My goodness, it certainly is beautiful up here. I was led to appreciate the scenery from down below in Interlaken, but this is nothing less than astounding. There are the tops of mountains all around me, shining in pure white. They tower upwards and around each other. Their lower slopes pass through several shades of green and are dotted with small farmhouses and tracks, with tiny dots, which I suppose are cows, and with various waterways running across them. And it all extends as far as the eye can see. To the other side is the lake, running up to, what was its name? Thun, that was it. Beyond that, I can just make out the railway line snaking into the lower hills which lead back to Bern. I can see the lower lands beyond the Alps but that far away, there is a heat haze which stops me making it all out. I'm truly grateful to see all this. It certainly does give some credibility to what Jessica keeps lecturing us about and it has also, incredibly enough, distracted me from the unbridled fear which was consuming me until now.

I suppose nothing lasts forever. Daniel's voice returns.

"Congratulations, ja? Vee are now airborne and sitting comfortably. However, Harris is a bit below us so Jezzica, you must descend, ja?"

"OK," replies Jessica and leans into the descent.

She drops quickly towards me, her yellow canvas drawing tighter than ever behind her as she comes closer and faster. Daniel is starting to say something, no doubt concerned with her approaching me a shade closely, when she executes a sharp turn to the left and leans back, drifting down to my level around sixty yards away. Honestly, is there nothing she can't do better than everyone else? What a little show-off. If only someone else were interested in the finer works of Chopin or Vivaldi. Then I might make a mark.

"Ferry good, Jezzica!" Daniel is evidently more impressed than I am. "Now let's see you turn, Harris."

I pull on the right-hand cord. Nothing much happens except that I feel rather ill again as a hilly range looms up directly underneath my right side with nothing between it and me except a lot of thin air.

"Nein, nein, Harris. You must not turn vithout a bit of speed, ja?"

No, I mustn't, yes? Is this man talking in positives or negatives? Still, I think I get the message and lean gently forwards before drawing back my right hand while keeping my left stretched forwards. I turn to the right although rather more gently than Jessica did when making her turn. I follow an arc around.

"Harris, stop your turn, ja?" instructs Daniel.

I release the pull on the right cord. My turn continues which is rather unsettling. However, I do recall that such would be the case and indeed it is. The rate of the turn slows down and I end up facing the lake, heading towards Thun.

"Zat is good, Harris," Daniel tells me. "Just turn around again so zat vee are facing back tovards Interlaken since vee must land zere, ja?"

I increase my descent then turn left. Then right. Then left again. Getting this thing to line up properly is much more difficult than it looks. Eventually, I find myself more or less lined up on Interlaken though again, somewhat lower than my fellow paragliders. This does not last for too long as Jessica suddenly gathers speed and shoots underneath me, at least so it seems. She jinks right and then turns left again, extremely sharply, I think.

"Jezzica, vot are you doing?" comes Daniel's voice, sounding genuinely annoyed for the first time.

What exactly is she doing, I wonder. I can't see any reason for her to be antagonizing Daniel or even just ignoring him. Knowing her, I would have thought that she'd be delighted to drift down and enjoy her beloved scenery for as long as possible.

"Oh, yeah, sorry, Daniel," comes her reply. "I've got this really bad wedgie, and I thought that it might clear up with a good, hard turn to the left. But I didn't realize that I would pull myself back in my seat so much which is why I leant forward to counteract it."

"You vere pulling some centrifugal forces," explains Daniel. "Like in military aircraft ven zey go round a turn and zey, how do you say, pull some Gs, ja?"

"I've seen, 'Top Gun' so I know what you mean," responds Jessica. "This harness is really pulling on my groin when I pull a sharp turn. Talk about hitting the G-spot!"

I can hear her and Alice both giggling away at this piece of completely unnecessary smut. You would have thought that up here, she might at least have managed to take things a little more seriously than usual.

Except, I wonder. Except that Daniel has stopped paying quite such close attention to her rather reckless manoeuvring. Could it be that she has another agenda?

"Erm, Jessica," I intervene, "I'm just wondering if we really need to be taking such an aggressive approach here. Are you trying to prove something?"

Amazingly enough, she seems to get my point. What's even more amazing is that I managed to ask the right question in the first place.

"Yeah, Harris, I think we need to push ourselves a little to make sure we can really make the most of this experience."

"Zat is enough!" cuts in Daniel. "Jezzica, you are doing ferry vell, but I am ze vun in charge here, ja? You vill not engage in needless conversation vit Harris!"

"I'm sorry, Daniel," I intervene. "I think that was actually my fault. I do apologize."

All of this has helped me to discover that despite my initial terror, I think I can really do this. I don't feel as confident as Jessica appears to but that's hardly restricted to paragliding. We're in her world and anything I can do, it seems, she can do a hundred times better. That said, I am somehow getting down to the bottom and Interlaken is still more or less in front of me.

We carry on like this for around another twenty minutes or so. Daniel chips in now and again although he seems rather put out by Jessica's over-confidence in particular. The fact that I myself am making a bit of progress but without having to try to become an amateur fighter pilot almost appears to be making me Daniel's favourite now. He keeps on talking to me in a slightly more friendly way than he does to Jessica although, as you might have expected, she gives the distinct impression of being unable to care less.

Our arrival in Interlaken is tricky. We come in what seems relatively high over the main park and Daniel tells us to slow down as far as we can. I end up drifting over a supermarket a short distance away but Daniel orders me to stay there for a moment. He then explains that we need to go down relatively slowly but just fast enough to descend in a tight spiral into the park where two of his colleagues will catch us. I need to start the descent in a straight line, to get over the park from the supermarket area and then go into the spiral. Jessica, of course, pulls it off like the top of the class. I seem to be going everywhere.

"Harris, you must turn more tightly, ja?"

More tightly? This is as tight as I've done all day but if I have to, I suppose I have to. I grip the right cord and pull for all I'm worth. Terror suddenly grips me again as I feel as though I'm growing very dizzy very quickly and I head for the ground. I also appear to be over a bus stop, not the park.

"Harris!" barks Daniel. "You are not over ze park! You must come in to land in a straight line or you vill land on top of a bus, ja?"

On top of a bus? I don't like the sound of that. I stop turning as fast as I can and then remember that you're not supposed to do that in the first place. A gentle correction encouragingly enough has me heading in to the park at a very low height. I think I may be pushing my luck as somebody looks out of an upper window and waves as I float past but more by luck than judgment, I somehow end up over the park. I sit back and pull back on the cords, slowing down. I can feel a seemingly gentle descent underneath me which becomes abruptly less gentle as my bottom makes a jarring connection with the ground below me, right where Jessica kicked me onto the train in Geneva two days ago. I really am taking a hammering to my rear end on this trip. Again, I'm sure the other two no doubt find this quite hilarious.

All the same, I'm down and I'm still alive. I actually feel a degree of elation. Jessica tried to encourage me earlier by telling me that this would be what she called, "quite a rush" and to be fair, I think she was right. I do feel good about it and quite invigorated. I don't know that I'm necessarily looking forward to doing it again, but the feeling of overwhelming dread has gone.

Daniel circles down with Alice and lands perfectly in front of us. I can hardly be surprised that he should pull it off expertly. His expression indicates that he has not been too impressed by the way in which we – notably Jessica – have taken advantage of his initially good nature to indulge in some quite reckless adventurism but I can appreciate, I think, what was really going on up there. I don't know if we're necessarily qualified for what comes next but at least we're as fully trained as we can hope to be.

Chapter 18
PLAN D GETS OFF THE GROUND

Jessica

It's been a strange sort of day. It's meant to be the big day, and it is. It's just that the big bit doesn't really start until the early evening. That may not be an entirely accurate description since the paragliding was hardly dull and I have to admit, I loved it. I wanted to do that since forever and unlike a lot of things, it was one which absolutely lived up to every last bit of expectation I ever had when I got there. The scenery was incredible and the sensation of floating over some sort of mountain paradise was everything I could have wished for. I'm so glad that the sun was out and the weather was perfect. We had no choice with the timing on this one. In fact, we were very lucky because if it had been raining, the whole thing would have been cancelled, and I do not know how we would have managed this plan without any training or experience at all. We're not exactly the Tom Cruises of fabric-arrested descent after half an hour in the sky over Interlaken but we're eminently better qualified than we were at breakfast time. All that aside, everything went just right with that part of the plan and if I run into God at any time and get the chance, I'm going to thank Him profusely.

That said, it was about the only part of the plan which has turned out as it should have done. The afternoon was more another exercise in frustration. Predictably enough, the range of cold weather gear available in the shops is a shade limited when the summer temperatures outside are reaching the low 30s. You can't really complain too much either since unless you're planning to go ice-climbing, you shouldn't really need that sort of clobber in the first place.

Complaining will draw attention and that we do not need. The idea that we're a squad of ice-climbers with a high degree of technical training, proficiency and experience is about as probable as the notion that we're here for a conference on how to sell air fryers to elephants.

We staggered around and picked up the various insulated jackets, trousers, boots, gloves and headgear which we would need. All at massively inflated prices which made Harris blanche. I'm not quite sure what the budget ceiling for this trip is but it's getting high enough for him to have second thoughts on the level of outlays. Of course, he already has a tan verging on sun-burn so when he blanches, the net result is that his face looks a bit like someone lighting a torch inside an empty packet of tomato ketchup-flavoured crisps. Or perhaps a Chinese lantern would be a kinder and more appropriate description. Either way, he looks hot and cold at the same time.

Getting the paragliders was a whole lot harder. It seems that you don't technically need a license to own one, but you do to use it. As a result, you can buy one without ID although you look suspicious as hell. We clearly screwed up in the first store since we just backed off when they asked if we were licensed to use them. That in itself was probably suspicious enough. Again, not illegal but they no doubt wondered what on earth we were doing or worse, planning to do. Harris suggested that we go to a sailing shop, buy a couple of mainsails and then sew them together into makeshift paragliders. I have to wonder, is he the world's least funny piss-taker or its greatest ever idiot? What the hell goes on in his brain? Sure, the works of Handel take some intellectual awareness to understand. Loving Isabel as intensely as he claims must be the driving force which most people seem to need in life. But how are these things enough when you can hardly find your way to the toilet without straining your IQ or when you need a super-computer to work out how to buy a bus ticket? They tell me that I'm shallow but at least things happen when I'm around.

On that basis, we – more like I – came up with the plan which got us equipped with the full set of flight gear we now possess. Hardly genius really but it revolved around buying each thing we needed in a different shop. This attracted a whole lot less attention because what's illegal is paragliding without a license. You therefore look dodgy if you buy an entire paragliding kit. If you simply buy the ropes, the harness, even the chute itself, that doesn't look nearly so dire. If you ask a helpful question like, "So, is this compatible with harnesses in Graubünden Canton?" then the impression that you're just getting some bits and pieces for someone else or at least for another venture miles away is sufficient to allay any reservations which people might have. Even when we tried on flight helmets according to our own sizes, nobody asked questions. I told Alice that it was OK to use her head as a trial for one helmet because she had the same head size as my sister. I so hope that's a blatant lie since I'm sure that Alice must have considerably greater mental processing capacity than Bethany, but you never know. I suppose Bethany must need some space for all that air.

The one piece of equipment which we had to do without, which is a bit of a pity, was the communications set. The shopkeeper showed us the various radio sets which individual paraglider pilots could use to talk to each other and provided a detailed – and somewhat tedious – explanation of how it all worked. However, he then added how it also included a very accurate transmission capacity so that rescue services and the police could keep track of us and respond to any emergencies. I said that I didn't think that would be entirely essential and he looked at me as though my parents were single-celled organisms. Or as if I was Harris. Or maybe both. Much of a muchness really. Obviously, it was necessary. It was a legal requirement, wasn't it? I nodded nervously at this point and pretended that I knew that. What he was promising was simply an unparalleled quality of transmission since not all of the emergency services back-ups were all that amazing. I affected to wake up suddenly and point out that of course, we already had a decent set of communications equipment so shelling out a whole lot for a better quality of emergency transmissions maybe wasn't quite our priority. The shopkeeper wasn't all that impressed, but we still managed to part on friendly terms.

This is definitely a pity. If it's impossible to get helmet-mounted communications equipment without broadcasting our technically illegal activities and precise location to law enforcement, then we're going to have to go without. I did wonder about simply using our phones, but I doubt Harris will manage that for more than twenty seconds before dropping his. So what's the point? We'll just have to fly down to Interlaken and signal each other by hand.

Alice is going to be flying with me. She wasn't able to train herself this morning. And if we have to use a two-person chute, then I weigh less than Harris and had less trouble learning the basics of paragliding during our one-off class. It makes sense. At least, as much as any of this lunatic scheme makes sense but that's another question. And if I want to be really cynical about it, in the event that Alice gets killed or injured, I'd like to be sure of being at least as equally badly off myself when Bethany learns about it. Being in full health myself at that point would be suicidal. But I'm not going to discuss that with anyone.

Following an afternoon of wondering all over Interlaken, pulling together enough gear for an airborne assault by professional paratroopers, we're now heading back to Captain Borisovich's. Our flight is booked and pre-paid so it's time to head. The feeling of anticipation which has been there all day is coming to a head for me. It's been easy to act cocky so far. I've been doing it deliberately to maintain morale and boost confidence but it's getting harder. It's not that I'm afraid or even less sure of what's planned. Honestly, it's not. It's more just that it's getting real. Somehow or other, I realize that the sensation of nearness is quite different to considering something in theory, even when you know that the theory is going to be reality soon. It chips away at the excess cockiness. I suppose that's a good thing. I just don't want it to affect the others. Let's hope this goes smoothly.

Some hope. The captain is sitting at the open cabin door of that visually unappealing contraption he calls a helicopter with one leg bent at the knee, the other hanging out of the door down to the ground. He looks at us with a worryingly smug grin on his face. I don't like the look of it. Smug grins are always bad news.

"Good afternoon, my English friends," he addresses us, sounding exactly like a Bond villain from the Sean Connery era. Can't these people ever watch anything and maintain a sense of irony? Or do these ones just fail to watch them at all? It's estimated that around half the world's population has seen at least one James Bond film. Why do I have to keep meeting the other half?

"Good afternoon, Captain Borisovich," I reply as neutrally as possible. "All set?"

He pauses and looks around the mountainsides surrounding us. Too exaggerated. Then he looks at us and his gaze is equally slow. I am very much not enjoying this.

"I'm not really sure," he responds eventually. "That depends."

"Depends on what?"

"Well," he says, looking upwards. "I might have under-estimated the real cost of this expedition. Reaching the height of glaciers puts a real strain on the helicopter airframe after all."

I'm no aviation expert but I know my bullshit and this stinks of it.

"Look, we have a deal," I remind him, "and we already paid."

"Yes, but it will cost more than that," he says curtly, looking at me without blinking. I don't know how the casting crew on, "The World Is Not Enough" missed this guy.

At this point, Harris strides forward. He has a surprisingly annoyed, even aggressive look on his face and his body language indicates that he is, well, angry. I've never thought of Harris as being genuinely angry and it seems entirely inconsistent with what I know of him. Fair enough, one month ago I didn't even know that he existed, but I still feel as though I've spent a fair amount of time getting to know him of late. I can't say that I've greatly enjoyed the experience so far but maybe there's more to it than I realized. I'm clearly about to find out.

"Now you listen to me, my man," he blares, again surprisingly angrily.

"I don't think so-," Captain Borisovich starts to reply in his smug manner before Harris cuts him off mid-smirk.

"I don't myself give a hoot what you think," he berates the captain. "That is not my concern right now and it need not be yours either. A deal is a deal between gentlemen and that, my friend, should be final between us."

Actually, I was the one who struck the deal. Harris only paid for it. And there are multiple reasons for not considering me a gentleman but now is not the time to air them. Still, who cares? Harris clearly doesn't and all of a sudden, he's taking the lead. The whole day is lurching from one level of unexpected to the next, always increasingly so, it seems. Alice and I simply stand there, incredulous observers and no more. We glance at each other. Alice stares at me with her mouth wide open. I roll my eyes towards Harris and shrug slightly. I really don't know, girl, is what I'm indicating. Let's see how this one goes. More likely, I look like a stoned koala who's just sat on a thorn bush but either way, the point is that this is now entirely Harris' show for the moment.

"I don't think so," Captain Borisovich comes back again but gets no further.

"It really is of no interest to me whatsoever what you think," Harris retorts loudly. "I don't see why my rights should be beholden to your greed and self-centred lack of awareness of the world around you or even common decency."

"Common decency can go–" starts Captain Borisovich but Harris, amazingly enough, strides right up to the man and stares him directly in the face.

"You'll wait until I'm finished!" he barks. "If you don't even have any basic manners, it's easy to see why your behaviour as a whole is unworthy of an inmate or a common interloper!"

What does Harris read in his spare time, apart from, "The Weekly Journal of Classical Music Hits"? "The Charles Dickens Guide to Insults"? "Upper Class Idiots in da Hood"? Whatever the answer is, it actually seems to be having some sort of effect on Captain Borisovich who, for the first time, looks just faintly concerned.

"I will not stand for this sort of disrespect!" Harris continues, pausing only for an angry breath. "I fully understand your position and that you are running a commercial venture with limited customers and very high overheads. Trust me, I do. If you perform opera, if you make your living from touring string orchestras, you face very similar problems. Talent does not come cheaply but sadly, the numbers willing to pay to enjoy such delights are regrettably not nearly as high as I do believe they should be."

They're probably higher than the numbers wanting to make an illegal evening landing on a glacier about four kilometres above sea level but let's stick to the big picture for now.

"In that regard, I think we both understand each other very well," adds Harris brusquely. "But what does not happen among those who appreciate the arts – these being all very respectable people – is a recourse to extortion and frank dishonesty. It is an unspeakable insult to those who have negotiated with you in good faith and does absolutely nothing for your own reputation or integrity!"

At this point even Harris needs to breathe, leaving just enough oxygen in his immediate vicinity for Captain Borisovich to respond.

"I'm not sure, my friend, that our situations are quite the same," he says. I wouldn't say that he's intimidated or such, but the overall smugness has evaporated. "My difficulties in making a living as a professional aviator are not those of your average violin player."

"An average violin player!" Harris explodes. "An average violin player, you say! We are talking about some of the greatest talents on this planet! Even these people struggle to make their way in this day and age and we are talking about people of such exquisite ability that they are unique in their class!"

"Those who pass aviation training are a tiny fraction of those who apply."

"I really don't care! The world is full of aeroplanes and pilots! I can tell you on one hand just how many truly great violin players I would consider to be alive and active at this moment, and name them too! How dare you claim to be somehow superior?"

"I wasn't claiming that, just–"

"Oh do be quiet, you stupid, small-minded, distasteful, little scoundrel!"

Screw me, Harris is on form. The guy has depths which have been completely unknown to me up to now. I can't see why he bothered with all this clarinet nonsense and didn't merely go up to Isabel's dad, slap him around the face, pull out a DIY marriage certificate and then bonk her on the floor in front of him. Just to make his point. Actually, that's not a very pleasant, mental image. I saw Harris without his shirt on at Heathrow Terminal 2's security gates and it wasn't something to raise the temperature of your flushes.

"OK, look, the deal's off!" Captain Borisovich scowls. "Just clear off and go to hell!"

"Well, you can return my money and pay us an extra percentage or two for the interest!" Harris replies fiercely.

"OK, OK, I'll get the funds now." Captain Borisovich backs off towards his hut.

"Hold on there, my man! We didn't fix the interest rate yet!"

"Go to hell! You get your money, and you get out!"

"I will not!" Harris booms. "You, sir, are a ne'er-do-well of the worst possible kind and you will abide by the terms I have set!"

I would have thought that serial killers, drug lords and war criminals might count as ne'er-do-wells of even worst kinds but again, I don't need to quibble over the technicalities. Unfortunately for Captain Borisovich, he seems incapable of doing so either.

"But I have no extra funds!" he wails.

That was a stupid thing to say. The fact that he did at all is, well, incredible.

"Well, that's just too jolly bad for you," Harris says in the manner of an unimpressed schoolteacher. Even he must draw on experience sometimes. "I'll just have to wait here until you get to the bank and back."

He proceeds to sit down on a small barrel near to the helicopter. Not the most comfortable seating arrangement but Harris' bum has seen some serious discomfort to date on this trip so it's maybe becoming immune.

Captain Borisovich says something under his breath in his native language which none of us can understand but that's maybe just as well. I don't want to be recording some serious profanities here and I'm fairly certain that's what's coming out.

"And if I don't?" he asks, somewhat hopelessly.

"Well, let's get to know one another a shade better because I think we'll be here quite a long time," Harris says with a degree of indifference before adopting a more studied and pompous tone. "My name is Harris Beadlesby, and I am a graduate and teacher of the arts of classical music."

We're supposed to be broadcasting our names and any other identifiers as infrequently as possible but it's a moot point now. Besides, neither Alice nor I really know what the hell to say at this point.

"In my opinion," he continues, "the real transformation of the ancient art of music-making came with the Renaissance from around the late 1400s. There are, of course, many who claim that the Medieval period produced the true roots of what we now consider classical music, but true polyphony did not really make an appearance until the Renaissance. The latter, as I implied a moment ago, is considered to have started in the early 1400s but even then, it is not as if polyphony simply appeared out of nowhere. It needed to be codified and transformed into a coordinated structure, capable of immediate replication by multiple performers who did not necessarily know one another and who may well have never even encountered one another. That is the logic for my own, admittedly debatable view, that the Medieval and early Renaissance evolutions were simply the culmination of the many roots which led to the emergence of today's classical music. The roots, needless to say, go back until several thousand years BC, but they all, in turn, developed ever further towards codified polyphony, which is what I would consider to be true music in the classical sense. Hence, if anything, the Medieval and early Renaissance compositions might be considered the birthing cries of the nascent development which became the true wonder of composition which first saw light back in the fifteenth century.

"If we look next at the Baroque period–"

An anguished scream suddenly breaks into this – at least to me – incomprehensible monologue.

"Oh please, no more!" Captain Borisovich yells at the top of his voice. "Just stop talking!"

He strides over to me and stares into my eyes.

"OK, you win!" he snarls. "You make him stop and keep his mouth shut. I fly you to the top of the Upper Grindelwald Glacier. You get out. I fly away. I keep the money you already paid. And that is that. No more, no less. We never see each other again. Do we have a deal?"

"Are you willing to shake on it?" I enquire primly.

He spits on the ground in front of me and growls, "Just get into the aircraft."

I really need to do more of this aero-tourism in the Alps. Hiking is great. You see some truly amazing sights. However, what I've seen today from that paraglider and now from this helicopter are awesome. The cabin door is wide open, possibly to facilitate our exit later but it could also be because this clapped-out contraption is too knackered to have such refined features as locking doors. But I'm liking it. Actually, I'm loving it. It may be partly the novelty value, to be fair. I sort of know what to expect when I hike up a mountain. It's wonderful but it's not wholly unexpected. Not that it's a bad thing. I mean, tourists know pretty much what to expect when they go to the Sistine Chapel but that doesn't stop them being entranced. The difference today is that I have never seen the Alps before from on top. The peaks themselves spread out below me with all the valleys linking them like some sort of organic mapping, set apart by a combination of forests, lakes and Alpine pastures. I can see places where I've hiked before and never realised quite how close they really are together. You wouldn't see that on the ground when there's a massive ridge in-between. Conversely, I can also see routes I've taken which truly were a very long way to go. I'm quite proud of myself really. Then there are the places which I've never been able to reach because they're simply inaccessible without either professional qualifications and equipment or, as now, air transport.

All of this I can see passing behind us. Captain Borisovich has flown quite high as we traverse the Grindelwald Valley. For understandable reasons, I suppose that's normal for what's supposed to be a tourist trip. However, he's flying at more or less the altitude of the glacier itself, which we're approaching. What's in front of us is even higher while what lies behind is truly below us. It just makes it even more incredible to think that what we're flying into is increasingly that bit more spectacular than what we're passing over just now.

It also makes it a shade scarier. Because while I've seen plenty of routes which I've hiked before, they're all down there. As in down there, some way down there. And I thought I was high up when I hiked them. Today, we're about to be dropped off on a sheet of ice at least a kilometre higher, or quite a bit more than that, depending on what you're looking at. And it's fricking cold. We just about sweated our guts out down at the airfield, getting into all that cold weather gear before we boarded. That was only about fifteen minutes ago but right now, I feel as though all that sweat is about to freeze itself down the small of my back. For once, Bethany might actually have been on the money as to what's needed. All three of us are smothered in enough layers to start our own winter sports shop if we wanted to strip off and just sell the gear but even so, I'm vaguely trying to think of Tim's hottest shirt-free moments in both, "The Living Daylights" and "License to Kill" for no better reason than to generate a hot flush or two to keep me warm. It's the only reason not to like the scenery since it keeps distracting me.

All good things come to an end though, and in this case it's a very abrupt end. The helicopter takes a sudden left and appears to veer straight towards a towering cliff. The scenery below us turns to rocky scree, soon mixed with ice and quickly thereafter to pure ice. For reasons I don't want to consider in too much depth, my stomach tenses up and somewhat oddly, I find myself picturing those photos you see of the Viet Nam War with rather bemused, American GIs sitting in a helicopter, about to jump out at their drop zone and go into combat. There may not be any Viet Cong down there, but I don't feel quite as secure as I normally do when in the Alps. However, got to act confidently. Harris might have led the charge on Captain Borisovich but going by the return to his more usual, anxious expression, I figure it's Captain Jessica who's back in the leadership role again.

The helicopter lurches upwards briefly. Why it's doing this with its nose pointing upwards and its underside running roughly parallel to the glacier edge, as opposed to rising with its rotors, I can't tell. I hope there's a piloting reason for it and not just that the desktop fan impression which passes for its engine has suddenly gone on the fritz. Either way, we ascend up the side of the glacier and then level out over what might be described as a flatter plateau at the top, if you allow yourself some poetic license. Note the comparative, "flatter". It's definitely not flat, just not the full-on sleigh run descent of the lower edge which overlooks the way back down the valley to Interlaken.

Captain Borisovich turns round to us and yells, "Twenty seconds to landing! Get ready to jump!"

Yes, sir. Whether "Platoon" or, "Apocalypse Now", it seems we're definitely back in 'Nam. Only it's got a hell of a lot colder since the Americans left. You know global warming is really their fault.

The helicopter touches down on that flatter field. Captain Borisovich turns around again and shouts another instruction, but the whirring of the rotors makes it impossible to hear. However, the gesture of a raised middle finger makes that an unnecessary requirement.

As per our forty second pre-flight briefing which Captain Borisovich was generous enough to provide, we hurl our three substantial bags out of the cabin door and then jump after them. Alice and I fall deliberately onto our right sides and roll over three times to minimize the impact. Harris falls flat on his face and starts trying to make snow angels while he looks for his glasses.

By the time I look up again, the helicopter is already at least a hundred metres away and accelerating rapidly around the peak on its extended route back to Interlaken. Strangely enough though, I don't feel alone or abandoned. My mind is clear and unconcerned about my fears. There's a job to do and it's time to get on with it. I know what I need to do next and that's good enough for me.

Chapter 19
PICKING THROUGH THE ICE

Harris

There isn't much conversation. This might be quite a hair-brained and hastily contrived plan but even Jessica, Alice and myself have enough sense between us to have talked through what we need to be doing now that we're finally on this glacier. As usual, I was treated as needing to be lectured repeatedly as to what I would need to do but I do believe that I have a reasonable handle on it. Fair enough, I suppose, I could imagine the eyeballs rolling with that little stumble out of the dratted helicopter but once I found my glasses again, I rose back to the moment and assumed my role.

The overall plan isn't really that complex. We each have a metal detector to locate the parts of the clarinet. Charles provided a very loose description of where he thought the instrument landed after its descent. It's strange to gaze up there and see that peak where Givret's clarinet was last touched and from where it fell to its new location. Or locations, I should say, since if Charles is to be believed, it's resting in more than one place. Taking Jessica at her word, that may be a good thing. According to her, if the clarinet had been a single, indivisible piece, it might well have shattered. Being a composite of five pieces, that should have allowed the shock of the impact to be absorbed through it splitting into the different elements. It just makes our job that bit harder now.

Again, I hope that Jessica knows what she's talking about on another, at least equally important topic. It's not that I don't believe her honesty, but she is a professional linguist. That much has been made clear on enough occasions to date. However, it does make me wonder why I should be intrinsically trusting her supposed expertise on everything from the science of physics through geography to public transport. Does she imagine that nobody else knows anything else? I shudder to think that just maybe she does.

My immediate concern is that I do hope that her meteorological assessment is correct. Going by sources of information which I do not know or would not even hope to understand, she determined that since the clarinet landed on the glacier, there were a few colder days with rainfall over the region, followed by mainly blazing sunshine. If Jessica is to be believed, then that means that the clarinet pieces should have been frozen in ice during the overnight periods which immediately followed its fall. With the onset of the warmer weather, the glacier will have been slowly melting each day, releasing water which flows down the mountains and into the valleys. This is apparently quite normal and is the main source of freshwater in these parts. The glaciers expand and trap water through the winter and then release it slowly over the course of the summer. However, the nights remain freezing cold, even in summer and so the rate of melting can vary. Jessica claims that we have been exceptionally lucky since the initial cold snap will have prevented the clarinet pieces from being simply swept off the glacier during the daytime melting, but the warmer weather will then have left them near enough to the surface for us to find and retrieve them.

At least, as she herself admits, that's the theory. The problem is, of course, that none of us knows just how close or not the pieces are to the surface. There's a risk that they've already been swept away although that seems unlikely. The more likely problem is not knowing how far down we will probably need to excavate to extract them. Ideally, they'll be near enough to the surface, but we simply don't know. The metal detectors are powerful, but the reality remains that the bulk of the clarinet is composed of wood. Very well laminated wood, thank goodness, but still wood. The metal of the keys and the frame which attaches them is a relatively small amount. If the pieces are buried too deeply, then the detectors will have a considerable challenge to find them.

All things considered, however, it's still a wonder that we're here at all. The sheer improbability of most of what has occurred since I left Bristol is quite incredible when I consider it. In which case, pulling the world's most expensive wind instrument out of an Alpine glacier should probably not be inconceivable. Even for a secondary school teacher, accompanied by one of his students and her thrill-seeking aunt. I really must pull myself together and stop thinking about things quite so rationally. It just isn't helping on this trip.

Jessica has determined the starting point, using my account of the basic description which Charles provided. This met with a predictable torrent of sarcasm as to its general uselessness, but I must concede that Charles could have been a bit more specific. It has put us towards the top of what is roughly a diamond shape, longer at the top end than at the bottom, with the longer end tailing away towards the cliffs which surround us on two sides. We're standing relatively near to the bottom of the cliff on our right, the top of which is where the clarinet fell from. I would say that we're in a field of ice except that most fields are relatively flat. This one proceeds on a slope whose highest point curves around the base of the cliffs and then proceeds downwards from there, with the lowest point at the corner of the diamond. The slope itself is gentle enough for us to walk on, but this is still dangerous, and we each have a pointed stick to support us and to prevent us from sliding. We should, again according to Jessica, have two sticks each but since we have to carry our metal detectors as well, we're limited to one each. Apparently we can get away with this because the immediate surface area is a form of slush. It feels icier than snow underfoot but is not rock hard and slick like an ice rink. Underneath, that hardness is apparently very much present, but it allows us to walk for now, provided that we're careful on the slope itself. Whatever else, I'm following orders at this point. I'm an expert on sonatas and concertos. All this mountaintop adventuring is someone else's domain. Which is why I really do hope that Jessica knows what she's talking about as much as she gives the impression of doing.

One of the more worrying aspects for me is the light. It is starting to fade and while genuine darkness may yet be some way off, a sort of dusk is already settling in. Like the other two, I'm wearing a head torch but have not yet switched it on. I would honestly love to but Jessica says that the battery will not last all night so we can use these things from around ten o'clock onwards. That's still a few hours away and I hope we're not going to take that long but since it's possible, I suppose I just have to do what I'm told. Again. I really am starting to wonder if this is how citizens feel in the world's more authoritarian countries.

We spread out from the starting point, roughly equidistant from each other. We each take an axis moving out from the centre towards the edge of an imaginary circle surrounding the starting point. Once we each come to the edge, we move right to scan the segment created between our own axis and that of the person to the right of us. With nothing found, we move further out, scouring a wider circle. In the event that somebody finds a piece, that will become the new starting point, and we'll go from there. It's a painstaking procedure and one which seems highly likely to take a very long time for next to no gain but it's the best we have.

An hour and a half later, there's still nothing to show. Absolutely nothing. I am not enjoying this sensation. I'm colder than I can remember ever having been in my entire life. I've fallen I don't know how many times, and my right elbow is aching severely. All of this I could take if I felt some degree of hope, but the worst aspect right now is one of an increasing hopelessness. What if this is all for nothing? I may not even get down from here again alive. And then what? I suppose Charles could eventually explain to Isabel why my frozen corpse should have appeared mysteriously in Switzerland, but I really do not know what she would make of that. But overall, it's just the feeling of putting in all this effort, taking all these risks and enduring so much discomfort for nothing whatsoever which is what I find truly soul-destroying. The light is much worse than previously, but it doesn't even matter since if my metal detector finds nothing, what am I supposed to see in any case?

At the same time, I can't stop. At the most basic level, there's no real reason to stop. What else is there to do? I could try to keep warm somehow, but it doesn't feel quite right. The other two are still hard at work. I almost hate to admit it but that is maybe the main motivation. I thought that love would take me anywhere and in terms of the overall perspective, it does. It's why I'm here. Yet it feels a little remote at the present moment. Is the concept of love enough to make me want to keep ploughing through this endless plain of ice? I can't say that it does without that feeling a little artificial. It's not even the scorn I would no doubt endure from the other two if I were to quit now. That would be dreadful but even that fear is not what's driving me. Strangely enough, it feels as though their own persistence and their dedication set an example of how to be behaving. Neither is doing anything for their own self-aggrandizement. Neither is trying to impress anyone. They don't even seem to be paying much attention to what anyone else is doing. They're just getting on with it. What they're doing simply seems to be what's expected of each of us. I just keep doing it.

It's dark now but the head torches are still not switched on. Without clouds but with a low, full moon, the effect is to make it quite easy to see what is happening. There's a dark blue effect to everything. Even Jessica has permitted us a twenty-minute break a short while ago, but the mood is subdued. We're just not getting anywhere. I said outright that I was feeling exhausted during our break. Jessica was sympathetic. That itself had me worried and still does. If we really had a good chance at this point, I would surely have received an earful of abuse.

The light of the stars is beautiful. If I stop for a moment to focus on one, what's amazing is how more and more just become visible. There are more and more of them out there which you don't even see until you focus on a brighter one and then gradually appreciate quite how many more are surrounding it. It's not just the moon which is illuminating us. If I weren't so uncomfortable and so increasingly pessimistic, I would enjoy what I'm seeing hugely. I do wish that it would show us something though. Once more, all I can do in practice is to keep looking.

"Auntie Jess! Auntie Jess!" Alice's shout rends the air out of nowhere. "I've got something!"

I don't know what it says about me that I'm slightly put out that she only bothered to call on her aunt and not me as well, when I should be simply overjoyed at the prospect of something turning up. Jessica isn't even as close to Alice as I am at this point. Honestly.

Inhibitions aside, I make for Alice, trying not to skid as I approach her from slightly higher up the slope. Jessica's form rises from below, a little to my right. Alice is trying to clear the ice away from a small crevice, her detector bleeping intermittently. Jessica charges in, unhooking an ice pick from her side. She's the only one who is carrying one of these tools. The shop refused to sell one which a child might use and both Jessica and Alice considered it to be tempting Fate too far to equip me with one. And they wonder why I feel disrespected on this expedition.

Jessica pushes Alice gently away from the hole she's been clearing and taps at it with her ice pick. She isn't swinging it hard, which is something. I did warn her when she bought the tool that going in full force would risk accidentally damaging the clarinet itself. She even thanked me for the advice. And apparently I'm the one who can't be trusted with these things? I ask you.

A few minutes later and she pulls out a small piece of metal. Two interlinked hoops. A look of incredulous horror, mixed with anger sweeps over her face.

"O M f'ing G!" she howls to nobody in particular. "We spend four hours beachcombing the only serious competitor to Antarctica for the world's most frozen hell-hole to find a fine example of the classical music world's most intricate engineering, and all we end up with is a frickin' bottle opener which some yobbo probably discarded after a barbecue karaoke party! What are we going to find next? An old tinny? A used condom with the contents frozen inside in case anyone wants a bit of free IVF once we get back down to warmer temperatures? Bloody sodding hell!"

She looks as though she's about to throw the offending article away in no particular direction. However, Alice cuts in.

"Hang on, Auntie. What would some yobbo be doing up here in the first place?"

"I dunno. Smoking pot, looking for a kebab van, trying to get enough signal to watch the footie. Whatever they do."

"But, Auntie, nobody would be doing any of that up here! It doesn't make sense," Alice responds. "Here, let me take a look."

Jessica hands over the piece to Alice who eyes it curiously.

"I don't really know," she confesses. "I don't think it's a bottle opener though. What do you think, Mr Beadlesby?"

It's nice to have somebody notice that I exist for a change. I take the piece in my gloved hand and raise it to my face. I can't see much in this light, so I switch on the torch on my head.

The rush of blood nearly knocks me over. I don't believe it! Surely not! Straight away, all of that hopelessness has disappeared as though it had never even been there in the first place. I turn round to the other two.

"This is incredible," I announce. "This is nothing like what you imagined at all!"

"So what is it?" asks Jessica. "One of those puzzle things you get in Christmas crackers with two rings which nobody can separate except for the family idiot? I didn't realize that Santa's grotto was located up here."

Her words are the usual sort of irreverent commentary you would expect but the tone is more one of exhaustion, not spitefulness. As usual with such remarks, I just ignore it.

"These pieces are the keys from the barrel of a clarinet," I explain. "I can't be certain, but I think that they're made of solid silver. If so, then this can only have come from Karl Givret's clarinet!"

Jessica and Alices' heads both look up sharply, their eyes focused on me. The atmosphere has changed completely.

"One question," Jessica says. The tone is questioning but not challenging. "I thought the keys were supposed to be attached integrally to the clarinet. Why are these ones separate?"

That is a good question. As ever, the woman is not stupid. I stop for a moment to think.

"I would guess," I start, in a knowing but humble tone, "that since the barrel is one of the shortest pieces, that the keys might have worked their way loose on impact. The joints are longer and would probably hold their keys while the shape of the bell would prevent the loss. As for the mouthpiece, I can't really say. So that would mean, at least, that the barrel should be close."

"All right," Jessica replies. "We found it at a depth of about forty centimetres, so I'm guessing that must be the rough depth at which to look. I'm going to carve out some circles around here with the ice pick at that depth. You two use your torches to scout inside them and see if anything shows up. If the clarinet is black, then it ought to show through to a reasonable extent."

It doesn't take that long. Twenty minutes later, I myself manage to see what looks like a shadow to the outer left of the third circle which Jessica has carved out in a concentric pattern around the spot where we found the keys. It's slightly uphill from there.

The feeling is wonderful. I simply cannot describe what it feels like to hold even just that barrel in my hands. The barrel of Givret's own clarinet. How, how, I cannot say really. Amazing, incredible, indescribable – none of them does justice to my feelings.

Jessica, by contrast, is more practically oriented.

"So, Harris," she interrupts, jerking my attention away from the wonderful images in my mind, "is this thing screwed, or will those keys fit back on? I mean, if it's landed in bits and pieces, then are we just going to be picking up the remnants in order to pull together the world's most expensive Ikea kit of a once prized, musical instrument?"

Another fair question, phrased once more with the delicate sensitivity of a common street criminal.

I look again at the barrel. Its condition is not actually too bad at all. I cannot say myself, but it looks as though it somehow bounced on the ice with the keys forced off in a single motion. I remove these awful gloves for a moment to place them together. The feeling of agony on my fingertips is excruciating. The sensation is like having water forced under the nails, which is immediately frozen. I cry out in pain but at the same time, I see the keys slip back over the barrel. The effect is perfect.

Jessica kindly takes the barrel from me and lets me get the gloves back on. I still cannot feel anything in my hands but at least the pain is diminishing. In the meantime, she turns away and starts to confer with Alice. I cannot make out what they're talking about but given the fairly serious tone and the various gestures up and down the slope, I assume that for once it isn't some infantile exchange about teenage sex or Alice's parents. If only the two of them would grow up. At least for Alice it isn't too late yet, but I can't speak for her aunt.

The two of them come back over.

"How are the hands, Harris?" Jessica asks.

"I think I may recover some sensation shortly," I reply, perhaps a little curtly.

"Well, let me know if you're having any serious problems," she tells me.

"Now," she starts, launching into her assumed leadership role again, "this is very helpful. Going by the angles of the two bits we've found, I think we can narrow down the area to search into a corridor stretching from up there to down there."

She indicates two corresponding points above and below us.

"Let's hope that the rest of the pieces haven't separated. We're lucky that we were able to get both parts of that, what was it? Anvil?"

"Barrel," I correct her.

"Yeah, thanks. The barrel. Still, as you say, Harris, with a bit of luck, the other pieces will at least be in one piece each. I figure that each one we find ought to narrow down the area we still have to search so as we progress, we'll get them faster and faster. Head torches on at this point, I think, and if you need any ice picking, just give me a shout.

"We'll sweep the corridor in a diagonal motion from side to side. Harris, you go downhill from here, Alice uphill. I'll take the further bit past Harris since it's getting steeper there.

"Any questions?"

None is forthcoming.

"Then let's go!"

An hour and a half more is all it takes. There was nothing further uphill from where the barrel landed, which is a credit to Alice. She missed nothing in the first place when she was sweeping outwards from the starting point. I found the lower joint next about twenty-five minutes later, Jessica the bell shortly after that. Going from there, Alice was reassigned part of the downhill sweep, which was a very good thing. The area covered was broadening and it was off to one side where Alice found the mouthpiece. After covering my own area until it met with that covered by Jessica, I expanded the search to the right of her part of the corridor and eventually located the upper joint. Unlike the barrel, each of the other pieces was fully intact.

I am now sitting in front of the five pieces of the clarinet, and my breath is coming quickly. I do so wish that there was a possibility just to feel relief on this expedition, to rejoice in a job well done. Even if only for a few minutes. I do know that we still face a daunting task in getting the clarinet back to Bristol and that spending the night up here is not going to be a walk in the park. But it would still be nice to do nothing but bask in the moment of recovering the clarinet. The question now, however, is whether these pieces still work together. This is critical, so as to ensure that we have the full set of what constitutes the clarinet.

Ever so carefully, I push the barrel into the mouthpiece. It simply won't fit. The feeling of horror is like a cold hand sweeping over me. I would have thought it impossible to feel anything even colder at this juncture, but such is somehow the case. If the pieces won't fit, then there's no clarinet, just a set of useless pieces. This can't be happening. Not at this point. No. No. I repeat, no!

I don't know what to do. I just sit there in horror. I have no idea what to do, what to say, even what to feel.

"What's the matter, Harris?" Jessica's voice cuts into my reflections. Her tone is casual, far too casual to my way of thinking, but not disrespectful or cruel. "Having trouble getting what you want out of your bits and pieces?"

Still the tone is not unkind although I do note Alice sniggering quietly at what I suppose was probably some sexual double entendre. Perhaps Jessica only meant to lighten the mood, but it's lost on me.

She stoops down and picks up the two pieces. She holds them up in turn and examines them with a look of vague interest as one might a lampshade in an average department store.

"Bit slushy," she remarks to nobody in particular before turning to me.

"Tell me, Harris," she asks, "is this thing precision-engineered?"

I sigh inwardly.

"Hand-crafted is the term more commonly used," I tell her, "but with an inordinate degree of precision, yes."

"Well, that's probably your problem," she replies. "You've only cleared out the slushy bits from the top ends of each tube. If you look closely inside, there's still some crap lodged in the gubbins there. It's melting at different rates which I would guess also affects the relative sizes of the bits and pieces to fit together."

I can't believe the crudity and complete lack of awareness in her description of the internal workings of one of the finest musical instruments on this planet. However, she somehow inspires hope at the same time.

"You have two problems here if you want to get this thing working. First, you need everything to be at a reasonable and consistent temperature. Second, you have to be able to take your gloves off to work on it without losing your fingertips to a case of frostbite which you would only be able to get otherwise by giving Frosty the Snowman a handjob."

Predictably enough, Alice has a small fit of hysterics at this staggeringly low level of humour.

Jessica continues, "Let's just get to the next stage of the plan and bed down for the night. We all need to get together and snuggle up close under our survival blanket. That, in theory, will generate enough warmth for all of us to have a good night's sleep. Or at least a good couple of hours' sleep in the time before the summer sun dawns on us all. Assuming all that works, it'll also provide just about enough warmth for you to warm up the clarinet and check that it's fully functional and that we can get out.

"All good?"

Almost every turn of phrase she employs seems to be incredibly crude, but I still can't help but be assured by the content. It's very strange. I confirm that it is all good.

"Great!" she says. "Then it's bedtime for everyone!"

Chapter 20
THREE IN A BED

Jessica

Sleeping together. It's a phrase with several connotations, some enchanting, some horrifying, some which prick your curiosity, some which make sure that you just don't want to know. Obviously, the primary connotation is a sexual one since it actually has very little to do with anybody sleeping in a bed so much as what they're doing in it before or after the actual sleeping bit. It can even indicate something considerably less sexually-orientated. After all, on various summer holidays as a child, my parents would sometimes book a twin room for me to share with Bethany, and I would never in my wildest nightmares claim to have slept with her in the sense which Colin does. Or maybe to the extent of the sense in which Colin is equipped to satisfy her desires – cue malicious smirk – but no more than that.

For me, the attraction in being able to sleep with somebody could be summed up as a sense of intimacy, of being able to trust another person enough to be completely vulnerable next to them and also for them to trust me. Obviously, if that somebody were Timothy Dalton, I wouldn't hesitate to ask any questions. The main problem would be that I'd be too excited to do much sleeping. Then again, if Tim were interested in something else apart from the actual sleeping in his bed, you wouldn't catch me complaining. I'd be sleeping on the back seat of his Aston Martin DBS if that was what it took. My 007 fantasies aside, however, that feeling of complete intimacy and trust is, I think, what really makes it an attractive proposition.

It's also why I feel that the concept of a one-night stand is just a bit cheap.

I'm not one to condemn others for simply feeling different about something to how I feel. Far too many people are given to doing that and belittling others' choices. In questions of taste, it's just ridiculous to my way of thinking. I don't for a moment appreciate concertos or symphonies, but I won't put down Harris for liking them, for example. I just wish he wouldn't be such a monumental prig whenever he's discussing them. In questions of politics, it can be harder to accept the right of others to think differently but I get around it, mainly by not getting into political discussions with other people if I can, and also by trying to recall that everyone has the right to an opinion while what really is offensive is a mindset which thinks that deliberately hurting other people for your own pride or benefit is somehow OK. In terms of morality, where two things are technically legal but one clearly more ethical, again I have to accept the need to live and let live so long as nobody is getting hurt by virtue of another's targeted meanness or blind stupidity. Hence the attitude to one-night stands. I don't see them as really being beneficial to anyone beyond the physical endpoint and have too often seen them ending them up as emotionally messy for all concerned. However, I'm not going to condemn you if that's what you're into. So long as it doesn't involve children, animals or me and not necessarily in that order. Also, provided that it doesn't involve Jöchi. I may only have met him for a total of ten minutes of my life, but it was a scarring experience.

All of that aside, however, the term, "sleeping together" seems altogether unsuited for what's going on now, on top of the Upper Grindelwald Glacier except that in precise terms, that is exactly what we're trying to do here. Though without much success. In fact, this is so uncomfortable that I'm even starting to wonder if a one-night stand might not be a preferable option. At least so long as it's not with Jöchi. Compared with that horror story, sleeping together with Alice and Harris inside the belly of a great white shark would be a preferable option. Even a great white shark with a serious case of gastroenteritis. That great British tradition of a bad Saturday night – fish 'n' shits.

Where I am just now is underneath a survival blanket on top of a padded sleeping mat, more or less spooning Alice with Harris on the other side of her.

We figured that the child among us deserved the most warmth, and it also prevented me from having to spoon Harris myself. While I don't want anyone to think that I simply passed the buck on to Alice with this one, it did seem at least a positive side-benefit to the genuine need to ensure that she stays warm. Or at least, as warm as possible in this icy hellhole. By my calculations/best guess, this should be just about enough to keep us alive. Comfortable is way out of our league. A survival blanket, for those who don't know, is a metal-covered, plastic sheet which basically reflects back at you around 90% of the body heat you lose. You can think of it as being loosely akin to wrapping yourself up in tin foil as you would a turkey at Christmas before you stick it in the oven. The great thing about survival blankets, however, is that vegetarians can use them too. So, in theory, this blanket should trap the heat which we're losing collectively and reflect it back onto our spooning selves. Since the dawn will come pretty early at this time of year, it only needs to keep us going for a relatively short amount of time.

The problem is that on a field of ice at this altitude in the middle of the night, we're already losing so much heat that even the aforementioned 10% of it is enough to power your house for a week using a solar panel. Even with all the precautions we've taken, it's cold. Bloody freezing cold.

Harris pipes up, "My goodness! I don't believe it's so perishing up here! How it could it ever reach this sort of temperature? Did you see this coming?"

Is he accusing me of somehow getting us into a freezer compartment impression by virtue of ignorance? Cheeky sod.

"I don't think it's all that surprising, Harris," I start in a tone which is sympathetic though probably a bit artificial. "After all, we're almost a mile above sea level whereas you normally live in Bristol which is at sea level. We're also hundreds of miles from the sea here, which means that the insulating effect you're used to is sadly absent. That's why I wouldn't say that it being a shade colder is necessarily a huge surprise."

Unfortunately, that was probably a bit patronizing.

"Jessica," he sniffs, "I'm a schoolteacher. I do have some awareness of basic geography."

Oh yeah? You seem to lack a basic awareness of anything more complicated than wiping your nose.

"You're a music teacher," I reply. "That doesn't necessarily mean that you need to be any more aware of geography than anyone else."

"I am very much aware of the world beyond music," he says, quite snootily. "Despite what you seem to imagine, I have just as much knowledge of the world at large as any other, normal person."

This is getting too much.

"Look, Harris," I start roughly, "you are not normal."

Luckily, it occurs to me that a slightly more conciliatory tone might be best here. He is pissing me off massively but at the same time, I suppose this petty streak more just reflects his own anxiety. I'm going to have to balance things out here.

"What I mean," I add before he can object further, "is that you are quite clearly a man of intelligence and integrity who dedicates himself to sharing with others what he finds truly important."

How nice of me. But that's enough diplomacy. Time to shut him up.

"But what you are clearly not is normal."

"Meaning what, exactly?" he snaps out of nowhere.

"Meaning that we wouldn't be sleeping out on a freaking glacier if you hadn't spent a quarter of a million pounds on a wind instrument which some idiot friend of yours managed to take to the top of an Alp and then drop overboard in the process. Meaning that we wouldn't have less than forty-eight hours remaining to get back to Bristol if you hadn't assaulted a retiree and exploded an extended cabin cruiser by launching her dog over the edge of Cheddar Gorge. To take a couple of examples."

"Well," he comes back in a subdued tone, "they weren't all entirely my fault."

"Oh, never mind. Let's just stop snapping at each other, shall we? We're not going to make this work any better by squabbling over what's already happened. We're actually making some progress and we've got the clarinet, amazingly enough. Let's just focus on what we still have to do."

That much, at least, seems to lighten the atmosphere. I might be a sarky, little git most of the time, but I can make friends when I have to.

"Talking of the clarinet, Auntie, I think it might be about ready to try out again," Alice chips in.

I almost forgot. Alice's main job at this point is to supervise the warming up of the clarinet pieces and call time on when to try them out. Each of us has some part of the instrument lodged between our thighs inside our trouser legs. It's one of the warmest parts of the body, believe it or not. The other two parts are under two armpits, one Harris', the other mine. Yes, I know. I think it's gross as well and no doubt Karl Givret is throwing up in his grave at the thought of it. I just hope nobody had the supermarket takeaway enchilada option for dinner. If they did, then the likely gas expulsion via Givret's instrument will probably result in a parp gigantic enough to bring down an avalanche on our heads. And you thought it was bad when your partner farted under the blanket at home.

We extract the various parts from within our outfits and hand them over to Harris. There's a slight stickiness on the lower side of the one from my crotch which I examine quickly in passing. The light is hardly amazing, but it feels strangely warmer than it should. What exactly is this? My mind goes blank for a few seconds before a horrible realization sets in.

I've just started my period.

Oh please no. Of all the things which could have happened, which Fate could have delayed for at least just another twelve hours. Right here, right now? I knew it was due sooner or later, but this is taking the piss. Or worse than that. I suppose it might explain my snappiness of late although I'm not usually one to get extra-grumpy in the run-up to the monthly event. Maybe I'm just a pissy person anyway. Best lay that train of thought to rest quickly though as it certainly isn't going to improve my mood. A quick reflection does, however, reveal why that paragliding harness felt quite so tight around my undercarriage. Ouch. Just the thought makes me squirm now.

Not wanting to make a big deal out of it, at least not quite yet, and in fairness to the other two, I grab a handful of ice to warm in my hand. Then I quickly wipe off all the traces I can see of bodily fluids on whatever part of the clarinet has just been subjected to a flow of female intimacy such as not even a Premier League footballer would enjoy. Together with the slightly whiffy but drier piece from under my armpit, Harris now has all he requires to re-constitute the world's most expensive wind instrument. There's a huge variety of things in what's gone through my head over the past minute. You have to wonder.

Like all good women, I obviously carry a set of tampons and sanitary pads on me at all times. You just never know. Going by that logic, I suppose I shouldn't complain about being surprised now. But given how just about everything else seems to have been plagued by near disaster, somehow in my mind, even if a bit illogically, I just assumed that the statistical chances of this actually happening couldn't be that high. I probably should have stuck with the logic that if it can go wrong, it will. A bit like supermarket queues. It doesn't matter which one you pick. It's always going to be the slowest one. Even if there are only three people in front of you instead of six in the one to your right, you're going to get the one with a checkout assistant so short-sighted that they start trying to scan their own lunchbox, and the clueless wonder who's trying to use their debit card for the first time in their life and eventually resorts to paying in one-pence coins, counted out one by one until the full eighty-eight pound bill has been accounted for. And then they start re-loading their trolley. It shouldn't be guaranteed. It just is.

At this point, I really wish that I'd gone up to that war criminal look-a-like I saw leching over me in some pub in Liverpool last week and tried to get pregnant. I don't tend to get a lot of unwanted attention, certainly not around half past seven in the evening as was the case when this happened. However, this guy had all the sex appeal of a jellyfish with syphilis. He must have figured that his only chance to get some action was to make a blatant approach to anyone more or less female whom he encountered in order to find the truly desperate one. He hardly stood to lose a lot. A quick G&T in the face persuaded him that I wasn't on the desperate list but I'm starting to wonder if a quick impregnation in the disabled toilet round the back might not have been a preferable experience to what I'm feeling now.

Anyway, just go with the flow. So to speak. Where did I leave those tampons? I think for a moment. They'll be in my little toiletries bag. That much is obvious. The question is where did I put said bag? Since arriving on the glacier, I haven't bothered with such niceties as brushing my teeth. Not because I'm British and therefore oral hygiene is an optional extra, thank you very much. We all know what anyone thinks who's seen an Austin Powers movie. Simply because until bedding down under the survival blanket, it was preferable to keep my nose and mouth wrapped tightly under a scarf. I perhaps should have paid more attention to the deodorant but that's Harris' problem now, I grin to myself.

Of course, the sodding bag is probably lodged right in the middle of my hiking rucksack. It's not a huge bag but it's black and therefore next to impossible to find anything in at night without emptying most of the contents. If I'd been smarter, I might have placed it closer to the edge but now that I think about it, I deliberately put it in the middle in order to reduce the chances of any of the liquids inside it getting frozen. The rucksack is currently lodged between my legs, which is a bit ironic since that's ultimately where I'm going to need a tampon to go. However, it's further down than where the clarinet part was. It's nearer to my shins.

I stretch down to reach it, and Alice reacts huffily.

"Auntie Jess!" she complains. "You're sticking your elbow into my ribs!"

"Sorry, Alice," I mumble, "slight emergency here."

"Like what?" she demands. "I'm already freezing and it's even worse with you bent over like that."

"It's…ermm…. a problem which Harris won't have," I state between gritted teeth, in a knowing tone. Alice doesn't get it.

"You mean like using common sense?" she asks. "I don't see how you're doing that right now."

I ignore Alice for the moment. I've reached the rucksack and am scrabbling around inside it, working my way through the water canister – now frozen stiff -, the first aid kit, a spare sandwich which is likely inedible by now and other bits and pieces. I grit my teeth in frustration at the one thing, which I actually want, completely failing to make an appearance. You get used to this when you hike a lot. You just don't usually end up doing so in what feels like a night out gone wrong at the Sir Edmund Hillary tribute park in Nepal. But I'm an experienced hiker and I know that sooner or later, I'm going to find it, and I do. My fingers grasp the toiletries bag. Bracing myself against the necessary, icy agony, I remove my right glove for a moment and gasp as the cold sears into my fingers. Alice looks over my shoulder curiously, but I brush her away.

The toiletries bag is like a mini version of the larger rucksack. How much crap have I packed in here? Toothpaste, a toothbrush (there you go – I'm not as bad as you were thinking a moment ago), lip salve, moisturiser, insect repellent. Pretty much everything you could want other than something to stick up your crotch. And if you are into any sort of practice which involves sticking one or more of those things I just named from my bag up your crotch, then I really don't want to know. Finally though, my now virtually senseless fingers grasp a tampon. I don't have much choice, so I stick it between my teeth while using my hands to re-pack the bag.

That done, I put my right glove back on and remove the left. There's only so long you can go with your flesh exposed, which is something I'm about to find out in the most grotesque way as I pull down my trousers and underwear. If ever you want to kill your libido, I don't think I can recommend a better way. All I want to do right now is pull everything back up and nestle its contents in a tiny, little ball of cosiness never to be disturbed again. Even the thought of Timothy Dalton performing the most passionate acts of delicate and loving caress as we move to consummate the undying love he has always carried for me is not enough. I just want to keep the contents of my knickers well and truly ensconced here. No way, never coming out, sorry.

In practice, it's not as though I've never applied a tampon before, so the overall procedure takes somewhere between five and ten seconds. I don't stop to worry about any escaping blood. It'll probably all freeze against my thigh before it even has a chance to stain my clothes. However, the tampon itself feels like a nine millimetre pistol cartridge, just with less absorbency. That said, it does hit the mark and my clothing flies back up, fully in place.

"It fits!" screeches Harris at the top of his voice. "My wonderful goodness! It fits perfectly!"

How the hell does he know? I didn't even tell Alice what I was just doing. I'm certainly not going to discuss my menstrual exploits with this Brahms-addicted bozo. I look up to see what's going on.

Harris is waving around the full clarinet. Well, I'm glad of that but like the moron he is, he swipes one of the pegs we've used to secure the survival blanket in place, and one corner of our makeshift protection is now flapping in the breeze. I lunge across both Alice and him to grab hold of the peg, but it's already slid out of sight across the ice in front of us. Having spent a few hours trying to find the various pieces of the clarinet, aided by its metal components, I am sure as hell not going back out there in an attempt to locate a plastic peg.

Damn. Frickin' damn.

Harris doesn't even look apologetic. He's entranced by having finally got the stupid thing back together and seems to be playing some sort of jolly jig on it. I look at him and want to punch him in the face and use the clarinet itself as a replacement peg. We're facing imminent death from excessive hypothermia and he's playing the theme tune to Noddy? And this from a guy who ten minutes ago was lecturing us about how normal he is? He's about as normal as an Elvis impersonator from the planet Jupiter landing in the local park to give you a lecture about supermarket discount vouchers in the Islamic Republic of Iran. And even then, if asked for the more abnormal of the two, you'd have a choice to make.

I breathe deeply and ignore him. We have no spare pegs, so the next best thing is going to have to be one of my precious hiking sticks. I jam that into the ground next to him and pull the clarinet out of his gob.

"Listen to me, Harris," I state, clearly and in a measured pace but with all the menace of a mafioso enforcer giving some poor schmuck their final warning in a New York mob movie, "you have almost killed us right now by wrecking part of our shelter. I'm going to repair it with a very valuable piece of equipment. If you should destroy, damage or lose any further piece of equipment which we require, I will seriously consider shoving that wind instrument so far up your alimentary canal that you'll still be able to blow into the mouthpiece while the music sounds from out of your rectum. That is not an idle threat. Do I make myself clear?"

I think he can tell when I'm really mad because he looks downwards and refuses to meet my gaze. Instead he just whimpers, "Yes, Jessica. I'm really very sorry."

I clamber back over him and Alice, hearing her grunt some colourful phrase which I doubt she uses very often at school and certainly not in her piano lessons. Given the duress we're all under right now, I don't see a problem with it myself. She's only articulating what's going through my head at present as well.

Finally, we're all back in position as before, only with the clarinet wedged between Harris and Alice and a tampon wedged where needed in my nether regions. I think we're done with disasters for the evening and can finally try to sleep a bit.

Oh dear, Jessica, you just can't learn. Otherwise, you would never, ever tempt Fate with a thought like that. What you just thought is probably what some engineer was thinking about on the Titanic after fixing a steam valve problem down below, about ten minutes before the ship ploughed into the iceberg. Only it doesn't even take ten minutes in this case.

Alice's phone rings. She shuffles awkwardly, her knee quickly making this one of the least comfortable periods I have ever suffered. She looks at the screen and turns to me in horror.

"Auntie Jess! It's Mum!"

Bethany? Holy freaking crap! Bethany? Bethany! How much more disastrous can this night possibly get? Why can't she just have sex with Colin and leave us in peace?

OK, Jessica, forget the self-reflection. We need a plan, and we need it now. As in right now.

Well, this worked a few weeks ago. If it ain't broke, don't fix it.

"Alice, answer the phone and hold it close to your face. Tell your mum that you're in bed in Taunton after a heavy day."

Alice knows better than to start a debate when time is of the essence. This may not be the best plan but it's a plan and she trusts me that it'll work. Let's hope she's right.

"Hi, Mum!" she beams into the phone she's just picked up. "How are you?"

"Oh, there you are, Alice! My goodness, I've been trying to get hold of you all evening!"

Yeah, and I bet Colin has been doing something the same to you, Bethany.

Get a grip, Jessica. We don't have time to sit around and be sarcastic. I get my own phone and start looking up cheap hotel rooms in the Taunton area. Thank goodness Switzerland is so small in a horizontal sense that the phone network signals reach pretty much everywhere.

"Oh sorry, Mum, it's been quite heavy here and I was spending a lot of time in the bath, just relaxing. Maybe I didn't hear you call."

"Are you all right, darling? Is it wearing you out too much?"

I roll my eyes to myself.

"Oh no," Alice responds. "I'm holding together fine. I just need to relax a little bit. That's why I've gone to bed a shade early."

It's worth bearing in mind that the time in Switzerland is one hour ahead of that in the UK.

"But how is the contest going?" Bethany finally asks. Don't worry about whether Alice might have tripped over a pebble, you stupid cow; try asking her if she's actually made progress in a serious competition. Takes a while to get there but that's my sister for you.

The problem, of course, is that Alice has already been out of the competition for some time, given that she never actually qualified in the first place. She looks over at me with a questioning look on her face.

"Well, Mum, I'm not quite sure how to describe it," she replies hesitantly, playing for time.

"Down but not quite out," I whisper over to her. "You're in until Sunday but unlikely to make the top spot."

We cannot have Bethany expecting to see her back in Bristol tomorrow, but we also don't need the maternal moron waiting to see Alice come back with the trophy in her bag. Alice does a good job of filling her in on this point. What a girl.

"Anyway, dear, what's your room like?" asks Bethany after a while.

I don't really know why this matters but at least we're ready for it. Alice spins her camera round to mine, which has some generic photos of the inside of a hotel room somewhere near Taunton. Why I've bothered to look up Taunton and not just pretty much a generic hotel room anywhere in the world, I'm not sure. At least this way, there's minimal risk of a random guide to the New York Subway lying on the side table or a leaflet for the Golden Passion Massage Parlour in Bangkok, which might give the game away a bit.

"And where is Mr Beadlesby?" Bethany enquires.

"Oh, he's right next to me," says Alice, a little too quickly.

"What?" Bethany reacts violently. "I thought you were in your bedroom? What on earth is he doing there?"

Playing with his instrument, which is probably longer than anything Colin has, you daft bint.

Focus, Jessica, focus, I remind myself. Thankfully, Alice recovers quickly enough to correct the error herself.

"I mean, he's in the room next to me, Mum," she says, talking as someone would correcting a mistaken dimwit. Which is probably pretty easy under the circumstances. "I think he may have gone to sleep by now. He was quite exhausted too."

"Well, if you're tired, darling, I really do think that you should get some sleep now. Maybe I should just pass on Dad's regards, and you can talk to him tomorrow."

"Yes, that would be a good plan," yawns Alice, winking at me. "Also, tomorrow's schedule could be quite packed so it might be best if I call you when it's a convenient moment."

Allowing for one mistake, Alice has otherwise handled this impeccably. That last comment is pure class. Even if Bethany probably doesn't like it as there's a risk of Alice calling while she's trying to shag Colin. But I'm much less concerned about that schedule than about ours. If we can just remember to call my sister at some point by the evening, this could be our ticket out on the Bethany front.

So long as we don't go and crash headfirst into the side of a cliff on our flight down to Interlaken. That'll really upset Bethany.

Which means it all works out for the best one way or another, I suppose.

Time for some sleep if we can.

Chapter 21
QUEEN OF THE AIR

Jessica

It's go time. Launch. No need for a highway to the danger zone. The danger zone is right in front of us. It's a downward stretch of ice which stretches out some way but gets progressively steeper. Heading down that can only lead to an airborne descent. The question now is whether said descent is controlled and navigated as hoped or ends up in an embarrassing impression of a berry jam at the bottom of the valley in less than a minute's time. It's a sobering thought.

Not that there's any need to sober up. I may feel a bit under the weather this morning, but it isn't due to drink. Nor, as might be the case after a night on the town, is there any trace of any unintentionally released body fluids anywhere in my vicinity. Well, only if you count the rather long and bright red popsicle impression snaking down my inner leg. But let's not dwell on that. I certainly don't want to.

The reason I'm feeling a shade rough is, understandably enough, due to a total sleeping time of about an hour and a half last night with the rest of the time spent reflecting on whether I still had any extremities. And trying to ignore the fact that the tampon I'd inserted was feeling like a surgical implant from a cold weather outlet next to where only penguins with heat intolerance hang out.

However, as planned, it didn't last too long, the sun usefully rising at around five in the morning. As far as I'm concerned, the sooner the better. The other two are helpfully enough still alive and that's about all we need. I may feel like an arthritis sufferer and hungry as hell, but we have the clarinet and we're on course to make our way out of here. The only underlying assumption where there may be a serious miscalculation on the part of yours truly, is that we may be on course to kill ourselves while trying to reach Interlaken. Apart from that, the plan is well and truly on the money. So far.

On getting up, we quickly spread out the paragliders and strapped on what was left of the kit. I wondered if it was worth ditching things like the metal detectors on the glacier but the hiker in me rebelled against the thought of littering the Alps. You just don't do that, even if you can. Besides, it might be genuinely held against us in the event that the forces of law and order, for whatever reason, investigate what we've been up to and discover such littering. The Swiss will do you over properly for that sort of thing. Maybe not as harshly as in Singapore but only just. Finally, the vast bulk of our equipment consists of the paragliders themselves so who really cares? What's left over is hardly going to make a significant difference. Might as well reduce the criminal penalties by a couple of hundreds francs if nothing else.

The peaks are standing over us, glistening in white though with some rocks pointing through here and there, this being the height of summer. After last night, that takes some convincing to believe, trust me, but I do know logically that it's the case. There's a real serenity up here as there usually is first thing in the morning. Nothing moves but the sun's rays just increasingly light everything up, not rapidly but steadily. Normally, I would say that it's beautiful but there's an implicit threat here. I can easily respect the mountains but it's harder to love them when you consider that each snowy top in front of you might become your headstone within the next five minutes. But come on, Jessica, get with the programme. They're magnificent and they're the background you need to look your greatest and perform at your best.

Harris, of course, had no clue how to strap himself in. At the point where they did this during the training flight, he was probably too busy trying not to brick himself to pay the slightest attention to what was happening. Luckily, Alice had the presence of mind to record the procedure on her phone and between that and my own memory, we've got Harris strapped in and ready to launch. Alice and I have got ourselves almost all in as well. Very fortunately, she followed in detail what Daniel was doing when he got ready to launch with her yesterday morning. Was it only so recently? Time is passing at a very slow pace here. Since this time yesterday, I've been hit on by Switzerland's most randy and physically disgusting teenager, learned to paraglide over some of the greatest scenery I've ever seen, acquired a shed load of equipment which I have no license to use legally, landed on a glacier from a helicopter, discovered the world's most expensive wind instrument ever and spent the one – and I hope only – night of my life in sub-zero temperatures. Never mind menstruation and Bethany. That's been enough for me.

Except, of course, it isn't. Now I have to throw Alice and myself off a cliff and get all three of us through an illegal flight into the centre of Interlaken so we can make a run for it back to Bristol. Just gets better all the time.

OK, final checks on Harris complete. Final checks on Alice complete. Final checks on equipment loads complete. Final steps in strapping myself in. Click here, click there, click on the crotch strap – bloody hell, I wish I didn't have to do that. The manufacturers would have you believe that any woman can do whatever she wishes without discomfort when she wears these tampons. If I weren't experiencing the example of a technically illegal activity, I'd feel like writing to somebody to complain about false advertising. Still, final checks on me complete. Let's go.

Harris is due to launch first. He's the one who's more likely to need some sort of supervision or guidance so it's best for him to be in front of Alice and me. If we launch first, we risk losing track of him entirely. He's on our right and looking as though he's on his way to his own execution. Alice and I are carrying the clarinet since, according to Harris himself, he's more likely to die than we are and if that happens, he'd like us to present the clarinet to Isabel as a final demonstration of his undying love for her. Unfortunate adjective to use under the circs but you have to admire his resigned courage. He knows this is a shade riskier than a bike ride (unless you're a dog on a skateboard next to the school where he teaches) but he's going for it without complaining. It occurs to me that if he dies but we don't, talking our way out of Switzerland with the clarinet but not getting noticed is going to be hellishly harder than it would be with him. He's the only one who knows a damn thing about it. Also, he hasn't given us Isabel's contact details. But I suppose we'll catch up with her if we're not too incarcerated in a Swiss jail to attend the funeral. Romance is so much harder when you bring practicality into the equation. But I don't want to kill his vibe so I'm keeping my mouth shut.

I give Harris the wave off. This is a kind of mock salute, waving the hand from the level of the eyes with the elbow bent, down to a forwards level with the arm outstretched. I don't really know what it means but I've seen fighter pilots taking off from aircraft carriers doing it on TV and it looks cool. I could probably have been a navy pilot myself, you know. I just didn't fancy the underwear. All that getting strapped in between the legs would be a real killer and once a month, as I'm discovering today – oh yes, as I'm damn well discovering today – it would be hell. Especially if ever I did need to eject, and knowing my luck that would definitely be at the wrong time of the month. It just doesn't bear thinking about. I'd rather go down with the jet.

Harris, needless to say, fails completely to look remotely cool. He totters down the slope, his neon orange paraglider trailing slowly behind him. What is it with him and neon orange? I dunno. Alice and I have a more modest blue, in case you're wondering. He's swerving from side to side in his efforts and I'm worried that he might even get his chute cords tangled up. That will be a literal killer but there's nothing I can do about it now. He's on the slope and his forward motion can't be stopped. Thankfully, that feature is what saves him as he skids and falls over forwards. Despite what you might think, this is not so bad. It just looks it. He slides along on his front, giving Alice and me a nice view of his rapidly receding backside as he accelerates down, clearly out of control. But right now, that doesn't matter. He flies over the edge of the glacier and disappears downwards. However, his chute follows him and then billows open. I can just see the top edge floating away. At least for now, he's airborne and he's not plunging to his death at terminal velocity.

So far so good. Time to go. I can't pick Alice up as Daniel did. I'm just not strong enough. We have an alternative arranged where we both jog forwards twenty paces, roughly to where the slope of the glacier becomes so steep that we're committed whether we like it or not. Together, we call out the number of each pace and on twenty, Alice launches herself backwards into my lap as I sit down. I immediately pull in the straps which will hold her tight against me. Our forward momentum is enough to keep us slithering and soon screeching down the slope at an ever-growing speed. Before we hit the point where Harris lurched over the edge, I do what he should have done but probably couldn't because he was lying prone on his stomach and pull the cords forward as violently as I can. This is just enough to expand the chute above us. We keep driving forwards though still just about on the ice and I can feel the chute tauten above me. Shortly before we cascade downwards, I pull back on the cords and lean back. This should result in a small climb. That doesn't exactly happen, presumably because we're too heavy, but the net effect is that we take off forwards above the ice, following a loosely flat trajectory. I look round to check and can see that the first peaks are moving past behind us while the glacier falls away beneath us. We're flying.

I run a fast check of the basic systems requirements. The cords are intact and working. The straps around Alice and me are holding fast. My view is not obscured – Alice is strapped slightly lower on me. In another life, I'd be pausing at this juncture to take in the scenery and admire its grandeur. Still, you've probably heard enough about blue skies, gleaming white peaks, Alpine meadows and forest lines, and just want to get to some of the action. It's the same for me right now too.

First things first. Where the hell is Harris? The basic plan is to descend fairly quickly to the level where the glaciers start along the mountainsides. This should give us a decent, forward momentum but keep us going at a reasonable height until we can see Interlaken in front of us. Then we'll have to balance descent, giving us forward speed, against sufficient height so that we can keep going long enough. This should be roughly intuitive, especially after yesterday's experience although at that point, as the one who figured it out yesterday, I'll be leading, and Harris will be following.

That said, it's damn hard work today. Having Alice strapped on in front of me is making this a hell of a lot tougher to control than my single seat gig yesterday. The paraglider still more or less controls OK but once it's going up, down or to one side or another, you have to apply quite some effort to rein it in.

Anyway, controls aside, at this point Harris is meant to be in front of me. Somewhere. So where has he got to? There's no sign of him to the front and I can't see anything above. I look down in dread but thankfully, there's no indication of a neon orange crash site, either recent or imminent.

Alice is looking around too. She looks over my shoulder and suddenly shouts in my ear, "There he is! Look! He's behind you!"

What is this? A frickin' pantomime? I check behind to see and indeed, he's there. About sixty metres behind us and the same distance higher.

Dimwit! He must have gone over the edge and then yanked back on the cords in fright at the speed of his fall. That would have stopped the fall and made him climb, but it would also have slowed him down considerably. Alice and I must have flown right underneath him on our launch. I offer a small prayer of thanks that he wasn't hovering right in front of us when we first took off.

So now what? The distance between us and Harris is increasing. He must be near stationary. I use my own speed to bank sharply to the left and pull back on both cords as we come around. This brings us into a climbing turn. Our speed is bleeding off but we're rising to just about Harris' level. On closer inspection, he's not quite stationary but is drifting forwards and starting to descend at a slow rate. Hardly enough for the plan but enough to let me get onto a loosely parallel flight path.

"Harris!" I yell.

No reaction. I pull in my breath and let go another shout.

"Harris!"

What's his problem? We don't have any engines behind us, and the only wind noise is that caused by the air flowing past us. I suppose the helmets are padded, since the main design concern would be to hear communications through the built-in earpiece and mic combination which, of course, we're not using. Damn. You'd think he might have seen us though. Alice and I are not flying in a stealth bomber. I bank to the right towards him. With a bit of luck, the movement might catch his attention.

It does indeed as he turns round and looks up as though we were the last thing he ever expected to see. You'd think we were trying to shoot him down or something. I give up any attempt at vocal communication but try to indicate with my hands that we need to head down and that he should follow me.

I wish we'd worked on hand signals a bit more before taking off. Then again, it's always easier to be wise after the event. If I ever find myself paragliding illegally with a total dork again, at least that's one lesson learned.

Harris cups a hand to his ear and shrugs, as if to indicate that he has no idea what I'm trying to say. He then banks left towards us. This is very bad. We're drifting closer together and will soon collide. It's not evident to Harris because his gaze is fixed on Alice and me but if you look upwards, you can see that our two chutes are not that far apart. If they become entangled, we're going to be literally hitched for the rest of our lives. All twenty seconds or so which will be left of them.

I point downwards once more, as emphatically as I possibly can, then bank left and start a gentle descent. Quickly, I bank right again to correct back onto my original direction of travel but maintain the descent. I hope that he'll follow me at least. I look back and see him give a thumbs-up. He's understood something though I'm not sure what.

That becomes immediately clear as he pitches down and descends. Rapidly. I can only assume that the plan itself has evaporated out of his ears. He's suddenly shooting downwards, heading well below the glacier line and picking up speed like some sort of air-launched missile. What on earth does he think he's doing? We might just make Interlaken that way but the lower you go, the less room for manoeuvre you leave yourself. Nor will you look like a regular paraglider to the local cop shop.

Harris, however, is scooting straight down towards the Alpine meadows level. He looks as though he's hellbent on breaking an airspeed record. If he carries on this way, I have no idea how he plans to land. These things can literally land in a public park – that's the plan, if I recall correctly – but not if you come in on an approach speed which needs half the runway at Zürich Airport. At this rate, Harris is going to spread what's left of him from one end of the park to the other.

His speed must be insane. I would have thought he was terrifying himself, but the remaining altitude will be reducing the impression of forward movement right now. Once he's level with the treeline though, it's going to look like he just took up F1 racing. What he'll do then, I hate to think. This has to be stopped as soon as possible because he'll probably fill his pants and try to brake in a heartbeat. That will leave him with little speed at a low altitude a few clicks before Interlaken. Then we're truly screwed.

There's only one thing for it. I push forward on the cords and dive towards him, keeping to his left. Actually, I soon find myself having to dive behind, not towards, him since it's only by taking a steeper angle that I can hope to generate enough speed to catch up with him. This really is scary. I'm looking downwards, watching the valley floor grow increasingly green and narrow as the mountainsides move in towards me. I hit the level of the meadows and pull up gently. Too fast a pull-up will kill my speed, and I still have a reasonable amount of horizontal space between us and Harris which I have to cover. But at least I should have time to descend the last small difference at a slightly gentler rate.

We're catching up with Harris now. The meadows below shoot past. Cows, tree clumps, sheds, paths, they're all a near blur. I may have been there before, but I have no idea and am not interested right now. Alpine meadows are not flat and I'm climbing and diving solely to keep aligned with them. Harris is still off to our right, towards the valley, and marginally higher than these changes although he's drifted further to his left. That's why I've been forced to fly over the meadows as I'm approaching from the side so as to get his attention. I should have switched to his right and back over the valley but too late now. It means going even faster than he's travelling which is why I feel like an Alpine bullet.

We finally draw level with Harris and wave vigorously. As before, it takes about twenty seconds for him to notice us, but he finally manages. I sincerely hope he does not start drifting left towards us this time since we have very little room left before colliding with the side of an inclined meadow and milking a cow with our fractured skulls.

Harris looks around. I give him another wave, trying to indicate that he should now keep his speed up as far as he can but also his altitude. I yank bank fast on the cords to skip over a small copse of trees and race over somebody in a sleeping bag. High altitude homelessness or a cheapskate hiker? Don't know, don't care. We shoot past but we've fallen behind Harris again. The moron has gone even lower now, meaning that it's impossible to catch up with him and avoid the meadows. The only solution is to overtake him above or below and then get to his right. Above seems like the better option since we're already up there. There won't be any climbing involved anyway, which would make us decelerate. I lean forward and dash across the top of his chute, executing a break to the left as I cross his path to align with him again. This cuts the speed slightly, causing us to descend without having to decelerate with the cords and we end up flying to his right, where we wanted to be. Damn, I'm good at this. The problem remains, however, that crackshot paragliding is not very inconspicuous.

Harris remains the principal problem, however. I point downwards and then draw my finger across my throat. The combination of the two gestures is supposed to show that heading downwards, at least just now, is not a path to take. But it's obviously too much for Harris to grasp as he doesn't get past part one and goes nose down even further. He banks right in order to round an escarpment jutting out below us.

My existing momentum means that I'm forced to take a violent left turn to avoid him, heading behind him and back into the area above the meadows. This slows me down and I take the opportunity to try to reacquire Harris' track. I can just make him out as he swerves around the escarpment. Nice technique but entirely the wrong idea in terms of height.

"Auntie Jess, look out!" screams Alice.

Holy crap! We've still been descending ourselves and that escarpment is looming right in front of us. The slowdown hasn't been nearly as dramatic as I was thinking and what suddenly looks like an entire forest is racing up and into my face.

I haul back on the cords and lean backwards for all I'm worth, pulling slightly to my right. We start to rise above the trees, and a slither of sky appears above them. We're slowing down but it may not be enough. I can see individual branches and a scared sparrow throwing itself into the sky to avoid our approach.

The tops of the trees are heading right towards us now. But they're also heading more to my midriff, to my thighs and then to my shins.

My feet brush a handful of branches, and I raise them as high as I can. Alice and I seem to stumble in mid-air but we're still there. In mid-air. Our speed is at its lowest since we left the glacier and we're floating only a few metres above the forest on the other side of the escarpment but we're still floating. A bit of a correction is needed, and we require more speed. I start a slow descent, moving down as quickly as we can without ending up like a couple of Christmas tree fairies on top of a random pine tree.

That was close.

Alice and I are both breathing heavily after our narrow escape. I suppose it's good to be reminded that I'm not as great as I think although I could do with a lesson which doesn't wave death so closely in front of me that I can literally brush it with my feet. If I was feeling cockier, I'd say that I'd kicked its ass, but humility feels more the order of the day right now.

Re-appraising the situation, I start feeling positive for the first time since taking off. There's Interlaken. About two clicks ahead down the valley. I can't believe that I'd ever be pleased to see that place in front of me but right now, I could only be happier if it were Timothy Dalton's warm embrace and look of passionate desire in front of me.

But where's Harris?

Killing the vibe is his speciality. My positive feelings disappear entirely as I see where he is, way out in front of us and racing past. He's about halfway down the forest line, flying at a speed which would probably let him get back to Bristol in about half an hour if he could keep it up. Which, of course, he can't, as he's at far too low an altitude. I'm no expert but it looks very hit and miss as to whether he'll make Interlaken and even then if he can get far enough to land in the park or if he's going to end up literally on the next train to Italy.

Pull up, man, pull up! At this point, you could still manage a gentle rise and then glide down to the park. What has possessed Harris to go with this all-out speed plan? Fair enough, it seems to be working in the sense of actually getting there but when is he planning to slow down? And where? Given that he seems incapable of making any sort of meaningful deceleration, the only alternative that leaves him with is a very sudden and very painful assistance by the ground.

In the meantime, Alice and I have the opposite problem. We're still some way out of Interlaken but travelling at quite a low speed. Unlike Harris, however, we do have a bit of altitude on our side. I move into a steeper glide downwards but still considerably gentler than what Harris has been employing. He seems to be approaching Interlaken like a bloody dive bomber though, so no wonder.

It does give both Alice and me the chance to see how Harris is doing. That really is quite staggering. "Keep it low key", "Try not to attract too much attention", "Look like a regular paraglider." Not this guy. True, he's heading back into Interlaken but that's where the theory and the practice diverge completely. Getting into Interlaken subtly should not involve making a beeline for the high street down the centre of town. It should also not involve almost castrating yourself on the chimney of a hotel.

Harris tears down the central concourse with all the subtlety of a cruise missile on its terminal approach. It may be first thing on Saturday morning but there are still enough people around to see this as he zooms along. He passes two supermarkets which haven't opened yet. The same is not true of the three hotels he passes as some bleary guests wake up to the sight of a slightly overweight schoolteacher zipping past the balcony. They must be wondering what the hell someone slipped into their fondue last night.

And he keeps descending. Are his cords locked or something? Does his belly flop over the front by default and drag him downwards? Whatever the cause, he jinks left to avoid a bus. Having passed its rear end, he only just corrects enough to avoid landing in a shopfront at the speed of a rollercoaster. The fact that it's the very same shop where we got his paraglider from in the first place only adds to the irony. It's hardly going to be a good ad for their products if we buy a chute on Friday afternoon and Harris' corpse rocks up, strapped into it fresh on Saturday morning. Frickin' hell.

Some old biddy steps out of a traditional baker's with a coffee in her hand and some pastry or other. She looks up to see Harris approaching like a thunderbolt coming down the street. He's now so low that if she doesn't shut her mouth and duck, she may be literally biting off more than she can swallow. Some people will do anything for a blowjob these days. Credit to the lady – she moves aside quickly enough that the only damage is when Harris kicks the coffee out of her hand.

By now, he's about to start running down the high street. That is not going to be easy when you're already travelling at some forty clicks an hour (rough guesstimate). Finally, though, the berk somehow wakes up and heaves back on his cords. He takes off, literally scraping the top of a car's windscreen with his bum and rising to the truly impressive height of the second floor of another hotel.

The horror we've been feeling at this display of aerial ineptitude is not good for Alice and me. We've been that intrigued to follow what was going on that we've allowed ourselves to drift a bit lower than we should have done. We've shifted to the right of Harris and are still on course to make a reasonable landing. Only we're too far east, heading for Interlaken Ost station. Touching down in front of the 06:34 to Bern does not carry the best chance of survival. I yank back on the left cord to bank sharply to that side and then back on the right cord as well, turning our bank into a climbing turn over the station. We swoop over its roof and head down for the Höhematte Park.

Dammit, we're on course but we're too fast ourselves now. I can't just head down into the park at this speed with Alice in front of me or at least one of us is going to end up on an accident and emergency ward at best. Gaining altitude remains the best way to kill the speed of the chute so I pull back hard on both cords, leaning back until we're halfway to facing upwards. That's when the cords suddenly go slack in my hands and it feels as though we're falling. Oh crap! We're stalling! With enough height, this wouldn't be a problem. We'd fall but only until the cords stretched back far enough to catch us. But right now, it's very bad. We don't have the luxury of height beneath us. I shout to Alice to lean left and do so myself, dragging down the left cord as far as I can at the same time. The chute tightens in my grip, and we go into a spiralling descent. I think the recovery is working. The only thing is that the spin is getting out of control. I can't rein it in. We just keep whirling round to the left and now we're getting caught up in the cords and the other ropes. It was easier yesterday but with Alice as well, the combined momentum has thrown me and I've over-controlled.

What would have been fatal with further to fall becomes what saves us at this point. The manoeuvre has killed the forward momentum, and we smack down onto the grassy surface of the park with only a couple of bruises. But we continue to roll over. That centrifugal force feels impossible to resist until our motion stops. Now Alice and I simply can't move. We're enveloped in a mesh of ropes and rigging which has trussed us up like flies in a spider's web which has just rolled up on itself. I'm spooning my niece in the middle of a public space in German Switzerland and there's nothing I can do about it. They say that happy families should be bound together but this is ridiculous. On the plus side, we're both still alive. So perhaps an overall positive.

The torrent of surprises doesn't stop for a moment. The next thing I know, Harris pitches up, standing over us and looking down with a concerned expression on his face. How the hell did he both manage to land and, hugely embarrassingly, do so more proficiently than Alice and I managed to do? I really can't answer that although the completely smashed advertising board on the far side of the park is a fair indication. Who cares? It's not my prime concern right now.

Nor, does it appear, is it Harris'. He eyes us with clear worry and asks, "Is the clarinet still in one piece?"

This is too much for Alice.

"Mr Beadlesby, we're trapped inside an imploded paraglider and for all you know, one of us could be dead or seriously injured! Shut up about your stupid clarinet and get us fucking out of here!" she screams in fury.

Harris is quite taken aback.

"My goodness, Alice!" he retorts. "I would never have expected this sort of –"

Children these days. I can see where this is going and we don't need it, so I cut in, "Never mind all that, both of you!"

"Harris, there's a survival knife in the side pocket of my rucksack. Can you see it?"

"Errm, I'm not really sure."

"Can you see the bag?" I ask, trying to keep as measured a tone as possible.

"Ah, yes, I do believe so. Would you like me to pass it to you?"

Please spare us. This guy can be such a vegetable that a vegan vampire could drink his blood all night without compromising a single principle.

"No, Harris." I grit my teeth. "Just get the knife out of the pocket and then cut the ropes which are between Alice and me. Strain the knife into the ropes, in a direction which is not pointing directly towards either of us or back towards yourself. Do you think you can manage that?"

"I really don't know. This isn't my usual line of work," he pleads.

"For frig's sake! Nor is paragliding off glaciers but you somehow managed that! Just cut us out!"

As ever with Harris, once there's no real alternative, he does somehow manage to follow instructions. Thankfully, my knife is a good one and the paraglider cords are not designed to entrap anyone, especially when not stretched taut, and we end up rolling out onto the grass.

"Thank you, Harris," I remark, doing my best to sound as genuine as possible before I turn to both him and Alice. "Now get this stuff wrapped up and let's head!"

The wrapping up goes smoothly enough. Harris is reunited with the clarinet which he insists on carrying himself. That doesn't bother me at all. We're soon ready to head but Fate still hasn't got over that bad curry last night. A siren wails a short distance away and I turn to see a police car racing down the high street towards us. It screeches to a halt on the far side of the park and two cops spring out, heading our way.

Oh damn.

"We'd better head a hell of a lot faster than under the original plan!" I order. We run.

Chapter 22

INTERLAKEN'S MOST WANTED

Harris

We run from the park down to the river. It flows along the side of Interlaken, next to the mountainside. The police from the park are chasing after us and another car is approaching the bridge up ahead of us.

I don't see how we can keep going. Jessica and I both have large packs on our backs. I suspect hers is heavier than my mine but only because we all know that she's fitter by a long way. Alice has a smaller but still substantial pack. We're also still dressed in the clothes we came down from the glacier in and the heat is overwhelming. After last night, it's a strange sensation but it's the least of my concerns.

We're going to be held at the bridge. Even I can see that. But then Jessica darts to the left, heading into the street where the hotel is which we stayed in two nights ago. The whole place is lined with shops, hotels and restaurants. There seem to be almost no private houses. I don't know what to make of it. Where can we fit in?

I'm gasping to myself as Jessica leads us onto a side street and charges ahead. How can I keep up with her? The sound of a police siren is a sufficiently strong motivation, but I do not know where my energy is coming from. We continue down this street without any immediate pursuit in sight but that doesn't last for long. We pass a small clump of trees to one side, and I glance back as we make another turn. At least two policemen are haring down the road after us.

The endless twisting and turning doesn't seem to be getting us anywhere.

Those police simply seem closer each time they round the last corner behind us. Sooner or later they're going to catch up.

I don't know if Jessica has realized this or not, but we suddenly come back onto the high street, further down than where we landed in the park. That was near to the river. Now we're down towards the valley from where we arrived. Jessica changes tack and accelerates straight down the pavement. She's going too fast for me to keep up now but I'm doing my utmost. She and Alice are getting ever further ahead of me, and the police are slowly but surely gaining on me.

Jessica disappears around a corner suddenly and Alice follows her a moment later. I keep following and round it myself. There's no sign of them. Now what? Where do I go? I can't see any better choice than to run straight ahead.

I pass a small lane to my right and a shadow steps out next to me. Jessica grabs me and yanks me down the lane.

"What?" I start but she cuts me off.

"Shut up, Harris! Right now, they haven't seen where we are so let's put some space between them and us."

She takes off again, twisting and turning down various passageways. I have no choice but to follow.

A corner appears in front of us, and we rush round it. I feel as though I can hardly breathe any longer and I do not know how much further I can keep going. But nothing is stopping Jessica and Alice, and moving forward is still the only thing left to do. I don't have a lot of time for reflection as it is.

A narrow alleyway stretches before us, running between two large buildings. One of them has a staircase on its side, leading up to the first floor. Jessica suddenly moves towards it and hisses forcefully, "Quick! Up here!"

I have no idea what she's doing but I'm not going to ask questions. We race up the stairs and into the hallway of what appears to be a hotel. It's similar to where we stayed a couple of nights ago. It's decorated in something approximating to a stereotypical, old style, Swiss chalet look although I suspect that may not be very authentic. The reception area is empty although there's a dining room to our left, overlooking the road which we just turned off. There are a few diners in there but not many and nobody appears to have paid any attention to us.

Jessica charges through the hallway with Alice and myself in tow. What on earth is she doing? She goes straight to a stairway on the right-hand side at the end of the hall and heads up it without hesitating. I cannot figure out for the life of me what's going on, but I have no choice but to trust her.

We go up two floors and into an empty corridor. Jessica runs to the end of it and tries a door. It's locked so she moves to the next one along. This is also locked. The following one is open, and she pushes in. Alice and I follow. Jessica barks an order, and Alice closes the door behind her. She and I stop to catch our breath.

"Here's the plan," Jessica starts in a tone without any malice, but which does not brook dissent. At this stage, it doesn't make much difference as I can hardly muster enough breath to say anything anyway.

"We've rounded a few corners without the cops following us and having the chance to see where we went. I'm guessing that they'll be assuming that we keep moving. Instead, we're going to lie low here for a short while and then move on. With a bit of luck, they'll be looking much further away by then."

"How do you know they won't look in here? Whose room is this anyway?" asks Alice.

"I can't be certain," Jessica admits. "I'm no criminologist but checking into a passing hotel probably isn't the standard escape route for your average felon. Whose room this is, I don't know but they didn't lock it and let's just hope that they don't come back any time soon. We won't be here for long."

She looks around the room at this point. From the door, we came in and down a narrow passage of a few feet with a wooden partition on our right. Further in, the room broadens to reveal a double bed against the right-hand wall with a desk and a chest of drawers on the left. Behind us and to the right is an en suite bathroom, which is nestled behind the partition. On the far side is a window, stretched between the walls behind a net curtain. There are a few bags and items of clothing lying around. This isn't an unoccupied room. I'm wondering if parking ourselves here is all that wise an idea. Alice puts the same question to Jessica.

"It's a bit of a gamble," she admits, "but I think we could be in with a chance. If we hole up in the bathroom, then even if somebody checks out the room, it's going to look like somebody's already checked in – which they are – and there won't be much obvious point to checking the bathroom too. The main risk is if the actual occupants return but we only need about twenty minutes so I'm willing to risk it. I daresay we can bluff our way past a couple of tourists if we have to. They'll be too surprised to do much and it's not as if we're going to nick anything."

On entry, the bathroom consists of a little toilet on the right, slightly offset from a washbasin. On the left side is a small shower. The room as a whole does not appear to be intended to accommodate more than one person at a time but Jessica herds us all inside and closes the door. All of our baggage is deposited in the shower, and we huddle up together as best we can. It reminds me a little, in fact, of last night under that makeshift canvas on the glacier. I take the chance to sit on the toilet itself with Alice standing next to me in front of the washbasin while Jessica crams herself into the shower door.

There's a moment's pause while everyone reflects. Having recovered slightly after a long pause, I do want to work out just where we stand now.

"Tell me, Jessica," I ask, "just how much trouble are we in? We only made a little, unauthorized landing in a public park after all."

She reflects for a moment before replying, "First of all, this is Switzerland, German Switzerland. You burp too loudly in a public space and you're facing two years without parole. Second, we didn't just make a little, unauthorized landing in a public park. We landed illegally on a glacier, we violated half the civil aviation code of the country in the space of about ten minutes, we caused a public disturbance in a public area, covered up – or at least tried to cover up – the evidence and we resisted arrest when we took off at pace from the local police. That's maybe not the worst ever charge sheet, but it will probably still get us a night of free accommodation in the

Interlaken cop shop together with some guy called Otto who's in there for cow-beating and bizarre, sexual practices. Given that between you and me we probably cover most of the orifices which he'd like to plough, that means that at least one of us will have a hard time standing up again by this time tomorrow."

Alice is looking decidedly worried, so her aunt adopts a new tone.

"Of course," she adds hurriedly, "Alice probably won't get charged with anything as a minor and just an accomplice. They'll get her a nice room in a local hotel and it'll probably be quite a sweet deal from her point of view."

She looks back over at me and continues, "I doubt you get serious jail time for illegal paragliding though. The problem, as you know, is that if we get hauled in by the local police department, they're going to start asking other questions such as what we're doing outside the UK with Alice and why we're running around Interlaken with a musical instrument worth a quarter of a million quid which was brought into Switzerland from Italy without ever being declared to customs. The fact that we're planning to continue said misdemeanour by getting it into the UK on the fly as well is not going to help us. I understand that you'll also face disciplinary charges from your place of employment since you're not supposed to be any further from Bristol than Taunton for the next six months. Right now, we're about seven hundred miles away. So we're in pretty serious trouble if we get caught.

"At the same time, there is a plus. Outside the Canton of Bern, the forces of law and order are not going to be quite so concerned about what this far they only know to be a case of illegal paragliding. The cops here are probably only bothered because it makes them look a bit stupid. Assuming we don't get caught in Bern, if we can then keep a low profile, ideally until we're out of Switzerland, then I think we stand a reasonable chance of getting away. The trickiest bit right now is simply to avoid the police. Sadly, I don't think this crowd are going to be talked out of applying due diligence with another Emmental burrito line so we're going to need a bit more effort and fast-thinking."

"But why are they on to us?" I ask. I'm really quite confused. "You said that we would look like ordinary paragliders coming into Interlaken and nobody would pay much attention to us. Why are they suddenly chasing us as if we're career criminals?"

She gives me one of her more supercilious stares.

"Harris," she begins, "I was never entirely sure that we would get away with our descent. Also, you maybe forgot about it, but I did try to point out that normal paragliders come in at a relatively sedate and gentle pace. You tore into Interlaken at the speed of a bullet train and passed down the high street at an altitude equivalent to a double decker bus. You arrived out of the sky in such an abnormal way that I'm surprised they've only assigned the local police to investigate it and not Mulder and Scully."

I wonder if I should point out that despite a bit of awkwardness in my flying, I did actually manage to land in the park without injury. The demolished billboard might admittedly prove witness to not everything having been perfect. But I still think that my four turns around the edge of the park were actually a more proficient way to land than the corkscrew landing which Jessica and her niece pulled off, tying themselves up nicely and almost literally hoisting themselves by their own petard. I think I'll gloat over that at some other point. We don't need an argument just now.

"I'm sorry," I offer in what I hope is a conciliatory tone. "I suppose not everything was perfect. That said, what do we do next?"

Jessica thinks again for a moment before responding.

"We need to get out of here when things get quieter and then ditch the equipment we don't need. A lot of it may have some sort of manufacturer's code or equivalent on it and that could be tied back to who bought it if anyone cares enough to investigate. Losing it in the forests might work but I would prefer to sink it in the lake or even burn it somewhere if we can get away with it."

"Why don't we just burn it here?" I enquire. "We could get a little bonfire going in this shower cubicle."

She looks at me with one of her most piercing stares. I consider what I've just said and start to develop a nasty idea of what is about to come next. I'm not wrong there.

"Do you take some sort of medication to inhibit common sense? The partition behind you is made of wood. Half the building is made of wood. If you set fire to something in here, it's going to spread. If the hotel goes up in flames, and this being at an early enough time of the morning for several guests to be still asleep, then we'll probably add arson and manslaughter to our charge sheet. That will at least put illegal paragliding in the shade, but it will probably expand the serious attention of Bern's police to those of every Canton across Switzerland and probably Interpol as well."

She rolls her eyes and sighs.

"Right now, let's just chill out for a few minutes and then take a raincheck out of the window to see if things look a bit quieter. Then we'll try to head out of town and see if we can get some transport from a smaller location down the road."

There's a moment's pause as everyone stops to calm down briefly. Then Jessica suddenly looks up.

"There is something which I could usefully do while we're here," she starts in a surprisingly modest tone. "I need to deal with a, well, woman's issue and apply something in an intimate area. Do you two think you could turn away and face the wall behind you for a couple of minutes, please? It won't take long."

This is completely unexpected but having stopped to work out what she's talking about, it seems like a fair request. I do not envy the ladies the serious inconvenience which their reproductive organs must cause them once a month.

I get up from the toilet and turn around with Alice behind me, facing in the same direction. The conversation stops.

All of a sudden, things go very wrong. There's the sudden sound of the door to the room opening and a man's and a woman's voices intertwine loudly. They're laughing together and making some rather obscene remarks. I can understand this because they're using English. The accent sounds as though it could be Australian although I can't rule out the southeast of England either. They both sound somewhat alike to me.

Curiously, the woman's voice seems to change in tone. It's almost as if there are two of them. It's not easy to tell, however, since there's a lot of noise from bangs and thumps with considerable laughter. I really cannot tell what's going on. I do wish I could check with Jessica but for obvious reasons, I cannot turn around and she isn't saying anything.

"Go on, love, grab the lube!" shouts the man and a woman giggles in response.

The next thing I know, the bathroom door flies open to reveal a completely naked woman standing in the doorway. She gasps in horror, which is not surprising. I accidentally turn ninety degrees to my right and realise that she's looking at Alice and myself rammed up against the toilet, with Jessica next to us, her trousers lowered and her hand at work in a place I would prefer not to mention. Then there's a shower full of paragliding and survival equipment. Whatever this woman might be trying to do right now, I doubt this is what she was expecting to see.

I look over her shoulder to see the man lying on the bed. He too is completely naked and tied by his wrists to the two bedposts. He's covered in a kind of whipped cream as well. A second woman, also lacking any modesty, is sitting between his legs and ingesting the cream from an area which I'm sure cannot be considered hygienic. The three of them appear to be maybe in their twenties or early thirties. Beyond that, I do not know what else to make of this.

I cannot say who is more horrified, them or us. My brain is simply swimming.

"Who the bloody hell are you?" screams the woman in the doorway in a very distraught tone.

As ever, taking the initiative falls to Jessica. She makes some jerking movement with her arm and swiftly brings her trousers back into place.

"Hi!" she beams. "Are you the guys who ordered the gear from tightlywrapped.com? We got an order for some really good stuff, and I can assure you that the ropes here will fasten up like nothing else. I've even tried it myself!"

She winks knowingly at the woman in the doorframe.

"Will you get out now?" yells the man. I do hope they dry clean those sheets before the next guests are booked into this room.

"Oh sorry," breezes Jessica before turning to Alice. "You daft girl! I told you the order was for the room on the fourth floor!"

"Well, I did tell you that I was pretty sure this wasn't where the Jehovah's Witnesses prayer meeting was taking place either!" retorts Alice.

Jessica forces Alice and me through the doorway and past the woman who's standing there. She skids on some whipped cream on the floor and falls backwards on top of the man. Somebody yelps and curses in some very undignified language. I do hope the impact doesn't hurt too badly.

Once back in the corridor, we have no choice. Jessica shepherds us along the corridor, down the stairs and out of the door, back into the street.

Thankfully, there's no one to be seen at this juncture. Nobody says anything but Jessica leads us off at a fast jog. Here we go again, I suppose.

Chapter 23
AND YOU THOUGHT PLAN D WAS BAD

Harris

Having exited the hotel, we are now making our way carefully through the side streets of Interlaken. It's not a full run any longer but more a measured jog. Nobody is in immediate pursuit of us, at least not for the moment. At the same time, we must look somewhat conspicuous with our huge, colourful backpacks. These are even bigger than they were earlier since we used some of the time inside that little bathroom to shed the outer layers we were wearing and strip down to something a little less exhausting, stowing the previous layers in the bags.

That is maybe just as well. The sun is rising quickly. The temperature down here in the valley was maybe quite pleasant at the break of day but the further it goes on, the hotter it gets. In fact, I must confess that I really am sweating quite profusely now. Assuming I can see clearly enough, it would seem that Jessica and Alice probably are as well except that, predictably enough, they don't appear to care. I do but that certainly doesn't bother anybody else.

I've lost track of where we're going at this point. My only point of reference is that we appear to be heading back towards where we came from with the paragliders. So, we must be heading towards the south side of town. Beyond that, I'm simply aware of more absolutely gigantic mountain ranges looming over me, all apparently covered in dense forests. If I hadn't flown in over them earlier, I would never have known or even believed that they give way to meadows above those trees. Equivalent ranges lie to the left and behind us with another range away to the right, over the lake which is immediately before us. We're getting closer to the water now. I can see that through gaps leading off the streets we're following but Jessica is keeping us away from the more open lakeside. No doubt deliberately. I do believe I'm getting slightly more idea of how she thinks in terms of concept. What she's actually going to come up with, however, remains beyond me to figure out.

After what feels like an hour but has probably been more like ten to fifteen minutes, if I look at my watch with a sense of honesty, we emerge at the corner of town. We're next to where a valley emerges in front of us and a mountain ridge begins to the right of it, rising steeply. In front of that and to our own right, then further behind us stretches the lake – the Thunersee if I recall correctly for once – from where we emerged two and a half days ago. Where to now?

A rail line stretches in front of the foot of the ridge, snaking along the side of the lake. That was what brought us here. You'd think it might be the way out. I ask Jessica.

"No," she replies curtly. "The police will be covering the immediate routes out of town and the only two ways onto that train are in Interlaken West and Interlaken Ost stations. If we pitch up in either of those, we might as well just hand ourselves in now and forfeit our own bail."

"So where do we go?" This is Alice asking now.

Jessica turns to respond but a shout cuts across everything else. I can't understand it but it's in German and it sounds angry. I turn to see some more police officers heading our way.

"Somewhere else!" shouts Jessica. "Follow me!"

With that she tears away, heading to the right and onto a path leading into the forest. It's easy to follow in the sense of navigation, tortuous in terms of effort required. What makes it easy is that it's well marked, a clear, light brown path, leading between the overhanging branches of pine trees with a reasonably generous space between them. What makes it excruciating is that the entire way is designed to take the walker uphill at this point and it just goes on upwards, without ever seeming to stop. And it's steep. Jessica adds to both of these features. It's hard to lose her bright blue pack, bobbing and up down ahead of us. But she will keep up a pounding pace which is simply killing me.

Yet I can hardly blame her. The forces of law and order are back on our heels. A problem with a path which is easy to navigate, I daresay, is that it makes it fairly simple for someone else to follow where you've gone to. A bit like a trumpet. It makes its way clearly but it's hardly a subtle instrument. Subtlety is lost on us as well as we belt through the woods. They're pretty but they all look the same to me. Greens and browns, twists and turns, and occasional glimpses beyond of the sky above and the ever-receding lake below.

Just when I feel as though I simply cannot continue, I lose sight of Jessica and Alice. I round a corner by a large boulder when a hand reaches out, covers my mouth and drags me over onto my back behind the boulder. A large branch is immediately brought down over my face.

I look above me to see Jessica's face with Alice's next to her. Jessica is the one whose hand is clamped over my mouth, and her other hand is holding the branch. Alice is looking down at me with her finger to her lips while Jessica scours the path back down the hill from the opposite side of the boulder.

A few moments later, the sound of rushing footsteps approaches and some tense exchanges in German. I can't follow them, but the speakers do appear to be hesitating in front of where we're hiding.

Jessica releases my mouth and picks up a small rock. Keeping an eye on the speakers in front of us, she twists herself around and launches it high into the forest above us. It lands with a small crash which immediately grabs their attention. They swap pleasantries for a moment and then one of them waves back down the hill to somebody before they turn back uphill and keep running.

Jessica springs out from behind the boulder and back onto the path. Alice and I follow at a slightly slower and clumsier pace. She's studying her smartphone. This takes a moment before she then looks up.

"There might be a way out here," she says, pointing to the screen although it cannot be more than a gesture. There's no way Alice or I could read a map at this distance. "This path branches slightly further along and goes in two directions. One goes straight up. That's where I threw the rock to so with a bit of luck, that's where they'll think we've gone. The other follows the line of the ridge for a while before it then forks either up or down. We're going to follow the lower path until we hit that fork and then re-group."

This doesn't sound like much of a plan to me but I'm going to have to assume that re-grouping means more than just having a nice sit-down. I do wish that were the case but even I am not naïve enough to believe it, only to hope for it. We start moving upwards again but thankfully, it isn't too long before we reach a split in the pathway and take the less vicious incline which leads right. A little further along, we round a corner and crouch down in a hollow next to it. Or, to be more accurate and perhaps more honest, Jessica and Alice crouch down while I just about collapse into it. That's what it feels like.

No rest for the wicked, of course. And now that my love for Isabel has turned me into a fugitive in at least two different countries, I can only consider myself wicked, I suppose. It's of little consolation that the same thing happened to many of literature and operas' great lovers – Sir Lancelot, Romeo, Tristan, Don José, to name but a few. At least they had the time and pathos to reflect on the enormity of their crimes, passions and who they had become or were destined to be. They did not, as far as the texts set out, end up leaping off blocks of ice, careering into advertising billboards in the local park and racing around mountain pathways like characters in some sort of demented "Carry On" film. The indignity is insufferable.

On the other hand, my humility must remind me, they did all end up dead or, at best, cast into abject misery. Jessica may be reducing us to an amateur assault course, but we do have that clarinet and have not so far wound up in custody. I must no doubt give credit where it's due.

These thoughts have passed through my mind in about fifteen seconds, I think. That's clearly too long for Jessica.

"Harris, you berk, wake up!" she hisses in my face. "You can fall over if you want but if you feel like having a sleep, you can do it in the holding cell of the Interlaken PD while Leutnant Dudelberg records your basic details on the charge sheet and the British Embassy staff in Bern call up their counterparts in Benidorm to find out what the usual procedure is for dealing with badly behaved, British twats."

"OK, OK," I stammer, completely out of breath still. "My apologies. Please explain the plan."

Jessica turns around to face both Alice and myself. This is relatively easy to do without being seen since Alice is already perched slightly above me, so our faces are more or less aligned in the vertical. I suppose this is what constitutes re-grouping in Jessica's world. It's another lesson in abject humility for me.

"As I mentioned before, we have to get not just ourselves out of here but also the gear as well. Some of this we still need, notably our passports, cash and the clarinet, without which we cannot complete what we started. We do not, however, need the paragliding equipment or the cold weather gear or the other bits and pieces we picked up for last night. At the same time, we can't just ditch them in a local bin since they may be found, and someone may tie them back to us.

"We could take care of all this if we could get off this mountainside. It's making us harder to find but we're hemmed in. The police will be blocking all the ways in and out except maybe at the top. That will take ages for us to reach though–" she glances disapprovingly in my direction –"and will be blatantly visible to anyone above the treeline within about twenty minutes of us emerging from it. Instead, we have to play to what we can do best.

"What we can do best is to transform ourselves. They think they're looking for a group of three, Caucasian, one man, two women, one probably younger than the other two. A bit overdressed and carrying huge packs. Since we're being sought in the first instance for illegal paragliding, it doesn't take a genius to figure out what those probably are.

"The first thing is therefore to dress down. It's a hot day and getting hotter so get into some lightweight, walking clothes and stuff the rest into the backpacks we have. Next, we split up temporarily."

"You two walk back down the path we just came up without any backpacks. If you meet any cops, just say, 'Grüzi!' in a friendly tone of voice and then keep walking. You could easily be a couple of walkers who were already heading along this way before the police started chasing anyone. Pretend to be an uncle and niece or something if anyone bothers to ask."

"How can I pretend to be her uncle?" I ask. "I don't even have the same name!"

Jessica rolls her eyes and gives me a very off-putting stare.

"Her mother could be your sister, who got married to someone and took his family name," she explains in a menacing manner before accelerating into a zone where I think she's on the brink of losing her patience. "Or you could just bloody lie! What do you think I've been doing for the past half week?"

I should have learnt by now just to keep my mouth shut at this sort of juncture, but it really does offend my better sensibilities.

"Jessica!" I intone. "I appreciate what we have to do but I should reiterate that I am a man of principle, for whom honesty carries a certain value and–"

"Will you shut the hell up?" she shrieks in a relatively quiet but furious, fearful screech. "Does Isabel know about the tax dodge on the clarinet? Does your employer know that you're a shade further away from Bristol than Taunton? Are Alice's parents fully aware that she never made it into the Young Pianists Finals of the West Country?"

I do so hate having my shortcomings highlighted in such a forthright manner. I avoid the rest of Jessica's stare and look down in sheepish submission. She hurries on.

"In the meantime, I will strip down to my underwear, which, being designed specifically for sports, comprises a relatively substantial set of shorts and sports bra, which pretty much looks the part for someone to be out jogging in. You do get some lunatics who go jogging on hiking paths, so I'll try to look like one of them. Just maybe without an obviously demented expression on my face.

"According to the map, a little further up this path is a little zig-zag path which goes down to the bottom of the slope. If we can tie up all the rest of the luggage into one big package, then I can roll it down in front of me. If there's anyone coming up from below, I can roll it off whichever stretch I'm on, straight down through the trees. I can then recover it from somewhere near the bottom of the next stretch. We'll stick some branches and moss over it, so it won't be immediately obvious to anyone.

"Once we're all at the bottom, we can meet here," she passes her phone to Alice who takes note of where "here" is. Nobody bothers to consult me. "We'll get the equipment and re-distribute it, taking special care to separate out what we need to lose. From there, we'll see if we can get some sort of watercraft out onto the lake. I reckon that if we can use a boat to reach some small bus stop somewhere, we'll be able to catch a ride where nobody's looking. We can also ditch the unnecessary equipment with a few rocks included into the lake so that it disappears for at least as long as anybody will be trying to find us. I mean, it's not as if we murdered anyone, right? They're hardly going to be assigning a whole squad of specialized scuba divers to help track us down. Any questions?"

Alice pipes up, "Auntie Jess, if we do get a bus somewhere, won't they still be covering the transport routes like you said?"

Jessica reflects for a moment and then responds, "Yes, but again, I don't think we're going to look like their target. We'll have ditched most of the baggage and we'll be dressed lightweight. We'll also stay quasi-separated until we're further away. What's more, they're no doubt checking Interlaken and then probably the bigger gigs too like Spiez, Brienz and Meiringen but the smaller stops in-between will be too unlikely. So one or two people getting on there who don't fit the profile probably won't attract much attention. It's not foolproof, I admit, but it seems reasonable. From there, we basically get a string of buses through the back end of nowhere until we're far enough way to get back onto mainstream transport and catch a flight from there."

Alice seems content with her aunt's explanation. It sounds risky but reasonably so. Not that I consider myself an expert on the ways of fugitives in the Alps, of course.

"I have one question myself," I ask. "What happens to the clarinet?"

"It goes into the baggage train with everything else," Jessica responds straightaway. "That thing is the most unusual aspect of our whole retinue. It will draw attention very easily. Since the baggage pack is going to be a liability anyway, it might as well form part of that.

"Besides," she flashes a brief, reconciliatory smile, "we'll take care to wrap it up tightly."

Ten minutes later and all three of us are standing in the path, considerably more lightly dressed than we were ten minutes ago. Alice has on her hiking trousers and boots. Her top half is adorned with a T-shirt, a picture of a female opera singer on the front of it. There's a man kneeling before her, his face at a slightly lower level than her midriff. The caption reads, "It just gets aria all the time!" I do so hope she wasn't planning to wear that in Taunton.

I was intending to wear another pair of those rather stylish jodhpurs I picked up before leaving but Jessica forbade that immediately, together with the orange beret. I do not understand how she can have such little sense of haute couture. Her rationale was simply that we would have to have something less conspicuous and memorable and so I've been relegated to the grey under-trousers I wore on the glacier and a rather anonymous, off-white shirt. I shan't end this escapade with a shred of dignity at this rate. I do manage to put the most stylish of my clothes into the small rucksack which I'll still be permitted to carry once we link up again at the bottom. Maybe something for later?

Jessica's clothing edits do not stop with me, however, as she turns to Alice.

"Sorry, darling, but you're going to have to lose the shirt."

Alice looks askance.

"It's not that it isn't funny–" I beg to differ but have learnt enough to keep quiet – but it's too easy for someone to remember. Put on something a bit more anonymous."

Alice sets about finding a less colourful T-shirt in more senses than one. Jessica works with her to finalize the re-packing. She herself is wearing an olive-coloured set of shorts and what I can only describe as a half-cut vest on top. Apparently they're known as a sports bra and pants. They don't cover a great deal although they're not quite as revealing as regular underwear would be and according to Jessica, they're not that different to hot weather running gear for women. I myself have no idea about any of this.

Once again, Jessica bids us both turn away while she attends to her womanly needs. These are certainly rather more than I need to be at all aware of. But I suppose that I must concede that it's not something fully within women's control. It certainly isn't within mine as I barely understand it. I'm not a biology teacher, after all.

All of this having been completed, and with more voices encroaching upon our location, Jessica waves us off. The intention is to re-group at the designated point in half an hour. Allowing for complications, whoever gets there first should just wait for the others. It sounds like a decent enough plan under the circumstances.

Alice and I set off back down the path. My nerves are jittering. What if these policemen recognize us? Will they expect us to speak German? Will I have enough money with me if I have to pay a fine?

Alice attempts to set my nerves at ease although I fear that she may be losing patience. You can increasingly see the likeness of the aunt in the niece's sarcasm. According to Alice, we just have to do what she refers to as winging it. This means that we don't worry about being recognized. If that's going to happen, then it will happen. There's no reason for them to have any particular idea as to what nationality we are and if they want to interrogate us badly enough, they'll be quite capable of doing so in English. No doubt fines can be paid later on through bank transfer if needs be. This is, after all, a country known for being at the cutting edge of banking practices. I'm not certain that all of these responses are necessarily very comforting.

We round a corner and run into a couple of officers walking up the path. They don't appear to be in a particular hurry, but they are interested as to who we might be.

"Grüzi!" Alice salutes them jovially before moving to pass them by but a swift instruction in German follows. Alice stops. They're asking something but I don't know what.

"I'm terribly sorry," I begin, "but I don't really speak German."

They look at me briefly and then glance at each other with quizzical looks on their faces.

"So what are you doing out here?" asks one in what sounds like a perfect, American accent.

My mind goes blank.

"Well, I was out for a stroll in the morning after some…er…breakfast and, you know, all of a sudden–" I begin before Alice cuts me off.

"Oh, Uncle!" she beams! "You're such a bumbler sometimes! We're hardly fugitives, are we? We're just taking a morning walk in the Alps! These guys are only doing their jobs and keeping the place safe."

She pauses for a moment before continuing in a concerned tone, "Who knows? They might even be on the tail of those ne'er-do-wells we saw racing up the path in the other direction. I told you they were a bad lot!"

She turns to the policemen.

"Sorry about my uncle," she explains. "He has quite a nervous disposition. He got into a little trouble back in England over some silly accident which wasn't really his fault at all, and ever since then he's had this paranoia about getting stopped by the police. You wouldn't believe it.

"Anyway," she continues, "how can we help you?"

"You are tourists on a hike?"

"I wouldn't say hike," Alice responds, "more just a walk. I mean, we're hardly carrying any serious backpacks or equipment around with us. But, yeah, we're tourists.

"I do love this country," she adds, gazing around us in admiration. If she's anything like her aunt, it might even be genuine. Genuine or not, it's certainly convincing. "Do you all come from here yourself?"

"Yes," replies the police officer who's been speaking, sounding slightly confused. "I'm actually from Sigriswil myself."

"Sigriswil!" Alice smiles. "I love that place! That suspension bridge you have is awesome! And the way it sits up there and overlooking the lake is just beautiful!"

"Indeed!" The officer seems to be warming to her. "I take it you've been there once or twice!"

"At least! It has everything you want as a tourist, just without being tacky. You should move back there from here." She stops and indicates Interlaken with her arm.

The other policeman looks rather disgruntled but the one who has done all the speaking cuts him off with a grin.

"Careful what you say, my girl! This guy here is from just outside Interlaken. Any more gags like that and he'll be writing up your charge sheet!

"But I agree with you!" he adds in a mock, conspiratorial tone. "It really is a dump. Long live Sigriswil!"

Alice winks back at him. He straightens up and says something to his colleague in German. The latter broadcasts something over his radio to other colleagues and then the first one turns back to us and salutes informally.

"Very nice to meet you both!" he smiles. "You have a good day now!"

Alice thanks him for his generosity and says how much she hopes to catch him again soon. I do rather hope it isn't that soon.

We set off again and pass two more corners before she turns back to me and says, "And that, Mr Beadlesby, is how we do that kind of thing! Just get into character and into the zone, and you'll be fine."

I don't know if I agree with that fully. Yet I can't deny that whatever it is she and Jessica have been doing up to now has clearly been working.

We continue down the path, keeping the exchange of pleasantries to a minimum. I do like Alice as a girl. At least, I do normally like her although I have to confess to being somewhat intimidated by her rougher attitude, no doubt acquired from her aunt, when in said aunt's company. Her foul mouth under pressure is also something of a surprise. Despite all that, she is not an unlikeable child, clearly just a strong-minded one. Nevertheless, we keep the conversation limited since Jessica has told us how sound can carry a long way without other sounds competing and we do not want to risk accidentally giving away any more than we have to.

This works well enough until we come round yet another corner and there in front of us is a man in probably his 50s, standing at the side of the path and urinating freely. The more personal elements of his anatomy are on full display, and he appears to have no shame. I had heard that foreign countries might have lower standards than what we're used to in Britain, but I'm nonetheless taken aback.

"Goodness! Is that normal?" I ask Alice.

"You tell me!" she replies. "I haven't seen all that many to date. I'm only fifteen, you know! What sort of a girl do you think I am?"

The man himself simply stands there, continuing to look at us with a small degree of resentment. We stare back, trying to focus on somewhere other than just below his waist. This continues until a similarly aged woman emerges from just down the path behind him and says something to him in German before pausing for a moment as she looks at Alice and me. She then screams something, whether at him, us or all three I don't know, and whirls him around so that we are unable to see his nether regions any longer. She may not have realised that he was still in full flow since another scream of rage follows promptly and the poor man is twisted round a third time so that he is flowing into the woods next to the path. I do hope he doesn't collapse from vertigo. He eventually stops, at which point she forces him to clothe himself fully again and then marches him off up the path, passing us with a very dirty look. I still don't really know what either Alice or I did.

"You meet all sorts sometimes," Alice comments absently before we set off again.

The earlier run-in with the law must have had some benefit since we pass another two couples of police officers on the way down, a woman and a man in the first, and two women in the other. Both groups refer to someone on their radio who may be the one whom Alice befriended. Both then let us past. Other than them, it's a relatively quiet walk, all things considered.

We reach the meeting point, according to Alice, about ten minutes late and take shelter in a disused hut overlooking the lake. It's a three-walled shelter, presumably used by fishing aficionados. It sports a nice view and is quite peaceful. Interlaken lies immediately to the right of us, curving around to form the end of the lake with the opposite shore stretching out from it and curving back round opposite us on the other side. Above that are some lovely gorges, full of forests and the start of the meadowed level above them. The lake stretches away to the left, curving around the gentle landscape which makes up this side. It follows a roughly straight line on a larger scale but still undulates sufficiently to provide a series of tiny marinas and swimming points based around various jetties and miniature harbours. I suppose true seafarers would expect considerably more but this is a landlocked country which only has lakes. I doubt anyone seeking seafaring thrills comes here on holiday in the first place.

The opportunity to sit down properly and rest my legs is something I've been missing since I sat on that toilet during our illegal venture into the hotel bathroom in Interlaken and that must have been a good two to three hours ago. It's the best thing to happen to me since finding the clarinet. I don't recall ever enjoying the sensation of relaxation so much before.

It doesn't last, of course.

Jessica rounds the side of the hut and dumps the bag of equipment next to us. Only now do I appreciate how huge it really is. Even if a lot of it is simply paraglider cloth, she has still transported a considerable amount of material here.

She sits next to Alice and grabs a water bottle from somewhere inside the bag.

"Everything OK?" she asks.

"Yeah, no worries," Alice replies.

No room for small talk, I note.

"OK, let's work out the next bit of the plan. I'm a bit worried that the cops may be paying more attention to the water routes than we were expecting.

"Harris," she addresses me unexpectedly, "do you still have those binoculars you brought anywhere?"

I have to confess to feeling a sense of near satisfaction at having finally contributed something of value. I don't know why I should care that Jessica of all people should need something which I've managed to bring along, but it does feel good. Unfortunately, it does also take a full two or three minutes of rummaging around in the bag to locate anything beyond a paraglider and an ice pick but eventually I come up with what she requested.

"Thanks." She takes the binoculars and trains them onto the shore of the lake to our right, essentially that formed by the town. She skirts them right round the shorelines and then checks the landscape behind us before lowering them to her knees.

"Dammit! They're clearly watching the lake, and they also have cops positioned at the stations behind and in front of us. I was hoping that we could get over to the pier in Interlaken where the various Thunersee ferries run from but that's about as much use as walking into the police station and asking if they have a spare room for the night. They're going overboard and I'd be surprised if they don't have people searching the trains going through Spiez and elsewhere too."

She curses a couple of times more and looks around. A worried silence descends on us. Nobody breaks it for at least five minutes.

At that point, a sideways grin envelops Jessica's face, and she turns to us.

"OK," she breezes, "sorry for the delay. The plan had to be recast a little, but I think we're onto something now.

"First things first, get the gear out of the big bag and spread it out on the floor of this hut, ideally not too visibly."

We follow her instructions in conjunction with her own actions. She nods her appreciation when the job is done.

"Now we take the critical things which you guys need and put them into the two smaller packs which you brought with you. I mean passports, money, water bottles, first aid kits. Just enough to keep us going until we can get back to Bristol tomorrow.

"And, before you ask, not including that crappy novel, Alice."

Alice gives her a look of mock aggravation but proceeds as ordered.

"And the clarinet?" I ask.

"Coming with me," she responds. "You two are going to rent bikes from over there on the edge of town. We've seen that you look inconspicuous, dressed as you are, so you can stay that way. It makes no sense that fugitives from Interlaken would be cycling back into Interlaken as well. So bike in and get round to the northwest side under Harder Kulm. There you can get a bus up and via Habkern to Beatenberg, which overlooks Spiez. It's just a bit further down the cliffside from where we jumped off with Daniel. Get the funicular railway from there to the bottom and then take the ferry across. And remember to pay cash."

"But Auntie Jess," Alice asks her, "what's the point? None of that makes any sense. It's a totally round the houses route."

"Exactly," Jessica tells her. "And that's why nobody is going to be looking for you on it."

"And what happens to the clarinet?" I cut back in.

"Good question," Jessica turns back to me. "The problem with that clarinet is that you stick out too much with it and we need as low a profile as we can manage. That's why we incorporate it into the part of the plan to do with me.

"There's a technique which I learnt several years ago when I was part of the cadet force at school. You can take a waterproof material and if you know what you're doing, you can actually wrap up things inside it in such a way that they can be immersed in water and remain dry. No joke.

"Now that you and Alice have your essentials, we'll pack up the rest of the stuff, except for my essentials and the clarinet, into one big bag. My essentials can go into my own, smaller rucksack. Then I'm going to waterproof both bags and the clarinet. Following that, I'm going to rent a paddleboard from over there," she indicates a small booth advertising rentals of paddleboards, whatever they are. I ask.

Jessica explains, "A paddleboard is a bit like a surfboard except that you can easily sit or even stand on it when afloat, at least in calmer waters. It's more stable, just heavier. You can use a paddle to propel and steer it in the same way as you would a canoe. They're used all over the Swiss lakes for recreation purposes.

"I plan to fasten the water-proofed packages to the underside of the paddleboard. I'll tie both the bags on with a couple of bits of rope. The clarinet I'll fasten on directly with some super-strength tape. Then I'll chill out on the lake for an hour or so. That's about the last thing anyone would expect from us. Then I'll just 'wake up' and set off for a bit of gentle paddleboarding. What I'm actually going to do is to get round a spur of land sticking out into the lake, where I'm not so visible, and dump the big bag, with the crap we don't need, at the bottom of the lake. I'll just hide the paddleboard underwater at the side of the lake. You'll lose your deposit, Harris, but that's small change beside the cost of the paragliders which you wanted to set fire to earlier, so I assume you'll live. I'll land in a quiet spot and get changed into my hiking gear, then go hell for leather along the lakeside until I can meet you guys in Spiez. We can meet at the marina there and figure out a way home. Probably a local bus from nearby will do to start with. If we can make it by around lunchtime, we should still have enough time to get out and back, possibly even by this evening."

She's already busy, packing up bags and wrapping them up in the various waterproof materials left over from last night. I can only assume that in terms of the great plan, we weren't being consulted, simply told.

Chapter 24
UNLICENSED TO KILL

Jessica

This is a very odd sensation. I'm lying on my back on a paddleboard, wearing nothing but my underwear, my watch and my sunglasses, with my passport tucked into the left-hand side of my sports bra. I point out that it's a sports bra since that means that the passport is hidden. All my other worldly possessions outside Liverpool are tied below me to the underside of said paddleboard. Not very far away are several law enforcement officers who are actively seeking to have me incarcerated. And now I'm sunbathing.

You can't tell under the sunglasses, but my eyes are very much wide open. There's no risk of me falling asleep with so much danger clear and present. I ought to be near-on exhausted after everything which has happened during the last twenty-four hours, even just twelve hours, but the adrenaline kicking in is removing that possibility. All of which is making it quite uncomfortable to be lying here. I so wish I could at least roll over, as you tend to do when you can't sleep. The problem with that is that if I do, I'm going to roll face first into the lake. I'm also not going to look like a random paddleboarder without a care in the world who has all day to get from here to the whole of fifty metres further down the lake. I have to leave a reasonable space of time before I get up and start to paddle gently away. Who would have thought that being a master criminal could be such tough and demanding work? You never see the villains in movies having to undergo such physical discomfort until the last couple of scenes when their plans all go to hell.

At least I can move my head from side to side and admire the scenery. I'm lying with my head at the back of the paddleboard, which is pointing away from the shore and towards the other end of the lake from Interlaken. There has to be something in this for me after all and I have a nice view of the Thunersee's north shore. The route up to Habkern looms over me, from where you can hike right up and over the saddle above it, then down into the Justistal valley, past the Niederhorn to your left and out over Sigriswil. It's a lovely hike on a good day and I certainly envy Alice and Harris at getting to see half of it close up on that bus trip via Habkern to Beatenberg. They're basically taking a shorter corner within the broader curve which my hike would have involved, passing in front of the ridge instead of going behind it, and then pitching up in Beatenberg, overlooking Spiez. Apart from the questionable smell of a pig farm in the middle, it's an almost perfect hike. The thought cheers me up until I recall again that I'm not there and am not going there. Back to grumpy.

I lie here and work on my tan for a few more minutes. I'm not someone really into tanning myself. Wandering around with the hue of a traffic cone is not what I consider overly attractive and I'm more into practical than beautiful at the best of times. I usually end up with a fairly tanned face and forearms over the summer season by virtue of my outdoor habits but not because I sit and slow-cook myself like a hog roast in a bathing suit with alcohol addiction issues. Working on my tan just now is more necessary since it's something I can do while keeping tabs on the law enforcement situation without appearing suspicious. I'm not sure quite how innocent I look but nobody has bothered coming out to get me so far. I doubt it's standard police operating procedure to leave highly wanted criminals in peace to top up their tans just because you can't be bothered to get a rowing boat.

The main question I have is how long do I need to wait before I can make a move? I literally don't have all day, but I don't want to take off down the lakeside too soon. It's a tough call. I can see police poking around in the rubbish bins at the lakeside over in Interlaken itself. Exactly how they think we would have got anything in there, I can't say, but they're clearly wise to the idea that we might have tried to ditch the evidence somewhere. There are doubtless enough of them scouring at least the lower mountainside for just such material as well. Still, there's no way anybody was around at the right time to see us tying all such incriminating evidence onto the bottom of this paddleboard or else I'd probably have about three heavily armed patrol boats surrounding me and telling me to lie on the board with my hands behind my head. In all the official languages of Switzerland plus English. These guys know how to do things properly, at least when it's going their way.

Therefore, I must be in the clear but that doesn't answer the question of how to stay there. Damn, I'm just going round in circles in my brain.

It seems I'm not the only one out here. I hear the noise of an approaching engine and some enthusiastic yells. They're the shouts of people enjoying themselves though, not enthusiastic, young police officers with the scent of a crook due a good kicking. Reminding myself not to react too swiftly, and hence suspiciously, I prop myself up on one elbow and look around.

There's a motorboat approaching from behind and to my left, close to the shore. It must have come out from Interlaken itself and has just dropped a girl in the water nearby. At least, a bikini-clad figure. I don't know if she'd prefer to be referred to as a "girl", a "woman", a "person" or even just "a humanoid life form with a Y-chromosome deficiency" in this politically correct age. I don't have all day to talk to myself, however, so I'm just going to refer to her as a girl. She seems young enough for it to be credible and she's not here on my paddleboard to complain.

She's holding on to something and as the motorboat approaches, a rope starts to rise from out of the water behind it. I think it goes back to her. On board the motorboat are two guys (I'm not going to bother listing all the different ways in which I should possibly be referring to them), one driving and one feeding out the rope. He sees it rise and feeds out a bit more. It sinks back into the water and the girl yells something at him. I can't make it out. His friend – I assume they're on speaking terms at least since they're both drinking together – starts a slow turn to the right, crossing in front of me, heading out towards the lake. The girl shouts something again. I don't know how they can hear her since they're further away from her than I am and right next to their engine but maybe the guy at the back is an expert in long-distance lip-reading.

Or maybe he and his pal are just piss-drunk. Either way, in an apparent response to the girl's shout, the motorboat changes gear and accelerates away.

All of a sudden, I feel a sudden jerk beneath me. The paddleboard lurches forward. The jerk is followed by a second, slightly less marked but still noticeable one. The paddleboard is being hauled to the right and I'm leaning along its right-hand side, my head at the rear, my elbow in the water and holding on for dear life with my left hand and my knees. I'm trying to shift my weight to the left side of the board, which is rising out of the water, when the whole thing more or less flattens out suddenly and takes off into the lake, following directly behind the motorboat. The semi-fall has maybe been a good thing for me since it lets me swivel myself around so that I'm lying on my stomach, facing forwards. If I'd still been flat on my back in the opposite direction, I'd probably be swimming by now while all the equipment and the clarinet would be racing off towards Meiringen without me.

What is going on?

I look behind me and there's that girl, apparently standing up and following directly behind me on some sort of platform. Oh, hold on, it's not a platform. It looks more like she's on skies. That's it – she's water-skiing. Fair enough but her stupid friends must have snagged the two bags of equipment under my paddleboard when they were pulling out and extending the rope underwater. My bags were hanging there like a couple of mooring buoys just beneath the surface. Since they weren't actually moored to anything, it seems I'm along for the ride.

She's looking pretty unhappy about all this from the small amount which I can see. Well, steady on, girl. I didn't ask to be here and I'm in full period flow right now, so we all have our crosses to bear, all right? I look round to the motorboat where it seems that her genius friends either haven't noticed a single thing or they're too wasted to work out that they're towing two female followers at a nerve-wracking speed. I don't recall going this fast even when paragliding although that might have been a question of perspective. Unlike Harris, I didn't fly into Interlaken at a height where I could tickle a salmon along the way.

Before her friends can help us all out by applying the freaking brakes, Fate intervenes. There's a sudden popping sound and the larger equipment bag shoots out from beneath my paddleboard and flies out behind me. It collides neatly with the girl on my tail, knocking her clean out of the water and skating across it for a few metres. I assume she's going to end up swimming but alive, but I have no time to reflect further. What I can see is the bar she was holding. It's shooting forwards towards me, coming up from my left rear quadrant. The motorboat is still ahead and marginally to the right so it's going to fly over me.

Something tells me that I need that bar. This board is still attached to the motorboat by the second bag caught in the towrope. So long as the board remains attached to the boat, along with its precious luggage, I have to keep hold of that rope. I'm not necessarily thinking quite that straight, but I know that I have to stick with the board and the boat. I hold up the paddle which is attached to the board, and it snags the passing end of the rope let go by the girl. This is just as well since it's what is attaching the bar to the motorboat. It has somehow snagged the underside of my board as well. I don't know how. The other connection to the motorboat via the second equipment bag, however, snaps suddenly as the first one did. The second bag launches itself into the sky behind me and tears down towards the tow path at the side of the lake. It smacks into two passing mountain bikers, knocking them both off their mounts and through the doors of a public lavatory. Talk about taking the piss.

I'm not left with any time to reflect on such developments. With the other connections to the underside of the paddleboard gone, the remaining rope is now snaking outwards at an incredible rate towards the motorboat, the slack being guzzled up like a worm caught in a whirlpool. It's going to go taut in a matter of seconds.

As soon as it goes taut, my arms holding onto the bar are almost ripped out of their sockets. I've jammed my feet into the foot slots on the paddleboard and am standing on it, grasping the bar for all I'm worth while I try to stay with the board. With nobody else in tow, the speed is tremendous now. The water rushes past in a blur of blue brilliance. I can see the shoreline pass me by a hundred metres or so to my left, but I can no longer make out any details.

What those buffoons on the motorboat are thinking, I have no clue. Are they actually so trollied that they haven't noticed that I'm not their girlfriend on her water-skies? Were they even looking backwards for the past twenty seconds or so or did all that switcheroo just pass them by in a drunken haze? If such is the case, then they're very likely heading for a waterborne DUI since the boat is heading out into the centre of the lake and just seems to keep accelerating. The water below looks like a sheet of white. There's nothing blue about it any longer whatsoever.

I'm jumping from side to side, trying to avoid the various, minor wavelets which seem to keep cropping up. It's not as though there's a tide here, but I think the boat is going so fast that I'm getting caught in the disturbance of its wake. Maybe if I can veer to left or right by some way, I can scoot along beside it and keep out of the way.

I suddenly realize that I'm water-skiing and I'm actually doing it pretty well. The thought which follows, predictably enough, is that of course this is what Timothy Dalton did in, "License to Kill" when James Bond escaped from the drug deal at sea, water-skiing behind a floatplane until he managed to get on board, throw out the drug-dealing pilot and take off with a few million dollars' worth of illicit narcotics money. If only I could be that cool. If I could get a couple of million dollars' worth of illegal funds off that motorboat, at least we could forget Harris' sodding clarinet. Nice idea.

That said, I think I am being kind of cool here. I dodge around a couple of buoys and cut over the motorboat's wake another time. The James Bond theme is starting to sound at the back of my mind and I'm trying to remember what Tim did. Probably just as well as it helps to distract me from how bloody scared I am otherwise. But Tim wasn't scared. He was too cool. Come on, Jessica, you know he'd be impressed by you now. Just hold it together, girl!

Oh crap! I don't recall the bit in the film when a pedalo with two senior citizens suddenly appeared in front of James Bond! Even if I can dodge around them, there's a fair chance that the rope will decapitate them. Chalk up another success to those motorboat morons. What to do?

Going by my earlier paragliding experience and hastily derived understanding of the physics of fluidity, there seems one option. Let's hope I can make it work or those two are going to have a very short retirement ahead of them.

Shortly before hitting the pedalo, I lean forward and force the front of the paddleboard nose first into the water. This jars me badly, but I manage to hold on. Just. It also creates a small swell in front of me. I lean backwards a moment before reaching the pedalo and haul on my rope, bringing up the nose of the paddleboard as I plough into the swell and take off. The paddleboard hurtles into the air and – presumably because I don't hear the crash of paddleboard and skulls – clears the pedalo and its occupants. The spine-crunching jolt on landing probably reduces my physical height by a couple of centimetres but at least that's one more manslaughter charge avoided.

I hope I've done something to earn Tim's undying respect in the unlikely event that I ever meet him. I'm not just in it for the sex, you know. Not that I'd turn him down if offered, of course. Just in case Tim's reading this.

Getting laid is not my primary concern for the moment. Not even a secondary or tertiary. Not getting myself killed, not getting anyone else killed and somehow reaching dry land with that clarinet are pretty much topping the list. I split my legs, raising the right one high enough to get past another mooring buoy, narrowly avoiding an intimate introduction with a bright orange, plastic globe. Especially today, that would have hurt like hell. I dodge around a couple more by skirting to the sides and finally seeing that there's nothing in front of me likely to cause instant death if I hit it within the next ten seconds, I take stock quickly of where the hell I am.

The Niederhorn looms on my right across the lake. The Niederhorn? Already? I wasn't expecting to get here until at least this afternoon. How fast is all this going? Where the hell are these nutjobs trying to get to? You can buy booze quite easily in either Spiez or Thun so I'm guessing it's one of those two. If I can just hold on long enough, I may yet live.

For reasons best known to them – or maybe not even since their brains may be too liquified at this point – these nautical wonders suddenly decide to head towards the Spiez marina to our left. I'm pulled out to the right and so move to swing left, back in line. Maybe they're going to stop in Spiez. Great!

But why aren't they cutting their speed? Spiez's marina is full of sailing boats and other pleasure craft. You can't just pull up at the speed of an F1 supercar and pull a handbrake turn like some kind of aquatic A-Team impression. Not only is it blatantly illegal but you'd probably end up spread across the crazy golf course in however much was left of your boat after the inevitable crash with the shoreline.

They can't be so drunk that their blood is 90% proof yet, since at the last minute, they veer to the right in a sharp turn around the edge of the Spiezerberg. This is a small, wooded hill which lies between the town of Spiez and the lake itself. It runs down to the edge of town and out into the lake as the lakeside arm of the marina. The boat is angling to pass it by.

This is going to cause me problems. I'll have to pull a very sharp turn to keep up and I hope I can do so without smacking into the shore. I pull back as hard as I can on the bar and lean over, slewing round to the right faster than I've yet done today. So far so good but it's going to be close. Very close.

Oh shit.

Oh shit!

OH SHIT!

I'm on the lakeside of the Spiezerberg arm but the bulk of the hill is still in front of me. Of much greater concern, the breakwater in front of the hill is right in front of me too and I have no way of avoiding it! No way at all!

I smash straight into the breakwater and leave the water entirely. Congratulations, Jessica, you've just become the Thunersee's first naval aviator.

A sea of green branches fills my vision, and I crash straight into it. At this point, the rest of reality simply turns blank.

Chapter 25
LIKE AUNT, LIKE NIECE

Harris

I rather doubt I'm ever going to discover quite what Jessica's fascination is with the Alps. I can visualize it, that I do not deny. Each time I've come up here, I have been able to see just how magnificent this landscape can be. However, I understand that Jessica finds some form of relaxation, even release up here.

This is now the third time I've climbed into these mountains in the course of the past twenty-four hours, and I have felt no sense of relaxation or release. I am not an idiot, and I do know why. The first time, I was en route to learn the art of paragliding, something which I would never even have contemplated trying out until my life entered the realms of the truly bizarre a few short weeks ago. The second time, I was in a helicopter, heading up to spend the night at heights way above those where normal people dwell, to be followed by more paragliding. Both times, it was quite clear why I might not be able to appreciate the experience as Jessica would have done. Now I'm making my way up to the edge of the ridge which overlooks this lake. It isn't all that far from where we took the paragliding lesson in fact. Alice and I are on board a public bus and the idea is to descend simply by public transport. You might imagine that for once, I could take stock of the scenery and enjoy it for all which it is.

Except that this time, I'm a wanted fugitive. I just can't shake the thought. I'm in a position where I never once imagined over the course of my life that I would find myself. It's a new perception of reality. The colours around me are still the same. The sounds I hear are no different. Yet it all feels somehow as if everything has changed. Nothing is as it used to be. I suppose it's similar to a momentous event. Falling in love was like this for me. As soon as it happened to me, I saw everything in a whole new way which I had never perceived before. On a sadder note, a bereavement can have quite a similar effect. Whatever else may be of concern, if you receive the news of a sudden loss, it colours absolutely everything and the other factors simply aren't so important anymore. What is truly concerning at this point, however, is that for some reason, I'm using the experiences of true love or heartfelt loss as a means to describe my situation now that I've landed illegally in a public park, accidentally broken into an orgy and been chased up and down a mountain track with an unlicensed paraglider on my back. How has such a sequence of silly goings-on come to colour my whole life like this?

Perhaps it's the prospect of incarceration. Like many things, it doesn't seem so intimidating until you're staring it in the face, until it's much more than just a theoretical construct. The idea of actually spending some time behind bars with no freedom to decide what I'm going to do next is quite chilling. Maybe it's the thought of how others will regard me. I have a reputation to uphold. I'm a proper gentleman, at least in my own mind. Or I was at least until around two days ago, if I'm honest. It's part of who I am, and I don't want to throw all that away in a heartbeat.

I don't know but it's weighing on me. The bus is lurching from one side to the other of what seems to be a single-sided road. How we've avoided plunging over the ever higher precipice beneath us, I cannot tell but I must be consumed by my thoughts because I'm not afraid. I really have greater worries. It makes no logical sense. If I die, I can't go to jail, and my reputation will be of little consequence. Yet that potential sentence is what's concerning me, not the massive drop which is only slightly to one side of me.

At the same time, I suppose I should be positive. I still have a way to follow, and I must. As usual, Jessica seems to have got the practicalities correct. Alice and I managed to make our way to the other side of Interlaken and out again on bicycles and then get this bus up into the mountains on the north side of the lake. She also predicted that if we left the bus early, we could walk to the funicular railway which would lead us down to the lakeside, from where we can get a ferry back over to the other side and meet up with her. There are all sorts of names for where we're going but I'll be blasted if I can remember any of them. Alice seems confident enough of it all so I'm just following her. We aren't exchanging pleasantries but that isn't because of any particular ill feeling between us, merely to avoid presenting the other passengers with an obvious pair of English tourists to remember. The curse of being a fugitive once more.

The bus stops climbing and passes into meadowland again. It isn't flat this time but rolls up quite a steep slope for the most part. Chalets of varying sizes, built on a series of roads and lanes, snake along the hillside and merge with each other at different points to form a village of sorts. It follows a main road which seems to run the entire length of the ridge. The view out over the lake is more or less the same one which we saw when learning to paraglide except that we started a shade higher then. It's still extremely impressive. I vaguely recall Jessica telling me that one man apparently dedicated a vantage point to posterity up here, having found it to be the most beautiful spot in the world. I don't know if I would necessarily agree with him. It's majestically attractive but I'm sure there are many like it, even in Switzerland alone, never mind the rest of the planet. Still, it's something which could be considered seriously, I'm sure. Of course, this is all something which I could find myself considering rather more meaningfully if I weren't coming to terms mentally with being very much on the wrong side of the law.

Ultimately, it's Alice who succeeds in distracting me. I manage to make out that we've passed a road sign welcoming us into Beatenberg. I don't know if that has anything to do with Battenberg cake. It sounds similar but not quite the same and my knowledge of German just isn't up to it. Whatever the case should be, it does ring a bell as a name which Jessica mentioned. Next thing I know, Alice is nudging me in the ribs and indicating that the next stop is ours. I'm in no position to argue.

We exit the bus at a small stop on what is presumably the outskirts of Beatenberg. Like I mentioned, we were already following an urban settlement along the side of the ridge so I'm assuming that Beatenberg and its neighbouring town or village must merge into each other in practice, even if not administratively. Such things really are beyond me.

Alice pulls a pair of sunglasses out of her pocket and dons them. It's turning into a very hot day although up here it remains a little fresher which is nice. The ridge looms over us to the right and Alice turns in the direction which we were following in the bus.

"This is the way, Mr Beadlesby. Let's go," she says without waiting. "According to the phone, we can make Beatenberg Station in about twenty minutes and get the funicular railway from there. When we get down to Meiringen, we'll be just in time to catch the ferry over to Spiez."

None of those names means a great deal to me although I vaguely recall Jessica discussing the merits of Spiez when we passed through on the train from Bern. It feels like a lifetime ago, so I don't remember many of the details. Not that it would matter much now as I just need to follow on.

My goodness, Alice is walking quickly. The road is flat by relative standards, but those standards are relative to the mountainside where we find ourselves. There's still a lot of up and down and it does take a toll. This pounding pace is making me breathe very hard and I'm sweating profusely.

"Do we have to go so quickly, Alice?" I ask breathlessly.

She turns her head without slowing down.

"Yes," she replies abruptly. "That ferry only goes once every two hours. If we don't make the funicular in time, then we'll never get to Meiringen in time. That means a two-hour delay before we can meet up with Auntie Jess. And we're meant to be getting out of here as fast as possible."

"But is it really that far?"

"Not if you go in a straight line, no. But the reason we got off the bus when we did is because the police may be checking buses coming into the station from Interlaken. We got off early so as to avoid that. If we then just roll up straight behind the bus, coming from the same direction a few minutes later, the cops are going to have to be pretty dim not to think about checking us out. And I don't mean ogling my top."

Like aunt, like niece it would seem.

"What we need to do is to loop round the station and approach it from the other side. We'll look like a couple of folk out on a walk, coming in for a ride back down. Problem solved. At least, that's the theory."

"That's fair enough, Alice," I gasp. "Just please try to take into account that I'm maybe not the fittest of walkers."

She looks back at me with a strange combination of pity, sympathy and contempt. I think I can see all three somehow although I may be imagining it. She turns her gaze forwards again and I inhale as deeply as I can while trying to wipe another, seeming handful of sweat from my brow with my basically sodden handkerchief. What I would give at this moment to be back on that glacier.

I'm suddenly extremely grateful to Alice. For a few minutes there, I realize, my mind was completely focused on something other than my criminal status. It might be that physical discomfort is a wonderful source of healing for the mind. I can't say for sure but up to now, since we left the bus, I forgot all about being wanted. It comes back now, as I march onwards, but it's a slightly dulled sensation. The exchange with her extended that and made me consider how other factors might matter as well in this life. There are other concerns going on which never crossed my mind. Ruefully, I can see why Jessica might not have bothered to brief me on the need to loop around the station. I sincerely doubt I would have remembered that. But Alice did. There's a lot going on at any one time of which we're all blissfully unaware, even when it's happening next to us. If we're completely caught up in our own lives, be that due to joy, sorrow, pain, pride or anything else, it's worth remembering that there is a world out there where we are not at the centre.

Philosophizing helps considerably but only to the point where I trip over an uneven paving stone, fall forwards and sidewards to the right, then ricochet off a low wall and collapse next to a small, stone water faucet, which is dispersing water continuously into a stone trough in front of it. Alice rolls her eyes but stops for a moment and swings down a water bottle from her small pack. She fills it from the faucet and drinks a long draught.

"What on earth are you doing, Alice?" I ask in horror as I pick myself up. A skinned elbow but nothing worse than that, thankfully. "You can't go drinking out of random taps in the street!"

"I'm not that stupid, Mr Beadlesby," she groans. "You see how it's labelled, 'Trinkwasser'? That means drinking water in German so it's perfectly OK. You should have some yourself. It'll do you good. Just hurry up about it."

No doubt she picked all of that up from her aunt, so I suppose it's credible enough. I lay down my bag and start to rummage through it in search of the water bottle I know that I have there somewhere.

"I said to hurry up," she remarks tetchily. "We don't have a hell of a lot of time."

There is only so much of this I will take. I look up from my bag and round on her.

"Now you listen to me, Alice!" I tell her. "We might not be in school any longer, but I am still a teacher, and you are a pupil. You are not in charge here and I will not be spoken to in that tone any longer. I am a good sport and a team player, and I will play my part properly in our endeavour here. Don't get me wrong. But I demand a little respect. And if I need a couple of minutes to catch my breath and have a little refreshment to sooth me, then I think that I jolly well deserve it at this moment in time."

I pause for a second to draw breath. I think I've made my point.

Or perhaps not. She comes up to me fast, her face a matter of a few inches only from mine. I don't know when I last saw such a look of total venom in another's face. Maybe when Jessica rounded on me in the plane, but this is worse. For reasons I cannot quite understand, this is a genuinely terrifying moment. It has certainly wiped all other concerns from my mind.

"Who the hell do you think you are?" she demands. The sentence is announced at a slow but steady pace but with the volume and intensity building with each word from a low but menacing growl to a piercing shriek of wrath. "I'm not in charge here, am I? Well, who is? I'll tell you this much – it's not you! Auntie Jess is running this and we're following her orders! We're helping you, you clueless cretin and my auntie is the only one who knows what we have to do! We trust her and we do what she tells us!

"You think you need a rest? Oh really? Cry me a river, you lazy waster! Auntie Jess has been giving this everything. She got us up and down the glacier. She found the way out of Interlaken. She got the heavy stuff up and down the mountain and she did all the running. Now she has to get all that crap out of the lake and around it on foot to Spiez. She's going above and beyond but you can't even be arsed to walk for twenty minutes to catch a train and a boat!

"You're the problem! She's the solution! And so long as I'm the one who remembers what she told us to do and knows how to get it done, then I am in charge. And if I say we get to that station in twenty minutes round the back way, then you don't stop to ask me how, why or where. You get off your backside, strap up now and follow me round there! And if you really can't do that, I'm off to get a nice flight back to the UK with Auntie Jess and I'll let Mrs Bodega know that she should expect a quick phone call from some Swiss German cop on Monday morning to explain why you might be a bit late for work!"

That hurt. Those were all quite valid points although I could have done without the last sentence. I look down for a second and then re-pack my bag, forgetting about the water bottle. I still can't work out where I put it.

"I'm sorry, Alice," I say. "We don't have time to discuss but you're entirely right. Please accept my apologies. This is hard work, but I will be behind you."

To her credit, her scowl melts and she grins.

"I know. Everyone just needs a kick up the ass at one point or another. Let's go."

I feel absolutely exhausted, as if my inner organs have somehow been removed and my muscles simply refuse to work any longer. However, we have reached the station, and the funicular railway is about to depart. The doors are still open, though only just, and with what must be a superhuman effort, I throw myself towards and through them. Alice steps through afterwards, giving me one of her more quizzical looks. The doors slide shut another ten seconds or so later.

Doing my best to retain some shred of dignity, I pull myself off the floor and lean back against the window behind me. The train is following the track down the side of the mountain, spending most of the journey inside the treeline. Hence the scenery probably isn't up to Jessica's preferred standards, at least not compared with the cable car which runs on from the station up to the Alpine peaks above. However, there are glimpses downwards of the lake beneath us, flanked behind by the soaring heights of the mountains on the other side. It was in their shadow that we first arrived from Bern in Interlaken. I'm quite impressed with myself for getting this much of a grasp on the local geography. I may not know every last twenty-something-syllabled village as well as Alice's aunt does but within a couple of days, I feel as though I'm making reasonable progress.

Not spending too much time on reflection, I quickly arrive at a new question. Where's our ticket? How do we buy one? There are only two other people in this carriage. Presumably at this time of morning, the popular route is up the mountain so that the masses can hike. There can't be many heading downwards. Such being the case, I think I can risk putting a question or two in English to Alice.

She glances up and down the carriage before coming back in a low voice, "We should have bought the tickets from the machine at the top, but we didn't have time. You could buy them with the app on your phone if you had it but by the time you've downloaded it, created an account, entered our details, keyed in your credit card number and actually bought the ticket, we could have travelled to and from Zürich about three times. So just leave it. It's really unlikely that there'll be an inspector anyway. If that happens, we just act like dumb tourists and offer to pay in US dollars. That'll throw them enough that they probably won't want to bother any further."

I'm shocked.

"But that's rank dishonesty! It's fare-dodging!"

She looks up but for once I can anticipate what's coming and I respond in advance.

"Oh, OK, I know. We're already in plenty of trouble with the law and we –

notably your aunt – have been lying our way across half of Switzerland since the middle of last week. I suppose it's just one more example of improper behaviour to add to the list."

Alice rolls her eyes but smirks briefly afterwards.

"That's about it, Mr Beadlesby. You can't have everything so just enjoy the view. Some people pay a fortune to see this place. Consider it a perk of the trip."

At this point, we're not far off the bottom. Alice scans ahead for the apparently improbable though not impossible presence of ticket inspectors. My heart skips a beat when she announces that she can see some, but she goes on quickly to point out that they're checking the crowds heading upwards just now, not the dregs coming down.

The train comes to a halt inside the station, such as it is. Basically two platforms carved into a steep slope in the shape of a staircase, either side of the single track which accommodates the train. Cables between the rails pull it up and down the mountainside. The ticket inspectors and the crowd are on the opposite side to that where we get out. It's a clean exit for once.

Alice strides quickly down the stairs and out into the sun. The lake glistens ahead of us on the other side of the road. We cross quickly and make for the nearby jetty.

True to Jessica's reading of the timetables, a ferry looms from the left, coming from the direction of Interlaken. It's a medium size boat, maybe a hundred to a hundred and fifty feet long. I can't really be sure. What I can tell for sure is that it seems to be heaving with passengers. I do hope they even have space for us.

Alice heads straight towards a ticket machine beside the jetty and punches in some instructions to place our order. She turns to me and asks for ten francs, explaining brusquely that Jessica had ensured that I would have a few hundred in the local currency before we even headed for the glacier. Somewhat embarrassingly, a quick perusal of my wallet reveals that Alice is quite right, even though I'd forgotten that detail. At least we have valid tickets for this part of the journey. Alice explains that they always do check tickets on the way on and off the ferry service so it's best to be equipped here.

The boat pulls alongside, its engine now in reverse and it draws to an expert halt in front of us. The gangway is lowered, and it feels as though somebody has opened a human floodgate. I certainly don't need to worry about finding space on the boat. I just need to be concerned about not being swept away in the tidal wave of people exiting. I can only imagine that they're going to form the next few intakes on the funicular railway heading upwards. All this mountain hiking must really be a popular pastime after all. Every five minutes I seem to discover yet another reason not to doubt a single thing Jessica tells me. The torrent does subside eventually, and Alice and I manage to board the boat.

For once, something actually seems to go to plan without any upset. It's a magical trip over the lake. My earlier concerns have lessened their grip on me and I'm actually doing no more than to enjoy the experience for what is one of the few times since we left Bristol. The boat pulls away from the jetty and sets course across the lake for Spiez. Alice and I proceed up to the front. I know it has some other, properly nautical term but I have no clue what it is, so I will just refer to it as the front. The sun shines down from a perfectly blue sky. I don't see a single cloud. That may have made the hiking hard work but here on the lake, there's a solid breeze coming straight in our faces and the temperature is just where you would want it. The water broadens out behind us in concentric wavelets. It's amazing how clean it is. You can actually see well below the surface in the undisturbed patches too. Beyond our immediate surroundings, the surface is dotted with buoys, boats and watercraft of various types – yachts, windsurfers, pedal boats and various others, their respective areas all properly marked out of course. There are swimmers closer to the shore as well. Framed by the Alps along its two lengths, with the lake extending into a minor heat haze at each end, it really is the sort of setting you would expect to see in a painting or perhaps in a romantic film set in the Alps.

The journey itself is only supposed to take around ten minutes, but it is worth every moment in my view. It's only as we approach Spiez itself when something strange occurs. The ship's horn suddenly blares angrily. I can see a couple of crew members coming out onto the walkway next to the bridge (I think that's the correct term for the control room with the steering wheel) and shouting quite animatedly at someone on the lake. Alice and I look round and see what appears to be a speedboat racing out of the area of Spiez and round in front of us to our right, following the side of the lake. A couple of seconds later, a figure appears, being towed on a rope behind it, travelling at what I can only describe as a very unhealthy speed for someone who seems to be riding a small surfing board or the like. This figure shoots over the surface, giving the impression of holding onto the rope in front for dear life, until suddenly colliding with something in the water just before the forest which juts into the lake to the right of the Spiez marina. The figure promptly flies out of the water, together with the board and disappears into the forest. As far as I can tell, the speedboat is carrying on along the lake as if nothing untoward has happened. How very strange.

Neither Alice nor I know what to make of it, but Alice is worried. Jessica was out there on a board. She wasn't supposed to arrive in Spiez like that but given how many things have not gone quite according to plan, no doubt anything is possible. Alice has little to say on the topic, but it doesn't take many words.

We arrive in Spiez shortly afterwards. A string of wooden walkways stretches out to form a makeshift docking area in front of the hotels and rather expensive-looking apartments on the actual land which forms the lakeside arm of the marina. Behind them looms a large castle at the base of the slope which turns into the hill on which the forest grows. The marina is busy with yachts and their owners milling around and on the other side, I can see an artificial beach which, on a day like today, is clearly packed with people. It's odd to see something which looks so much like a picture from beside the sea when you only have to look up a little higher to see all of these landlocked mountains rising above it.

Alice has no concern for any of this. No doubt she's seen it before, but she has other things on her mind as she charges along the walkways to the concrete wall which joins the two arms of the marina. It's clearly the rendezvous point which Jessica had in mind. Alice scans this peremptorily and then turns her gaze onto the lakeside path leading into Spiez from the direction of Interlaken. She sees nothing.

"Dammit backwards!" she hisses to herself, clearly distracted. "There should be some sign of Auntie Jess by now!"

She pulls out her telephone and tries to call her aunt but to no avail.

"I don't like this, Mr Beadlesby. I'm going into the woods to see if I can find whoever crashed there. I don't think it will take that long. If it's not Auntie Jess, we can be back here soon enough. Do you want to come?"

I'm not sure I'm being given a genuine choice, so I acquiesce accordingly. I can't think what else I would really do of any use if I did have such a choice. And I don't want to find out that I never actually did in the first place.

Chapter 26
WHICH PLAN ARE WE ON NOW?

Jessica

I'm lying on a forest path on the far side of the Spiezerberg from town, which runs next to the Thunersee. There's a paddleboard located at a very awkward angle on top of me which is definitely not helping to ease my period pains in the slightest. What just happened to me? It takes me a moment or two but now I can remember. I was like Tim in, "License to Kill", wasn't I? A smile comes to my lips briefly and then immediately evaporates. If I recall correctly, Tim didn't end up with a distinctly bloody elbow and a stinging nettle hanging menacingly over his naked shins.

Nonetheless, I should consider myself lucky. I manage to withdraw my shins from underneath the local fauna without being stung and despite the superficial pain in the elbow, my arm still works. In fact, so does all of my body as far as I can tell. No broken limbs, no collapsed lungs. I assume the liver and kidneys are still doing whatever they do. A massive lump of earwax detaches itself from my inner cochlea and adds to the odd hue of my right shoulder but if that's the worst of my injuries, then I think I'm doing pretty well.

I feel quite light-headed and it's hard to focus for the moment. I need to stop trying to work out exactly what happened to me at the point where I crashed and afterwards. Somehow or other the paddleboard and I ended up here on the forest path. I don't know how but so what? I don't need to know how, so I'm going to forget about it. What I do need to know is whether the guys on the motorboat noticed in time to be coming back for me or if anyone else is on my tail. A quick glance around would seem to indicate a negative to both of those questions, at least in the here and now. I take a seat.

What next? Ah yes, the clarinet. I know that the two equipment loads were snapped off the board by the various ropes involved but the clarinet was strapped directly onto the underside in its own wrapping. With a bit of luck, it'll still be there. Given that it accounted for some 99% of the value of everything attached, that's quite important. I turn the board over and amazingly enough, there it is. It's still wrapped and attached as done originally and even looks undamaged despite everything else, myself included, taking quite a whack or just getting lost entirely. Chalk up one for the team, then. We're on a roll.

Or, that reminds me to ask, where exactly is the team? What time is it? Going by the sun, it's late morning so if Alice and Harris made their way as planned, I suppose they should be nearby but once more, it's getting a bit difficult to calculate everything. This is when I notice that amazingly enough, I still have my watch attached. Would have helped to notice that a moment ago. I let my mind go blank for an instant.

I immediately wish I hadn't. There's the sound of footsteps coming along the path, moving quickly. Alice or Harris? Random hikers? Or law and order? I have no idea, but I don't want to find out the hard way. I kick the paddleboard over the low clumps of bushes and into the lake. Except that the damn thing floats, of course, doesn't it? It's hardly surprising on reflection but I do wish it would sink. It's about two metres long and if it just floats there, I may as well run up a flag with my face on it and an arrow pointing down, announcing, "Hey, guys! She's down here!" The area of my crash landing includes some flattened bushes and a fairly indented piece of walkway which I stand no hope of flattening out in the thirty odd seconds it's going to take for those footsteps to reach me. I guess I'm going to have to run for it although doing so in bare feet on a stony path is not going to be comfortable and I won't reach full speed.

Once again, watching Bond films comes to my aid. This is going to be one of the most expensive tributes ever to, "Dr No" but if it worked for Sean Connery, it'll work for me. In, "Dr No", Bond and Honey Ryder hide from the eponymous villain's rather dim-witted henchmen (and they are men; I'm not being sexist, just saying it like it is) by concealing themselves under water and breathing through bamboo sticks. I don't have any bamboo to hand, but I can unscrew the bottom end of the clarinet. It's a watertight tube. Grabbing it in my right hand and holding on to the rest of it in my left, I leap back out into the lake, passing over the now stationary paddleboard. Slick move, Jessica, at least it would have been if the lake were more than knee deep at this point. Sitting there with my knees wrapped round my chin and the various parts of a wind instrument worth more than where I live, with lake water lapping round me, I must look like a complete dimbo but that wouldn't have bothered Sean, would it? I roll onto my front and sink beneath the water, only the wider end of the lower piece of the clarinet still above the surface. Its other end is in my mouth, forming what has to be the most expensive snorkel in the world.

Nice idea, Jessica but clearly both totally ineffective and totally unnecessary. Two figures emerge above me, standing on the shore on the other side of the paddleboard. The shorter one picks up a pebble and lobs it my way. It's quite substantial and lodges itself in the small of my back. I convulse without meaning to but stay under the surface. A second follows, bouncing off my left bum cheek. That hurts too and I suppose that my assailant must have seen me, so I float up to the light. Which takes about five seconds.

"What on earth are you lying around there for?" demands Alice.

I look up. I place the clarinet parts on the paddleboard and put down my hands and knees which reach the bottom of the lake long before the rest of my body is even submerged. I must have looked like a bit of an idiot, splayed out next to the paddleboard like a wannabe corpse in a naff detective show. Alice and Harris are stood there, neither appearing very impressed.

"Is the clarinet all right?" Harris virtually yells.

I just crashed, airborne and doing about fifty clicks an hour, face first into a forest. Is anybody vaguely concerned about my welfare?

Apparently not.

"Did you retrieve the whole thing?" Harris follows up. He could hardly be more worried if he were female, nine months pregnant and had just gone into

369

labour. I wish I hadn't thought of that. Things coming out of my more feminine passageways are another worry in my head which doesn't seem to be of the slightest interest to anybody else.

I drag myself, the paddleboard and the clarinet out of the water and onto the path. Ouch, ouch and thrice ouch! As Shakespeare might have put it if he'd had the misfortune to be me right now. I forgot about those damn nettles, but they've got me now. Again, it's not as if anyone cares. Harris grabs the pieces of clarinet from me, re-attaches them with the finesse of a jeweller tending to a 3000-carat diamond, and then proceeds to play a small pirouette or whatever the technical term is. Like I could care less in a billion years.

"You really are funny, Auntie Jess!" Alice giggles. "You were lying there, next to the paddleboard like an underwater chav who lost her tenth drinking game and all her clothes at the same time! This is Bern, not Benidorm, you know!"

As her principal mentor, I'm in no position to criticize Alice's expertise in the art of sarcasm. Before I can even think of a pithy comeback, she hauls the paddleboard over to the other side of the path, drags it up to a thicker group of trees, and stows it at their base, where there's a more substantial and heavier clump of bushes.

"Where'd you put all the equipment?" she enquires.

"Oh, I lost it all when I got snarled with some boat," I tell her, still somewhat vaguely.

"The whole damn lot?" she asks. "You mean you don't even have any clothes apart from what you're wearing? Or your boots? Or your wallet? Or your phone? Or anything?"

Alice's words are hardly reassuring. She's bringing home to me the fact that I'm currently on the edge of a small town in central Switzerland with nothing to my name other than a single set of sodden underwear, my watch, a damp passport stuck to my left boob and – if you'll excuse the language but I'm under a bit of duress right now – a fucking clarinet. And, by the way, I could not right now give a rat's ass if Karl Givret once used it to play the most haunting introit, if Beethoven performed his most intense sonata on it, or if

Harry Styles happened to have stuck it between his bum cheeks one time to blow out the theme from, "Star Wars" to a particularly pungent aroma.

"I'm maybe a little under-equipped right now, Alice," I admit. "But at least we can re-group and get moving now. In fact, we'd better. Fast."

"But aren't we safe here for a bit?" Harris asks. Nice to see that he's finally acknowledged my presence once more. I've only just nearly died twice and risked getting jailed for a few years in order to save his sorry rear end. Pity his questions remain those of a complete imbecile.

"OK, let's get this straight, shall we?" I'm doing my best to keep a calm demeanour. "Right now, we need to be discreet and place as far a distance as we can between ourselves and the forces of law and order in Bern, who would doubtless like to detain us for a few days. Days, I may add, which we don't really have right now if you and your clarinet are to make it back to Britain in time for the wedding bells to peal."

"Why on earth would the state authorities in the capital be so concerned?" asks the brains of the team.

"I mean the Canton of Bern, where we are still at the moment."

Harris laughs nervously. It's nice to see that even he can acknowledge now and again that he's asking a stupid question.

However, that doesn't last very long.

"Goodness me though, it's a bit like the inverse of one of those films where the pilot guys have to escape from France or Germany into Switzerland, isn't it?" he asks.

I believe he's referring to, "The Great Escape" and similar stories of World War Two derring-do by shot-down Allied aircrew. Honestly though, if I'd been in the Luftwaffe and had known that shooting down that bomber was going to land this dimwit on my head, I'd have let him fly back to England unopposed.

Thankfully, Alice breaks in at this point.

"But, Auntie Jess," she asks, "I still don't understand how we're going to get home then? Won't the other countries want to catch us too? Everywhere we go, our profile as international criminals just seems to get worse."

"Chill out, Alice," I say as reassuringly as possible. "Like I've told you before, we've only really embarrassed the Swiss, principally those round here. They won't want to alert other countries since there are far worse things for them to worry about and this will just make them look stupid. If we can get to somewhere in France or Germany, then we can probably catch a flight without getting the third degree from a stoked Alsatian dog and a female impersonator of the Incredible Hulk with a pair of rubber gloves and an evil glint which says, 'The lube is optional.'"

I think that's quite an amusing description, but it isn't reassuring Alice too much, so I change tack.

"It's quite easy, really. We get out of Bern, find a quiet border crossing point into France or Germany, get a couple of buses to the nearest airport and head for home. I mean, it's not a million miles to Lyon and that's a hub for the ski season in winter. It's well connected to most of the London airports, and we can probably get back via Gatwick, Stansted or – save us – Luton."

"But won't we look a bit strange with a really expensive clarinet?"

She's got a point. I really do love Alice. Always comes up with the more intelligent questions. Not that the competition on this trip is all that high, mind you.

"We'll have to consider that," I reply. "Perhaps catching the Eurostar train from Paris might be a better plan. Then again, they have border controls a bit like the airports these days. We're going to need a way to clear those, unless we want to pay some human traffickers for a minimum safety trip over the English Channel and then get beaten up by a bunch of Daily Mail readers and card-carrying Brexit voters who need to find somebody new to hate this week."

"Perhaps I could interrupt this enlightening discourse on the state of today's British politics for a moment?"

Sheesh, this guy is pompous sometimes. If we do end up spending the night in the hospitable clutches of the local PD and sharing the cell with a very large man with flexible, sexual preferences, I'll happily be his wing when it comes to finding the most satisfying orifice of Harris' body to poke.

"As I see it," he pontificates, "we simply need to move quickly and discreetly."

No doubt took a double first from Cambridge to figure that one out.

"So let's rent a car."

"With what? Your driving license? Which will have your name, address and date of birth all over it? As well as your photo which will probably match any CCTV records which might have been recorded in Interlaken."

"Oh right," he responds awkwardly. "Best head for the station, I suppose."

I start to pray. Please God, give me the strength I need not to tick one more box on my growing list of felonies under Swiss law by decking this twat. Probably not the terminology God is all that used to hearing and unlikely to show up any time soon in the Church of England's Book of Common Prayer, but at least it's heartfelt. In fairness to Harris, he's not a malicious or ill-intended guy. Nonetheless, right now, if I had to decide between punching him in the face or beating up a serial killer, human rights abuser or sex offender, I'd have a choice on my hands.

"No," I start in my most patronizing tone of voice, "they'll very likely be looking out for us at the exit points of public transport and since all of the trains and buses depart from Spiez Station, that's probably the first place the cops will be covering round here.

"What's more, if I rock up in a soaking pair of underwear and not much else apart from the world's most unnecessarily expensive clarinet –" he winces at that one, much to the pleasure of my meaner side –"I suspect we may attract a fair bit of attention.

"So the next step is that you and Alice get yourselves into town and buy me a set of clothes and a pair of boots!"

"Why both of us?" asks Harris.

"Because I need you for the money and her to make sure that I don't end up dressed like a colour-blind gay parade participant with a fetish for 15th century leisure gear!

"I also need some very important equipment for the period of the month which I'm enjoying right now, and which is designed for exclusively feminine usage. Harris, just shut up on this one and buy what Alice tells you to. She'll know precisely what I'm talking about.

"A sandwich and a drink would be nice too, by the way," I add. "Just nothing with too much green stuff in it. I don't trust greenery."

Let's show him who's wearing the trousers round here. Oh yeah, except I'm half-naked so it's not me, is it? Why do I always need a better plan?

Finally though, he does manage to ask something sensible.

"What sort of clothes do you want, then? I mean, how do you propose we get out of here?"

I already know the answer to that one, but he doesn't and he's not going to like it, so I pause a moment for dramatic effect.

"We hike."

Finally, a little peace and quiet. We've come into Spiez and rocked up at the marina. My arrival in the forest on the Spiezerberg has left such a crash site in its wake that the best way to avoid arrest just now may as well be to hide in plain sight. So now I'm taking a moment to rest my weary body on the concrete palisade which joins the two arms of the Spiez marina. It lies on the edge of the concourse which borders the lake, with the public park opening up on its other side. I can't see anyone in pursuit or even looking suspicious at this point so I'm taking the chance to lie down and close my eyes for a few minutes, simply leaving the warm sun to wash over me. Together with the breeze from the lake and the sound of the gentle lapping which comes up from it, it's a very relaxing setting and just what I want right now. After that dramatic arrival in the Spiezerberg, we can't risk touching public transportation until some way out of town. We have to move quickly but for the short duration while Alice and Harris are off shopping for me, I intend to make the most of it.

My main concern is that I might fall physically asleep and completely miss something important but it's a risk I'm willing to take.

"Hey! Grüzi wohl-a!"

Screw me, that was quick. I might have been worried about falling asleep, but I could swear that was only about thirty seconds ago and already I must have drifted off and ended up in a full-on nightmare where that pratt Jöchi crops up again.

Unless…

Oh for the love of all which is holy! No. No. No!

I'm having a vaguely Shakesperean day. How would the great bard have put it? Once more do I see the sphincter of Fate loom broad above me, clenching and unclenching its foul opening to let loose another steaming nugget in the foot course of my life.

I'm a vulgar person with an education.

None of the above saves me from the fact that that self-centred, seriously over-pimpled and dangerously over-testosteroned teenager has emerged from who knows where and is now homing in on me like a sex-addicted, guided missile launched from one very phallic-shaped fighter jet. I really need to drop it with the poetic similes and just get to the point. Otherwise, I fear that Jöchi's point may be getting to me while I'm still not paying attention properly.

Where the hell has he come from anyway? Shouldn't he be serving coffee to the unfortunate guests for whom he has the hots in that hotel in Interlaken while ignoring the ones he doesn't fancy? What's he doing in Spiez? Presumably, it's his day off and he lives here or something. I don't know but since I'm not supposed to understand German, I'm in no position to ask. I'm not sure I care enough to do so anyhow.

"Tu hast mich verlassen!" he says loudly, in a mock hurt voice. I left him. Yes, that's true. Only it wasn't meant to be a joke.

What now? Stick to playing dumb, I reckon.

"¿Que? No entiendo!" What? I don't understand. This has to be one of the most useful phrases in the entire, Spanish language.

"Was denn?" he asks. "Tu no verstehst? Es gibt den amor! Der ganze mundo versteht el amor!"

This is another piece of grammatical vandalism of two languages, loosely expressing surprise at how I could fail to understand love, which all the world understands. I wonder if it would be better to use the Spanish or the German for, "total bollocks", in response, to ensure that my point is properly made.

I don't get the chance.

"Es un Tag des amors," he tells me. It's a day for love. Or something like that. Having nearly died twice today already, the idea of there being a quick bit of nookie on the side as well doesn't do a great deal to make me believe that it's really any more extra-special by now.

Any sign of Harris or Alice anywhere? Predictably enough, no, none whatsoever. If I run now, we could spend ages trying to track each other down again, not least with my phone now somewhere at the bottom of the Thunersee. So what to do now? What would a nice, but clueless Hispanophone immigrant say?

"Hey!" I try. "¿Quierres el arroz?" Would he like some rice?

Borderline racist in its stereotyping but keeping things woke is the least of my concerns.

"Ah!" he beams. "Was für eine Romantika! Un Ros, meine Querida!"

With that, he starts looking around for a rose, which is, according to him, a sign of real romance. For me, his desired one. I roll my eyes while he heads to the nearest flowerbed. For once I'm grateful to whatever higher being may be overseeing my existence right now. If the Spanish for "rice" had sounded like the German for "penis", I hate to think what sort of situation I'd be in right now.

The cheapskate returns with a somewhat manky tulip which looks as though somebody's dog probably took a piss on it about half an hour ago. What a romantic indeed. What's your encore, dude? An intimate dinner lit by a battery torch, consisting of oven chips with economy lemonade? You really know how to sweep a girl off her feet.

Which is fast becoming clear is his main objective. He nods towards the Spiezerberg forest?

"So, Querida, vamos die Wunder del Amor im Wald hacer!"

He's suggesting that we make the wonders of love in the forest. I suppose it's an improvement on, "rumpito pumpito" in poetic terms but the net effect is much the same. It's about as attractive a proposition at the best of times as getting a pedicure with a chainsaw and this is not the best of times. I'm trying to avoid getting too close to the scene of my existing crimes in the forest. Having a quick bonk in public just round the corner is unlikely to reduce my jail time.

I need to find something else which works. Maybe the age gap.

"Errm, hay un problema," I begin. There's a problem. "Eres muy guapo, pero…"

I've told him he's very handsome. A lie but at least maybe just a white one. However, I have my reservations. I glance him up and down and then look at myself before continuing.

"No quiero un niño."

I don't desire a child. It doesn't take me very long to figure out that that was a very stupid thing to say since it can be interpreted quite easily in more than one way. His interpretation is quite predictable although his enthusiasm is a shade overwhelming.

"Hey!" he responds immediately and with a rather artificial level of concern in his voice. "Das non machen wir!"

We're not going to do that, he says, and with that he whips out of his pocket a string of condoms. This guy travels prepared, at least for what he wants. Might be more helpful if he carried some pimple cream, but I don't want to give him a complex, so I don't say so. Plus I can't remember what the Spanish is for, "pimple" either.

Either way, I'm quite taken aback. When I said that I didn't want a child, I meant not on the way into me although now that I think about it, he's quite right in that I didn't mean one coming out of me either. Perhaps we can just agree to keep people significantly younger than I am out of my nether regions altogether. There's already been enough going on down there since last night and it's making me distinctly uncomfortable. Could be a get-out line, even a true one. Let's see.

"Sería incréible!" I start. It would be incredible. OK, so let's get going with another, blatant lie before getting to the true bit. "Pero hay algo más allá abajo. No sería fácil acomodarte."

There's something else down there. It wouldn't be easy to accommodate you. How true. How bloody true.

He stares at me uncomprehendingly for a moment and then his eyes widen.

"Algo más?" he asks. "Du hast schon ein Niño dabei?"

Something else? Do I already have a baby on the way?

For frig's sake! If there's one thing I am definitely not right now, that's pregnant. There's probably a liquid trail of menstrual blood all the way down the Thunersee from Interlaken to Spiez which can attest to that. I mean, what a misogynistic, little git! As if women are just there for his pleasure and to be cast off in favour of the next one once a slight inconvenience occurs, such as the conception of a child. I'm starting to wonder if feminism has more going for it than I was thinking. It's not as if the men I've encountered in the course of the past week or so have done their gender many favours. That stuck-up prig Daniel, Captain Borisovich, Jöchi. If I didn't already know Colin, I'd have thought we were scraping the barrel in Interlaken. The most impressive man I can recall talking to since last Wednesday is Harris. What does it say for the male sex when that clueless wonder is the best ad you have for the Y chromosome? If it weren't for Tim, I'd be considering de facto lesbianism for the rest of my life. Oh yes, Timothy Dalton. Damn, I wish Jöchi would sod off so I could lie here and fantasize a bit about Tim for a few minutes before the next bit of hard work starts.

Except that next bit of hard work may be closer than I'm thinking. Two burly individuals, one woman and one man but both equally touting the physique of an overweight grizzly bear, are heading this way with a purposeful stride. The fact that they're both wearing police uniforms and carrying all of the associated apparatus, from a 9mm automatic through a vicious-looking taser, right down to a cheese sandwich is also testifying to the fact that they're not just here to patrol for random crims. Of which there are obviously a hell of a lot in a small, reasonably well-off, Alpine town like Spiez. I can't be sure since their eyes are covered in military-looking shades, but I think I may be a particular point of interest for them. Why? I don't know but it might be that although those idiots in the motorboat didn't realize it, that bit of high-speed water-skiing and forest-crashing which took place a short while ago may have attracted a bit of interest from local law enforcement. Not least after their colleagues in Interlaken maybe put out an alert for a man and two women currently wanted on suspicion of illegal paragliding activities in the town centre. And a woman on her own by the lake in nothing but what appears to be swimwear might well present an interesting consideration. Not just for pervs like Jöchi either.

Jöchi? My brain whirs. They're not looking for a couple, are they? But that means…

I swallow back the rising bile in my gorge and grasp Jöchi's cheeks in my hands with a breathless gasp of, "Mi amor!" I then proceed to stick my tongue into his mouth and try to do something to clean his teeth with it. My arms wrap themselves around his torso and I hold on tight.

I don't know if I have ever felt more disgusted in my life before by something which I'm doing myself. Perhaps if I commit a war crime one day or drop kick a baby over the edge of a suspension bridge I might top this but right now, it's all I can do not to spew down Jöchi's throat. The sensation is not being helped by the fact that he seems to have the longest tongue in history. Less romantic descriptions of acts of passion often refer to sticking your tongue down somebody's throat but in this case, not only has he done that but I'm worried that if he goes much further, the tip of his tongue may show up at the other end and he'll be literally kissing my ass. I can only assume that mouthwash is an alien concept to this grotty individual as well since I feel as though somebody is trying to suffocate me by blocking my windpipe with a decomposing chipolata. His hands are all over me too, grasping what he apparently thinks is my pregnant stomach as though he's a cross between a midwife and a marine, and wants to get the little bugger out and into the real world as fast as possible. The only comforting factor is that I would still rather he should be trying to get something out of there than into there.

Just as bad is the nagging feeling of guilt at my shamelessly opportunistic behaviour. I'm usually quite pleased with my ability to find a way out of almost anything. I don't feel guilty about showing Bethany pictures of places hundreds of kilometres away where she imagines Alice to be. Needs must and Bethany is only ever a killjoy in the first place. But this feels, well I can't quite say, but odd. Am I prostituting myself on behalf of Harris? Am I somehow taking advantage of Jöchi's probable desperation to find a girlfriend, even if the roots of said desperation are painfully easy to identify? While many of those I went to school and university with are now settling down to happily married life and even the joys of parenting, is this all I can make of the joys of union between a woman and a man? I can't say that all this is top of my mind, nor that such reservations are necessarily more important to me than staying out of jail, but I am still feeling just a bit cheap which doesn't lighten the mood.

A sudden order in a stern voice puts a stop to this hybrid of, "Gone with the Wind" and "Alien". Jöchi somehow extracts his tongue from the lower regions of my internal organs and stares round at the two cops who have just come up to us. I do my best to look as though I'm hopelessly in love and not about to lose all voluntary control of my intestines in at least one direction, possibly two.

"What are you doing here?" demands the policewoman. The conversation is in German, but I'll use the translation for the sake of convenience. There's no Sperman involved, thank goodness.

"What does it look like?" responds Jöchi in a highly disrespectful tone.

"It looks like a compost heap making love to itself," smirks the policeman.

I don't know whether to laugh or be outraged. That's quite funny inasmuch as it applies to Jöchi. I wouldn't have thought it would apply to me unless I've already caught his pimples. Oh no… For some reason, I desperately want to find a mirror and possibly the local pharmacy asap.

"I'm here with my darling girlfriend, trying to make the most of my day off by appreciating her beauty," pouts Jöchi. Unusually poetic for him but maybe he can express himself a bit more coherently if there's no Spanish involved. Or if he thinks he can get laid.

"Oh, I'm sure!" grins the cop. "You mean you can't afford a room but the marina concourse in Spiez is free?"

"Shut up, Franz!" scowls his colleague. Going by the stripes on her shoulder, I imagine she's the senior one here. She turns to the two of us.

"How long have you been here?" she demands.

"¿Que? No entiendo!" I respond. What? I don't understand. Might as well stay in character. I don't need Jöchi coming to the realization that I can understand German a whole lot better than I suggested previously, at least not in front of police officers who might find all that just a shade suspicious and worth asking more about. Appearing totally clueless at the same time might help as well since it makes me seem like less of a master criminal. Just think of Harris for inspiration.

"I've been here all morning," Jöchi informs her, maintaining his childishly grumpy attitude. I'm not sure if he's meaning to but he's clearly helping me out. Chances are he's just trying to get rid of the cops so he can carry on snogging me as soon as they clear off and he can get his tongue back out of his own gob. But nobody's forcing him so I'm not complaining. Not for now at least.

"And she's been here the whole time? Why doesn't she speak German?"

Bloody woman, won't she just shut up and move on? It's not like I'm guilty. Oh yeah, except I am, aren't I? I suppose I can't really take issue with her trying to do her job properly. I just wish she was making a living selling ice-creams instead.

Undeterred, Jöchi comes back full swing, telling her, "What do you think? That I just picked up this stunning woman and paid ten francs for her company? In which case, I suggest you get on with clearing up Spiez's prostitution problem and quit bothering law-abiding citizens like me and my beautiful, Spanish girlfriend!"

Steady on, dude! Do I look I'm putting up sexual favours for sale here? I glance down at my semi-naked anatomy and have to admit that, well, yes, perhaps I do to a certain extent. No make-up or high heels though, and my hair is no doubt a disaster zone at present so I can't completely match the stereotype, I hope. And even if I did, ten francs? Is that all I look like I'm worth? Ten frickin' francs? I admit to not being au fait with the current rates for a paid shag, but I'd like to think that a good time with me might at least generate more than you'd need for a meal deal in the local supermarket. What sort of bloody cheapskate is Jöchi? I'll tell you this, matey: if – and I stress, "if", because it is never going to happen in reality – you were ever to get into bed with me, don't think you'd be seeing change of a one hundred franc note any time soon. Ten francs? What the hell, some people…

It occurs to me that I should get over my pique at being considered several pay grades lower than what I think I should deserve to earn as a whore because the policewoman is talking again. And when it comes to sex and violence, I get the distinct impression that the latter is more her speciality. She's asking in rather dubious tones if Jöchi and I saw anyone arriving in town at speed off the lake? He shrugs and I respond by glancing around with another, "¿Que? No entiendo!" look on my face. The female police officer snarls nastily at my top and heads off with a sniff. I may even be offering some mild cause for jealousy. I wouldn't say that I'm more than adequately endowed, and she likely has more on top than I do but on the other hand, when you have the overall physique of a main battle tank, you probably need a pair of 38 Triple Ds before anybody's going to notice that there's anything standing out at all. Her colleague casts a look in a similar direction but I think he's just ogling. Pervo. It's almost like somebody recruited Colin to maintain law and order round here.

None of this is bothering Jöchi. Perhaps he feels like I owe him one now as he swirls round to face me and immediately glues his face to mine with what feels like an industrial strength suction pump attached to my mouth. I can feel his gigantic tongue inside of said pump and can once more taste old corn chicken slices. Makes you wonder if it would be worse giving medical treatment to this guy as a proctologist or a dentist. What's even worse than that is that I can feel his greasy arms holding me in a distinctly unromantic embrace while his hands work their way steadily up my midriff. I take it he rarely trims his nails. I feel as though my ribs are on the verge of being sandpapered smooth. The smell of cheap booze and a lack of deodorant is growing stronger and I'm starting to feel a very unwelcome protuberance pressing on the side of my thigh. If I were in a dark and lonely place, I might actually be feeling quite frightened. In the bright morning sunshine, on the promenade in front of the Spiez marina with hundreds of people around, including a couple of cops who only left us about twenty seconds ago, I don't feel quite so threatened but I'm hardly comfortable. My key concern though is how to get out of this mess without drawing undue attention to myself.

You'd think that Jöchi must imagine that we're in a private wedding suite or something. I haven't read the Swiss legal code in detail, but I have a fair suspicion that displays of public nudity are not welcomed in this country and that intimate relations are best kept out of the public sphere. That's why I'm rather horrified to discover that his hand is working its way right under the edge of my bra.

I can feel the little git's hand passing under the elastic and trying to get a grip. Any further, pal, and you're going to be feeling part of me right in your crotch which I'm sure you're not looking forward to, namely my knee. I'm all set now simply to throw him over the edge of the promenade and into the water, then make an all-out run for it. Not entirely legal but I'm well beyond caring at this point. If I have to choose between that and a public indecency charge, then he's going straight into the yachting zone with a testicle swollen to four times its natural size.

Once more, everything changes in a heartbeat. Something slides over his hand which isn't my breast and falls out of the left of my bra, down onto the ground. Jöchi draws back briefly, allowing me a few seconds to breathe through my mouth once more. He looks down and I follow his gaze.

There on the ground is my passport.

All of a sudden, I'm entirely free again. Nobody is touching me at any point, least of all trying to swallow my head in a failed gesture of human affection. Jöchi has sprung back. He stares at the passport and then looks up at me, real fury burning in his eyes.

"You bitch!" he screams in English. "You total, lying bitch!"

See? I told you they could all speak fluent English. Never try to act dumb in the language of the Brits and Americans. Most people expect it anyway.

"You told me you were Spanish!" he shrieks angrily.

Well, not exactly. I never said that I was any nationality and if you want to go into the details, I was actually basing my Hispanophone persona on an illegal, Mexican immigrant character I saw in an American movie once.

However, I don't think this is quite the time to go into questions of geopolitics and national cultures.

"You are English!" he bawls. "You never admitted that!"

Hold on, I never said that I wasn't English, did I? I just sort of pretended that I couldn't understand any language other than Spanish. Besides, that's a UK passport so technically I could be Scottish, Welsh or Northern Irish and therefore not English either. Once more though, I don't think this is the time for political nuances.

More pressingly, is he ever actually going to give me a chance to say anything, whether in Spanish, German or English? Or Germanish, Spanglish or even Sperman?

"What did you think you were doing, you dreadful ball of greedy lust?" he continues. "I promised you my undying love! I was going to be your shining, Teutonic prince! The answer to your dreams! You took the seed of my passion and gobbled it down for your own, passing pleasure! How could you be so cruel to a young boy?"

I'm not often stuck for words, but this is mind-blowing. Never mind the ins and outs of Mexico, England, Spain or Switzerland. What difference does it make when you're currently resident on some far-out planet in the galaxy far, far away from reality which this guy inhabits? Did I draw a comparison to the film, "Alien" a short while back? I'm wondering if I was actually a lot closer to the mark than I'd realized. Did I just snog a Germanic E.T.? I hope I didn't get pregnant through some form of extraterrestrial spermatozoidal osmosis which replaces sex out there. Oh yeah, I can't have done. I'm on my period. I forgot about that for a few minutes. Always look on the bright side of life and all that, I suppose.

"Well, you English cow," he roars as he backs away, "you look at these!"

He pulls up his T-shirt and indicates a set of ribs which look like the remains of a chicken after a date with Colonel Sanders.

"And weep!" he snarls. "Look at my face! Go on, look at it! You could have had this, all this love, innocence and devotion if only you had been ready to give me your honesty and not your lying lust!

"Go to hell and enjoy whatever the rest of your horrible life has in store!"

With that, he storms off towards the open-air court where a bunch of much fitter teenagers are playing volleyball. I'm left standing there, my jaw hanging open and my passport lying on the ground next to my still damp feet.

Did I just get dumped by Jöchi? Am I meant to consider him another ex-boyfriend? I barely said a word to him and those I did say were all out of a GCSE Spanish phrasebook. It's not as if we had a meaningful relationship. He compared me to a hooker but even then, there are probably prostitutes who have more meaningful relationships with one-off clients. I don't even know what his surname was or where he lived.

So why do I care? It's not as though I wanted to date him. I was desperately trying to work out how to get rid of him when the intervention of my falling passport did it for me. He may have accused me of being some sort of serial paedophile abuser but almost everything he said was blatantly incorrect.

Except that I did lie to him or at least take active steps to deceive him. Not in order to get off with him, as he seems to think. Quite the opposite really. But I have just been dumped because I lied. Again, why do I care? I've been lying so much since we left Bristol that I can barely remember what the truth about anything even is anymore. And that's quite sad. I'm not sorry to have got rid of Jöchi. I'm certainly not remotely sorry that my underwear has remained essentially unentered by anyone other than myself. I just wish that somehow or other, I could have ended it on my terms and without having all his stupid accusations thrown in my face. Including the one that I lied, which is the only one which was true.

None of this makes sense. I pick up my passport, sit back down on the concrete wall and look out over the Thunersee. Normally I love this spot. I could spend hours sitting here on a day like this. I just don't know why I suddenly feel so empty.

Chapter 27

I HATE TO GO A-WANDERING

Harris

This is hard work. That's putting it mildly. In actual fact, it's hardly an accurate description at all. I've worked hard throughout my life. I was a choirboy at the age of five and had to attend singing practice five times a week. I had to use special mouthwash and gargle, then make sure that I practised whenever I was in the bathroom. I mean that in both the British and American English senses. That was hard work, to be sure. I still remember the ghastly way the other pupils would treat me when I was working on my alto rendition of Meder's, "In tribulatione invocavimus" in the boys' room at school. Still, that was their loss and my gain. Only I know that fine piece now.

That I would call hard work. I worked hard too on my studies. Nobody would ever call me a slouch. I didn't take things for granted. I learnt them and learnt them well. The mockery I seem to be receiving right now for my ignorance of German would be immediately tempered were we to find ourselves in the lands of Ancient Greece. Talking one's way out of a romantic encounter with a lustful, Swiss teenager, or negotiating the purchase of a paraglider which you hold no license to use may be considered achievements by some. Yet they hardly compare to the rush of appreciation you feel coursing through your blood when you hear the wisdom of Plato in the original language. However, that takes hard work.

And then, there's my love. What would we be without love? That is a question I have so often asked myself across the span of my life so far. I worked hard, I worked assiduously, I worked with no expectation of gain, except that I wanted to know what it meant and why it mattered so. It may sound naïve to some, even quaint and faintly ridiculous but I felt in my soul that it was an answer I needed. Then I found Isabel. My hard work was rewarded. I still struggle to express what the torrent of affection and mutual linkage of our beings say about our very existence, but I know, I mean I really know, how crucial it is to me, to her, to us both. I must still work so hard to make her mine, but I have no doubt of the quality of my ability or the strength of my passion. There may be a range of factors which have driven me forward over the past couple of days, including, I must admit, embarrassment, coercion and blind fear but behind it all, I do believe, has been the fact that I am doing this for that love I feel and for all I must give for Isabel.

All these and more have been hard work, hard work which has found its goal and continues to build, to sustain and to enrich my existence.

What I'm going through right now, however, is sheer torture. Even if it matters, and I suppose it must, it is an effort which defies the description of hard work. It's about as enriching as the contents of a foal's stable after it has enjoyed a good feed. What's worst is that it is actually necessary but beyond that, I see little blessing in it.

I have no idea where we are other than that it's somewhere in a valley. No doubt Little Miss Action Hero could pinpoint where we are in some node of geography with a name which sounds like someone gargling with bleach. It's all I can do to remember where she was at least five minutes ago and try to reach the same point.

My reward for agreeing to clothe her at my expense in some frightful outfit which appears to be a hangover from a long-forgotten military conflict? Something in which I would not be seen dead myself although I suppose somebody must have once done so, since that's presumably where it last came from? My reward is to be told that apparently we have to escape from the Canton of Bern on foot. Once we reach the next Canton, whichever one that is, we might – I stress might – just be able to take a local bus. And of course, we have to do so at near on lightspeed because of the timetable for which I'm responsible.

"Oh, don't worry. It's just thirty clicks or so up that valley. Then we get over the pass at the top, scoot round the forest and come out at the butt end of the ravine down that side. Shouldn't take too long."

For someone who works in professional linguistics, she really does have a vulgar turn of phrase, I must say.

The worst of it is that there simply isn't any end. They say that you can endure just about anything if you know when it will end, assuming that it does. The resilience of medical patients who are given a harsh course of treatment which should cure them is usually quite remarkable. They often push through much more bravely and strongly than anyone might have first imagined. I understand that marathon runners can force themselves to great levels of achievement by pacing against a known quantity. The music heard in some communities in the Pacific Islands is haunting but exquisite and it lasts for what seems a divine eternity. The effort required by those playing is, though, apparently excruciating due to the physical postures involved but they see the goal and they achieve it magnificently.

The difference I'm feeling just now is that there is no endpoint, at least nothing beyond, "the butt end of a ravine" which may as well be twenty thousand leagues under the sea for all the reality it holds for me. We're walking through woods. I asked why we shouldn't just walk along the road at the base of the valley, but it seems that it would make us more visible and we're much better off sticking inside the treeline. I admit that I can accept that logic. I just do wish that the route through the treeline wouldn't have to be halfway to the top of the mountain ridge above us, nor that it would keep climbing. The path itself just winds along like an endless serpent, swallowing up all the effort I make for no real gain. Every now and then, I see the peaks beyond us, which are the nearest thing we have to a target. That awful ravine is on the other side of them, I understand. It's hardly a comfort since it means that even if I do survive to the point of reaching them, I'm then going to have to get over them somehow and down some new incline on the other side.

And all at the pace of an over-excited gazelle. This I do not understand. I can accept that it's necessary right now. For reasons I do not comprehend, I can force myself to endure this, at least until I collapse physically. But that woman? She does this as a form of relaxation? It defies all logic.

For sure, she and I are not of a kind. Her tastes are lowbrow. She seems to think that she still has her dignity so long as her underwear is intact. Her ignorance of anything refined is excruciating. And her preferred mode of self-expression, that persistent, petulant sarcasm, is something of which I would be utterly ashamed if I were in her position. To her credit, I suppose, she is helping, and she doesn't display a meanness of spirit. It's not so much a case of what she is which I find a shade distasteful, more a case of what she could be but isn't because of her acceptance of the lowest common denominator.

I pause for a moment. A horrible sensation grips me and despite the staggering heat, I can actually feel a drop of cold sweat. What have I just been thinking? "Persistent, petulant sarcasm"? Is that not what I've just been employing?

After only three or so days in her company, am I turning into Jessica?

Goodness me. I mean to say, I don't hold anything against her. I don't regard her as anything but a good person at heart. I just really could not bear to think of myself as being like her. What would Isabel say if I expressed myself in a stream of similes largely concerned with bodily fluids, pure idiocy and acts of sexual perversion? Despite what Jessica may imagine, I have worked out who the character James Bond is, but I would hardly equate a spy film to a Concerto by Bach in terms of enjoyment.

Is it something to do with the surroundings? I'm cursing to myself as I struggle up these mountainsides and somehow my mind is focused on all these things which are distressing me. However, if I stop to think, I should be quite pleased, I daresay. I'm actually holding Karl Givret's clarinet in my hand. His actual clarinet! I would have been amazed even to touch it for long enough and now I own it! Not only that, but it's less than academic now that despite all the odds, I have it literally in my grasp. And torture though this may be, if I trust Jessica's word, then we are en route to getting back to Bristol with it. So, is the physical discomfort really that bad? That's just the thing. Despite everything which has finally worked out – I won't say gone to plan since that would be over-praise, but we somehow have a result – I feel as though I just want to give up. I can't face much more of this. I thought that the fast walk in Beatenberg was heavy going but this? This is like nothing I could ever have imagined. And it's supposed to take most of the day, according to Jessica. The fact that it's cancelling out the positives which I should logically be feeling is, I think, testament to how painful it is, not to how little I value those positives.

However, it doesn't explain why I should be emulating Jessica. Incredibly enough, she enjoys this and undertakes it as a form of relaxation, or so she claims. It defies all belief. To relax truly, I would recommend something like a summer's afternoon, swaying lightly in a deckchair with the sweet smell of roses seeping over me from a flowerbed a few feet away. Digesting a fine lunch of feta, almond and bruised tomato galette, followed by a delicate clafoutis, I lie back and close my eyes. The sound of Purcell's, "The Fairy Queen" flows around me while the sweet taste of a fine Bellini graces my tastebuds. Bliss.

What I would definitely not call relaxation would be some hoo-yah, twenty-miles-in-half-an-hour, let's-scale-Mount-Everest expedition in baking heat, up a never-ending slope with the only breaks being to drink out of a mountain stream which, in my view, is ominously close to a herd of cows. I admit that the views are breathtaking at the top, but I could quite happily enjoy the photos in my English country garden. I was very curious to see the photographs which were taken when oceanographers discovered the wreck of the Titanic, but I didn't decide to take up deep-sea diving as a result either.

Even the military don't do this sort of thing for fun. They do it for professional reasons. So quite what this lunatic sees in it, I really do not know. I'm lost for words, and also for breath and probably any further fluid left to sweat out of my exhausted body. No, I can't be empathizing with Jessica on account of being in the Swiss Alps.

Does her influence simply spread through some form of telepathy? Again, it defies all logic, but you have to consider Alice. I've always liked Alice. A spirited girl and never afraid to ask a difficult question but never rude or disrespectful. She would speak her mind, but you could hold an intelligent, even quite mature conversation with her, which is more than I can say for some of her classmates. Such was the impression I got in school.

Put her in the presence of her aunt, however, and it's almost as if you've cloned the elder one. Sarcasm, vulgarity, a quite immature sense of humour and an unquestioning loyalty and acceptance of whatever orders Jessica should issue. Every time I've been left with Alice, she has never once questioned an instruction left by Jessica and it's almost like listening to the older one speaking through the younger. I concede that she still speaks her mind and doesn't hesitate to question her aunt, but it remains clear who the leader is and who the sidekick is as soon as we go into action, or a decision has to be taken. Jessica's affection for her is obvious which must be how they accommodate each other so easily, regardless of the bluntness of expression which each possesses. And then there's the matter of Alice's parents. I've met them a couple of times at parents' evenings at school. Somewhat cold but otherwise upstanding people, I've always thought. Yet the level of disdain, nigh on contempt, in which Jessica holds her sister is simply awful. As for her brother-in-law, I can only describe her attitude as loathing. And bizarrely enough, not once have I heard Alice even murmur any dissent. She doesn't merely acquiesce in Jessica's abuse. She clearly agrees and laughs along.

Except... But... It makes me very uneasy even to consider this but there is a certain superficiality to Alice's parents. I don't know them well at all, but they do come across like quite a few of the more clearly better off couples with children at the school. They're happy to talk to me but as a mere teacher, I do wonder if they would really want to mix socially. The clothes are exquisite, as are the manners, but they still just come across as that bit cold and remote. I don't know why I should think this. I have no right to judge or criticize these people. The problem is that now I've encountered Jessica and also Alice, the latter in the capacity of her aunt's niece and not her parents' daughter. Superficially, they're almost unbearable, at least together. I have no idea what they're discussing half the time. They both laugh at a series of in-jokes and anything vaguely approaching a sexual double entendre. And they don't hesitate to criticize or shoot down anything they consider stupid, mainly by their standards. And yet, they're the ones on my side. They don't pretend to be anything they're not – at least, not unless Jessica is lying through her back teeth to get us out of a sticky situation but I'm not counting that. They tell it like it is and most importantly, I can trust what they tell me. The strangest thing for me by a long way is that however much I dislike her behaviour, however distasteful I find her ways of expressing herself, and however wilfully ignorant she is of most of what matters to me, I can't help but respect Jessica. I just really don't know why.

She shouts something back down the slope and tells me to hurry up. Probably something more vulgar than that in direct speech but I'm too through to notice.

Apparently we're a couple of clicks in now.

Chapter 28
HIDDEN IN PLAIN SIGHT

Jessica

Well now, this is more like it, isn't it? I'm actually quite glad for a change that the original plan went to hell because I wasn't expecting to get a decent hike out of this, but you never can tell. In fact, the list of plus points is growing right now. I never came out here expecting to get to go paragliding – twice – but I can tick that one off the bucket list. I've had some nice dinners. Thank you, Harris. The ham and cheese sandwich from the Spiez supermarket wasn't too bad either. And now I'm getting to hike the length of half the Simmental. Not bad at all.

Admittedly, things could have gone slightly better in the fashion department. Probably thanks to Alice having been there, it wasn't a total disaster but I daresay she could have done a bit better in guiding Harris. Mind you, the guy really can be stubborn when you just don't need it. I now find myself hiking through the Alps dressed like a medical orderly in the Second World War. No disrespect to the women and men who did such sterling service in the 1940s, I hasten to add. It's just that Harris must have forgotten everything I ever told him about practical, hiking attire when he bought this stuff. Although it maybe never reached his brain in the first place, going by his attempt to get around some of Europe's highest mountains, looking like a Che Guevara glo-stick in a show-jumping contest. I myself am now wearing a short-sleeved, tan shirt with breast pockets which mis-align with the natural curvature of my body to give the impression that I'm wearing a bra about five sizes too small. At least the shirt lets my skin breathe. The sensible, olive-green shorts are marginally too big at the waist, meaning that they hang off my hips slightly and descend to halfway down my kneecaps. If I were to wear the accompanying stockings to the top of my shins as intended, I would look like I had a real Enid Blyton addiction problem but being me, I have them scrunched down to my ankles, just above the brown boots which – believe me, I'm soooo glad – fit me perfectly. So hardly ideal but it could have been a lot worse. Just take a glance at Harris to see how.

By my reckoning, if we can make some godforsaken piece of real estate between Zweisimmen and Boltigen by dusk, we should have a reasonable chance of getting on board a Postbus heading over the Cantonal border into Fribourg without the forces of law and order getting in the way. From there, we head to a quiet border crossing with France and make for an airport where we can find a flight going on Sunday afternoon to either Bristol or somewhere close enough. One of the London airports will do if we can't find anything closer and there are always loads of flights to those. It probably means spending the night in a bus shelter somewhere between here and France but compared with last night, that'll feel like a five-star hotel. At least Alice and Harris managed to get me a proper box of tampons. A higher temperature and less blood down my legs should let me sleep better too. Add an extra star to the accommodation rating already.

Fair enough, it hasn't all been the greatest trip of all time. Criminality, near death experiences on a regular basis and the most revolting and unromantic encounter of a quasi-sexual nature which nobody else has encountered who isn't into bestiality while wearing a leather thong and an Elon Musk mask. So they tell me, I mean. All of those I could have lived without. But you can't have everything.

Right now, I'm all in for enjoying it. It's an easy enough walk. A fairly constant climb but nothing breathtakingly steep. Most of it through the treelines but still with a decent viewpoint now and again. It's for the best in any case. The heat is sizzling and since we won't be all that high up, the shelter of the forest is about the best relief we're going to get. And we have to keep up a decent pace, no slacking. The quality of forest pathways is usually quite reliable so that matters too. There are also a fair number of minor waterfalls and fast streams so keeping up the intake of fluids isn't a hassle. And finally, if we stick inside the treeline, nobody searching the peaks above us is going to look down and say to his or her fellow cop, "Oh look, Hans! There are three people heading along there! Two look like quite fit women while the third is a totally unfit waster wearing some really stupid clothes from the 1800s. Does that remind you of anyone we're supposed to be trying to arrest today?" That's an important consideration at the moment.

Speed is very much of the essence. The early evening bus into Fribourg Canton will be the last one of the day. I daren't take the train, at least not from anywhere still within Bern Canton, since the things are full of very diligent inspectors. The bus drivers, however, are a little less worried so long as you sling the correct number of francs at them for the ride. By my reckoning, that should get us near to Jaun, from where we can get the last bus of the day down to Bulle. As a relatively major centre, Bulle will still have some transportation running which will let us reach some nowheresville in the northern Canton of Neuchatel. It's far enough away from the Interlaken region that nobody will care about us anymore by then and especially not if we can get into France. Both countries being part of the Schengen zone, the border controls between them are minimal and on Sunday morning, it'll be as easy to cross as it is to find a kebab in Liverpool on a Saturday night. As in you'd need to lack at least two senses completely to have a chance of failing. The main trick is going to be not looking suspicious, particularly when we have to fly, in having next to no luggage – none at all in my case – but a clarinet which Jeff Bezos might consider a shade over-priced. Standing out at border controls is rarely a good idea unless rubber gloves with industrial lube, if you're lucky, give you some sort of sexual thrill. And when it comes to sexual thrills, unless they're being offered by Timothy Dalton, I have no further interest in the faintest possibility of receiving them for the immediate future, thank you all the same. Not even Pierce Brosnan. Only Tim.

As a result, the lack of luggage is both a help and a hindrance. Like Tom Cruise in, "Top Gun", I feel the need, the need for speed. In fact, I know that we desperately need speed so not having a lot of luggage to lug along is critical right now. I say, "not having a lot" even though I technically don't have any. Why? Because Tom had one advantage over me. He had Goose in the back seat of his F-14, not Harris. I'm carrying Harris' small rucksack myself at the moment because it's about the one thing I can do in a practical sense which might move his lardy arse slightly more quickly along the path here. He's insisting on carrying the clarinet at all times now. I suppose he took offence at me having used it as a DIY snorkel earlier. Whatever. It doesn't weigh that much so he's welcome to it. What I can't afford is that he slows us down any further.

Honestly, if it were left to Harris to determine, we'd be going at a speed which might just about have reached the edge of the Spiez suburbs by now. Our best chance of reaching Bristol before tomorrow evening would be to invent a time machine so as to give us another month to cover the distance. About fifteen minutes ago, I saw a grandfather overtake him, pushing his granddaughter along on a little, plastic cart. I wonder if it might be quicker if Alice and I were just to hijack a shopping trolley, bundle him in and then push him to Boltigen. We could probably push him halfway to Paris in the time it'll take him to reach Boltigen. No joke.

Still, for now, apart from yelling at Harris to get a move on every few minutes, I am determined to enjoy myself. I can and I will. In fact, I should make the effort. If I dwell on what's annoying me, I'll get annoyed but there are so many good things out here as well. Isn't that why I come up here usually? Come on, Jessica, wake up and smell the pine needles. It's summertime in the Alps. Nice weather, pleasant enough path and decent scenery, not least when the trees thin out now and again. And even when they don't, you can still see down between them to the valley floor which is always a decent sight. I start to wonder again what it must be like to live in the chalets which you see down there and on the lower slopes. When you're ooh'ing and aah'ing over how awesome the views are and the magnificence of the mountains, you always think that it must be some kind of neo-divine experience to live there. Only, if you're a bit more honest about it, you have to recognize that we all come to treat the regular and normal as, well, regular and normal. So if I actually did live down there, would I just end up treating all this as par for the course? No big deal. Those mountains didn't choose to be there. They just are. What's so special? Would I be that bit more impressed by the ocean? By the seaside next to Liverpool even? Do the people who live up here wonder in awe what it would be like to live where I do? Near to the sea and to where John Lennon and Paul McCartney used to get an ice-cream on a Saturday afternoon and you can pay us three hundred pounds for an autographed ice-cream cone to prove it? Except that for me, it's just the same old. Is it the same thing for people who live next to Niagara Falls, the Andes, the Taj Mahal, the Great Wall of China or whatever else? It's an interesting thought. I don't know the answer.

There you go. The Alps can make a genuine philosopher of me. I wish I could discuss all this with Alice but racing along these paths at breakneck speed doesn't create a decent environment for a meaningful discussion.

"You OK, Alice?" I ask. Need to check in.

"Yeah, fine, Auntie," she comes back, a shade breathlessly but with no indication of needing to stop any time soon.

"You needing a break soon?"

"No," she grins then nods her head backwards down the path towards Harris, "but I think he will be."

"So what?" I snort with perhaps a hint of derision, but he can't hear us. "He's been needing one since about five minutes after we left Spiez."

"But we'll have to stop sooner or later for him."

She's quite right. He will need a break. So will Alice and I eventually but that much we can manage. The problem with Harris is that if we give him a break too soon, he'll be subconsciously expecting them that bit sooner every time. But if we don't, he'll likely collapse from heat exhaustion. What a choice.

We keep going for a couple of minutes but then an idea occurs.

"I know," I tell Alice. "What we'll do is extend the drinks breaks by a couple of minutes when we stop by the waterfalls. No new breaks but give him the margin he needs."

She raises her eyebrows slightly questioningly, but I think she agrees. It's better than nothing.

About ten minutes later, we reach another waterfall. Fast-running water and a rock bed mean that it's reliable enough to drink out of without too much risk of looking like the Russian secret service just stood us our last round. Alice and I bring out her water bottle and we both take a good swig. I don't have a water bottle any longer so I'm dependent on her. However, it's not as if the waterfalls are going to run dry any time soon, so big deal.

We're still waiting for Harris to pitch up when some dog skirts around the corner. I give it a dirty look. As you may have gathered by now, I'm not the world's greatest dog-lover and I certainly don't appreciate people who fail to follow the rules of hiking, including that you keep your dog on a lead. All right, so you're not really supposed to crash into hiking paths on a paddleboard either, but it's not explicitly banned. Letting your dog run all over the shop quite definitely is.

This grubby, little example is one of those dogs which make you wonder why people bother. I don't like dogs much, but I wouldn't call myself a rabid hater. Not until I get bitten by one at least, and then it'll be literally too late. Anyway, I'm able to appreciate that there are some sweet dogs out there and people must enjoy sitting around, snuggling up with them and stroking them behind their cute, little ears. That must provide some justification for all the hassle. But then there are the frickin' ugly, ungainly and/or generally unpleasant specimens. The ones which look as though they just swallowed a fat person's life jacket while trying without success to reflect on the meaning of reality TV. The ones which want to tear your throat out because you "infringed on their territory", to quote the morons who insist that they can do no wrong, basically meaning that you breathed a bit too much oxygen ten minutes' walk away. The ones which seem to have no control of their bowel movements apart from those associated with ingestion. All these just make me wonder, what's the point? You have to march them out of the house at least four times a day, come rain or shine, to keep them toileted and exercised. You spend half your free time cleaning their hair off the furniture and your clothes, two-thirds of it in springtime. You spend more of your disposable income on their food than on your own, twice as much if you're vegan. And for what? A so-called best friend who either tries to eat your human friends for you or sits around dozily and raises a leg to fart when feeling energetic enough. And that's most of them.

This one seems to be of the lazier variety. At least, it doesn't give the impression of wanting to eat Alice and me for lunch. That may be because it's reasonably well-behaved or because it just finished a sandwich twenty minutes ago. A short while later, a somewhat rotund, short lady toddles up. She looks slightly askance at Alice and me but gives us a, "Grüzi!" as she should. Good to know she follows some of the rules.

At this point, I realize that there's a tension in the air. She's staring at Alice and me in a slightly passive aggressive manner. Why? I look over at Alice and then consider myself and I can see why. We're both transfixed on her and her dog because, as it's just occurred to me, they're virtually identical. They're both small, podgy and, well, I don't want to be insulting or anything but... a bit ugly. It's actually quite amazing. She looks just like her dog. You really can't tell the difference. I just hope her husband can or goodness knows how many legs the kids will have.

I manage to pull myself together and start smiling instead of gawping.

"Lovely dog!" I grin. "Where'd you get her?"

"Him!" she growls, side-eyeing me with a definite air of dislike.

"Oh sorry!" I do my best. "You mean she's a boy?"

That probably wasn't the smartest thing to say. She looks as though she's going to set the dog on me for insulting it. Given that the dog doesn't seem to care a hoot, that's an odd scenario. Anyway, if she does do that, I'll set Alice on her. I can drop kick a dog, but she won't have much chance of doing that to Alice.

The brewing Swiss-Mexican stand-off is deflated by the appearance of Harris. He staggers round the corner and almost trips over the dog himself. Thankfully, the canine wonder decides that our company isn't really for her –

sorry, him – and waddles off. The owner looks back at me, as if to mutter a curse should she be a medieval witch. Going by looks, either she or the dog certainly could be. But enough witch-burning entertainment for now. We need to get Harris sorted out.

Harris all but collapses by the side of the waterfall. I fill up his water bottle for him and this time he drinks without even stopping to complain about the possibility that the liquid might have passed within a couple of kilometres of a cow at some point in history. Going by my understanding of geophysics, over the past few millenia, it's probably passed through at least twenty-eight dinosaurs, I don't know how many mammals, plus some caveman called Bob but I'm not an expert and we have more important things to discuss.

"You know, Harris," I start, in as kindly a tone as possible which nonetheless brooks no dissent, "we're not even halfway there yet. Are you sure you can make this?"

He looks up at me with a faraway gaze, as if I'd spoken to him in Arabic. Or Swiss German. He has about the same chance of understanding either.

Nothing. I cough.

"Well, do you?"

He stares straight ahead and then says with no emotion, "I'll do whatever it takes."

I'm not convinced that this is enough.

"Harris, my question is not whether you have the willingness. My question is whether you're simply able to do this. An honest answer would be vastly more helpful than anything else."

It's at this point where, if we were in an animated kids' movie made from about 2005 onwards, he would come out with the response, "I got this." Not only meaningless but grammatically incorrect as well. There's a reason why I was glad when Alice grew too old to want me to take her to see such cinematic crap anymore. Intellectual snobbery aside though, we don't got, I mean have, anything much at all to go on right now.

"I told you," Harris says irritably, "I will do whatever I must."

"Fine," I sigh. This is getting us nowhere, quite possibly literally. "We don't

400

have time for extended breaks so let's go. I'll make sure we stop to drink but otherwise we don't let up."

If you'd only just joined the conversation, you'd think I was organizing a hen party. Time to go.

Around forty minutes later, Alice and I are waiting for Harris again at the side of another stream. Not really a waterfall this time but fast-flowing and cascading over loose stones and rocks, which is always good for ensuring that the water is effectively cleaned by nature. This is Switzerland, of course, so there are fewer used condoms floating around in the waterways than elsewhere, especially at higher altitudes. Whether there's a higher pregnancy rate up here or people are just better behaved, I can't say but at least I feel more relaxed about drinking what nature provides. My principal concern, however, is not the risk of possibly catching syphilis as part of the drinking gig. Again, this isn't a hen party. It's the fact that Harris is now at least fifteen minutes behind us, probably more.

"We're just not going to make it on time, are we, Auntie?" asks Alice.

What can I say? Mathematically at least, she's entirely correct. We simply don't have the margin.

"Do you think we can get a train or a bus yet?"

I don't know. I wish I could say yes but I don't feel happy about it. If we were to hike just a bit higher up, we'd still be able to see the side of the Thunersee in the distance. We're not yet that far from Spiez if you count the distance by any other measure than how far we've come on foot. And public transport would be the main artery to be watching if I were trying to catch us, I know. Maybe cars and bikes as well but pretty much any sort of mechanized transport. Hiking is such a stupid idea that it's about the only one which we stand a good chance of getting away with.

Harris pitches up eventually, now about twenty-five minutes behind and clearly in bad shape. You'd think he was suffering an asthma attack from the way he's breathing although he assures us that such is not the case. At least, that's what he says when he can say anything. He is literally drenched in sweat, and his hands are shaking. Let's face facts. This plan simply isn't going to work. Still, that hardly makes it unique on this trip. The question, as usual, is what's the alternative. How else can we travel?

My mind flits around the possibilities but there don't seem to be many. I even find myself wondering once more if we could commandeer a shopping trolley from a supermarket down in the valley and push him along in it. Logistically, it could work but, I realize, it would leave us wide open to being seen from above and we would certainly attract attention. Get with the programme, Jessica. We need something better than that.

"Let's head for the valley," I say out of nowhere, getting to my feet.

"But won't we stand out then?" Alice asks, not quite aghast but heading that way.

"It's a risk," I concede, "but it's the only alternative to continuing up here and this simply isn't an option any longer. We're that bit further out now so it's the best chance we have."

And so we take the next turning downwards and head for the valley floor. I don't really know what I'm doing but I'm not going to admit that, certainly not yet. While there's time to think, there's always the possibility of a good idea.

Or even a crazy one. We exit the tree line a few minutes later and set off across the fields at the base, on the other side of which lies the main road down the middle of the valley. The fields start on a slope, so we still have a reasonable view up and down the valley for a moment and I stop to look round. Nice place, the Simmental. Fairly typical, Swiss mountain valley with a river running alongside a well-kept road down the middle, surrounded by neat farms running up the sides to the treelines and then these run upwards to the meadows above. Maybe not outstandingly different to various others in the same area but there's nothing wrong with any of them per se.

However, it's not the view which catches my attention for very long at all. At the far end to my left, coming up from the Spiez end of things, is a police car. Alice spots it too and her immediate reaction, like mine, is to run back into the treeline as fast as we possibly can and lie low. The problem is that there are a few people out on farming duty, tending the fields. Right now, we look a trio of hikers. Well, maybe a duo of hikers plus somebody who looks as though he ought to be trying to flag a ride to the nearest morgue, but you probably can't tell that from where they are. We're not suspicious. However, if they see us run like hell when the local PD approaches, then we are, and the chances are that everyone knows everyone around here and they'll helpfully inform their buddies in the car. Said buddies, no doubt on the alert from Interlaken and Spiez for three characters of dubious appearance and behaviour, will have to be pretty thick not to join the dots. And once they do, we're screwed. Harris couldn't outrun a stone statue at the moment, never mind a fit and capable police squad.

But give me a box and I'll think outside it. It's often a bad habit but it can also be a useful one. We'll stand out if we travel by public transport, by car or by bike, will we? Likewise if we hike up the road? What does that leave? Air travel, I suppose but been there, done that, and as a result, now more wanted than a supermodel's tits. Not much opportunity either right now unless someone has a combine harvester which can sprout wings but not even James Bond ever managed that.

What about public services, however? Inside an ambulance, a fire engine or even, if you think about it, a police car? But approach a police car? What sort of crim would try that in their right mind?

What sort indeed? They wouldn't, would they?

I turn to the other two and order them sternly, "Make for the road! Now! Fast!"

We tumble down the field. These things always look easier to cross than they are in practice. The grass rises to halfway up your knees at least and the ground is far from even underneath it. What looked like a few strides' quick march to reach the other side seems to take forever. No doubt Harris is on the verge of giving up completely, but I'll just have to hope. I can see the police car drawing closer down the road and I reckon we only have a minute or so to make it. Harris simply won't make it, so I run the briefing past the two of them on the hoof.

"We're going to flag down that car," I tell them in my best this-might-sound-like-sheer-lunacy-but-just-shut-up-and-do-exactly-what-I-tell-you tone of voice. "I'm going to claim that we need a ride to the nearest pharmacy down the valley to get the asthma medication which my daughter desperately needs."

"What daughter?" asks Alice.

"That's you, of course!" I tell her, rolling my eyes. Get with the party, Alice. "You're going to have to breathe heavily like you're having an asthma attack."

Harris would probably be a better contender for the role of an asthma sufferer right now but once he's got his breath back, I simply can't rely on him. Instead, I stick my face forcibly into his and tell him in the most menacing manner I can, "You will get into the car and do exactly what I tell you, no more, no less. You will take zero initiative, you will not think of anything, and you will keep your mouth firmly shut unless and only if I tell you to say something. If you say one word without my permission, just one word, I will ram that clarinet so far up your bum that you'll be able to play your own funeral dirge on it when the mouthpiece appears under your nose. Is that entirely clear?"

He nods helplessly so I sprint for the road. Alice and I make it just as the car rounds the last corner before coming level with us. This is arguably the stupidest move I've pulled all weekend but it's the only one I can think of which might just work out. That maybe shows how fine a line we're treading, or it maybe shows that I need clinical help. Maybe both, I dunno. Guess I'm about to find out.

I flag down the car and it halts beside us. Harris hasn't caught up yet but I'm going to have to talk my way in. That should provide the extra time he needs. Translating from German, here goes.

"Good afternoon, Lieutenant!" I beam while trying to look a bit desperate as well as fetching.

"Sergeant," the policeman corrects me.

Good. Always aim high if you don't know. You're much less likely to insult them than if you screw it up the other way round. The sergeant is sitting on the passenger side. Going by the relative numbers of stripes, I'm guessing he's the senior one.

"I'm so sorry to bother you," I continue as quickly as I can, the idea being to leave minimum scope for questions to be posed to me. "I'm in a bit of a bother and was wondering if you can help me. It seems that most of the pharmacies round here have closed by Saturday afternoon, but my daughter really needs some emergency medication for her asthma attack."

I nudge Alice. "Asthma," remember? It's the same bloody word in English and German. You can hardly have missed it. Still no reaction. A much more brutal application of my elbow to her ribcage produces the necessary result.

"You must think I'm a terrible idiot and awful mother," I blush. "I just didn't realize what a severe, allergic reaction she'd have. I wasn't expecting such heavy pollen until later in the year."

This piece of informed bullshitting kind of works. I know for a fact that the pollen is always much worse earlier on in the season, but I'm not entirely prepared for the reply from the sergeant that as far as he knows, it isn't that much worse this year than it usually is. I keep it ditzy and explain that it must just be so much worse than it is back home in Germany. That's a smart move. It explains why my accent is not local although I speak the lingo and also increases the underlying impression of me being a bit thick. They won't admit it, but the Swiss do have a certain superiority complex vis-à-vis the Germans, at least on their home turf. It gets reciprocated on the other side of the border so I wouldn't worry too much about the political incorrectness.

"Anyway," I continue, "there should be an emergency pharmacy a bit further on down the valley, isn't there?"

Once more, my local knowledge kicks in. The Swiss maintain rigorous schedules of all pharmacies in a given area so that at least one is always staffed and ready to open at any time of day or night. The same is true of Germany so that once more, my local knowledge is easily explicable even though I'm an airheaded tourist. I should really be in Hollywood with these sorts of ad lib acting skills. I'd think about it seriously if Tim hadn't retired already. No disrespect to the man but Daniel Craig just isn't such a tempting prospect for me.

"Well, the nearest emergency pharmacy is back that way in Erlenbach," replies the cop, indicating the road behind. "We can take you back along there in a few minutes if it helps."

Oh bloody hell. Of all the bad luck. Got to think fast.

"Oh that's so kind of you," I gush, "but it was actually them who told us that we would have to get to Zweisimmen because they were out of the meds she needs. She's a bit peculiar. Any chance you might be going near to Zweisimmen, even just part of the way?"

I smile as sweetly but cluelessly as I can. It's probably vaguely what Harris looked like when he was about two days old. Alice is looking around and appearing a shade too healthy for my liking, so I elbow her again. The ensuing gasp is like listening to a Harrier jump jet taking off. Don't overegg the pudding, girl! At this rate, you can hardly see the pudding for the omelette on top.

Apart from Alice's total ineptitude where acting is concerned, things are actually looking up when the usual source of disaster on our travels appears. Harris staggers up, panting more heavily than even Alice is managing.

"Hi," he starts before I stick my other elbow into his ribcage for good measure. Bloody hell! That was the elbow I skinned on my landing in the Spiezerberg! Holy crap, does that hurt!

"Shut up!" I hiss under my breath. "No English!"

"What a family!" I grin sheepishly, addressing myself once more to the two policemen who are both now quite intrigued by the threesome in front of them. "You can tell they're related, can't you? I guess she gets the allergy from her father. I've always been fine!"

"That's your husband?" asks the junior officer.

It pains me to affirm this. Being married to Harris may be Isabel's great ambition but so what? Colin's great ambition is to spend a weekend of passion in bed with my sister but I'm in no hurry to do that either. The only plus point re Harris is that it's not as bad a proposition as snogging Jöchi and I somehow survived that encounter. When it comes to Colin, I'd have a decision to make. I bring up a mental image of Timothy Dalton without his shirt on in, "License to Kill" and tell one of the most whopping lies yet since I arrived in Switzerland, namely that Harris is the object of my life's affection.

406

"And why's he carrying an oboe?"

My attention is jerked back to reality. Thank goodness he's talking in German. If Harris had understood that question, he'd no doubt be jumping up and down, pontificating about the difference between an oboe and a clarinet and asking how the policeman could possibly have made such a gross error. Being me, I appreciate that there are worse problems than that to consider.

"The thing is," I start, "that my husband has a very unusual hobby. He's a musical naturist."

"A what?" The sergeant looks extremely unconvinced.

"The theory goes," I explain, "that music is actually just a form of capturing soundwaves which form an underlying communication pattern throughout nature. There are some obvious examples like the songs which whales use to communicate over hundreds of miles of ocean or the high frequency sounds which bats use. You see, there's a lot more sound in nature than you might think.

"In the Alps, there's very little human-induced sound so it's possible to tap into all this. Musical naturists use wood instruments to mimic the natural soundwaves which are all around us to communicate with the natural world. They shed their clothes so as to maximize their natural connections.

"That's why he's dressed so badly. My daughter and I go walking while he removes his clothes, which are designed for easy application and removal, and communes with the natural world all around."

They look highly sceptical but it's obviously puzzling them as to why anyone would make up such complete bollocks in the first place, not if they're doing it to distract their attention from a serious crime or two. I mean, coming up with all this crap is hardly the SOP to escape from Alcatraz, is it?

"Anyhow," I continue, re-applying my good elbow to Alice's midriff, "we've hit a real problem today so do you think you'd be able to drop us anywhere near Zweisimmen, please?"

The sergeant looks round at his subordinate who simply shrugs.

"Yeah, OK," he says. "We don't have much else to do today. You haven't seen any shifty-looking sorts in mountain gear, have you? They've got us looking for some illegal paragliders and water-skiers of all things. If you think musical naturists are a bit of out of touch with reality, you should try our colleagues in the Interlaken and Spiez police squads. What a crowd of hopeless airheads."

I shrug as if to say that I wish I could help them but sorry, just don't know.

He reaches behind him and unlocks the rear door.

"Come on then. In you get."

Chapter 29
BREAKING NEWS

Harris

It's an unsettling sensation to travel in the back of a police car when you're a wanted lawbreaker. It's even more unsettling to do so when you're sat next to somebody doing her best to sweet-talk her and you out of it, but you haven't the first idea what she's actually saying. It doesn't help also that these police officers will insist on scouring the local radio stations for something to listen to while they travel, clearly passing over two operatic renditions plus a Schubert sonata in favour of some soulless rubbish which the less educated children listen to where I teach. All of this combined with the stifling heat in the car, and the smell of severe body odour does not result in a pleasant trip.

Not that any of this seems to be bothering Jessica, needless to say. While Alice sits and does her best to wheeze and snuffle like a chronic asthmatic, and I sit and try to stop wheezing and snuffling like a chronic asthmatic, Jessica is blithely chattering away to the two policemen like their long-lost sister. You'd think she was planning to marry one of them, the way she's laughing at every other thing they say and responding in kind herself. Except that I believe she's already told them that she's married to me. What a thought. Given the lowbrow level of humour which both she and Alice usually seem to enjoy, I can only imagine the level of Teutonic smut being bandied around in this vehicle. Surely I don't look like someone who would be half of a marriage at that level? How can they believe any of this?

I simply don't know. It's easier to stare out of the window and try to recover my breath. That much I think I may eventually achieve, slowly but surely. I suppose that once again, it was nearly thanks to me that everything didn't work. We could have escaped on foot had I been fit enough. I shouldn't have complained about the water quality from the streams which turned out to be fine in the end. I should have paid attention to Jessica's guidance on active breathing, and the need to force out sufficiently large breaths as well as to bring them in. I considered this a patronizing luxury but on reflection, it might have helped us. Or maybe not. Perhaps I was simply never up to the challenge in the first place.

I do wish Jessica would sometimes stop to reflect occasionally on what has actually gone before. I do not believe that I am quite the pampered idiot she considers me to be. I am well aware that in terms of practicality, I do not have her skillsets. Yet such an awareness does mean that I know that I have to learn things and, again slowly but surely, I hope that I do. If nothing else, I am at least learning not to question direct orders from her when she is in one of her authoritative modes. It has just never worked before, so I know the best way to proceed. For Jessica, however, nothing ever seems to matter except for the next ten minutes. It's all about the immediate future and how to get a result. Hence whatever's already happened is of no consequence. I don't know how she therefore learns anything although I suppose she must, even if perhaps only in a practical sense. It does seem to blind her to the fact that some of the rest of us may just need a bit longer to develop. That's not the same thing as saying that we can never do so.

Then again, on reflection, we only had four and a half days to pull this off so what use is someone who needs a couple of months to be anything other than a liability? And how exactly am I going to spend six months learning to perform to order? Jessica's order, that is. She's a hard taskmaster but in this instance, that's what's needed. I'm just going to have to learn to like it.

I sit and continue to observe the passing scenery. It's all beautiful, all serene and all very much like what I've been seeing ever since we left Spiez. I don't know why I keep coming back to Jessica as some sort of default value for reference these days, but I will still question her devotion to the Alpine setting. I'm starting to wonder if it is a bit like a form of music. Isn't there a need for some form of variation? To me, a chamber rendition of a hymnal is exquisite, I mean absolutely exquisite. I'm also a devotee of piano concertos, the opera buffa and the grand opera in particular. I can take great joy in simply putting on a recording of something by Handel or Verdi, sitting back in a reclining chair and relaxing for two or three hours with my eyes closed shut but my mind fully switched on. But not the same thing each time. I think that the real appreciation of the greats is when they are interspersed with other fine works which may not be my most preferred, but whose contrast offsets the true greats with an alternative. Mozart's full genius is revealed partly when set against the comparative, even if slightly inferior, works of others. I adore the taste of mascarpone tiramisu, but I know that I would not appreciate it so much if I had it with every dinner. The blissful taste of a good red is all the better because I can compare it with the tastes of other liquors or non-alcoholic drinks. The variety is what makes the specials so special.

This is why Jessica's unwavering adoration of the Alps confuses me. It's as if there might as well not be any seaside views, any lower woodlands to explore, any grasslands or deserts. Certainly not any urban wonders to visit. So long as she has her Alpine vistas in sight, the rest of creation is an irrelevance to her. I can see myself, literally right here, right now, how magnificent they are but isn't part of what makes them great, that very difference between them and equally amazing, just different scenes of oceans, jungles, arctic plateaus or perhaps the likes of Paris or Florence?

On the other hand, and I'm prepared to admit where I might be wrong, does that mean that I should be sleeping with as many women as possible so that I can appreciate how truly amazing Isabel is? The logic may not be a perfect parallel. This is no doubt a moot point since I do not intend to test it in practice. Also, I suspect that if I were to enquire of Jessica or Alice about what chances I might have of seducing enough females to try it out, I doubt I would receive a very flattering answer. And I'm certainly not going to ask around simply to find that much out the hard way.

Still, I think the philosophizing has helped a little. I seem to have recovered to the extent that I can breathe without being heard across the car and I'm no longer quite as uncomfortable as I felt when we first got in. I should concede some value to contemplating the Alpine scenery after all. Maybe it has a capacity as a springboard to relaxing contemplation which is its real worth. Maybe. I'm still not sure that I can think or view things like Jessica can. To each their own.

In fact, the scenery is changing already. We're drawing into a small town of sorts. It's vaguely reminiscent of Interlaken, I think. I'm not going to canvas opinion on the topic, however. I shall just keep my head down and keep following. As a good teacher, I hope I should make a good student too.

We pass a few houses and hotels before turning into what seems to be the main thoroughfare. There certainly appears to be a kind of cartel running Switzerland's supermarkets. Even I, who only first encountered the country about four days ago, can spot the same handful of chains who seem to have a franchise in virtually every town of more than a couple of hundred inhabitants. It makes it easy to identify when you're in the high street somewhere, I'll give them that. In addition, there's a range of restaurants and other shops, most of them closed by now since it's getting to later on Saturday afternoon. According to Jessica, the countryside shuts up shop in most instances around now. Once more, I have no reason to doubt her.

The car draws to a sudden halt outside a small pharmacy near to the railway station. Jessica exchanges some more pleasantries with the police, none of which I can understand, and then nudges Alice in the ribs. Alice heaves into another case of what sounds like pantomime tuberculosis and gets out of the car on her side, followed by her aunt who has been sitting in the middle. I exit on my own side. My instinct is to say thank you for the lift, but I have direct orders to the contrary and am staying clean if I can.

Jessica marches us all over to the door of the pharmacy. It's closed.

"What now?" I ask quietly.

Jessica ignores me and rings on the intercom by the door. There's no response for a moment, but she turns round to tend to Alice in a maternal manner before waving dutifully to the two policemen, who have got out of the car themselves and are wandering over towards the station where a couple more of their colleagues are sitting. One of those colleagues is looking over at us a shade curiously though I can't tell why. It clearly hasn't escaped the attention of my co-travellers.

"Why are they peering over at us like that, Auntie Jess?" Alice asks in a low but clear and concerned tone.

"Not sure," Jessica replies. She sounds less worried but no better informed. "It's a bit strange. I would have thought that this far out from the lakes region, they'd have calmed things down. The two over there may just be the ones assigned to watch over Zweisimmen Station as part of the broader scheme."

"I don't think so," Alice comes back. "Look over there – there are two more cars on the other side of the station."

"Oh hell!" curses Jessica. "What's the deal?"

She stops and reflects for a moment.

"I suppose it must be that since Zweisimmen is a major transit point on the way out of Bern, that they're using this as a convenient base to monitor the comings and goings. So if we can just get past this, we may still have an easier ride ahead of us. What I don't understand is why they're getting their knickers in such a twist about a couple of minor joyriding incidents in Interlaken and Spiez in the first place. What's spooked them?"

"I dunno – SHIT!" Alice suddenly screams.

"Alice, shut up! At least in English!" Jessica barks but Alice has raced off to her right. Jessica is about to fly after her when the intercom suddenly buzzes and a voice asks something in German. Jessica whirls round and exchanges something there. I can tell that she wants to go after Alice except that her niece already turns up, right back with us. She's carrying something in her hands. I look over and see that she's picked up a newspaper of sorts from a distribution box at the side of the road, a little past where we're standing. I do not know what is going on further, but I think everything is moving a little too quickly for most of us now.

The door buzzes and admits us into the pharmacy. Alice is trying to get her aunt's attention, but Jessica makes it plain that she does not want to hear any more for the time being. We walk up to the counter of the pharmacy where a very stern-looking, middle-aged woman is standing and looking at us as though we really had just been arrested. I almost want to check that this is indeed a pharmaceutical establishment and not a magistrate's court.

Jessica nudges Alice into another coughing fit and makes a request. There is an immediate demand from the pharmacist. Jessica looks unsettled but launches into some lengthy explanation, ending with something which sounds like a plea of sorts. It has no effect. Her interlocutor barks something back. Jessica repeats her plea, as far as I can tell, and then seems to be requesting details. She receives nothing but a very similar-sounding refusal of whatever she's trying to get.

There's a slight pause and I'm starting to worry. The expression on Jessica's face is that one which clouds it before yet another lunatic idea comes her way. A sly grin works its way over her mouth in the flicker of an instant and now I'm scared. Given all which has happened since last Wednesday, I believe I am at least within my rights to feel very scared.

Jessica glances casually towards me and then looks down at her feet in a rather embarrassed manner. She proceeds to ask Alice something in a very low whisper. Alice looks up strangely and then goes over to inspect the dental care products. Jessica sidles up to the counter and engages the lady in a hastily-spoken, quite urgent conversation. The woman looks decidedly unimpressed and rolls her eyes at least three times. She also looks over towards me as if I were wanted on an assault and battery charge. This continues for a couple of minutes until finally, the pharmacist storms off into her back room. I look over to Jessica who indicates very clearly with her hand that both Alice and I should refrain from saying anything at this point. We stand and try to look as neutral as we can when the pharmacist reappears with a small box which she passes to Jessica with a sniff. She then keys some details into her till and asks Jessica for payment. Jessica looks into my bag, which she's still carrying, and pulls out one of the few Swiss banknotes which I still have. Or at this point now, had. She has nothing of her own any longer and the onus is on me to cover the expenses, I know. Nonetheless, I find this display of literally having me pay for everything just a little galling.

This performance complete, the lady directs us to the door with a tone indicating that she would be grateful if we could manage not to return for another millennium of two. Jessica smiles sweetly and chaperones the other two of us out of the door. I can hear it being locked firmly behind us within about ten seconds of our departure.

"Bloody hell, Harris!" Jessica smirks. "I wish you could be a bit more careful!"

We're far enough away from other people at this point so I ask in a sufficiently low voice, "What do you mean?"

"You saw that cow in the pharmacy?" she says. "Well, she refused to pay any attention to my request for asthma meds for Alice because I couldn't produce a valid prescription. She even cottoned on to the fact that Alice's performance maybe wasn't quite as Oscar-quality as it could have been."

"Sorry, Alice – no offence!"

"None taken," Alice replies distractedly, "but I think we have bigger problems."

"Huh? Like what?" Jessica asks. "Well, just to get to the point of the first story, what I ended up telling her was that yes, I made up the bit about Alice's asthma. I couldn't have her telling the cops that we were here on false pretences. Then I said that I did that because I didn't want to have to tell the police the real reason why we needed to get to an emergency pharmacy. Namely that my husband and I had a slightly wilder lunchtime than intended during our hike in the mountains, while our daughter was taking a nap, and now I simply have to get hold of a morning-after pill before Alice ends up with an unintended baby sibling early next spring."

"But you don't have a husband!" I start, uncomprehendingly before it suddenly dawns on me what exactly she must have meant. As a non-practised liar, these things don't come naturally to me.

"You mean you told her that you and I were…were…"

"Yes, Harris," she sighs. "Don't worry – I didn't want to have done it either. I just needed a good line. Look on the bright side, it worked in the end!"

Before she can gleam further at this triumph of hers, Alice cuts her short.

"Unreal, unintended impregnations aside, Auntie, I don't think you're going to like this too much."

Alice thrusts what seems to be a local newspaper at her. Jessica looks at it for a moment before her eyes widen in horror and the colour somehow drains from her sun-tanned face.

"What the bloody frickin' hell is this?" Jessica screams under her breath, if such a description can be considered accurate. She is very upset but to give her credit, she has the presence of mind not to express herself too loudly in English while the police are in wider earshot.

I look round from the side and see two photos on the front cover. Both are very grainy and of bad quality, but I can still determine what they're showing. The first is a picture of Jessica, Alice and myself beating a somewhat hasty retreat from the park in the centre of Interlaken after our paragliding descent and illegal landing. It must have been taken by a nearby camera. The second is a shot of Jessica, taken by a similar camera but some distance away from her, airborne over the Thunersee in her underwear, loosely attached to the paddleboard which she crashed a moment later into the side of Spiez. I doubt anyone could identify her from the photo alone but the three of us know very well what both of these shots are. The text is, naturally, in German but Jessica gives a real-time translation as she reads.

"'English Perverts Terrorize the Thunersee!'"

She looks up, "How do they know we're English? How do they know we're perverts?"

"Are we?" asks Alice. "I haven't done anything dodgy. As far as I'm aware, Mr Beadlesby hasn't, unless you count allegedly getting you pregnant over lunch. What have you done?"

The immediately expected riposte doesn't materialize which is quite strange. Jessica simply looks askance and goes back into the paper.

"'Terror struck the Thunersee region today as a crowd of hooligans from England ran rampant over Interlaken and Spiez, ignoring local laws, vandalizing property, almost causing a serious accident on the lake, and molesting local youth.'"

416

Jessica's face makes clear that she is not to be interrupted on pain of death at this precise moment.

"'They literally arrived out of nowhere. An illegal landing was made in Interlaken's Höhematte Park by an airborne terror squad. One of them even had the temerity to fly straight down the centre of town, assaulting innocent passers-by.

"'I was just sitting there, having my early morning milk coffee,' says Mrs Ingeborg Früggelberger, a retired wild goat control expert from the Diemtigtal. 'Suddenly this huge man, like the Incredible Hulk with a beard and some riding trousers, flew over my head and tried to grab my coffee.'

"'Local police attempted to apprehend the dastardly crooks as they knifed their way out of the Höhematte Park, but they were clearly no debutantes since they evaded capture and ran amok through the peaceful streets. At one point, they broke into a local hotel and tried to engage a group of innocent tourists in a vile group sex act.'"

Jessica is getting quite riled just now, but Alice appears to find it somewhat amusing.

"I'm glad they didn't get any camera shots of that bit!" she sniggers.

Jessica glowers but clears her throat and goes back to the paper.

"'After leading officers on a dangerous chase through the local forests, the group tried to escape by water, their ringleader hijacking a paddleboard close to the shore.'

"Since when was I the ringleader?" asks Jessica. Nobody responds so she continues.

"'In a brazen move, this delinquent caught a passing motorboat with her guy rope and attacked an innocent water-skier in its wake. The woman thus attacked, Gerlinde Mumpitz of Thun, was literally thrown off her water-skis while this shameless wrongdoer engaged in some highly illegal and hugely dangerous manoeuvres along the length of the lake. She almost decapitated one couple and came close to drowning a toddler in her tidal wake by the Faulensee children's play area. Police in Spiez were rapidly alerted but the woman in question had gone to ground in the Spiezerberg forest before they could catch up with her.

"'Shortly afterwards in Spiez, the same woman sexually molested a local teenager, Mr Jöchi Hägervongelschmidt, a waiter by profession but on his day off. Clearly distressed, Mr Hägervongelschmidt told us between tears that, 'She was very assertive. She just wanted my body. She viewed me like how a dog would view a particularly attractive chew toy. What was I to do? I'm only nineteen and lightly built, and yet this middle-aged, paedophile pervert, bulging with strength and dressed in almost nothing, threw herself over me and ravished me in ways no other woman had ever done before.'"

I'm not sure if I have ever seen anyone look quite as furious as Jessica right now but I also do not think I know anyone who would be able to contain such rage without expressing it, as she is somehow managing to do at this moment.

"Well, so what?" asks Alice casually. "He's obviously just making it all up and nobody will remember any of this guff by tomorrow afternoon so who cares? It's not like you really got off with him any more than you really shagged Mr Beadlesby."

There's an unexpected but very awkward pause. Alice looks around in bewilderment before her jaw drops wide open.

"You don't mean you-!!! Not Mr Beadlesby!"

"No!" Jessica and I both respond in accidental unison.

"You mean Jöchi?" Alice asks incredulously. "You actually snogged Jöchi?"

"Well, not quite like that," Jessica starts to reply, clearly quite uncomfortable. "It's not like I was getting intimate with him or anything. I just, sort of, well needed to distract the police and make it look like I wasn't on my own, and it seemed like a good idea. I mean, not a good idea per se, just a way of making the cops look the other way and think that I was there on a day trip with my boyfriend. Of course, he's very much not my boyfriend. Never has been, never ever will be. Let's be clear about that. But, well, yes, I did sort of have to pretend that I was well, kind of involved - to a very, very limited extent only – with the guy. I mean, it was nothing romantic or erotic. Oh hell, no. I'd rather get it on with a clinically dead orang-utan whose last meal had been a stilton cheese and red onion chutney sandwich, at least a month old. It was totally gross. The guy's tongue was so long, I probably won't need to wipe my bum for the rest of the day –"

"Please, Auntie Jess, that's enough!" Alice coughs, doubling over as if to vomit. "I get the idea, although I wish I hadn't."

Jessica looks away and then back to the paper.

"Middle-aged!" she snorts haughtily. "Middle-bloody-aged! Cheeky, little runt! Do I look like my sister or something? Let's see, what's next?

"'It was thanks to Mr Hägervongelschmidt that police determined the nationality of the terrorists involved. He confirmed that he had seen documented evidence to the effect that they were United Kingdom citizens and added that the ringleader had not denied being English when confronted with such evidence.'"

Alice blanches and says quickly, "So we'd better shut up completely as far as English is concerned. Thank goodness they think we're German."

A horrible thought crosses my mind.

"But what if Jöchi told them that you can speak German?" I ask, glancing over at the police officers gathered a short distance away.

A deathly silence descends. All three of us look at the ground. It only needs somebody to tie the various loose ends together now. Nobody says a word.

That is, until Jessica suddenly looks up and beams.

"Oh, hold on!" she exclaims. "If I recall, I never actually used German in front of Jöchi. He thinks I can speak English and Spanish, but I never spoke any German in front of him."

"You more or less understood it," Alice reminds her dubiously.

"So what?" breezes Jessica, suddenly back into her typical couldn't-care-less manner. Perhaps she's that relieved at the sudden mitigation of the threat. "He was probably too dumb to figure that much out and all he could really think about was what was in my underwear, not between my ears."

"Well, I don't mind telling you that I still feel quite uneasy right now," I come back. "What do you think our next steps should be?"

For once, I don't seem to have asked what is considered a question stupid enough to have been asked by someone devoid of any intelligence whatsoever. Jessica looks around the valley for a moment, lost in thought.

"Let's see," she finally starts again, taking up the paper. "According to this, they're manning all the checkpoints to ensure that the crooks don't get out of Bern."

She looks up and scours the railway station where there is quite a bit of activity.

"No doubt they're checking things diligently over there since Zweisimmen would be a significant crossing point for various routes coming into and going out of Bern. There's more to Bern beyond here but almost everyone over there will have come through here, if entering from the direction of Spiez. If we can get west of Zweisimmen, then with a bit of luck, we can make it to Fribourg without further mishap."

"Meaning what?" asks Alice. "How do we get there?"

"Go with what you know works," Jessica responds. "Let's ask the cops for a lift."

"Are you sure?"

"No, but I'm not very sure of anything else either. The station has too much paperwork being checked and if we start hiking at this time of day, we're going to look very odd, especially since we have minimum equipment but an expensive clarinet. I'm all for sticking with hiding in plain sight. We get over the Cantonal border into Fribourg, take late buses and night buses through Fribourg and Vaud to the Neuchatel border with France, then cross over tomorrow morning. That being Sunday, nobody will give a damn whether you walk over the border with a valid passport or drive over in a main battle tank with a North Korean flag on it. Jean-Pierre of border security will be too busy sleeping off his hangover to notice or care."

I never really know with Jessica what's fact, what's hyperbole and what's somewhere in the middle. I simply trust her, but I don't know if that's because I believe anything she tells me or because I just have no other choice.

Either way, Jessica waltzes up to the police and addresses them in her most cheerful manner. Their response seems initially rather taken aback but she soon has some of them laughing and a few minutes later, the same two who brought us this far have waved us back into their car. It pulls off and into the road, passing every roadblock on the way and attracting no attention whatsoever from any police control. We travel along a very scenic route through a mountain pass called the Jaunpass. It really is beautiful in the evening light. The woods around us keep gaining in darkness but the slopes above remain defiantly sunny. It's a strange combination. The police eventually drop us at the head of the next valley in the town of Jaun itself. This is a pleasant, little place, wedged between two, very steep inclines on either side of the head of the valley. It's a rural spot with a few hotels where hikers and others stay during the summer months, I understand. It's also where Jessica told the police we were trying to reach.

Finally, and very much to the point, it's in the Canton of Fribourg. A long road stretches away down the valley towards the town of Bulle, so Jessica tells me.

The police car having receded out of our view back towards Bern, Jessica turns to Alice and me.

"That road goes to Bulle, but we don't have to follow the whole thing. We just go down far enough to get a few buses and then get over the border tomorrow into the next country along. From there, we and the clarinet are going home."

Chapter 30
CHARMING

Jessica

Have you ever woken up on a bus shelter bench next to a secondary school teacher whom you're not dating and have no intention of dating? I hope that's not the case, especially if you're a pupil at the secondary school in question. Even for the rest of us, I can assure you that it's not an attractive proposition. If you also have what feels like a mini slaughterhouse on the go between your thighs, it's really not something to look forward to at all. The main thing in its favour is that it's not quite as uncomfortable as spending the night on top of a glacier. And that's more because of what the glacier is like.

Having rolled off the bench and onto the remains of somebody's unfinished Turkish beef wrap, I'm not in the best of moods. We're in Le Locle, a small town in the Canton of Neuchatel, next to the French border. Le Locle has a train station, from where we could travel over into France and catch the train to Lyon, from whose airport I intend us to catch a flight home. However, while they may be a lot more relaxed about apprehending the dastardly felons who trashed Bern with their illegal paragliding, water-skiing and perverted sex acts (bloody cheek), I don't want to take a chance on the border guard having been alerted at the main crossings served by public transport. Hence we're getting up and walking down to the nearby crossing at Le Chauffaud which can be literally walked over. We'll be able to see quickly enough before we get there if it's to be avoided before we try to cross. From there, we can cut up north for a couple of kilometres and get a train from the first station on the French side of the border. The chances of the French giving a rat's ass about non-lethal joyrides in the Canton of Bern is about the same as that of them caring about the availability of strawberry versus chocolate cornettoes in the same area, as in virtually zero. So all in all, not such a bad plan, especially at six o'clock on a Sunday morning.

Or so you might think. Unfortunately, it must take a bit of time for Harris to come up to speed with what passes for reality in his universe after he first wakes up. I explain the plan to him, but I suppose I'm competing with mental images of Purcell or Weber. Maybe Isabel but since he's only just woken up, that's not something I really want to ask. Not that I think he's a pervert or even a very horny guy, but Isabel is special and there are some things you just don't ask.

"And then we go over the border into France and catch a bus to the nearest train station," I finish after outlining the overall plan.

"Cross the border? Are you really sure about that now?" asks Harris, apparently horrified. "But won't they have guards and barbed wire and things like that?"

If I recall correctly, he has actually been outside the UK before this venture started four days ago. But you'd think his universe started and stopped in Bristol, going by how he talks sometimes.

"We're talking about the back end of nowhere in the countryside between France and Switzerland, which are both Schengen countries. We're not trying to cross the DMZ from North Korea into South Korea."

"What's the DMZ?" he asks, this time looking completely blank.

"The De-militarized Zone is the area of no-man's land which separates the two Koreas," I explain before coming up short. "You do know where Korea is, don't you? It's not just the name of a restaurant behind Sainsbury's."

"I have heard of Korea," he sniffs pointedly.

"Though I guess BTS or Blackpink are beyond the sphere of musical etiquette you inhabit," I mutter under my breath before sighing loudly and proceeding.

"The fact is, Harris, that nobody cares about the minor border crossings. You could just about drive over them in a runaway train and nobody would notice. If we can make it to Le Chauffaud, then we're well away."

Harris still looks very dubious but Alice chips in at this point.

"Look, Mr Beadlesby," she says, "Auntie Jess is right. Nobody has closed those borders since World War Two."

"Actually, the last time was because of COVID," I point out.

"What?" Alice looks up in true surprise. "They had COVID in World War Two?"

Oh please, Alice, don't you turn into a raving idiot. We already have one complete moron on the team. I don't need two of you.

"Let's just go," I say blankly. "Follow me."

"Welcome to France," I announce jovially.

"What? Was that the border?" Harris sounds incredulous.

It's half an hour later. We walked past a customs office and a guard hut. Admittedly, they were empty and Lieutenant Jean-Pierre, if he'd bothered to turn up for work at all, had probably been taking a six-hour liquid breakfast with a break for a cognac in the middle. But still, what did Harris think these out-buildings were? Probably what would have been useful conveniences to throw up in if the Lieutenant could remember where the hell he put the keys to them before he got sloshed.

"It's not very different, is it?"

"What do you expect? The border's only fifty metres behind us!"

"But this is another country, is it not?"

"Legally speaking and politically, yes, it is but that doesn't mean that everyone on that side is going to be dressed in a Teutonic waistcoat, mountain breeches and a William Tell hat, yodelling away and listening to some oompah-oompah brass music. Nor does it mean that everyone here is going to be wearing a stripy top with a badly fitting beret and a string of onions round their neck. That is no more likely than it is to find half of England on a Sunday afternoon full of people called Cecil doffing a nice Pimm's and tonic while watching some jolly good fellow step up to the cricket wicket and bid his associates a grand what ho."

Except that oh yeah, said stereotype probably is quite likely to feature in

Harris' world. I just cut short the conversation by adding markedly that, "Geopolitics and modern culture are slightly more subtle than that."

We proceed onwards towards the nearest train station. The countryside is pretty, if a little less impressive than what we were passing through in Bern and Fribourg. Gone are the looming heights. Instead we have a combination of rolling hills, mainly covered in trees and fields. Nice enough though nothing amazing. It's probably quite a preferable landscape for those who consider nipping down to the shops and back a hefty bit of exercise. People like Harris, who seems quite relieved at not having to trek through any serious mountains anymore. The hike is baking since there's no shade and the sun just keeps getting hotter. Given the time it is just now, by midday this place is going to be seriously uncomfortable. I'm not going to complain though. It might not be my preferred option, but we only have to walk for about another half hour, and we can be on a train. From there on, we're basically riding public transport so who cares? I like nice scenery out of my train windows but right now, I just want to get back with that clarinet and Harris in one piece. Well, two pieces, technically but you know what I mean. If we can pull this off, at least we'll finally have achieved something.

It's actually a nice thought, achieving something. It's not something I think of myself as doing that much. I do my work and devise advertising campaigns in different languages or put formal invitations into foreign prose or whatever. However, it feels more like merely doing my job. It's a decent job, I quite like it, and I get paid enough. I just don't feel as though I'm doing all that much which makes a particular difference. I don't mean that I'm desperate to save the world. I don't have to achieve global peace or find a cure for AIDS, not even in German. I just feel slightly uneasy whenever I see someone's obituary, if that's not too morbid a way of putting it. I know as well as anyone that obituaries are always focused on the positive side of things – how this was a dedicated and friendly person who always put family and friends first, who smiled at everyone and made them laugh, and who always considered what others needed. No doubt there are facts to back it all up and I'm not saying these things aren't true. Nonetheless, there must be someone out there who's a complete git, mainly noticeable by virtue of their body odour, with zero consideration of anyone else and about as funny as having somebody with extra manky hair go down on you and give you a case of nits in your pubes. So how come none of them ever dies and gets an obituary? If they don't, the composition of the living population is a truly frightening proposition.

What I wonder, getting to the point, is what would anyone write about me if I were to take an unexpected tumble off the side of an Alp or accidentally eat a hamburger laced with Novichok which some Russian spy had intended for the security chief sitting two tables down from me? "Jessica was a sarky, little git who liked hiking in the Alps because there weren't too many people there to get on her nerves. Please note that if you don't like salt 'n' vinegar crisps, then you shouldn't bother attending the wake after the funeral." Honest but not overly impressive.

However, if we do manage something now and Harris wins the love of his life, perhaps I'll finally accomplish a worthwhile achievement. I appreciate that it's a question of perspective. Isabel getting a lifelong, romantic fling with Harris sounds a bit like an act of cruelty towards the poor woman but if they're both genuinely up for it, who am I to judge? Love is a beautiful thing apparently. I remain to be convinced but if Harris is, then good for him. At least I can do something which makes a positive difference to somebody.

Such philosophizing keeps me going until we hit the station. There's no option round here to swap either Swiss Francs or US Dollars into Euros, so I just get Harris to buy us all tickets to Lyon from the machine on the platform with his credit card. A train in fifteen minutes? That's quite handy. I spot a baker's shop nearby and leg it over to get some homemade pastries and cakes. There's nothing else open on a Sunday round here and I haven't eaten for ages, so I intend to enjoy myself. I even remember to get something for Alice and Harris to have too. Again, having borrowed his card. I know I'm taking a security risk by doing that but I'm a generous individual. And I'm very tired by this point.

Twenty minutes later, the marginally delayed train rocks up. Despite my over-catering, we've knocked off all the pastries and cakes and although I'm not going to admit it to the other two, I'm actually feeling slightly queasy. Never try eating a pain-au-chocolat, a strawberry tart and a full millefeuille in under fifteen minutes in scorching heat. Even if you're hungry as hell, you're going to regret it. And unless I can keep it under wraps with a good drink of water, whoever sits next to me on the train may be going to regret it as well.

We board the train and take a right into a somewhat busy carriage. It's not completely full so we should get a seat but there is the most amazingly full luggage rack stretching from the door to about one third of the way up on the left hand-side as you progress up the central passage. This is hardly a concern for us since we have about as much baggage as someone rocking up for a dirty weekend in a nudist colony. However, this is clearly not the case for most people here. How much stuff do people need? The bulk of this pile seems to consist of mountain bikes and associated gear, which I suppose is fair enough. But besides that, there are more suitcases than you find in your average department store and then a range of quite bizarre items. Somebody has a very 1950s picnic hamper. I didn't realise that the Famous Five were still going strong myself but perhaps they just moved to France. Then there are a couple of Swingball sets. Don't people just buy these things for their back gardens, not to cart around half the country? This being France, obviously there are enough pétanque sets to provide the Russian arms industry with all the ball bearings it could possibly need for a year. There's even a sealed tank with some sort of snake sitting in it. What are these people smoking? I feel kind of sorry for the poor thing as it looks less like an exotic pet and more like an incredibly bored one. However, my sympathy diminishes when I see another animal cage a small distance along, containing a bunch of mice with rather worried expressions on their faces. No doubt that's the snake's picnic hamper. I'm not a vegetarian myself so it's a bit hypocritical to blame the poor reptile but the empathy I was starting to feel for it is now quite diminished.

We push on past all this and find the three seats we need just behind where the luggage rack ends. It's actually four seats, two facing forwards, two facing back, tucked into a quiet, little corner behind the luggage rack which is now ahead of us in the direction of travel. Our kind of place. Assuming Harris can keep his big mouth shut, I hope we can get by, largely unobserved and unnoticed.

The journey commences and the train trundles further through the French countryside. I won't digress with some lengthy disposition about how it's nowhere near as impressive as the Alps, how the rolling countryside with nothing much on the horizon is relatively boring and so forth. I'll just say that it's different yet actually quite charming in its own way. In fact, it's quite like many people's preconceptions of what rural France looks like. A lot of yellows from fields of mustard, interspersed with small areas of woodland and farmhouses plus enough green to offset the yellow. Where are all the pigs, I wonder? I didn't know the world could produce enough pork to require all the mustard France must be producing for ham and mustard sandwiches. It looks the part for sure. All that yellow stands out against the azure sky above with only the occasional tree breaking up the horizon. No mountains but enough hills to keep the broader landscape rolling and it certainly appears to go on forever. It feels like it too as I would rather we could just be in Lyon as soon as possible. The various villages we pass are picturesque, quaint and old style with a lot of white-washed walls, shuttered windows and red tiled rooves. The only bit at odds with the stereotype is that the people in them look up as we pass through and appear reasonably happy. You wouldn't think that they spend half the year on strike and threaten a new revolution every time somebody in Paris suggests that they might have to add half a centime onto fuel taxes because amazingly enough, you can't afford for the entire country to retire in their mid-fifties with pensions worth 120% of their pre-retirement salaries, full health care for free and an individual social care worker each time they trip over a dropped croissant in the street. But what the hell? It's the French way and it's worked since 1789 so don't touch it, all right? Vive La France and screw Les Anglaises. Works well every time. Unless you count 1940 but you don't make jokes like that unless you want a Napoleonic riding boot wedged firmly up your derrière.

Still, time to forget analysis of international relations. We have more immediate worries, not least the fact that there's a ticket inspector working his way down the carriage from the opposite end to where we boarded. He seems to be paying an inordinate amount of attention to his job, which I don't like at all, and for some reason which I do not understand, there's a burly police officer behind him. It may be no big deal though. He's spending a disproportionate amount of time giving anglophones a hard time, especially Brits and Americans, so he may only be doing it for a bit of a laugh and a good time at the expense of the NATO members whom he finds particularly irksome. He's hardly the only public servant in France who enjoys that pastime. If you think that US immigration officials are obnoxious, then you need to realise that they have plenty of competition in terms of civil service officials in several other countries. America does not necessarily have all the monopolies it believes itself to hold.

I don't know but I don't want to find out the hard way, so I nudge Harris into some form of awareness and tell him softly not to say anything, especially not in English.

I should have known better.

"What's that?" Harris asks at the top of his voice, suddenly disturbed from what was no doubt a mental session listening to Brahms' greatest hits in his head or something. "Don't speak English? Whyever not?"

You're about to find out, matey.

The ticket inspector, already quite close, looks up and grins evilly. He addresses the last few customers between us and him in French and is responded to in the same language, so he checks their tickets in the most perfunctory manner possible and legs it down to us.

"Vos billets, s'il vous plaît?" he demands with a knowing smile. Your tickets, please.

Well, I've got him on this one at least. They always do this when they're trying to nail a Brit or a Yank – pretend to speak zero English so as to throw them completely because they don't know any French. Not this time, pal.

I show him our tickets, responding in fluent French that he's very welcome and remarking on what a pleasant day it is.

That was maybe just a bit too cocky. He starts off taken aback, then recovers his nastiness and eyes Harris suspiciously.

"You speak Eenglish, monsieur?" he asks in a probably exaggeratedly heavy, French accent. Like something out of one of the "Pink Panther" movies.

"Well, I do, yes. Quite well too, I might say," Harris replies.

You dolt, Harris. He wasn't asking if you were able to speak English. He was checking that you basically only know how to communicate in that language and that you are indeed English. Because that confirms that you're a legitimate target in his eyes. He only needed that because I had temporarily rocked the boat by knowing French.

He sees the clarinet in Harris' hands and asks if he might see it. Harris hands it over and he turns it over quite gently, looking at it with an expression which starts curious and becomes increasingly impressed.

"My gootness, zees eez an impressive piez of werk," he remarks.

"I'm pleased to see you know your instruments!" Harris beams. "Not everyone is as cultured as they should be!"

I am not remotely pleased. Not because of Harris' implied, sarky critique of my lack of sophistication. More because if this guy really does know what he's talking about and he realises the actual worth of that thing, we are going to look a shade unusual to say the least.

"Vairy valu-abble, Eh must zay," the conductor continues.

"Absolutely!" continues Harris, somehow thinking he's found a new friend. "It's in the region of - "

He stops abruptly as my foot connects violently with his shin.

I pitch forward exaggeratedly, covering up the fact that I just kicked him with an attempt to look as though I suddenly fell forwards. I'm in one of the backward-facing seats so how convincing that is, I hate to think but at least it serves as a distraction.

The inspector could hardly care less.

"So vot eez eet vorth?" he asks again.

For once, Harris shows some presence of mind as he replies, "Oohh, somewhere in the region of eight thousand pounds, I think." Pretty good actually. Hardly an astronomical sum but more likely than saying ten quid fifty, two for fifteen.

"Eh rather eemagine eet may be vorth more zan zat," intones the inspector in a sinister way. Why does every other individual we run into on this trip sound like a villain out of a Bond film? I feel like I've met half the friggin' cast of people I don't fancy without ever once getting an eyeful of Tim. It's just not fair.

He gives us a very evil eye.

"Eet may bee vorth several zousands, Eh theenk," he remarks, turning it over again, before turning to us very suddenly. "Zo vat are you three doing veez eet? Who are you really?"

Oh for frig's sake. How many of these unexpected crises do I have to deal with in the space of four days? Or is it five now? Is there no limit to how much Fate can churn out of its rectum?

Apparently not. Harris leaps to his feet.

"Now listen here, my good man," he begins, in a tone which Boris Johnson might consider a bit over-posh and pompous, "I really don't appreciate your tone at all. We have every right to be carrying this fine piece of musical craftsmanship. In actual fact, we ourselves are representatives of a distinguished corporation –"

What the hell is this? Look, Harris, I'll do the bullshit round here. That one is my department, got it?

Before I can think of a way to shut him up, however, Fate intervenes. It seems that the exchange so far was just an opening fart in what is about to become a full-on salvo of serious, faecal matter.

Harris has been accompanying his attempt to talk us out of this by adopting a quite supercilious but deliberately casual posture. He's balancing on his left foot, with his right folded behind it, lifted with the toe pointing to the ground. His upper body is leaning towards the end of the luggage rack, against which he is leaning on his outstretched, right arm. His head is tilted slightly in the opposite direction. The idea, I suppose, is to give the idea of being eminently superior in intellectual terms to this crass inspector while patronizing him into checking the ticket, forgetting the clarinet and sodding off.

If so, it doesn't work. I can't see all which is happening behind me but there is a sudden clatter as something gives way. Harris lurches to the right as his arm follows through on a falling suitcase and I look behind me to see a cascade of suitcases, all falling over like dominoes. The effect continues into the bike racks as mountain bikes clatter noisily and begin to strew themselves everywhere. Even worse, I suddenly see that glass tank clatter downwards and spring open. Something long, dark and apparently quite angry comes hissing out of it. There's a sudden gasp of horror and a marked exclamation of fear from some of the nearer passengers. The snake's hood expands in the direction of that noise which promptly turns into a scream of terror.

It's a cobra? A freaking cobra? Who, in the name of all which is holy, keeps a cobra as a pet and moves it around in a glorified fish tank on public transport? And now it's ended up on the same train as Harris Beadlesby, a man so bereft of common sense that he makes brainless morons look like James Bond. Maybe not as played by Timothy Dalton. That would be too much. But at least Roger Moore or Pierce Brosnan. Fate clearly had one hell of a curry last night.

Somehow or other, I see an opportunity here. This is probably the most stupid thing I've done to date on this trip. In fact, it's probably the most stupid thing I've done to date in my life, and the competition is pretty intense. However, it might just get us out of this.

I spring upwards and twist around. I grab the clarinet from the now horrified inspector and yell at him in French that actually, we're special snake-charming emergency experts and we're here to respond to crisis events.

I've read somewhere that cobras are not remotely interested in the sound of a snake-charmer's flute. What entrances them is the motion as it sways back and forth, left and right. I bloody hope they're right or I may be signing my own death warrant with this stunt. I push my way past a couple of overweight, French ladies which is pretty easy as they're charging up the carriage in the opposite direction. I just have to wedge myself into the chain of a mountain bike to let them get past. That done, I settle myself in a crouch, rocking back on my ankles, and face what appears to be a very irritable reptile. I'm not entirely sure why it should be so pissy. After all, it just got freed from a transparent suitcase and given how scared those mice looked, I assume it was being kept reasonably well fed up to this point. Admittedly, the exit was a bit unexpected, and it may have knocked its hood on the way out but that doesn't seem to be such a bummer. It might not have a ticket but given the sudden terror on the face of the inspector I doubt it has to worry about incurring a fine.

Whatever the reason, it does not look happy and content. Maybe it's just the vibe on the carriage since nobody else appears too overjoyed either. But none of this is a major worry right now. My main concern is how to become a proficient snake-charmer with a combined experience of zero hours. Zero seconds more like, if you want to be picky.

How the hell do you actually play a clarinet? Well, you blow into it, no doubt. I raise the thing to my lips and blow as hard as I can, just in case the sound does help after all. There's a slight rustle and what sounds like a rhino with a serious wind problem. The main effect is to focus the cobra's attention even more closely on me. I go swiftly to the theory which I think I might vaguely know and start rocking from side to side. The cobra stands higher on its tail for a moment. Not sure if this is good as it might indicate an intent to strike in the near future but at least it looks slightly more curious than angry. Fantastic. Now I'm an expert in cobra body language. If this thing needs a psychotherapist, I may just have found a way out of this mess.

Got to keep swaying though. Perhaps the music does help a bit as well. Who knows? Just because I read it somewhere I can't even remember doesn't mean it's definitely not true. At least the rhythm might help me to sway in time. Let's try again.

The snake hisses suddenly and moves forward a little. I jerk backwards and let out a cry of alarm. At least, that's what I try to do but the mouthpiece is between my lips. I yell into the clarinet, and a strange, high-pitched roar emerges. The snake pauses and looks straight at me. Maybe the sound does help? I don't know but I go back to swaying anyway while I try another vocalized blow into the clarinet. This works as well. It occurs to me suddenly – it's like playing the kazoo. You semi-sing into it and a kind of music emerges. It's nothing like you would hear in an orchestra and no doubt Karl Givret must be spinning in his grave at this piece of musical vandalism but the thought that Harris doubtless has a similar opinion is enough to make me grin to myself.

I try manipulating the keys of the instrument. The sound basically grows worse. I don't really know what tune I'm trying to produce but it sounds like some sort of hybrid between the American national anthem and that song they use for the Cup-a-Soup adverts on ITV3. I'm busy swaying like a drunk scarecrow in a hurricane now and catch someone giving me a very evil look from the corner of my eye. Probably a US citizen who, with credit to his patriotism, is more concerned about respect for his country than dying of envenoming in the next ten minutes. Still, I don't want to have to choose between a serious dose of haematitic poisoning and getting beaten to death by an American patriot, so I broaden the repertoire. The new tune has a certain similarity to, "Take on Me" though with more of a "Bob the Builder" feel but at least it's less offensive in terms of international politics.

It also seems less offensive to the snake. I add in some back and forth swaying to complement the side-to-side routine and the cobra actually follows my lead. It still doesn't look like my best friend or as if it's considering whether or not it wants to offer me a drink back at its place after this dance is over but right now, it does appear to be marginally less inclined to end my life within the next minute. Or however long it takes you to die from cobra venom. My expertise in herpetology doesn't stretch beyond cold sore creams. Not that I get a lot of that sort of thing, you understand. Just saying. So I hear.

Perhaps this serpent is nonetheless concerned about catching a cold sore from me if it bites me on the face. Which, I hasten to add, is an entirely groundless concern. Again, just saying. Whatever its motivation, it does seem to be eyeing various parts of my body with what looks like a critical appraisal. If my dance floor analogy holds, then it's like the random pervo who gets a bit wasted and then thinks he has a right to check out your anatomy, piece by tantalizing piece. I just wish I could yell harassment and get a bouncer to throw him out. I swear though, if that thing strikes and goes for my menstruating crotch, then even if I die, I am going to make sure I murder Harris first.

For the moment, I seem to be holding it in sufficient enthralment for me to stay alive. It continues to follow me. The question now is how to get it to somewhere safe. I suppose its original tank is probably the best bet. It looks intact enough, only with its front door blown open. If I can get the damn thing back into the tank and slam the door shut, then all I need to do is find something substantial to keep it closed and we're all set. Good idea but how do I make the snake move? The tank is about ten metres down the carriage behind it.

I start off by swaying slightly more to the left than to the right. That works. The snake is moving off my central axis. If I move slightly to the left each time, then bit by bit, excruciatingly slowly but still noticeably, it and I move in a circle. I push ever so slightly forward so as to get it to sway backwards and away from me at the same time, giving me enough room to move around it until I have my back to the tank. You might be wondering why I don't just force it to move backwards itself without the turn, but the reason is that once I have it following me, I can move backwards myself, with the snake following me forwards. That I can do, covering a much more substantial distance in the same time. Getting it to move backwards itself is painfully slow. I'm now onto the theme tune from, "Goldfinger" with a shade of the ad for Bird's Eye Potato Waffles so my musical inspirations are running thin. My legs are also starting to ache like hell. I need to get this over and done with as soon as I can.

We're about halfway down the carriage, about five metres from the tank. I'm still trying to think of a way to entice the cobra back into it. This is not that easy when you're also trying to perform a busking act for a lethal predator without ever having earned even 10p with a similar act in Liverpool city centre. And given the quality of some of the acts which somehow earn cash in Liverpool city centre, that makes me astronomically crap. I'm hard at work, no doubt about that.

All of a sudden, the train lurches to a halt. Perhaps somebody finally figured out that there might be what constitutes an emergency going on.

Congratulations, guys. Obviously, France still has to reach Switzerland's standards of efficiency, but you got there in the end. Perhaps a relief to most people, the music comes to an abrupt halt, and I suddenly roll over backwards onto my back, my legs splayed in the air in front of me. I look up to see the cobra fly forwards in the air. Bloody hell! Am I about to get sexually assaulted by a snake?

Thankfully not, it seems. The snake skids briefly over my face. A lovely sensation. But it's still moving fast and skates straight over. Its momentum carries it right into the tank where it crashes into the back but twists around, its hood wide open and a furious hissing coming out of its mouth. Not good.

I look around and find a random pétanque ball sitting next to me. I pick it up and sling it at the snake. Predictably enough, it flies with all the accuracy of an empty packet of salt 'n' vinegar crisps slung by yours truly at a public bin and misses the reptile entirely. However, it does crash into the back of the tank and that distracts the cobra. It looks round to see what gives. This is my opportunity, and I lunge forwards and slam the tank door shut. A heavy suitcase next to it, rammed against the edge, quickly ensures that it stays closed.

I honestly wonder if I got bitten. Sweat is pouring off me like I just showered under my own armpit. My breath is coming so quickly that if there were any chance that I might be pregnant, I'd be worried that I'd gone into labour half an hour ago. I could hardly be flushing more hotly if Tim had just promised me a night of unbridled and uninterrupted passion at his place. However, I don't appear to have any bites on me (unless you count where a couple of those really annoying horse flies got me on the way over the French border) and there is no sensation of numbness anywhere. Maybe in the part of my brain concerned with common sense and self-preservation but what's new? I think that actually, somehow, I've just about survived this experience.

The clarinet is lying to my right. I reach over and pick it up, then get to my feet. Scraping my hair out of my eyes, I stride up to the inspector and look him directly in the face.

"Lieutenant Indy-Anna Jones, Special Snake-Charming Emergency

Response Squad!" I bark at him in fluent French and wave the clarinet in his face. He gulps visibly and backs away from me, his gaze rapidly descending to his feet. "Now piss off!"

In the end of the day, he doesn't even stamp our tickets. Am I the only one who does any work round here?

Chapter 31

I WOULD DO ANYTHING FOR LOVE

Harris

"So tell me, Harris, what do you actually do for a good time? I don't mean the big-ticket items, all that going out to the opera or performing in a four-hour gala festival of Mozart's greatest hits and all that sort of thing. Just like when you get home from work or when you have an hour spare. What sort of things are you into?"

Crudely phrased perhaps, but I suppose it's a fair question, and as far as I can tell, it's being asked with only genuine intent. We seem to have a fair bit of space to ourselves now since almost everybody else has quit the carriage with the cobra in it and we, or at least Jessica, are regarded as being somehow too tough for others to talk to. Jessica appears to have given up trying to convince the world that we're a family from France or Germany and seems content for us to hold a regular conversation, provided that it remains relatively unacademic. It makes a pleasant change to how we've been travelling over the course of the past week, so I see no reason to object.

The countryside rushes past, but I will agree with Jessica that it maybe isn't quite as visually striking as the Alpine scenery which surrounded us earlier. It's pleasing to the eye but even Jessica doesn't seem too worried about possibly missing a great view if she pays attention to the inside of the train for a few minutes. That is something I am definitely doing since I simply do not trust that crate at the other end of the passage to hold the snake. If it happened once, it could happen again as far as I'm concerned and I'm not going to relax until either it or we are off the train. Other than that, however, I am actually quite enjoying this trip to Lyon. Our water was running low earlier in the morning. We'd used up most of it by the end of yesterday after hiking through Bern and Fribourg and then finished it on waking up. However, Alice discovered a communal fountain next to the station which was an absolute godsend. A strange contraption, it resembled a fire hydrant in some ways, with a circular handle which had to be wound round in order to release water, but it worked as designed and Jessica assured me that the water was perfectly drinkable. They're common across France, she tells me. If so, then that's certainly something which I think the British should be adopting themselves. Especially on a hot day like this, you can appreciate how the French are one step ahead of us on that one.

I think for a moment before replying to Jessica.

"Well, I don't think I'm that different to other people really," I start. "I do actually watch television now and again!"

"That's reassuring. What do you enjoy? Dramas, comedies, documentaries, underwear commercials?"

"Well, musical broadcasts, of course," I say, studiously ignoring that last comment. "I do have quite a thing for period and costume dramas as well, in fact, so historical shows and documentaries can take my fancy."

"You mean you watch stuff like, 'Bridgerton?'" Jessica asks dubiously. "I would have thought that was a bit salacious for your tastes."

"Maybe so," I admit, "but like most people, I pick and choose within the genres. It's also worth noting that there was a real boom in quality, costume dramas in the 1970s and 1980s and I often find myself coming back to that."

Warming to my theme, I continue, "The adaptation of 'War and Peace' in the early 70s with Anthony Hopkins was marvellous, for example. Then there was, 'A Tale of Two Cities' as performed by James Wilby and Xavier Deluc in the late 80s. A truly spectacular performance."

Going by the blank looks on Jessica's and Alice's faces, I can only imagine that it wasn't quite spectacular enough to have garnered their attention. Nonetheless, I continue, describing my favourite performances and actors in the vague hope that they might have heard of any of them. Since I never have any clue as to what Jessica is talking about when she references popular culture, if I can find some commonality here, it's my best chance of identifying enough common ground for an intelligent exchange.

"Another I really loved was the 1983 adaptation of 'Jane Eyre'", I arrive at some five minutes later without much luck so far. "Stunning performances. Eyre herself was portrayed wonderfully by Zelah Clarke while I have never seen anybody deliver a better interpretation of Edward Rochester than Timothy Dalton."

Jessica almost falls out of her seat. I look over to make sure that the snake hasn't suddenly escaped.

"You're into Tim?" she gasps.

"He was, indeed still is, a renowned, Shakespearean actor," I point out. "He was an obvious choice for the role but even then, he still shone unexpectedly well in it."

"Oh yeah, that's cool," Jessica says hurriedly. "I know he's a talented guy but ultimately, he hit the jackpot of acting, didn't he? He was James Bond, for frig's sake!"

I do recall something about Mr Dalton having graced the lower realms of popular culture at one point and tell Jessica pointedly that we all have moments of ecstatic and lower, cultural milieux.

"Oh yeah, I know," she comes back. "That stint did he did in 'Flash Gordon' was not his best call. I'll give you that for sure."

I'm feeling as though I would really like to press on to another topic before the experience of watching, "Hamlet" becomes tainted beyond redemption for me.

"Of course," I begin, "there's always Isabel."

"Huh? Oh, right." Jessica's mind seems to be floating elsewhere. "What all do you do with her?"

"Auntie Jess!" Alice sits up straight and announces in mock horror. "That's not the sort of thing you ask a red-blooded male about his girlfriend! Do you have no sense of decency?"

"Chill out, Alice. I'm not trying to get the inside scoop on 'Debbie Does

Dvořák'. What Harris does in his private life is his concern but there may be a bit more to it than that. You may not realize but there is a greater spectrum of romance than what you read about in those soft-core teenage porn books you get free with bulk-bought discount eye shadow. Love can be a beautiful and soul-enriching experience for some people."

"Like you and Herr Rumpito Pumpito in Spiez?" smirks Alice.

"We all have our off moments," Jessica concedes, "but that's what makes the true thing so special. No doubt Harris can elaborate further."

"I'm not sure I necessarily want to hear about all that," Alice cuts in worriedly.

I'm not sure I want to describe all that, at least not in the sense to which Alice is referring.

"Well," I intervene, "I would say that Isabel and I are much like other couples. We do enjoy sharing the experiences of music and literature together, often over a glass or two of a fine red.

"Or maybe even three of four!" I wink knowingly. To no avail, it seems.

"We're always very excited at the start of the month when the next edition of WECPA arrives. We spend hours checking out what's coming up and planning our trips back and forth."

Jessica continues to look as though she has no idea what I'm describing. Maybe she finally knows how I've frequently been feeling for the past few days. Except that her life doesn't depend on this.

"Mr Beadlesby," Alice intones wearily, "I rather doubt Auntie Jess is going to be very familiar with the West Country Performing Arts monthly catalogue."

"And why not?" I ask, deliberately trying to sound a shade supercilious. "I suppose the performing arts are not really a significant concern of hers?"

"Because she lives in bloody Liverpool!" Alice retorts with considerable indignation. "She'd be quicker nipping over to Manchester for a gig than coming down to Somerset. The only real choice is whether she'd rather spend a couple of hours getting to a Mendelssohn concerto or a Take That tribute act."

That's a fair point. I will never for the life of me understand how others cannot appreciate the wonders of the classical composers. However, I must also appreciate their perspectives if ever I am to help them to appreciate such wonders. It's a difficult proposition.

"I tell you what," Jessica cuts in, speaking to both of us, "let's just accept that we all like different things but talk about them in a respectful way without anyone feeling that their tastes are worth any more or any less than anyone else's."

"Except where it comes to men you might pick up on the side of Lake Thun," Alice adds.

"Very droll," says Jessica. "That was a case of needs must. If you think you found it disgusting, you should have been sitting where I was and feeling his hand make its way up inside your lower bra strap."

"He what?" shrieks Alice. "You didn't mention anything about him getting his mitts on your tits!"

"He didn't!" Jessica responds hurriedly. "He just tried to!"

"So why didn't you deck him if it was so gross?" asks Alice.

"Because there were cops everywhere and anyway, I didn't need to as he backed off of his own accord."

"And then he just pushed off?" Alice asks.

"Yeah," Jessica says grimly, then grins. "And he didn't even call after that!"

And so the rest of the journey proceeds. We somehow reach Lyon with no further drama but with several insights into an eclectic mix of mainly European composers and the finer architecture of musical instrumentation, on one hand, and how best to experience the Alps and James Bond films on another. We also cover some details concerning home-brewed alcohol and erotic literature aimed at mid-teens. I suppose I should know about all this as a secondary school teacher but am very glad that I don't.

On reaching Lyon Station, Jessica shepherds us all out of the train and onto a red shuttle connection, labelled, "Rhônexpress", which she assures us will go straight out to the airport. Indeed it does and we arrive at what I think is late morning. I lost my watch on the glacier so can only confirm the time when we pass a clock.

We enter the main hall and look around. According to some research on Alice's telephone, there should actually be a flight leaving for Bristol at some point in the mid-afternoon. Our plan is to acquire tickets here and now, thus minimizing our exposure to online booking since we don't know how far or not anyone may be still looking for us. We just have to hope that it isn't booked out already.

There's a ticket desk ahead of us with two clerks on duty, a man and a woman. He looks like a very bored and uninterested individual. Quite young so I would have hoped that he would be trying to impress and make his way, but such does not seem to be the case. The woman is a shade older but clearly very efficient, going by the speed with which her fingers zip across the keyboard as she serves the only other passengers ahead of us, an elderly couple.

"Good," murmurs Jessica. "I want us to get as little attention as possible, just what we need. If that dozy dude can stay awake long enough to serve us, we'll be well away."

She marches up to the desk with Alice and me behind. An exchange in French follows. I can't follow it, but I know what she wants to get from it. However, she doesn't seem to be having much success.

I suppose her intention to avoid attracting any more attention than necessary has gone out of the window since she suddenly loosens the upper fastenings of the top half of her shirt and leans over the counter with a rather disrespectable amount of cleavage showing and a large smile on her face. I really do think that the women's rights movement is set back considerably by these supposedly powerful women who still insist on resorting to gross harlotry to achieve their goals. In fact, this really does quite annoy me. I am myself a strong supporter of equity among the peoples of the world, without discrimination based on sex, gender, ethnicity, religious belief or other distinction. We should be looking for the commonalities which bind us, such as music, in my humble opinion. I turn to Jessica to tell her this.

"Shut up, Harris!" she hisses as I get started. "We can discuss all this later if we have to!"

The employee at the desk suddenly adopts a more interested posture.

"You are all English?" he enquires in a very proficient tone and almost accentless English. "I had not realized the extent of your group."

"I can show you a grouped extent!" Jessica purrs in English now, struggling to find a way to get more cleavage out of her sports bra, as far as I can see. The clerk shows no interest and looks beyond her.

"What's the problem?" I ask.

"It seems that UK immigration has been complaining about APIs not being complete and demanding that they be entered at least 48 hours in advance of a flight, which means no possibility of selling tickets after that point."

"What's API?"

"Advance Passenger Information," Jessica tells me. "You're supposed to enter it in advance so that they can match the ID information against the passport which is actually presented. The thing is that it's not a legal requirement per se until the point where you hit passport control. The demand from the UK is more like a heavy-handed request but one which the airline doesn't want to ignore since they prefer to stay on good terms with airport authorities.

"I'm trying to see if I can persuade this little tyke to overlook that and use the override possibility to get us on board."

The said, "little tyke" cuts in, "I'm very sorry, madam, but company policy expressly states that I cannot sell you a ticket to travel before next Tuesday. I can also tell you that your rather brazen attempts to convince me of additional motivations are of no concern to me but—"

He pauses momentarily, looking at the passports offered for his consideration, Jessica's, Alice's and mine.

"This man," he says in a rather different tone, indicating me. "He is not your husband?"

"Hell no!" says Jessica before pulling herself up short into a more tactful mode of self-expression. "I mean, you are allowed to travel together without being married these days, aren't you?"

"Yes, yes, madam," replies the clerk, clearly finding her an unnecessary inconvenience. He then regards me suddenly and seems to look me over. A huge grin appears on his face.

"Oh-ho!" he says to nobody in particular. "You are telling me that this man is just your travelling companion?"

Jessica looks concerned, as if we are somehow being checked for law enforcement reasons or similar but Alice nudges her and whispers something, nodding towards me. Jessica gasps briefly and a very short conversation ensues between them. She then shrugs and turns back to the clerk.

"Oh, yes," she says. "My niece and I are just accompanying him back from a pride festival near Saint-Étienne. It can be quite intimidating for a single, gay man to travel around on his own, especially in another country where he can't understand the language."

What on earth is this? Why should Jessica be telling the world at large that I'm a homosexual?

The answer becomes chillingly clear as the clerk turns to me, all interest in either Jessica or Alice completely pushed aside. He has eyes only for me.

"I'm very sorry, my very good man – very good indeed – if you find our country at all intimidating. I myself know how awkward it can be when your sexuality is simply unappreciated, feared and even hated for no better reason than it being different."

I so wish now that I had not reflected on how wonderful it would be for all people to live in open harmony and security regardless of their gender preferences and identity. The problem with points of fine principle is that they can be so much more disconcerting when you have to do something with them rather than just talk about them. I sincerely doubt that I'll get much sympathy from Jessica on this one, however.

I now appear to be in a private conversation. Jessica and Alice may as well not be there at all.

The clerk looks intently at his computer screen for a few seconds and then looks up again.

"I see," he starts slowly. "This is a tricky problem, a very tricky problem."

"But do you think you can solve it?" I ask.

He breathes noisily through his teeth.

"I wish I could, I really do but I don't know….," he tails off before suddenly sitting bolt upright. "Actually, just give me a moment."

He sits and stares again at the screen, his fingers flying across the keyboard as he enters information and reads even more, all at a dazzling speed. I am truly impressed. If this man could play the piano with the skill he seems to exercise on a computer keyboard, he might be a real find. Eventually he finishes and looks back at me. There's a very odd expression on his face.

"OK, my man, I think I may have a solution, but it will take a lot of work, a lot of effort, and it will not be easy for me. I will be running a considerable risk."

"I'm terribly sorry," I say but he waves me away.

"A terrible risk, yes," he repeats warily, then more breezily, "but for a man like you, I think it is worth it."

"I'm flattered," I say. "I don't know that I'm all that important, I must say, but I do appreciate the compliment. However can I repay you?"

He suddenly leans across the counter and comes very close. His eyes bore into mine and his face is only a few inches away. I can smell something like salami and garlic coming from his mouth.

"I think we can arrange that," he says quietly but very forcibly. I wouldn't say that he's being aggressive, but his tone certainly brooks no argument.

"You are not interested in the ladies?" he asks, nodding towards Alice and Jessica.

"Errm, no, not them," I reply before realizing a little belatedly that I might not have provided the answer I would have wanted to.

"Then I think we have an arrangement," he continues in a knowing tone. "I will get the tickets all sorted out for you and your two friends here. You will just need to come to pick them up discreetly. You should come to the gentlemen's toilet facilities on the second floor in fifteen minutes. There are three closets inside there. I will be in one. Just ask softly for Pierre-Luc. Once you are inside, I will provide you with the tickets and you and I can enjoy the repayment you mentioned earlier. All good?"

I have a very bad feeling about this but don't suppose that there is a great deal else I can do about it right now.

"You've arranged to go cottaging to get the tickets?" Alice asks incredulously.

"Sorry, what's cottaging?" I ask.

"It's generally taken to mean going around public toilets to have homosexual sex with men," Jessica informs me.

"How come she knows that and I don't?" I ask tetchily, indicating Alice.

"Maybe because she lives in reality while you spend your time on Planet Nutjob where men court their future wives by impersonating famous musicians from Karl Givret through to George Michael!" Jessica responds.

We're just round the corner from the ticket booth. There are about twelve minutes left until I'm due in the men's toilets on the second floor and we clearly have a problem, me in particular. A very big problem.

"You could just take it up the butt," Alice suggests. "There's enough time before the flight leaves."

"How do you know how long a round of anal sex takes?" Jessica asks her niece suspiciously.

"I'm guessing Pierre-Luc can't have all that long if he has to be back at work before they notice that he's busy shooting his load into Mr Beadlesby."

"Excuse me," I interrupt "but do you two think we could avoid discussing the problem in such graphic terms? I would prefer to find a solution which does not involve my rectum being forcibly penetrated within the next half hour."

"We could buy some lube from the pharmacy down there," Alice nods along the concourse. "That would make it less forcible."

"That's funny, Alice," Jessica grins, "but I think we need something a bit less predicated on Harris simply taking it. There's probably not much point in saving his marriage if the first things he has to do on his return are to get tested for every STI in the book and apply a year's supply of petroleum jelly to his rectum."

"If he can get married, then who cares? I thought you said married couples didn't have sex?" Alice quizzes her.

"Well, that's usually after the first week or so," Jessica responds.

I'm failing to follow the logic of this conversation, but it really is not helping. I turn to Jessica who seems slightly more inclined to have something helpful to say.

"Now what?"

"All right, give me a moment," Jessica says, half to herself and half to me and Alice. She waves away her niece with one hand, presumably at the prospect of another supposedly amusing remark. I don't find her very funny just now and even if Jessica does, we simply don't have the time.

Jessica puts her hands on her hips and breathes deeply before exhaling loudly.

"We have little chance of convincing him that he doesn't want to go through with this before giving you what we want, since we won't get the tickets that way. And if we try to get the tickets and just run, then he can call in the cops on us and have the tickets invalidated before we even clear security. He won't technically have done anything wrong. So, unless you're going to take it up the bum anyway, we have to persuade him that it's just not an attractive prospect."

"Well, it isn't to me," I pout.

"Of course not," Jessica replies hurriedly, almost irritably before suddenly pausing and gazing at me. "Why not, precisely?"

I'm taken aback. What sort of idiotic question is this?

"Well, do you think being penetrated by a man's penis is an attractive prospect?"

"In actual fact, quite a lot of women do, you know," Jessica tells me pointedly, "but most of them prefer one hole over another and that's not least to do with the comfort factor.

"What I suggest is that you meet up with Pierre-Luc and agree to go through the motions with him. You just need to convince him to let you go first. You then make it as uncomfortable as possible for him, and he calls it off."

"You mean I have to penetrate him?" I ask in horror.

"Yes and no," Jessica replies. "Yes, you have to penetrate him but no, not with any part of your own anatomy. Something a bit more painful than that."

"Such as?" I ask then gasp.

Both Jessica and Alice are looking over at Karl Givret's clarinet.

"You cannot really mean to employ Givret's instrument in this way?"

"Well, Harris," Jessica says with no compassion whatsoever, "you've got about eight minutes to get into that cubicle. It's Givret's instrument or your glory organ. Take your pick."

My goodness me, what am I turning into here? They say that love transforms us into something we could never have imagined before. That much is true, I grant you, but I certainly hadn't imagined that I would turn into a lawbreaker under the legal codes of both England and Switzerland and, probably in the next ten minutes, France as well. Technically, I'm guilty of absconding with a minor, all sorts of aerial violations, breaking and entering, falsifying my identity to law enforcement officers and now, in a moment I suppose, soliciting sexual services in a public restroom. When I told Isabel that I would do anything for her, I certainly meant it, but this was nowhere near what I had in mind. I imagined the great, romantic heroes of opera but nothing like this ever happened to Aida, Carmen, or Tristan and Isolde.

There's little time for reflection. We reach the public convenience, and Jessica runs through the plan.

"Alice, you stay outside. For once, I am going to try to be responsible and keep you out of things which are not suitable for your age group."

"I wouldn't call them suitable for anyone," says Alice.

"Indeed," Jessica sighs. "But anyway, if this does all go south, we might at least be spared a couple of extra years in jail for bringing in a legal child.

"Harris, you go in and find the cubicle with Pierre-Luc. I'll get into one next to you. If there isn't one free, I'll wait around and then groan loudly when I'm free.

"You'll make small talk until I'm ready. Or French kiss him or something."

I wretch inwardly at this but keep my thoughts to myself.

"I will have the clarinet with me. You can't show up holding it without arousing his suspicions and they're not what we want to arouse. You need to get him to turn around to the wall and drop his lower garments. I can then push the clarinet over to you and you do the necessary. Once he seems uncomfortable enough with the idea of a quick shag, you apologize profusely that your kinky idea went so wrong and promise to call in again and do it properly when you're back next week."

"But we won't be coming back next week, will we?"

Jessica rolls her eyes and tells me with a degree of scorn, "I can't even remember the last time I told the truth. Probably last Tuesday. Now you just say as I say and do as I tell you. Got it?"

I nod.

"Then, with the quick shag having gone literally down the toilet, you get the tickets. By that point, he won't want to inform law enforcement or anyone else of what really just happened anymore than we will. That's the overall plan.

"Alice will stay outside with the baggage we have left in case we need anything or there's an emergency and she can help. I'll yell if we need help, OK?"

Alice acquiesces as well.

"Let's go," she orders.

I don't understand how Jessica will pass unnoticed in a men's toilets, but I don't have long to wonder. We go in and are faced by three cubicles, all with their doors shut. We've entered at the far end of the room and to the left of the door we entered by are four urinals along the wall and two washbasins at the far end between the urinals and the cubicles. These, being quite spacious, cover the width of the far wall. A condom machine adorns the near wall, immediately to our right. It has a customer who turns around embarrassedly and then looks quite confused to see Jessica there. He starts to say something in French but is cut off by Jessica who addresses him quietly but sharply, also in French. She pulls a condom packet out of his hand, helps herself to one, and then gives the packet back. He backs out of the door.

"What did you say to him?" I ask her softly.

"I told him that I identify as a man who happens to be stuck in a body with a woman's glory organs attached," she responds matter-of-factly. "When he objected, I told him to stop being a gender-discriminatory pig and demanded that he share his condoms as a sign of our equal need."

"What need?"

"This," she replies, and unwraps the condom. She then places it over the mouthpiece of the clarinet. "A much more sanitary arrangement."

I don't really know that much about what Karl Givret's character was like, but I can well imagine a degree of turning going on in his grave just now.

But it's time to step up to what I must do. I think of Isabel. This is for her and for her alone. A rather odd way for a man to consider a sexual assignation in a public toilet with another man he met no more than twenty minutes earlier, but it's the only way I can bring myself to face this.

"Pierre-Luc," I call a little less softly than I've been talking with Jessica.

No response.

"Pierre-Luc?"

There's a shuffle from inside the middle of the three cubicles. The door opens slightly, and a face appears behind the opening.

"Is there someone else there?" comes Pierre-Luc's voice.

Jessica has just disappeared into the cubicle to the right.

"No, not anymore," I lie. I hate lying but I can only do as she says and does.

"In you come then," whispers Pierre-Luc and opens the door briefly so that I can slide in.

The cubicle might be relatively spacious by public toilet standards but there is not a lot of room. It's deep enough for two people to stand, one in front of the other but barely wide enough for one to pass the other. The walls are a light grey colour, the door a fake wood. There's little outstanding about the lavatory itself. It reminds me of those at school.

Pierre-Luc is standing with his top half clad only in his shirt, which is fully unbuttoned. He has an inordinate amount of chest hair for someone with such a smooth face, I must say. His trousers remain around his waist although I note that they are unfastened. He tilts his head to one side and grins knowingly.

"I'm so glad you could join me, Harris," he says. I think the tone may be intended as seductive, but I'm not reassured. I want to think of Isabel but when I do, I can only imagine what she would say about all this and that is hardly encouraging.

"Come to me, you beautiful man," he intones, embracing me and kissing me on the lips.

I pull away which seems to upset him.

"What is the problem?" he asks with a sudden look of angry suspicion on his frowning face.

"Please can I have the tickets?" I ask. I'm impressed with myself suddenly. Finding a good excuse like that is usually Jessica's forte. I should be depressed at turning into her to some extent but for whatever reason, I'm feeling slightly relieved.

"Ah, yes, of course," he smiles, his worries subsiding. "Best not to forget what you need before we ensure that I get what I need. And you, of course. I assume this is not your debut?"

I'm trying to think of a good line to get around this when the sound of the bathroom door opening and closing sounds. Pierre-Luc freezes for a moment as footsteps cover the floor outside the cubicles and then the door of the cubicle to the other side of us from Jessica opens and closes. A groan emerges from there. That's something at least.

"We'd better get started," I tell Pierre-Luc. "We don't know how long it will be until this place is empty again and I've got a flight to catch."

"Well well, a feisty one," he comments. "Perhaps you can bend over then, and we'll get started."

"Actually," I say, "I find that it really is preferable to go first, if you don't mind."

I obviously don't want whoever is in the cubicle to the left to hear all this, but I hope Jessica has picked it up. Pierre-Luc appears surprised but then shrugs, kisses me again for a few seconds, then unfastens and lets slide his lower garments and bends over the lavatory with his head against his forearms on the back wall.

Jessica's head suddenly pops up above the cubicle wall to the right and she passes over the clarinet. I really don't know what I'm doing next. I can't picture anything else, not Isabel, not my dreams, nothing even to do with music, only the ghastly apparition in front of me. How can this be happening to me?

I pause suddenly as the bathroom door opens again and someone else enters. He (at least I assume it is he although going by Jessica's presence next door, I suppose anything is possible in this place) walks straight up to the door of Jessica's cubicle. I can hear it being torn open and someone almost launching himself through.

"Oh come on, my love, let's party!" says a voice. The language is English, the accent American.

What on earth is going on? The sounds of something akin to both a struggle and to a couple making love erupt from the cubicle next door.

"What the hell?" asks the voice suddenly. "You're not Brendan! You've got breasts!"

"Well you're not Timothy Dalton and you're about to have not much of a dick left, so let's call it quits!" comes Jessica's voice, followed by the sound of what's probably her knee colliding with part of the man's anatomy.

Pierre-Luc twists his head around and yells, "Brendan, you asshole! I told you not to bring your guys in here while I'm in with mine!"

A second American voice comes from the cubicle to the left, "Screw you, Pierre-Luc. You knew I was coming here just now! It was my turn! And are you in there with Oliver? He's mine!"

"No I'm not!" retorts the first American voice from the cubicle to the right. "I thought you were in here, Brendan, but it's some psychopathic woman!"

I hear the door of the cubicle to the right come loose from its hinges and crash to the floor, quite possibly with Jessica and her companion on top of it. Her voice sounds immediately.

"Harris! Just do the bloody business!"

"Who the hell is Harris?" comes Brendan's voice. "Are you cheating on me, Oliver? Or are we up for a threesome?"

There's only one thing left for me to do. I take the clarinet and hating every moment, I brace myself, get lined up, close my eyes to the sight, and ram it up Pierre-Luc's rear end.

Pierre-Luc's howl is tremendous. It is followed immediately by a massive gust of flatulence which releases what sounds uncannily like the sound of a foghorn from between his legs. He thrashes around and makes for the door. Jessica said to make him uncomfortable, so I suppose I have at least achieved that. He bursts through the door and out into the bathroom.

I follow him out to see Jessica picking herself up from the floor while a man, I assume Oliver, starts to rise from the floor, only to knock his head heavily on the condom machine and fall over again. Another man, who must be Brendan, emerges from the left cubicle with nothing on but his socks. It strikes me as being akin to Faustian pornography.

Pierre-Luc screams again as he backs into a urinal and the clarinet proceeds an inch or two further into his body. Jessica glances over and then her eyes widen and her jaw drops.

"What the frickin' bloody freakin' hell did you think you were doing, Harris?" she gasps. "You were meant to recreate a sexual encounter, not shove half of a seventy-centimetre clarinet right up his bum!"

"You didn't give very specific instructions," I sniff.

"Well how far do you think your average act of penetrative sex gets?"

"That rather depends on the glory organs of the one in question," I respond, a mildly ironic grin on my face.

"If you've got glory organs that long, I don't see that you'd ever need a clarinet to convince Isabel to take you without a second thought," Jessica comes back.

There's another groan from Pierre-Luc, followed by a massive burst of flatulence and what might be a chord in A minor.

"What in the name of all that is holy am I meant to be doing?" asks Brendan out of nowhere.

Jessica rounds on him.

"I don't bloody know and I don't bloody care! Get back into your cottage and clean your own glory organs with the toilet brush! Just sod off!"

She turns to me and says, "Well, nothing else for it but to extract the world's most expensive classical music-themed dildo."

With that, she grabs the clarinet and heaves. There's a sudden hiatus to the movement and then she flies backwards, landing on her back with the clarinet in her hands up to the upper joint. The mouthpiece and barrel have become detached and remain inside Pierre-Luc. From what I can see, extracting them will not be easy as only the lower half of the barrel is protruding.

Jessica picks herself up once more, wiping some moisture out of her hair. There's an awful lot of it and her hair is soaked. I don't ask. She strides over to Pierre-Luc who is now facing us, whisks him around and grabs the barrel. Pierre-Luc shrieks once more and there is another huge explosion of gas but the clarinet pieces remain firmly wedged.

"Dammit, we need some lube!" Jessica snarls and makes for the condom machine. She touches what I assume is the relevant button. The machine promptly falls off its fixing and knocks Oliver entirely unconscious. Jessica probes quickly but there seems little chance of getting anything out of it.

"Alice!" she calls. "Get in here!"

I don't know what use Alice will be but there's no time to ask before she appears at the door.

"What the fuck?" she screams, her eyes bulging as she takes in the sight of Pierre-Luc with a significant amount of a clarinet sticking out of his bottom. Brendan and Oliver, both near naked and the latter lying unconscious on the floor, only add to the ghastly scene.

"Language, Alice, please!" Jessica chastises her in a tone of mock disapproval.

Alice continues without paying any attention.

"I thought I'd seen it all in that hotel in Interlaken but that was just an hors d'oeuvre by the standards of this place!" she exclaims before adding coyly, "It's no bloody wonder Mum says you're a bad influence for me to be hanging out with!"

"What a cheek!" Jessica retorts.

"I'm seeing two of them from here," smirks Alice.

"Comedy remarks aside though," Jessica cuts in, "have you got some toothpaste there?"

"Toothpaste?" asks Alice. "What for?"

"Next best thing we have to lube."

"Who the hell uses toothpaste as lube?" Alice responds. "If you ever get a boyfriend, I will never brush my teeth in your house."

Jessica has been paying minimal attention to Alice's commentary. She has gone through my rucksack with great speed and pulled out the tube of toothpaste I brought. She then proceeds to apply it very liberally to Pierre-Luc's anus. He screams again and lets fly with another eruption of gas directly into her face but to her credit, she continues with the task in hand. Whether it's going to work remains to be seen.

She's not finished yet, however. Next she pushes Pierre-Luc against the one cubicle door which remains fully on its hinges, where Brendan is now sitting inside on the lavatory bowl itself. Paying him no attention at all, she reaches down to Pierre-Luc's rectum and, grimacing violently, reaches in until she somehow extracts the open ring of the condom which she used to cover the end of the clarinet. Pulling hard on the edge of the ring and ignoring Pierre-Luc's continued screeching, she pulls the cubicle door fully closed and then fastens the ring's edge to the door handle. Just as Pierre-Luc starts to turn round to see what she's doing, she lifts her knee and draws it back, then kicks the door open without any warning while grasping Pierre-Luc suddenly to prevent him following. The mouthpiece and barrel erupt from inside Pierre-Luc and fly into the cubicle where they appear to knock Brendan unconscious too. Pierre-Luc also seems to have fainted from the shock as he is now lying on the floor, breathing heavily with his eyes closed. Jessica retrieves the mouthpiece and barrel and hands them back to me to reunite with the other parts.

"I strongly suggest you use an industrial strength disinfectant before anyone puts this in their mouth again."

The thought had occurred, I admit.

"What about these people? They need medical attention!" I say.

"Like we care!" retorts Jessica. She skirts around the bodies on the floor,

456

checking that they're breathing and laying them in what I think is known as the recovery position. "This is yet another crime scene to add to our catalogue! Let's get the hell out. With all Pierre-Luc's screaming, I don't think it will be very long before some proper professionals are on the scene."

With that, she leads the way out of the bathroom at speed. Amazingly enough, the corridor remains clear but as we round the first corner, we run headfirst into some security guards. Jessica bursts into fluent French. I start to say something, but she kicks me hard in the shin while continuing to talk rapidly. The guards say something back to her and then start running to the bathroom.

"What did you tell them?" I ask her.

"I said that some German yobbos just beat up a bunch of airport personnel who were doing something very inappropriate in the public facilities," she says. "Since they think we're French, if we now get to the departure gate and turn into a respectable, British family, we might just get out of this."

Looking at the state of us and noting how people must be able to smell us on the other side of the airport, I don't know quite how incognito or respectable we can truly be, but I've learnt not to question Jessica's plans. I do what I'm told and follow on.

I love Isabel so and would do absolutely anything for her. What I do not know is whether she would genuinely appreciate that if she knew what it really involved.

Chapter 32

LAND OF HOPE AND GLORY

Jessica

Incredibly enough, the rest of our time in the airport goes almost without incident. Somehow or other, no law enforcement agents have so far communicated our credentials to either the airline or the French border security force and our passports take us through. Pierre-Luc could have grassed us up, of course, but the chances are he didn't. As far as he knows, he has even less reason to want to inform the airport security services about what actually happened inside the men's toilet than we do. When the uniforms showed up and asked if he and his "friends" had really been beaten up by some German thugs, he would have corroborated the story if he'd been thinking straight, crap puns notwithstanding. I don't know if his brain is fully functional yet, but it was his bum which took the hit so if he can think past the anal agony, we should all be back in business. Depending on your definition of that term as well, of course.

We pass security without too much of a glitch. It's nothing like Heathrow was but Alice and I have both impressed on Harris that he had better be on his best behaviour and that if he mentions his glory organs once, they will be on the receiving end of a thrust from one of my knees which will make Pierre-Luc's rectum feel like a minor itch. Security takes a couple of bottles of shampoo and skin cream from his rucksack, but he doesn't care, Alice and I even less.

The French border guard stamps us out of the Schengen area with the sort of bored expression usually reserved for Cambridge University professors who try to look cool by watching reality TV shows with their teenage daughters. And who fail badly. I can't say I really blame them, given the state of said shows these days, but given how smart they are in the first place, you wonder why they bother.

Now all we need to do next is get onto the plane. We proceed to the gate where the flight is, as far as I can see, only ten minutes late. In terms of airlines, that's pretty good and it won't matter at the other end where we have a leeway of about an hour and a half. That's cutting it fine if anything goes badly wrong but so far, we seem to be on the money. I'm very wary though. To date since last Wednesday, if it can go wrong, it has done. This is just too easy. I feel like a marine in one of those action movies where some military squad is creeping through a derelict base or an abandoned starship and you just know that some crazed terrorist, zombie or alien is going to leap out of somewhere and slash someone to death. The only comforting thought is that it's hardly ever the girl who dies first. I might have played gender-confused back in the toilets but I'm emphasizing my femininity now. Not that that's any too easy when you're dressed like a garden centre commercial and soaked in various, indeterminate, bodily fluids emanating from yourself and others. But there's got to be some guy out there who's into the contents of a drainage pipe with boobs.

Which reminds me, I need to change that tampon.

Perhaps Fate ran out of ideas with which to shaft us after Pierre-Luc. That one was pretty special, even by the standards of this trip. Near death by hypothermia, an erotic encounter with a teenage impersonator of Freddy Krueger and participation in a cottaging incident which left three unconscious bodies on the floor. That takes some beating. Oh yeah, I forgot the cobra too.

Or maybe Fate was just waiting for a truly great opportunity.

"Chuck us a tampon, will you?" I ask Alice.

She reaches into the rucksack and rummages around. She rummages around a bit more. Get on with it, for frig's sake. I'm not yet bleeding a waterfall here, but I haven't got all day.

"Oh sorry, is this what you're looking for?"

Harris sits up, an empty tampon packet in his hand and a vacant expression on his face.

"Yes," I growl softly, "and for your sake, it had better have one or two left."

"Oh, I do apologize," he announces. "I just used the last one. These things are surprisingly useful for cleaning the inside of a clarinet. I never realized. Did you still need them yourself?"

He's looking and sounding quite cheerful in a genuine way, but my own look must be turning very fearful now as I can see his cheerfulness draining away and becoming replaced by some serious concern. They talk about women's rights being belittled because of the cruel sexism of male chauvinists in traditional power roles across the world. No doubt that's true in several cases but as I've mentioned before, I reckon there's another problem of simply clueless, male wonders who have absolutely no bloody idea what it's like to be a woman. Partly because they don't think to ask and partly because they're so frickin' stupid. How you combat that is the real challenge which decades of feminism have still to find an answer for.

My preferred course of action right now would be to batter Harris around the face to an extent which would make Jöchi look like Pierce Brosnan by comparison. But I'm not normally a girl with a short temper and that's something I'm quite proud of. Instead, I grasp Harris by the collar and march him into one of those over-priced convenience stores-cum-newsagents which you find in almost all airports anywhere. Another triumph for the common, shared, global experience which cuts across people of all nationalities, politics, ethnicities, genders, religions and attitudes to Chuck Norris movies.

"Right, you, I need some more, intimate products or at least something which will do the job," I hiss, "and you're paying."

He gulps and starts looking around. He's probably too frightened to argue. I damn well hope he is. Unfortunately, this kiosk doesn't seem to go in for basic pharmaceuticals and sanitary products like many others do. The best it has is a stack of condom packets. What is it with Lyon Airport? Is this the aviation cottaging capital of Europe or something? Does nobody know how to pass the time while they wait for their flight except by getting laid? Perhaps that's why ours is delayed by ten minutes, because the pilot has to wait for his Viagra to kick in first.

"Oh look, how about this?" asks Harris, holding up a packet of paper tissues.

It's a start but we need something with a bit more absorption capacity. At least the tissues might hold it in though, so I take them in hand. A crap option is usually better than no option.

"Well, you won't run out with these!" announces Harris proudly. "You can bundle them up in tissues to make just what you need!"

He's holding up a family pack of marshmallows.

You have got to be joking. Does he think I'm pregnant and my kid can't wait to have a bonfire party in there?

I'm looking at him with incredulity written all over my face when our flight is called. Oh great. Now what? My brain whirs and there's only one thing for it. I push Harris over to the counter and get him to pay. Then we leave the shop.

"You stay here with Alice while I go to the toilet," I order him, taking the tissues and marshmallows. "Do absolutely nothing until I get back!"

I arrive back, smelling even worse than I already did and with a couple of flies buzzing around my crotch. I'm walking a bit funny too. I can assure you that it will be a long time before I ever even consider eating a marshmallow again. I'm distracting myself by reflecting on the unlikely event that the pilot announces halfway through the flight that due to a structural fault, one, heroic volunteer is going to have to jump out of the plane to their death in order to save the rest of the passengers from crashing. I'm fully resolved in my mind that if that happens, Isabel can have her clarinet but she's going to need a new fiancé. That guy is on very thin ice.

It seems that while I was away, Alice somehow found an airport kiosk flogging books in English and has equipped herself with a new novel for the rest of the journey. "Party On! Dance On! Tampon!" How apt. No doubt a work of great wit and humour, but I can't say I find its title to be particularly amusing right now.

We board the aircraft and find our way to the three seats assigned to us. Alice sits by the window while I take the aisle seat with Harris between us. He is now under the strictest orders to say nothing and to do nothing until we land in Bristol. He can breathe, he can read the safety instructions card, and he can look at the back of the seat in front of him but if he even dares to think about doing anything else, he is going to regret it in a way which he will shudder to imagine. And that is not an exaggeration. The scene in, "Casino Royale" where James Bond has his testicles given unwarranted attention by a carpet beater will look like a children's party game by comparison with what I have in mind for Harris if he steps out of line on this flight.

The other passengers seem to be hoping that the pilot will indeed be looking for volunteers to jump out of the plane, only they'd like three, not just one, those three being Harris, Alice and myself. The aircraft is nowhere near full, and the people seated near to us are demanding and receiving new seats as far away from where we are as possible. Someone even asks if they can use the emergency oxygen supply because the stench is so appalling. Blood, sweat and marshmallows. It's like World War Two, just less fun.

Thankfully, the crew don't eject us physically from the aeroplane and it takes off. As soon as it leaves the ground, I suddenly realize just how tired I am. I really haven't noticed up to now but all of a sudden, it's as if I don't have the energy to raise my arms or to keep my eyes open. Images of airborne descent, starlit skies, racing along a lake and a vile teenager flit across my mind but nothing makes sense. I try to think of Tim, but his face only just appears before a blackness descends.

I don't know how long it's been since I fell asleep but it doesn't feel as though the plane is descending yet so it can't have been all that much. I open my eyes and sit up. At least, I try to sit up, but I don't get very far. As soon as I start to lean forward, something snaps my head back against the seat behind me. It's not a pleasant sensation and the fact that my head is turned to one side makes it even worse because it means that I'm looking over at Harris whose face is worryingly close to mine. People might even think that we're in some sort of relationship together. And I can't reach over to the sick bag.

The smell is dreadful. I reach behind me and can't feel anything except my hair and the seat. My hair, however, is beyond matted. It's curled in on itself and is basically solid. The head cover of the seat is firmly ensconced within it.

I call across to Alice who leans over Harris to take a look.

"Bloody hell, Auntie Jess!" she tells me. "You're literally stuck to the chair! I suppose whatever it was you lurched back into in that toilet when you fell over has somehow solidified and merged with the material which the chair cover is made from."

She stops to inspect the covering and continues, "Yeah, it's something organic, at least partly. The dye in the cover has dissolved and run right down your neck so it looks as though there's been a full-on reaction of some sort."

Alice is doing GCSE chemistry and is very proficient at it, so I'm prepared to trust all this.

"How do I get out of this without a lot of pain and a resulting bald patch?"

"Tricky one," Alice frowns. "I don't think we have much which would dissolve it. Especially after they confiscated our shampoo at the security check. We need something with a bit of a kick to it and that was about the best we had."

Great. I probably won't even get back into Britain now because the photo in my passport looks nothing like Jason Statham.

"Do you think we can get anything on this aircraft?" I ask.

"If I might be allowed to intervene?" asks Harris, a shade irritably but still clearly somewhat wary of upsetting me. "I think there might be something."

"Oh yeah? What?"

"The drinks trolley is heading this way. It might have something we could use."

"Good call!" chirps Alice. "I'm not sure but I think I know what we want."

The trolley rolls up a minute later with two crew members asking if anyone would like any drinks. These are probably going to cost the equivalent of half a sports car for a Diet Coke but that's not much worse than getting your hair done most days, so I don't care. Besides, Harris is going to pay.

"Two cans of beer, please," announces Alice breezily.

The senior crew member, an older lady who sounds like a 1920s school mistress, eyes Alice suspiciously. At least I think she does. I can't actually turn my head towards the aisle right now.

"And how old are you?" she enquires sternly.

"Oh, I don't want to drink it. It's for my aunt," Alice tells her.

The lady says nothing for a moment and then continues.

"So why doesn't your aunt order her own alcohol? She looks to me as if she's unconscious already."

Kidnapper, trespasser, child molester, mugger and now a chronic alcoholic. I don't have much left to achieve beyond war criminal and Satanist. That said, I could still be a war criminal or a Satanist with a brain as an idea comes to mind.

I can't look at the crew members, but I state loudly, "I need the beer to sooth my stomach. If I don't get its calming effect soon, my lower intestines will explode, and the resulting gas cloud will envelop half the cabin. I'm very sorry but I suffer from a rare condition known as gastro-entero-volcaneritis."

It's pretty obvious that they don't believe a word of this except for the threat of me guffing big time if I don't get my booze. That proves enough for them to throw two beers at us and run like hell, not even hanging around to charge Harris the same as what he already paid for the clarinet.

Alice helps herself to the first beer, cracks it open, then leans over Harris and pours it over the top of my head. I feel like I'm receiving a libation on the grounds of a third league football club. Alice proceeds to work the beer into my scalp like a hairstylist. It's hardly a pleasant sensation but I can feel something loosening behind me. Alice forces my head as far forward as it'll go. This is not all that far but it's enough for her to take the second beer and pour it down the gap. I can feel it running right down my back and into the seat of my underpants. What with the marshmallows lodged in another area of the same garment, I suspect that I'm becoming Britain's least sexually attractive proposition after a sandwich toaster. And even then, you'd have a decision to make.

A sudden gust of turbulence jolts the aircraft, and my head moves upwards rapidly. I'm still attached to the chair but I'm becoming looser. Oh please, did I just think that? I suppose I'm allowed one per show. The sign to fasten seatbelts is switched on but Alice ignores it and continues to massage the back of my head, gradually pulling away tufts of hair until finally, I lean forward into clear air. Well, pretty stenchy air but not merged into the back of the seat. This is just as well since the fearsome lady crew member is rushing towards us, an evil glint in her eye at the sight of Alice not strapped in. We just dodge that bullet with seconds to spare.

A minute or two later, the plane begins its descent. We're heading into Bristol. So far, so awful but nonetheless coming out on top. I await to see what's next.

Passport control should have been dead easy with the electronic gates, whereby you can pass with your biometric data. Provided you're eighteen or over, of course. Naturally, I find myself heading up to the human check with Alice in tow. Harris is there too since he bruised his forehead in the cottaging bust-up and so, I guess, the biometric reader wouldn't work. Now he has to get checked in the old-fashioned way. I hope the UK Border Force doesn't have too much of a problem with someone entering the country who looks like he's just been in a bar fight. They probably do except that they'll be forced to let him in due to his valid, British passport. No doubt happens all the time when the Benidorm flights arrive, mind you.

Meanwhile, I am dreading the potential prospect of Alice's leaving the UK technically without permission having been reported. We reach the front of the line, and I hand over our passports.

"You two are together?" asks the guy on the desk, not in a suspicious way but hardly in a very friendly one either.

What does that mean? Does he think we're a lesbian couple? There's a bit of an age gap but it's not impossible. Except that would technically make me a paedophile on top of all my other misdemeanours. The thought occurs that within the last three hours, we were both in a public toilet where someone was getting buggered with a clarinet. I can feel my throat tightening.

"Well, not really, Officer," I stammer. "She's just my niece."

He looks at me strangely.

"That's what I meant," he mutters. "I didn't think you were married or something."

"Oh no!" I beam brightly. "I'm well into guys! Tell me, are you single yourself and maybe free this evening after work?"

If I weren't so exhausted, I don't think I'd be making such an idiot of myself right now, but I just want to find somewhere to collapse. Alice nudges me hard in the back of my ribcage and I stop talking.

The Border Guard rolls his eyes but says nothing and hands our passports back.

"Welcome home," he grumbles.

Incredibly enough, Harris passes through behind us with barely a murmur. It maybe helps that he's holding the clarinet which still reeks of Pierre-Luc's exit chute so that may have contributed to the Border Guard waving him through as fast as possible. It's a useful technique to remember.

We proceed past the luggage belts where we have nothing to pick up. When all you have are two, minor rucksacks, a clarinet and the odour from hell on you, checking in hold luggage isn't too much of a concern. Well, maybe it is for the other people with hold luggage who are astronomically grateful that you didn't check in anything to sit next to their suitcases, but you get the idea. Now all we have left is the customs desk.

Big deal. 99% of the time, nobody can be remotely bothered to staff the place, especially not for flights arriving from Europe. The number of people trying to smuggle in commercial loads of Italian fashion designs or Swiss watches just doesn't justify the salary of more than two customs officials a year probably. On the rare occasion when they do manage to catch someone with an extra bottle too many of Polish vodka, I doubt they file a report. They probably just down it in the staff room next to the toilets. Which would explain why you hardly ever see them.

Except, of course, today. The one time I need a quiet waltz through, there's some jobsworth on duty, checking everything out. There just has to be, doesn't there? Not only that but as we come round the corner into the customs room, Harris trips over a stray baggage tie on the floor and lurches forward, losing his grip on the precious clarinet. I spring forward to catch it before it falls to the ground and suffers yet another dose of near destruction, spinning on my heels as I catch it and coming face to face with a very austere-looking, older man in the uniform of a customs officer.

"Err, hi," I mumble. I'm not really sure what to say.

Harris pitches up behind me, looking suddenly relieved, doubtless because the clarinet is still intact. Whether I'm dead or alive is probably a secondary concern. Alice brings up the rear and comes over to stand beside me.

"What's this you're bringing into the UK?" demands the customs officer.

What does he think it is? An experimental lipstick applicator? Don't you just hate supercilious officials with no sense of humour?

"It looks to me like a clarinet," he cuts in.

Oh well done, Einstein. You've confirmed my suspicion that nobody can get a job as a customs official without first class degrees from both Oxford and Cambridge Universities.

"It also looks to me like a very expensive instrument," he continues, "very expensive indeed."

Well, I didn't get it for ten francs from one of those cheapy tourist shops in Interlaken, next to the plastic chalet glitter ball and a cuddly cow with what looks like a replica of genuine bullshit coming out of its rear end. I can get enough of that for free whenever I'm forced to talk to my brother-in-law.

"The thing is," he looks up suddenly with a nasty look halfway between fake friendly and very threatening on his sneering face, "I actually know quite a bit about wind instruments. It's a hobby of mine, you know."

You have got to be taking the piss. First the French ticket inspector and now this guy? Am I the only person on the planet who likes Bond films more than clarinets? This is like getting tipsy and falling off Blackpool Pier on the one day of the decade when a great white shark is swimming past the UK. At this level of bad luck, I'm surprised we didn't run into the yeti on top of that glacier and discover that he wanted the clarinet to use as a spare toothpick.

I wish I wasn't so tired. Inspiration is deserting me. Come on, Jessica, think.

"Well really," interrupts Harris out of nowhere, in a very unnaturally posh voice, even by his standards. "I might have expected you to recognize a couple of Poltovsky Folk Buskers then."

"What?" asks the official, clearly confused.

"You've never heard of Poltovsky Folk Buskers?" asks Harris, his tone akin to that of someone asking a child if they've never heard of brushing their own teeth. "Not that well versed in the world of wind instruments after all, I see."

"Perhaps you could enlighten me?" asks the official. His suspicion is clearly back in play although he doesn't sound quite so sure of himself either now.

Harris sighs and rolls his eyes. He's surprisingly impressive for someone who recently decided to don his neon orange Che Guevara beret again. I thought I'd told him to ditch that, but I don't care anymore. He's doing better than Alice or me. It's all I can do not to gape.

"Poltovsky Folk Buskers are an indigenous group originally from northeastern Transylvania," Harris explains in a patient but highly condescending tone. "They were virtually unheard of until UN peacekeepers discovered them when on patrol after the Yugoslav War.

"They speak a language which has nothing in common with any other in Europe."

He turns to Alice and me and grunts a few, nondescript vowel sounds. I respond hesitatingly with something I once heard coming from an unusually friendly chimpanzee in Chester Zoo.

"You see what I mean?" asks Harris.

"Perhaps," responds the official with a fair degree of incredulity, "but why are they dressed like tramps? And where's their luggage?"

"They hate attention so they're travelling light," Harris states before remarking pointedly, "At least, they were until you got yourself involved. We'll pick up their bags from a colleague of mine later on."

"And why the clarinet?" asks the customs officer, still not convinced.

"Oh for goodness' sake!" intones Harris. "A clarinet! Are you that ignorant?"

"I know a clarinet when I see one!" retorts the official.

"My good man," says Harris, "this is a cumbuglor. I grant you, it looks much like a clarinet and musical historians are sure that they're from the same family. However, the cumbuglor is a very rural variant on the theme. In fact, the best way to demonstrate it would be to try it. I assume you're familiar with a regular clarinet?"

"Of course!"

"Well, if you try this one, I think you'll soon appreciate the essential differences," Harris tells him and takes the clarinet from me. He offers it to the customs officer.

"Please go ahead and try it," he says.

It's probably just as well that Alice and I are meant to be eastern European peasants who are horrified at the idea of someone taking our precious cumbuglor into their unaccustomed hands, because right now we can only gawp with horror. He's not really going to put that thing in his mouth, is he? I mean, surely not! I have seen some truly foul things over the last couple of days. I have done things which I would never have dreamt of doing, even in a horror movie. I have been living in what feels like a film of bodily fluids, not all of whose originators I'm sure I know. But this is beyond gross.

The official eyes the clarinet curiously then raises it to his lips. Alice gurgles in horrified disgust and I have to kick her shin to shut her up. He draws a breath and immediately coughs. A note sounds from the instrument, somewhat ironically like the sound you might expect to hear from a rhino's bum – another bit of useful knowledge from my visit to Chester Zoo there. The man grasps the clarinet more tightly and wraps his lips around the mouthpiece. He then draws in another breath.

I'm sure I'm about to feel violently ill but he beats me to it. His face goes a shade of pale green, and he leans over the table next to him and vomits. Not just a little retch but what looks like the contents of everything which has gone into his stomach since about the time when we passed into Fribourg. He just can't hold it back. I'm starting to wonder if we should call medical services when he turns over and looks up at us with a look of pure hatred on his face.

"Just take your bloody instrument, get the hell out and never, never come back in here again!" he hisses venomously. Works for me.

We stagger out into the hallway of the airport. Alice and I gaze in surprised awe at Harris. He simply shrugs and steps back to inspect the clarinet.

"Just because I'm a teacher doesn't mean I can't learn as well," he says casually, "and I've had an excellent instructor since last Wednesday."

Chapter 33

IT ALL GOES SOUTH

Harris

"Yes, Isabel, my darling love, I'm on my way back now and we should be arriving in Bristol around half past five."

I pause while she speaks on the other end of the line. I feel the thrill running along my spine. Five days without her voice has turned me into a shivering wreck. It's a sound beyond price.

"Of course, I feel the softness of your cheek press against mine whenever I turn my head for a moment. I've spent the last few days with you constantly on my mind. My nights have been full of the vision of your face. Nothing else could distract me from the thought of your beauty and how we'll soon be spending our whole lives in each other's love."

The two laser stares of wide-eyed incredulity opposite me could probably halve an iceberg regardless of global warming. I squirm slightly and add away from the phone, "Well, yes, it's still technically true, just with a few extra bits left out."

Jessica and Alice seem far from impressed.

We've just boarded a train after taking a bus service from Bristol Airport to Taunton Station, a journey of about an hour. This is Jessica's plan, but it seems reasonably coherent. Now we catch the train back from Taunton to Bristol, appearing there as if we've just spent five days away at the piano competition. I'll admit to feeling very guilty, but we'll also maintain a slight pretence about having met with Charles in Taunton, where he gave us the clarinet, now back from mainland Europe. The only remaining piece of the puzzle is to come up with a cover story for why Alice and I look as though we haven't changed or washed for six months and have mislaid most of our luggage but we're working on it. Jessica will basically disappear and make her way back to Liverpool. I just have to get her a ticket.

In the meantime, Charles has let Isabel know that he has been making arrangements for me to pick up the clarinet and that I will be presenting her with it when I arrive. This is also more or less true. Again, it leaves out some of the finer detail from the explanation. It may also be a little tricky to explain how come it looks slightly the worse for wear and has a very odd aroma. The efforts to clean it up with sanitary products and in public conveniences have worked to an extent but it really could do with an overhaul by a dedicated expert in the maintenance, protection and preservation of antique, musical instruments. The worst damage, or at least the greatest risk of such, has actually come from the rapid changes of temperature. The clarinet has moved from sub-freezing temperatures on top of a glacier to the almost oppressive heat of an Alpine valley in full summer weather. In-between was a short period underwater at high speed. Not everyone may know of these things, but I am well aware of the effects of temperature changes on wind instruments in particular and the potential warping which can ensue. It's something which I certainly hope does not occur in this instance, not least because it'll be very hard to explain how the damage occurred in the first place, should we end up having to get it repaired.

All of this aside, however, I feel a sense of real trepidation now. It's almost like a moment of triumph approaching, an entry into Bristol Station with the goal of our endeavour held high in front of me. Indeed, after all the trouble it's caused us, I think all three of us could feel particularly proud of arriving back with our mission effectively accomplished. For some reason, I am gripped by a real sense of anticipation as often happens when a great achievement comes to pass.

At the same time, there's also a niggling nervousness. Everything going smoothly has not been a hallmark of this expedition and Jessica, in particular, seems very reluctant to assume that nothing else can go wrong at this point. Alice is just now on the telephone to her mother.

"No, Mum, the train is hygienic enough. I can't see any traces of bad behaviour or left-overs from people's lunches…Well, there's no sign of that for sure! You can be quite certain that I wouldn't be sitting on the same row of seats if there were!"

I can only guess what she's talking about, but I don't think I want to ask. Alice pauses and listens for a bit.

"Yeah, OK," she continues. "I suppose we can manage that."

She waits a while again before concluding.

"We'll see you at quarter to six? Great, bye, see you then."

She hangs up and exhales loudly.

"Let's hope they're as delighted to see me again as I am to see them."

"I dunno," Jessica responds wearily and looks at her watch which miraculously survived the Thunersee. "That probably leaves them enough time for a quick one before they have to leave to pick you up so they might be fully sated for a bit and delighted to see you."

"Why a quarter to six?" I cut in. "I thought we were due back at half past five."

"Yes, we are," Jessica tells me, "but we need to leave a window for me to get out of the station and out of sight of my sister. As well as that offspring of an ogre and a teenage mutant ninja stockbroker she's married to. It doesn't matter so much if Isabel sees me off to the side in the station since she doesn't know who I am. Just make sure that she doesn't see either of you engaged in extended conversation with me."

I consider replying with something about how it's always best to reconcile family differences, but I feel that it won't go anywhere meaningful just now. I don't believe it's a sudden and novel emergency either.

Jessica meanwhile has moved onto other things.

"So, our next biggest concern is how to explain to Alice's parents that the two of you have got back from your piano contest looking like you got run over by a milk float at Glastonbury and then spent half a week asleep in a manure tray before you noticed. Except, of course, that you've got a clarinet worth a quarter of a million quid at the same time."

There's a moment's silence while everybody admires the West Country scenery rushing past the carriage windows. I can always recommend my own part of the world to those who want something beautiful without having to endure the exhausting physicality of something like, say, the Swiss Alps.

"Why don't we say we got mugged?" asks Alice.

"Because then your mum will ask why you didn't call the police," Jessica tells her. "That woman would call the cops if she heard that somebody had stolen a nap for twenty minutes. She'll probably go dashing back to Taunton to demand that the local police force dedicate itself to arresting whoever pinched your Arctic dungarees or whatever. One thing we have to avoid is that she goes to Taunton herself in the near future if she's going to ask anybody any questions which would pre-suppose that you've been there."

"I know," Alice tries again. "We could say that we got caught up in an English Civil War re-enactment. Taunton was always being captured and re-captured by Royalist and Parliamentary troops in the 1600s and they're always putting on re-enactments."

"So why would you have taken off most of your clothes and lost all your luggage?" asks Jessica dubiously. "You look more like veterans from the sort of battles the English have been fighting regularly in Benidorm in the 2100s than in the West Country in the 1600s. And what would your role have been anyway? From what I've seen in museums, female teenagers in those days weren't there to fight so much as to shag."

"Well, that would explain how come I lost most of my clothes!" states Alice brightly.

"I rather doubt telling my sister that you lost your clothes by too realistically acting the part of a teenage prostitute in the 1640s is going to calm her down much more than telling her the truth about what you were doing in the Berner Oberland."

"It's no worse than what you were doing with that pimply teenager in Spiez!" smirks Alice.

Jessica makes as if to reply then seems to think better of it and just frowns semi-seriously. I decide to try to help myself.

"We could say that our luggage was taken by traffic wardens from outside the competition venue while Alice was playing inside," I offer.

I immediately wish that I hadn't. The gaze coming my way indicates that I might as well be sitting on a bus seat with a higher IQ than my own.

"Great idea, given that you could have taken it inside and that it's quite amazing that you didn't, given that you were never supposed to have rented a vehicle in the first place!"

It becomes obvious that Jessica is paying scant attention to Alice or me. She looks out of the window for a short while and then back to us with a curious look on her face.

"OK, I think I have this. It's pretty stupid but it should appeal to your dad, Alice. He thinks that anyone dwelling in rural parts has been left behind by evolution. According to him, you can't live further than two clicks from a supermarket without a similar distance of emptiness between your ears. This is one for him.

"According to research, plants are stimulated to grow by classical music. I'm not sure I believe that as you can research anything you like these days. Some dude in California looked into whether flatulence was produced as a self-defence mechanism while a team in Argentina demonstrated that Viagra could address jet lag in gerbils. So I suppose trying to grow parsnips with Puccini is no big deal.

"Anyway, we tell everyone that following the competition, you agreed to help out some local farmer with a nice bit of Schubert and so you ended up playing along in a field somewhere out there. A bull came along, tipped over the piano and got caught up in the straps of your bags. This caused said bull to stumble and roll along a bit until it fell down a ditch. At this point, there was no hope of getting the luggage back before it was time to go for the train, and you made your way over the field and onto the train in the state you're in now."

"That doesn't sound very plausible to me, Jessica," I note a little haughtily.

"True," she says, "but neither does my brother-in-law. And if he decides he wants to buy it, my sister will just go along with whatever."

"Very much so," Alice agrees but then stops short. "But what about Mr Beadlesby's fiancée? Isn't she bright enough to see past all this?"

"I'm afraid so," I begin but am cut off by Jessica.

"The thing is, Harris, you'll have Karl Givret's clarinet with you. Surely nothing else about you will catch the slightest bit of attention?"

"Oh come now!" I protest. "I think Isabel and I are a shade higher-minded enough to see our way past an immediate thrill and present victory. She will see in me a symbol of the culmination of a hard struggle and look further so as not to focus merely on the clarinet as though there is nothing else to capture her attention. A lot more can and will"

"Oh, all right," Jessica shrugs. "Just take off that stupid, neon hat and we'll get her fixated on the clarinet like we need her to be."

Bristol Temple Meads Station is at least old enough not to be just any, other, anonymous, concrete station, covered in graffiti. Built of a faintly red brick, it was constructed originally by Brunel in a Mock Tudor style in the mid-1800s. It was later enlarged in the Jacobean style and now forms a permanent edifice from the Victorian era, overseeing the trains of the West Country to which it once held the gate.

It does, however, still have relatively far-removed platforms with quite a bit of graffiti on them when you get closer, and it's to one of those where we've now been diverted due to some technical glitch in the covered area of the station. Not that this is bothering me. I know that Isabel must be out there somewhere. Where? Where? I ask myself again. I don't want to seem nervously dysfunctional and compared with the languid state of my female companions, I'm certainly more animated, but bringing the clarinet to Isabel is like a form of fulfilment, and it's about to happen. It's something which was meant to be a crowning achievement, then a dream never to be realized, and now something realized indeed through a combination of grit, sweat, love and dedication. Perhaps a few other elements as well but I leave that level of humour to Jessica.

Suddenly she's there. Wearing a light pink blouse under a dark blue cardigan, with a soft, yellow skirt down to just above her ankles and a pair of dark brown clogs. Her hair is caught in a beautiful bun, held in place behind the pink bonnet which almost matches her blouse. My goodness, she's like a goddess. Her eyes are standing out as they stretch along the side of the train, no doubt trying to locate me wherever I may be in view. She was standing a short space back from the train as we passed her by, her back to another platform and a track running behind her before turning into the main hallway of the station. A wall runs along the far side of that track.

In an instant, I simply can't take it any longer. We've just passed her and are about to stop. I will probably stop about two carriages' length down the platform from where she is. I cannot just sit here now, waiting for us to roll to a halt while the lovelight of my life is standing behind me, waiting for me to emerge. I stretch myself out and rise to a standing posture.

"Oowww!" comes a howl, "watch it, Harris! You just whacked me in the human delivery area and right now, that is about the last place I want to be taking a wayward nudge."

I turn round to see Jessica grasping her groin area with a look of serious discomfort on her face. I look down apologetically, but she waves me away.

"Never mind, Harris," she tells me, "you just go and play with Isabel. I'm sure her organs are much more glorious than mine at the moment."

That's not really the way I was thinking about things at all. I suppose it could make a fellow wonder for a moment. I pause. But no, I'm not one of those louts in the sixth form. Meaningful relationships are built on quite a lot more, quite a bit differently. I am a man of principle.

I look back down to Jessica and Alice. Neither seems remotely excited but I suppose that perhaps we're all just exhausted. The difference with me is that I have what I suppose must be an adrenaline rush which is keeping me going. I know what that can be like. When I played solo instrumentals on the viola, the oboe and the harp in my teens and early twenties, I would spend ridiculous hours rehearsing yet never be at all tired or lacking in alertness when my turn came to perform. But following the performance, I would be wrecked. I wonder how long I can keep going this time.

I stride up to the end of the cabin where the door leads into the tiny passageway, in which the outer doors are located. Moving into this small space, my way is blocked by a somewhat older lady, pulling a gigantic suitcase from the rack stuck against the wall on the opposite side of the carriage from the open door. I do not want anything to slow me down but part of me knows that morally, I should make the effort.

"Can I help you at all, madam?" I ask.

"What the bloody hell do you think?" she yells. "How do you propose to get in here and do anything useful, you stupid, great arsehole? Don't they educate anyone in universities these days?"

I'm rather taken aback. It's true. It would be very hard to fit anywhere alongside or worse, between her and the bag but it's not impossible to imagine. I certainly don't see any need to insult me for trying to help her.

"Well, I'm very sorry, Madam," I retort, as offhandedly as possible. "Certainly, nobody is going to force any assistance on you which you would not like to receive. You can simply help yourself."

I consider that quite a witty comeback, but it garners no response. My wit is nearly always under-appreciated, I think. However, it's not my main concern by a long way and I somehow squeeze past her towards the open doorway, the clarinet held out vertically in front of me.

There's a huge commotion from behind me. I spin around to see the older lady heave the massive bag, quite unexpectedly, right out of the rack and into space. She herself falls over backwards but the case continues through the air until it careens into my midriff. I'm standing in a somewhat twisted posture and so the force of the collision spins me back round towards the front and the open door. I'm knocked upwards and reach instinctively for something to hold onto. This motion causes the clarinet to be swung into the horizontal and also propels it upwards. It approaches the doorway at about shoulder height, stretched straight across it.

I must be fairly evenly in the middle of the doorway because both the mouthpiece and the bell at the two ends of the clarinet catch different sides of it at around the same time and lodge firmly. There is a massive, continuing momentum of that suitcase behind the clarinet and me. The force is tremendous, and the clarinet freezes for a moment in the doorway. Only for a moment though. Less than a second later, there is a seemingly ear-splitting crack, almost akin to what you would imagine a felled tree sounding like at the point where it is toppled. The clarinet splits clean into two halves in its middle, each half flying out of the door. They both skid across the platform and vanish over its opposite edge, down into the abyss of the track on the other side.

At that moment, another train pulls out of the main hallway of the station. It isn't a high-speed express but it's travelling at a fair and gathering speed and it has only left a few seconds ago. I manage to cross the platform just in time to see both halves of the clarinet lying there, each spread over a piece of track. The approaching train pulls alongside and promptly runs them over with a – to me – sickening crunch. I stand in numb shock for the twenty seconds or so which it takes the train to finish passing and then look down at the shards of clarinet still visible there. One or two of the metal pieces are still discernible but for the most part, it's almost as if nothing more than some valueless, spare parts had been left there accidentally.

It's all just gone.

The lady herself is shouting something, which is of no consequence to me. Out of the corner of my eye, I can see Alice and Jessica helping her to pick up what seems like an unusually large amount of lingerie from the platform before stowing it into the suitcase and sending her on her way. It's only going on in parallel to what I'm experiencing.

"Was that the clarinet, my poor darling?"

Isabel is always so tender, always so kind. I nod, almost without realizing.

"Well, it's almost quite funny, I suppose," she says in a rather cheerful manner.

Funny? What on earth is she talking about? This is Isabel, isn't it?

"Oh, I am sorry," she comes out with, a shade more contritely. "I didn't stop to think, and you wouldn't know. Let me explain."

She takes my arm and leads me to a nearby bench where she lowers me gently to the seat. Alice and Jessica are following at a respectful distance.

Isabel is studiously ignoring them, not in an aggressive or unkind way, just in a manner which somehow doesn't seem to register their existence at all. That said, I can't for the life of me imagine how she might actually know who Jessica is so this could be a confusing setting. In any case, she and her niece stand a respectable distance away from the bench, though probably just within hearing range. Isabel sits to my left and takes my hands in hers on my lap.

"You see, my darling, I know where you've been!" she beams.

"You do?" I croak awkwardly. How awful can this get?

"Yes!" she continues. "Charles told me!"

She rounds on me conspiratorially, tightens her grip on my hands, and moves her face closer to mine.

"According to Charles, you had a little bother with the government authorities in moving Monsieur Givret's clarinet from Italy over to here. So you took advantage of the piano contest to get out of town for an extra day or two to pick it up from somewhere."

"That's…uumm…all you know?" I ask hesitantly, my throat dry as a desert.

"Oh yes!" she says emphatically. "You don't have to tell me everything, you know. I'm not an idiot. I think I can work this out for myself. You and Charles somehow arranged for the clarinet to be shipped over here but you needed to get it from somewhere quiet on the south coast without too many questions being asked.

"Oh I say, you are naughty!" she gazes at me, wide-eyed but with a glint of complaisance in her eye.

"But it doesn't matter!" she says suddenly. "Really, not at all!"

I have to get this straight. Jessica maybe accused me of living outside reality at one point but even if I do, it isn't as far removed as we seem to be right now.

"Please, Isabel, listen to me," I manage to say. Maybe even a shade gruffly. "A couple of minutes ago, a clarinet worth a quarter of a million pounds was just smashed to smithereens. The house we hope to live in as husband and wife was mortgaged to buy that clarinet and all we have left now is a mortgaged property. I don't see this having been a very positive gain."

She draws back for a moment and looks me over, almost disapprovingly. Her expression changes to one of curiosity. It then reverts to innocent joy. She leans over and kisses me once, then draws back a small distance and continues to speak, adopting a kind but measured tone.

"You got that clarinet in order to bring our families to a point where we could be united," she says. "I still can't believe that you would really do such a thing, but you did. It was incredible! How many other men would have dreamed of trying to do anything like that at all?"

I have no idea, but I think it's a rhetorical question.

"I went to Father when I heard about this. I couldn't face the possibility of you failing and it occurred to me that there were just too many unknowns in this shadowy world of moving instruments around between Europe and here. And so I told him upfront all that you were doing."

I sincerely hope that was the version she just described of what I was doing.

"You'll never guess? He almost began to cry! Perhaps it was the way I told it, but he said that he had no idea just how dedicated you were. He said that he could not believe that a possible suitor would go to such lengths for me but that if I had indeed found one, I should be taking steps to make him mine forever now.

"I mentioned to him that something might still go wrong but he wouldn't hear of it. He started talking about how stupid and selfish he had been and how the only thing of any importance now was rewarding us as a couple with the recognition which the love and dedication deserve which we have shown each other. According to him, the clarinet does not even matter. It is our love which is the truly valuable, even the only valuable thing in this equation."

I'm flabbergasted. It seems as though the whole adventure has been a total failure and a wild success within the same five minutes. We completely failed to deliver what we set out to do but I proved everything I needed to prove. I simply don't know what to make of it.

"So, darling," Isabel somehow sits next to me and almost sidles up at the same time, "should we be planning a wedding soon?"

I haven't felt this overwhelmed by a sensation since...since...well, since…since jumping off that cliff edge above Interlaken tied to a paragliding chute. Which was only three days ago. Well, perhaps I'm getting a little caught up in everything which has been happening of late, but my point is that this matters. Like my life.

The comparison with Interlaken does make me pause for just a moment, however. I'd like to have this off my chest at an early stage.

"Errm, Isabel, there is one thing," I say, trying not to sound too cautious. "Like you said, I was maybe, well, a bit naughty in getting the clarinet here."

"Nothing too awful," I add hastily. That maybe depends on quite how you define, "awful," but it's not a certainty. "I mean, I didn't kill anybody or steal their things, or commit sex crimes or –"

"Harris!" Isabel breaks in sternly. "I could never for the life of me imagine you doing anything like that! What on earth were you doing?"

"Well, that's just it. Like I said, nothing too awful but perhaps we could just agree that those harmless, little secrets simply stay harmless, little secrets so that nobody ever needs to be upset?"

She looks at me suspiciously but then relents and leans in to kiss me once more. I'm savouring the instant when I hear a sudden commotion. Breaking away from Isabel, I see Jessica hurtle over the track where the other train passed and spring at the wall opposite. She clears it quickly and then falls off the other side. The ensuing squelch indicates that she probably hasn't fallen too far but may not have fallen into anything very desirable either. But why? What's she doing?

The answer is not long in coming as two figures approach from further down the platform.

"Alice! Darling! Have you been all right? I'm so sorry you didn't win! I know you should have! Those judges must be total dimwits! How could anyone not notice just how naturally talented you are simply by looking at you? When you play, it's simply exquisite! And have you been eating all right? Have you had the right amount of sleep? My goodness, you do smell rather ripe! Is everything OK? And where are your bags?"

I've only met Alice's parents a couple of times before, but I didn't notice that much about them. Right now, however, if this is her mother, then I suspect that even I may be starting to understand why Jessica might not be as fond of her sister as a lot of other women are of theirs.

Alice's father is standing there in some very expensive clothes and with a rather smug expression on his face, almost a casual sneer. Goodness me. I've learnt quite a bit about Alice over the past couple of days, but I don't see any particular semblance between her and her parents at all.

Alice herself is busy trotting out the line about an accident while performing a piece of Schubert on a farmyard, as instructed by her aunt. It sounds like the most terrible load of codswallop I've ever heard, and her mother clearly doesn't know what to make of it. Her father, however, seems simply rather bored.

"Oh, all right, Alice, we'll go shopping on the way home," he tells her and moves off towards the carpark. Her mother does little more than acquiesce and presumably stops worrying at this confirmation that Alice is healthy and unharmed. Given what their daughter has actually been doing since last Wednesday, that's probably for the best.

"Oh, I say!" Isabel waves and runs after them. Catching up, she asks, "My car broke down this morning, so I came up here by bus to meet Harris. Is there any chance you could give us both a lift to near the area of the school?"

I still need to get Jessica her train ticket back to Liverpool but I've no idea where she's gone to since scaling that wall. Nor am I in any place to start looking around for her. I do not feel good about this at all but then I consider the opposite. If I do anything which hints at her presence in front of her sister, all hell will break loose, and it would be one of the worst things I could possibly do. In fact, the best thing I can do right now is to get hold of Isabel as quickly as possible and tell her not to mention that other woman whom she saw hanging around with Alice earlier. I'll need to think how to explain that away later.

I glance over at the wall and wonder what lies on the other side. I can see absolutely nothing but apart from trying to glance respectfully, I just can't do anything to help.

Chapter 34
YOU NEVER GIVE UP

Jessica

"Oooh, do coom on, dearie! Get a firm grip and joost ram it in, there – go on! Imagine I'm woon of them barmaids with a ginormous tap of beer and you're joost slamming it into woon of them beer moog things!"

"Oh, do be a bit sensible! You know that if I think too mooch about that there Rhonda down the Pig & Blanket, I risk giving me sparkploogs a bit of a joomp ahead of time!"

How wonderful. Going by the sounds emanating from oopstairs, - sorry, upstairs – I get the distinct impression that the Montagues have been using the period of my absence in much the same way as Colin and Bethany were making use of Alice's. Either that or they're having a bit more fun changing a lightbulb than most people do. I do hope not though as I have enough to do next week without having to go to their funeral.

Either way, I hope they'll finish off soon. They're the last thing standing between me and the welcoming haven of my little place in Huyton. I'm finally back but lacking my keys. They have a spare set and always provide me, in a very kindly way, with what I need when I lock myself out, as happens a shade too frequently. The only thing is that I don't really want to go barging in on their intimate moment together. No doubt they're imagining that it truly is intimate and don't realize that most people on the street until at least halfway to Tesco's are getting a set of X-rated mental images which they'd really rather not be seeing in their mind or anywhere else. So I just don't want to disturb them. When I consider the last snog I got, I'm even jealous. At least whatever they're doing is based on genuine love and affection, and doesn't involve German Switzerland's least attractive, sexual reject. I think I'd rather be dick-picced by Heidi's grandfather.

As a result, I plant myself in the front garden and try to find something with which to block my ears. Or who cares? It'll be over soon. They lack the stamina. And if it really won't peter out after a couple of minutes, I can go down to the Pig & Blanket and ask Rhonda if she'll flash her thigh at the upper bedroom window for a few seconds for me. From what I've heard, that should do the trick and it'll be game over before you can change another lightbulb.

Most of me is simply too tired to give a damn anyway. It's Wednesday afternoon and I've been on the go since early Sunday evening. That's right – Sunday evening. You got that right. Why, you ask? Well, I shall try to explain.

At the usual, unwelcome approach of my sister, I realized I needed to be out of the picture pretty quickly, so I leapt the next railway track, thankfully now free of clarinet-cracking trains, and vaulted the wall. All in a day's work for Timothy Dalton, no doubt, but still quite an impressive display of gymnastics from someone with no pretensions to any skill in that field. At least, it would have been impressive if I hadn't landed in a huge rubbish skip on the other side. I'm still not sure what all was in it, but it was wet, it was sticky, and it squelched audibly as you descended into it, which happened with pretty much any movement more dramatic than breathing. It was also next to the car park. This meant that I had to stay and fester in there, until I could be sure that Colin and Bethany had driven off with Alice, and it was safe for me to go peeking out. For reasons I could not fathom, I could hear the two of them, mainly Bethany of course, yacking away, checking out Alice for any stray microorganisms which might herald a deadly strain of rectal influenza in Taunton, hitherto unknown in the rest of the UK, and so on and so forth. My nerves were screaming for them just to get into the frickin' car and get out, but my brain told me that I had to wait. For some, bizarre reason, I eventually heard Harris and, I think, Isabel, come up and get into the car with them. I suppose they must have needed the ride, but it was a shade unforeseen. If married bliss means hanging out with Bethany and Colin, then I'm afraid you've been on a journey to nowhere since last week, Harris, but it really is your problem now.

My problem was rather different. We'd just returned with more or less mission accomplished. Within about ten minutes, the mission had gone to hell with the clarinet's destruction, but the objective had nonetheless been achieved for some reason best known to Isabel. Everybody was on the money except for yours truly, who found herself sitting in a glorified sewage can, dressed in an outfit only otherwise sported by a mannequin in the Imperial War Museum, carrying a passport, and absolutely nothing else. No money, no tickets, no documents, no food, no extra clothes, no nothing. Unless you count a pressing need to get to Liverpool, which is about three hundred clicks away. For those who still think in imperial, that's almost two hundred miles. It's essentially the entire length of the country of Wales from the south end to the north. To people who like to bang on about how the UK isn't really that big a country, how places like Canada or Australia are vast by comparison or how we're just like a vibrant commune, I say try finding yourself at one notable point such as Bristol and consider how best to get to another notable point such as, oh I don't know, maybe Liverpool. On foot. There's a reason the Beatles didn't walk to Hamburg, you know.

No doubt others are thinking, but, Jessica, you're a hiker, aren't you? True enough, and I do like a good hike. You'll forgive me for being a bit old-fashioned though but a "good hike" to me typically means better scenery than the side of the A49, more comfortable places to sleep than Herefordshire bus stops and enough money to buy something to eat more substantial than a leftover packet which once had some crisps in it a week earlier. And even then they weren't salt 'n' vinegar. Let's get it straight. I can walk, and indeed I have just walked all the way from Bristol Temple Meads Station to where I live in Huyton. I just don't like it. At least, I don't like it when I don't have the equipment, don't have any money and am already worn out from getting chased all over the western side of the Alps. Don't want to put any avid tourists off the England/Wales area for proper visiting, of course.

I did try to get a lift at one point when I waved down a tractor which seemed to be going the same way as I was. However, that impression didn't last for long when I hopped on board and the farmer, with a beard which seemed to merge seamlessly into the chest hair of his open shirt, gazed at me hopefully and nodded at his dog.

"She don't be liking girls wid too many clothes on, you know!" he nodded to the dog while gurgling knowingly at me.

I jumped straight off and told him that he only needed one bitch on board, so I didn't want to take up space unnecessarily.

At least my period stopped at Shrewsbury. I had always been getting my own seat in bus shelters quite easily up to that point, since I smelled like a beery version of a Rocky Road ice-cream which had passed its sell-by date two months previously. By this point, the bus shelters weren't even really worth it anymore. I still had to go around with the stench myself which was worse than sleeping outside. After Shrewsbury, it wore off a bit to be replaced simply by standard body odour with a good bit of cheesy foot essence. As a hiker, I'm used to that much.

But none of that is why I'm really in such a foul mood. Actually, that's not very accurate. I'm not in a foul mood in the sense that there's a serious risk of me losing my temper with a passing cyclist for disturbing the oxygen flow I'm trying to breathe. I'm not angry with anyone. I'm not even annoyed at having to listen to the Montagues indulge in the delights of human passion with all the finesse of the local Church Coffee Morning. I feel a lacklustre impatience but mainly just because I need my front door keys in order to gain access to my shower, my bed and whatever may be left in my kitchen which is still more or less edible without the risk of giving me bubotic plague.

No, I don't resent the Montagues their intimacy. Not a bit. I'm genuinely glad for them that they're making each other happy. In much the same way, I'm very glad for Harris that he and Isabel are making each other happy. I have to confess that I was a shade surprised to see Isabel in the flesh finally, after all we'd heard about her from Harris. I would not say this in front of Harris, and I am simply being honest, not bitchy. So let me start by saying that she's not ugly. She's just…well…not quite as pretty as I'd been imagining that she would be when we returned in conquering glory from our European adventure. I suppose I'd somehow been thinking of all those photos you see of events like the end of the Second World War where the returning soldiers seem to have had their choice of the best of booty which 1945 could produce. Granted, the fashion was different then. You'd hardly be looking to score big time in a tweed jacket and clunky clogs twice the size of your actual feet these days but if you focus on the girls' faces, you can see what was in it for those guys. They quite probably had pretty big tits as well, I suppose, if anyone had been able to make them out under the tweed.

Isabel herself is not bad. I'm not in the habit of checking out women, I hasten to add. But like most people, it's not that hard for me to determine on a superficial basis whether someone is stunningly gorgeous, mediocre or as attractive as the prospect of having an enema performed with a wonky vacuum cleaner. Isabel does not qualify as the last by any means but after hearing Harris pontificate on the joy she brings to him and how the wonder of her being radiates into the sky around her, I suppose I'd somehow built up a mental picture more akin to a decent Bond girl rather than an unemployed traffic warden who just got a part-time job deep-frying burritos in a West Midlands chippy. Nothing wrong with people who undertake those jobs, I should stress, just you don't tend to associate them in your mind with someone about to get laid by Pierce Brosnan.

That said, it's not Isabel's looks which have been bothering me. Like I said, I'm glad that she and Harris are so happy together, regardless of what either of them looks like. The point of the whole expedition was to make sure that they would have the chance to live a happily married life of shared, passionate love together and we managed that. Except not really. Going by what I heard Isabel saying, it was all going to happen anyway. Harris never actually needed that stupid clarinet, which got smashed to smithereens at the last step, but his own love shone through and was recognized by Isabel and her family. That's beautiful, I know, and I appreciate it. It's just that, well, I don't know. How to put it? He never needed me in the first place. I never did a single thing which counted for anything. Everything turned out OK and the contribution of Jessica Morriston to making it all work was precisely zero.

Why do I care? That's not a pleasant question to have to answer but I suppose I have to since I've been feeling depressed by it ever since I climbed out of that garbage skip. You have to hand it to Fate: no respect but what a critic. It was horrible. Everything had turned out exactly as it was meant to. Well, at least it did if you count the end result. The rest of it was a bit of a farcical screw-up but in terms of the ultimate objective, it was mission accomplished and everybody was happy.

And I just wanted to sit down against the wall and cry.

Why? I dunno or at least, I tried to convince myself for half the way home that I didn't. After all, I got a free trip to Switzerland. I got accommodation (of a sort), food (give or take), two paragliding trips and a hike up the Simmental. I also nearly got arrested and killed on various occasions, as well as borderline sexually assaulted by Switzerland's most unattractive teenager, a venomous snake and a homosexual, American dude in a public toilet, but I figure I paid my dues. And I know that at least somebody finds me attractive. So what's the problem?

If I'm honest with myself, the problem is precisely that nothing I did made a difference, like most things I do. I suppose that I just wanted to be somebody's hero. Somebody's heroine? Whatever – I lost track of my gender identity in a public convenience in Lyon Airport. Let's just stick with hero. It sounds less like a narcotic substance. Yes, I wanted Harris to be happy. Sure, he pissed me off regularly with his overbearing pomposity on the subject of whatever he considered culture and his clueless inability to navigate his way along a one-way street. But he's not a bad person and he actually believes in something. I'm glad that he's happy but I just wish he could have been happy because of something for which I was partly responsible. Instead, I might as well not have bothered. Given all the messes we got into, it's more amazing that he's happy and settled not because of anything I did but despite everything I did.

So there you go. Dammit. I just wanted to matter for a change. I don't know why. Perhaps it was because for once I saw a chance to matter, or at least I thought I did. Normally, I don't care and nor does anyone else. It's not as though I'm a bad person. I'm just someone who doesn't matter because she doesn't make a difference. I don't suppose there's much new in that. It was just never shoved in my face quite so forcefully before. That's one lesson learned. If ever you think about hiking the entire length of Wales, make sure you have something positive and cheerful to reflect on before you set off.

"Shall we take a break joost now, loov? Me favourite baking show will be on in two minutes, and we can finish oop after that."

"Ooh yes, that's a good plan. I was joost thinking how I might need a biscuit or two at this point to keep going."

Tempting though it is to come up with some sarky jibe about the Montagues' love life, I'm holding off. It's not a very erotic, mental image or if it is, then that's your concern and I don't need to know, thank you very much. But at least they have each other and there's something there which matters. It might not matter to anyone else, but it's not meant to, and that, I suppose, is why any snide remark from my side would just be petty and pointless.

At least, however, if they're breaking up their copulating formation for a few minutes, I might be able to request a spare set of keys without interrupting at a critical moment. I don't think he's as obsessed with baking shows as she is, so I won't be causing an upset.

Back inside finally, everything I'm wearing goes straight into the washing machine and I go straight into the shower. I don't even stop to admire that picture of Tim on the way in. He can wait until I'm on the way out and feeling vaguely attractive again.

Two bottles of body wash and three rinses of my hair later and having probably used up about half the freshwater supply for the West of England up to October, I step out and start drying myself off. I'm in no hurry and gradually start to feel almost human again. I've forgotten what it's like to be able to raise my arm without the most vile odour being released and am pleased to re-discover the sensation. I no longer feel as though I'm sharing my underpants with a holiday camp of micro-organisms. I'm very pleased to imagine that my firstborn will no longer be able to grab a S'mores or two on the way out now.

Talking of food, what do I have of any sort of comestible nature in my kitchen? There are enough things which I could cook. I bet you thought that I would have no ability in that area. Well, not quite. I can run up a decent enough dinner when I need to. Right now, however, I basically want something edible which I can put in my mouth within the next ten seconds. I don't recall actually buying that Battenberg cake but I'm not into shoplifting so I suppose it must be mine. A couple of minutes later and it's an academic discussion since it's no longer available unless you're going to apply some pretty unpleasant surgery to my alimentary canal.

Having constituted a mug of milky coffee, I stagger off to the sofa, where I just about manage to finish the coffee and place the mug on the side table before closing my eyes. I recall nothing more.

It's about two in the morning and I wake up with a horrific crick in my neck, a twisted feeling in my left thigh which makes me wonder if I somehow gave birth without realizing that I'd been pregnant first, and a taste in my mouth of total disgustingness. The latter has to be down to what happens if you collapse into sleep immediately after shoving an entire Battenberg cake and a large milky coffee down your gob in the space of three minutes flat. The joint pains most likely have to do with not bothering to get comfortable on a couch or bed before embarking on an exceptionally deep sleep. Whatever the cause, I want to go back to the bathroom for a very long, very warm shower.

I get up from the couch and promptly fall flat on my face. Ow!. OK, so my body may not yet be fully ready to collaborate again. Maybe another sleep, just with a bit of attention to getting comfortable on first lying down. Oh yeah and maybe following a quick dose of mouthwash. The thing is though, that I suddenly don't feel so sleepy anymore. Tired, yes, but not sleepy.

I shuffle listlessly towards where I think I probably last left the remote for the TV, when my eyes fall on the pile of paper behind the door. Of course, the mail. In these days of the internet, anything actually interesting coming through which isn't a parcel is pretty much about as likely as winning the lottery and having Timothy Dalton bring the winning envelope to your house. However, it has to be dealt with and if I want to feel sleepy, then it could be the way to go.

Let's see. Utility bills, political pamphlets, an invitation to an annual festival party from the Jehovah's Witnesses. Nothing I'm too desperate to welcome. A plain, brown envelope with nothing more than my name and address on the front.

In a moment's panic, I wonder if this comes from some Swiss law enforcement agency and is my summons to appear before a court in Bern on a public disorder charge next Monday. Hold on, Jessica – it's been posted from within the UK and it's unlikely that the Swiss Embassy has nothing better to do than follow up on embarrassing incidents of policing ineptitude in the Canton of Bern. Fair enough, put the CPR gear on hold for a minute. But what is it?

Turning it over, I see a return name and address, the latter being in the Bristol area. It's come from one Mr Harris Beadlesby.

Harris? What the hell does he want? And how did he get this here just after I arrived or even before? Ah yes, of course, because I spent half a week walking up the eastern side of Wales. How did I forget that? Dear me, I really need to get my body and brain working properly again. I had no idea that paddleboarding and snake-charming could have such a devastating impact. Maybe it's just how I do them.

Anyway, let's see. I open the envelope, and a hand-written letter falls out. Quite a long one too. Various, smaller envelopes accompany it. Lucky me! Where to start?

I pick up the letter and shift back to the sofa, adopting a deliberately more relaxed posture before I start to read.

Dear Jessica,

I hope this message finds you well and safely returned home. I do apologize for the way in which you were left behind in Bristol Temple Meads. I just didn't see a way to get back to you without alerting your sister. While I cannot claim to understand your family dynamics, I do believe that this would not have been something which you would have considered a preferable option.

I am writing to thank you sincerely for everything you have done for me. We may have differed over a few points, but I have come to realize that the past week has been one of the most enlightening experiences of my life. That is thanks to you, and also to a certain degree to Alice, of course.

As you can imagine, I am utterly delighted that my marriage to Isabel should now be confirmed to go ahead. It is all I could I have wished for. However, it would never have happened without our adventure to Switzerland. This may not be obvious, but I shall try to explain what I mean.

You no doubt saw how the clarinet itself was not ultimately needed for the intended effect. What mattered to Isabel, and to her father, was that I showed myself willing and even able to achieve something in the service of what was genuinely important to me. I'm glad that they should think that but please let me assure you, I would never have believed that myself for one moment or made it work if it had not been for the time I spent in your presence.

What I believe I have learnt, which is much more valuable than even that clarinet, is that if I apply myself to something and if I can see things from more perspectives than merely my own, I can do it. This was something I could never have understood until I saw it in action. You were the inspiration here. It was thanks to you that we started our adventure after none of my pupils made the piano contest. You were the one who found a way to get onto the glacier and back. You were the one who worked out how we could escape from the police by getting a lift in a police car itself. And these are only a couple of examples. Had it not been for you, we would never have gone anywhere, and I would be simply lost.

I never thought that I would be proud of myself for lying but the couple of instances where I was able to contribute showed me that even I could learn to do the impossible. Hiking may not be a team sport, but every sportsperson needs a captain, and you have been ours. I don't know how I could have learned better.

You have one outstanding quality, of which I think you should be justly *proud. You never give up. Not once did you consider doing so, at least not to my knowledge. You applied every last ounce of imagination, intelligence and blind luck, and you somehow got us through. Nothing we faced was ever enough to make you turn round and quit. You just never give up and I admire you for it.*

Isabel and I would be truly honoured if you would like to attend our wedding this autumn and I enclose an invitation. Alice will be there as well, accompanied by her parents so I'm afraid we may need a cover story as to why I've invited you, but I daresay that between now and then, we can think of something.

I am also enclosing a couple of additional elements, one to compensate for the loss of your hiking equipment, the other as a sincere thank you, which I hope you will enjoy.

In closing, I would like to say that I hope very much that we can stay in touch. Maybe not on too frequent a basis since I think we would each drive the other insane but on a social basis every so often, I would be very happy.

Yours sincerely,

Harris Beadlesby

So what do you make of that? More interesting than a utility bill and I'd certainly rather go to his wedding reception than the Jehovah's Witnesses' party, but I suspect I'm meant to think something a little more mature than that. I don't really know what to say but I do feel somehow less disappointed with the outcome of last week than I was doing up until I read this. I'll keep it around and read it again to see if I can get the full gist. It takes me a bit of time to do deep and meaningful correctly.

In the meantime, let's check out the envelopes. The most obvious is the wedding invitation. He must have moved pretty fast on this if Isabel only agreed formally last Sunday but I suspect there was already something brewing. Either way, I see that there's an all-you-can-eat buffet. Provided I don't have to spend too long around Colin, I think I could have quite a good time.

The next envelope contains a not insignificant H&M voucher. Presumably, this is what I'm going to use to replace my hiking gear, which was lost on the floor of the Thunersee after it knocked some poor girl off her water-skies. But I ask you, H&M? Who goes to H&M to get hiking gear? You might as well go to HMV. Even Bethany wouldn't manage something that moronic. Still, it's the thought which counts and all that. When you think about it, I could use this voucher for my regular clothes-shopping and invest the funds thus freed in some truly ass-kicking hiking gear. My mind starts to fill with images of myself dressed as the ultimate action heroine, someone whom James Bond would ask for permission to snog before he got it on with her. And I'd only say yes if it was James Bond as played by Timothy Dalton too.

What does that leave? Going by the H&M voucher, I semi-dread to think. One last envelope contains quite a bit of documentation. I open it carefully and out fall two one-month country passes for Switzerland, valid from whichever day you choose to activate them on. One adult, one child.

One-month passes? This must have cost him a fortune. One month passes? Is this for real? This can't be true! This is something I only ever dreamed of having!

Thank you, Harris! Unless you could have got me a night of unbridled passion with Timothy Dalton in a luxury, mountaintop hotel suite, I can't think what else I'd rather have received. One-month country passes! Unlimited access to the whole of Switzerland and every form of transport other than air! And let's face it, I sure as hell do not want to be going anywhere with Captain Borisovich again.

This means Alice and I are sorted! Mid-July to mid-August should work. But then there's Bethany. Bloody Bethany. A whole month for her darling daughter to be away with her awful aunt. That's going to take some convincing story and a half.

I sit down at the kitchen table and start mixing together a white hot chocolate. About as healthy as a nuclear power station accident but I do love them. While hot chocolates, I mean, not nuclear power station accidents.

A short while passes before my thoughts come full circle. That's an idea, now that I think about it. Indeed.

They're always banging on about the safety of nuclear power plants in Britain. You'd think they were run by people who'd just failed their Aldi's exam the way some of the press goes on. However, that works for me. Switzerland has nuclear power reactors too but nobody in the British press ever mentions them and certainly not in a derogatory manner. So, all you need is someone in one of the waste disposal sites in Berkeley or Oldbury to drop their sandwich over a pile of fizzled out plutonium and some journo to blow it out of all proportion, and Bethany will think that anywhere in Britain west of Birmingham is one neutron away from the apocalypse. But it could be mentioned to her that Switzerland might be a safe place to sit out Armageddon until the local technicians have fixed it all. I have a couple of university friends who work in the media down that way, and I wonder what they might achieve on my behalf? I mean, it's only Bethany, for frig's sake.

I lean back and rest the back of my head in my hands, my gaze fixed on the ceiling. Quickly, I hook one ankle round a kitchen table leg to stop myself back-flopping onto the floor behind me, then re-gather my thoughts.

Yes, there could certainly be a way to make this one work.

You never give up, do you, Jessica?

A wicked grin spreads slowly from the corners of my mouth.

You never give up.

ABOUT THE AUTHOR

J. E. MacKenzie comes from Scotland, lives in France and works in Switzerland, just to confuse people. It may be worth pointing out that the border between two of those countries is only a ten-minute walk from where he lives.

A great fan of Alpine hiking, he rates all things Swiss, with the exception of the cowpats. However, if you're going to have Swiss cheese and Swiss chocolate, then you're going to need milk so it's probably fair enough. Nor is it any worse than in other countries with Alps.

He has a wife and five children, some of whom can be persuaded to join a 20-click hike with a 1,000 metre altitude difference, and some of whom are a bit more sane.

OTHER BOOKS BY THE AUTHOR

OF COURSE I LOVE YOU,
I just don't like you very much.

www.ingramcontent.com/pod-product-compliance
Lightning Source LLC
Chambersburg PA
CBHW020824030726
47496CB00001B/77